BOOKS BY BARBARA KINGSOLVER

Fiction

Prodigal Summer
The Poisonwood Bible
Pigs in Heaven
Animal Dreams
Homeland and Other Stories
The Bean Trees

Essays

Small Wonder
High Tide in Tucson

Poetry

Another America

Nonfiction

Holding the Line: Women in the
Great Arizona Mine Strike of 1983

PIGS IN HEAVEN

a novel by

BARBARA KINGSOLVER

HarperPerennial
A Division of HarperCollinsPublishers

Grateful acknowledgment is made for permission to reprint the following song lyrics:

From "Big Boys," by Barbara Kingsolver and Spencer Gorin, copyright © 1989.
From "Falling For Me," by Barbara Kingsolver and Spencer Gorin, copyright © 1992.

A hardcover edition of this book was published in 1993 by HarperCollins Publishers.

HarperCollins books may be purchased for educational, business, or sales promotional use. For information, please write: Special Markets Department, HarperCollins Publishers, Inc., 10 East 53rd Street, New York, NY 10022.

First HarperPerennial edition published 1994.

Designed by Claudyne Bianco

The Library of Congress has catalogued the hardcover edition as follows:

Kingsolver, Barbara.
  Pigs in heaven : a novel / by Barbara Kingsolver.—1st ed.
    p. cm.
  ISBN 0-06-016801-3
  1. Title.
  PS3561.I496P54 1993
  813'.54—dc20   92-54739

ISBN 0-06-092253-2 (pbk.)

02 03 04 05 ❖/RRD 30

FOR CAMILLE

ACKNOWLEDGMENTS

This book germinated under the warm encouragement of friends in the Cherokee Nation, especially Ron Watkins, Nancy Raincrow Pigeon, and Loretta Rapien. Regina Peace, Toby Robles, Carol Locust, and Donna Goldsmith patiently helped me understand the letter and spirit of the Indian Child Welfare Act. Joe Hoffmann, Georgia Pope, Frances Goldin, Sydelle Kramer, and Janet Goldstein helped the story find its way through the woods. Camille Kingsolver gave me five-year-old insights and reasons to keep writing.

The legal dispute described in *Pigs in Heaven* is not based on a single case history, but was constructed from the materials of existing law and historical fact, insofar as I understand them. The specifics of legal process vary among tribes. Other people would tell this story differently, and none of them would be wrong.

SPRING

QUEEN OF NOTHING

WOMEN ON THEIR OWN run in Alice's family. This dawns on her with the unkindness of a heart attack and she sits up in bed to get a closer look at her thoughts, which have collected above her in the dark.

It's early morning, April, windless, unreasonably hot even at this sun-forsaken hour. Alice is sixty-one. Her husband, Harland, is sleeping like a brick and snoring. To all appearances they're a satisfied couple sliding home free into their golden years, but Alice knows that's not how it's going to go. She married him two years ago for love, or so she thought, and he's a good enough man but a devotee of household silence. His idea of marriage is to spray WD-40 on anything that squeaks. Even on the nights when he turns over and holds her, Harland has no words for Alice—nothing to contradict all the years she lay alone, feeling the cold seep through her like cave air, turning her breasts to limestone from the inside out. This marriage has failed to warm her. The quiet only subsides when Harland sleeps and his tonsils make up for lost time. She can't stand the sight of him there on his back, driving his hogs to market. She's about to let herself out the door.

She leaves the bed quietly and switches on the lamp in the living room, where his Naugahyde recliner confronts her, smug as a catcher's mitt, with a long, deep impression of Harland running down its center. On weekends he watches cable TV with perfect vigilance, as if he's afraid he'll miss the end of the world—though he doesn't bother with CNN, which, if the world did end, is where the taped footage would run. Harland prefers the Home Shopping Channel because he can follow it with the sound turned off.

She has an edgy sense of being watched because of his collection of antique headlights, which stare from the china cabinet. Harland runs El-Jay's Paint and Body and his junk is taking over her house. She hardly has the energy to claim it back. Old people might marry gracefully once in a while, but their houses rarely do. She snaps on the light in the kitchen and shades her eyes against the bright light and all those ready appliances.

Her impulse is to call Taylor, her daughter. Taylor is taller than Alice now and pretty and living far away, in Tucson. Alice wants to warn her that a defect runs in the family, like flat feet or diabetes: they're all in danger of ending up alone by their own stubborn choice. The ugly kitchen clock says four-fifteen. No time-zone differences could make that into a reasonable hour in Tucson; Taylor would answer with her heart pounding, wanting to know who'd dropped dead. Alice rubs the back of her head, where her cropped gray hair lies flat in several wrong directions, prickly with sweat and sleeplessness. The cluttered kitchen irritates her. The Formica countertop is patterned with pink and black loops like rubber bands lying against each other, getting on her nerves, all cocked and ready to spring like hail across the kitchen. Alice wonders if other women in the middle of the night have begun to resent their Formica. She stares hard at the telephone on the counter, wishing it would ring. She needs some proof that she isn't the last woman left on earth, the surviving queen of nothing. The clock gulps softly, eating seconds whole while she waits; she receives no proof.

She stands on a chair and rummages in the cupboard over the refrigerator for a bottle of Jim Beam that's been in the house since before she married Harland. There are Mason jars up there she ought to get rid of. In her time Alice has canned tomatoes enough for a hundred bomb shelters, but now she couldn't care less, nobody does. If they drop the bomb now, the world will end without the benefit of tomato aspic. She climbs down and pours half an inch of Jim Beam into a Bengals mug that came free with a tank of gas. Alice would just as soon get her teeth cleaned as watch the Bengals. That's the price of staying around when your heart's not in it, she thinks. You get to be cheerleader for a sport you never chose. She unlatches the screen door and steps barefoot onto the porch.

The sky is a perfect black. A leftover smile of moon hides in the bottom branches of the sugar maple, teasing her to smile back. The air isn't any cooler outside the house, but being outdoors in her sheer nightgown arouses Alice with the possibility of freedom. She could walk away from this house carrying nothing. How those glass eyeballs in the china cabinet would blink, to see her go. She leans back in the porch swing, missing the squeak of its chains that once sang her baby to sleep, but which have been oppressed into silence now by Harland's WD-40. Putting her nose deep into the mug of bourbon, she draws in sweet, caustic fumes, just as she used to inhale tobacco smoke until Taylor made her quit.

She raised a daughter in this house and planted all the flowers in the yard, but that's nothing to hold her here. Flowers you can get tired of. In the record heat of this particular Kentucky spring the peonies have blown open their globes a month ahead of Memorial Day. Their face-powder scent reminds her of old women she knew in childhood, and the grave-yard. She stops swinging a minute to listen: a huffling sound is coming from the garden. Hester Biddle's pigs. Hester lives a short walk down the road and has taken up raising Vietnamese miniature potbellied pigs for a new lease on life after her stroke. She claims they're worth two thousand per pig, but Alice can't imagine on what market. They're ugly as sin and run away for a hobby, to root in Alice's peony beds. "Go on home," Alice says in a persuasive voice. The pigs look up.

"I mean it," she says, rising from the porch swing, her hands on her hips. "I'm not above turning you all into bacon."

In the dim light from the kitchen their eyes glow red. Pigs are turning out to be the family curse: Alice's mother, a tall, fierce woman named Minerva Stamper, ran a hog farm alone for fifty years. Alice picks up an empty flowerpot from the porch step and throws it at the pigs. The darkness absorbs it. She throws a dirt clod and a pair of pruning shears, which also vanish. Then a medium-sized aluminum bowl. Harland ordered the Cornucopia Of Bowls from the shopping channel for their wedding anniversary, so now their home has a bowl for every purpose. She picks up another one and gives it a fling. She'll have to pick them up in the morning, in front of God and the Biddles, but she wants those pigs out of her life. She finds a galvanized watering can and lifts herself on the balls of her feet, testing her calves. Alice is in good shape, despite her age; when she concentrates she can still find all her muscles from the inside. When her first husband left her the house fell apart but she and her daughter held up well, she thinks, everything considered.

She heaves the watering can but can't tell where it's gone. It lands with a ding—possibly it struck a member of the Cornucopia. The red pig eyes don't even blink. Alice feels defeated. She returns to the porch to collect her losses.

She's not walking away from here. Who would take her in? She knows most of the well-to-do women in town, from cleaning their houses all the years she was raising Taylor, but their respect for Alice is based on what she could tell the world about their basements. On Fridays, Alice plays poker with Fay Richey and Lee Shanks—cheerful, husky-voiced women who smoke a lot and are so thankful to still be married, if she left Harland they'd treat her like she had a virus. Minerva and the hog farm are both gone, of course, the one simply dead and buried, the other sold to pay its own debts. It depresses Alice deeply to think how people's lives and all other enterprises, like life insurance, can last long enough to cancel themselves out.

A mockingbird lands on the tip of a volunteer mulberry that has grown up through the hedge. Flapping to stay balanced, he makes the long branch bob and sway like a carnival ride. His little profile flails against a horizon the color of rising dough. In the few minutes it took Alice to make an accounting of her life, dawn was delivered to this address and the automatic spotlight on Biddles' barn winked off. No matter what kind of night you're having, morning always wins.

The mockingbird springs off his mulberry branch into darkness and then materializes up on the roof, crowing to this section of the county that her TV antenna is his and his alone. Something about the male outlook, Alice thinks, you have got to appreciate. She stands with her arms crossed against her chest and observes the dark universe of the garden, which is twinkling now with aluminum meteorites. She hears the pigs again. It's no wonder they like to come here; they get terrified down at Biddles' when Henry uses more machinery than he needs. Yesterday he was using the hay mower to cut his front yard, which is typical. The poor things are just looking for a home, like the Boat People. She has a soft spot for refugees and decides to let them stay. It will aggravate Hester, who claims that every time they eat Alice's peonies they come home with diarrhea.

The neighborhood tomcat, all muscle and slide, is creeping along the top of the trellis where Alice's sweet peas have spent themselves all spring. She's seen him up there before, getting high on the night perfume, or imagining the taste of mockingbird. The garden Alice wishes she could abandon is crowded with bird music and border disputes and other people's hungry animals. She feels like the queen of some pitiful, festive land.

Welcome to Heaven.

For the first time in years she thinks of Sugar Boss: her family tie. Sugar is a second cousin and the most famous citizen of Heaven, Oklahoma. Alice has her picture put away in the scrapbook with Taylor's high school diploma and whatever else there is in the way of family papers. It's an old picture cut out of *Life* magazine, summer of '55. Sugar posed for a photographer with a pop bottle raised to her lips and a crown of daisies in her hair, leaning against the WELCOME TO HEAVEN sign, and was seen all over everywhere in the advertisement. Alice saw her at the grocery checkout and couldn't believe her eyes. She sent a letter, needing no more address than "Sugar Marie Boss, Heaven, Okla.," and it got there, even though by then she was no longer technically a Boss but a Hornbuckle. Sugar wrote back.

They'd spent their last years of childhood together on the farm during the Depression, along with dozens of other people who showed up at Minerva's door once they'd run out of everything but relatives. Of all the cousins, Alice and Sugar were closest, born a mere month apart. At nine they could pass for twelve and got jobs at the mattress factory, where it was all young girls, sewing up the ticking and stuffing in feathers. Their arms grew muscled and the down stuck on their hair, making them look like duck girls. Those times made bonds among people. The clotheslines ran from house to house and the wash ran between families like the same drab flag repeated over and over, uniting them all in the nation of wash-tubs and rough knuckles. There was love in that life, a kind of solid hope. Children ran heedless under the flapping laundry in a nation of their own. But it's Alice's impression that most of them grew up with hungry hearts, feeling sure that one day they would run out of everything again.

After their chance reconnection, she and Sugar shared their memories in long letters pressed into fat envelopes, but once they'd finished with the past, neither one had it in her to sustain the correspondence. Alice suspects Sugar's life never reached the same elevation again; in her letters there was mention of daughters prone to pregnancy. Alice pictures a rattle-trap house and flowerbeds gone to jimson weed.

But Sugar once put Heaven on the map, and that has to carry some weight still. Alice stretches her legs into the pale orange morning that is taking hold around her, and it dawns on her with a strange shock that she is still the same person she was as a nine-year-old. Even her body is mostly unchanged. Her breasts are of a small, sound architecture and her waist is limber and strong; she feels like one of those California buildings designed for an earthquake. As surely as her organs are in the right places, she feels Sugar is still there in Heaven. She could write her today. She's kept feelings for Sugar, her long-lost relative who came home to her one day in the checkout line. Something like that is as bad or as good as a tele-phone ringing in the night: either way, you're not as alone as you think.

2

A MEAN EYE

"Look up, Turtle. Angels."

Taylor stoops to her daughter's eye level and points up at the giant granite angels guarding the entrance to the Hoover Dam: a straight-backed team, eyes on the horizon, their dark, polished arms raised toward the sky.

"They look like Danny," Turtle observes.

"Biceps to die for," Taylor agrees. Danny, their garbage man, is a body builder on his days off.

"What do angels need muscles for?"

Taylor laughs at the thought of some saint having to tote around the overfilled garbage bags of heaven. "They made this back in the thirties," she says. "Ask Grandma about the Depression sometime. Nobody could get a job, so they had this WPA thing where people made bridges and sidewalks and statues that look like they could sweat."

"Let's take a picture." Turtle's tone warns off argument; she means Taylor will stand under the angels and *she* will take the photo. Taylor stands where she's placed and prepares to smile for as long as it takes. Turtle concentrates through the rectangular eye, her black eyebrows stranded above it in her high forehead. Turtle's photos tend to come out fairly hopeless in terms of composition: cut-off legs or all sky, or sometimes something Taylor never even saw at the time. When the pictures come back from the drugstore she often gets the feeling she's gone on someone else's vacation. She watches Turtle's snub-nosed sneakers and deliberately planted legs, wondering where all that persistence comes from and where it will go. Since she found Turtle in her car and adopted her three years ago, she has had many moments of not believing she's Turtle's mother. This child is the miracle Taylor wouldn't have let in the door if it had knocked. But that's what miracles are, she supposes. The things nobody saw coming.

Her eyes wander while Turtle fiddles. The sun is hot, hot. Taylor twists her dark hair up off her neck.

"Mom!"

"Sorry." She drops her arms to her sides, carefully, like a dancer, and tries to move nothing but her eyes. A man in a wheelchair rolls toward them and winks. He's noticeably handsome from the waist up, with WPA arms. He moves fast, his dark mane flying, and turns his chair smoothly before the angels' marble pedestal. If she strains her peripheral vision Taylor can read the marble slab: it's a monument to the men who died building the dam. It doesn't say who they were, in particular. Another panel across the way lists the names of all the directors of the dam project, but this one says only that many who labored here found their final rest. There is a fairly disturbing bronze plaque showing men in work clothes calmly slipping underwater. "Poor guys," she says aloud. "Tomb of the unknown concrete pourer."

"Working for fifty cents an hour," the wheelchair man says. "A bunch of them were Navajo boys from the reservation."

"Really?"

"Oh, yeah." He smiles in a one-sided way that suggests he knows his way around big rip-offs like this, a fancy low-paying job that bought these Navajo boys a piece of the farm.

The shutter clicks, releasing Taylor. She stretches the muscles in her face.

"Are you the trip photographer?" he asks Turtle.

Turtle presses her face into her mother's stomach. "She's shy," Taylor says. "Like most major artists."

"Want me to take one of the two of you?"

"Sure. One to send Grandma." Taylor hands him the camera and he does the job, requiring only seconds.

"You two on a world tour?" he asks.

"A small world tour. We're trying to see the Grand Canyon all the way around. Yesterday we made it from Tucson to the Bright Angel overlook." Taylor doesn't say that they got manic on junk food in the car, or that when they jumped out at the overlook exactly at sunset, Turtle took one look down and wet her pants. Taylor couldn't blame her. It's a lot to take in.

"I'm on a tour of monuments to the unlucky." He nods at the marble slab.

Taylor is curious about his hobby but decides not to push it. They leave him to the angels and head for the museum. "Do not sit on wall," Turtle says, stopping to point at the wall. She's learning to read, in kindergarten and the world at large.

"On wall," Taylor says. "Do not sit on wall."

The warning is stenciled along a waist-high parapet that runs across the top of the dam, but the words are mostly obscured by the legs of all the people sitting on the wall. Turtle looks up at her mother with the beautiful bewilderment children wear on their faces till the day they wake up knowing everything.

"Words mean different things to different people," Taylor explains. "You could read it as 'Don't sit on the wall.' But other people, like Jax for instance, would think it means 'Go ahead and break your neck, but don't say we didn't warn you.'"

"I wish Jax was here," Turtle says solemnly. Jax is Taylor's boyfriend, a keyboard player in a band called the Irascible Babies. Taylor sometimes feels she could take Jax or leave him, but it's true he's an asset on trips. He sings in the car and is good at making up boredom games for Turtle.

"I know," Taylor says. "But he'd just want to sit on the wall. You'd have to read him his rights."

For Taylor, looking over the edge is enough, hundreds of feet down that curved, white wing of concrete to the canyon bottom. The boulders below look tiny and distant like a dream of your own death. She grips her daughter's arm so protectively the child might later have marks. Turtle says nothing. She's been marked in life by a great many things, and Taylor's odd brand of maternal love is by far the kindest among them.

Turtle's cotton shorts with one red leg and one white one flap like a pair of signal flags as she walks, though what message she's sending is beyond Taylor's guess. Her thin, dark limbs and anxious eyebrows give her a pleading look, like a child in the magazine ads that tell how your twenty cents a day can give little Maria or Omar a real chance at life. Taylor has wondered if Turtle will ever outgrow the poster-child look. She would give years off her own life to know the story of Turtle's first three, in eastern Oklahoma, where she's presumed to have been born. Her grip on Turtle is redundant, since Turtle always has a fist clamped onto Taylor's hand or sleeve. They cross through the chaotic traffic to the museum.

Inside, old photos line the walls, showing great expanses of scaffolded concrete and bushy-browed men in overalls standing inside huge turbines. The tourists are being shuffled into a small theater. Turtle tugs her in for the show, but Taylor regrets it as soon as the projector rolls. The film describes the amazing achievement of a dam that tamed the Colorado River. In the old days it ran wild, flooding out everyone downstream, burying their crops in mud. "There was only one solution—the dam!" exclaims the narrator, who reminds Taylor of a boy in a high school play, drumming up self-importance to conquer embarrassment. Mr. Hoover's engineers prevailed in the end, providing Arizona with irrigation and L.A. with electricity and the Mexicans with the leftover salty trickle.

"Another solution is they didn't need to grow their cotton right on the riverbank," Taylor points out.

"Mom!" hisses Turtle. At home Turtle whines when Taylor talks back to the TV. Jax sides with Turtle on the television subject, citing the importance of fantasy. Taylor sides with her mother, who claims over the phone that TV has supernatural powers over her husband. "Just don't believe everything on there is true," Taylor warns often, but she knows this war is a lost cause in general. As far as her daughter is concerned, Mutant Ninja Turtles live in the sewers and that is that.

Outside the museum, a foil gum wrapper skates along the sidewalk on a surprise gust of wind. A herd of paper cups and soda straws rolls eastward in unison. Lucky Buster sits on the ramparts of the Hoover Dam, trying to figure out how to save the day. People will throw anything in the world on the ground, or even in the water. Like pennies. They end up down there with the catfish. There could be a million dollars at the bottom of the lake right now, but everybody thinks there's just one red cent—the one they threw.

Lucky sits very still. He has his eye on a bright red soda-pop can. His friend Otis is an engineer for the Southern Pacific, and he's warned Lucky about pop cans. They catch the sun just right and they'll look like a red signal flare on the tracks. When you see that, you've got to stop the whole train, and then it turns out it's just a pop can. Bad news.

The people are all up above him. One girl is looking. Her round face like a sweet brown pie can see him over the wall. He waves, but she bobs behind the mother and they go away. Nobody else is looking. He could go down there now. The water is too close, though, and scares him: water is black, blue, pink, every color. It gets in your eyes there's so much light. He looks away at the nicer camel hump desert. Now: *go*.

Lucky drops down and scoots along the gray wall that runs along the edge. One side is water, fish-colored; on the other side you fall into the hole. He is as careful as the circus girls in silver bathing suits on TV, walking on wires. One foot, another foot.

A white bird with scabbed yellow feet lands in front of Lucky. "Ssss," he says to the bird, shaking his hands at it. The bird walks away fast, one spread foot and then the other one. Lucky is two steps away from the pop can. Now one step away. Now he's got it.

The bird turns its head and looks straight at Lucky with a mean eye.

The sun has dropped into the Nevada hills and rung up a sunset the color of cherries and lemons. Turtle and Taylor take one last stroll across Mr.

Hoover's concrete dream. Turtle is holding on so tightly that Taylor's knuckles ache. Their hypochondriac friend Lou Ann has warned Taylor about arthritis, but this snap-jawed grip is a principle of their relationship; it won Turtle a nickname, and then a mother. She hasn't deliberately let go of Taylor since they met.

The water in the shadow of the dam is musky green and captivating to Turtle. She yanks on Taylor's fingers to point out huge catfish moving in moss-colored darkness. Taylor doesn't really look. She's trying to take in the whole of Lake Mead, the great depth and weight of water that formerly ran free and made life miserable for the downstream farmers. It stretches far back into the brown hills, but there is no vegetation along the water's edge, just one surface meeting another, a counterfeit lake in the desert that can't claim its own shoreline. In the distance someone is riding a kind of small water vehicle that seems pesty and loud for its size, like a mosquito.

Storm clouds with high pompadours have congregated on the western horizon, offering the hope of cooler weather, but only the hope. The Dodge when they get back to it is firecracker hot and stinks of melted plastic upholstery. Taylor opens both front doors and tries to fan cooler air onto the seat. The ice-cream cone she bought Turtle was a mistake, she sees, but she's not an overly meticulous parent. She's had to learn motherhood on a wing and a prayer in the last three years, and right now her main philosophy is that everything truly important is washable. She hands Turtle a fistful of fast-food napkins from the glove compartment, but has to keep her eyes on the road once they get going. The Dodge Corona drives like a barge and the road is narrow and crooked, as bad as the roads she grew up risking her neck on in Kentucky.

Eventually they level out on the Nevada plain, which looks clinically dead. Behind them the lake stretches out its long green fingers, begging the sky for something, probably rain.

Turtle asks, "How will he get out?"

"Will who get out?"

"That man."

"Which man is that, sweetheart?" Turtle isn't a big talker; she didn't complete a sentence until she was four, and even now it can take days to get the whole story. "Is this something you saw on TV?" Taylor prompts. "Like the Ninja Turtles?"

"No." She looks mournfully at the waffled corpse of her ice cream cone. "He picked up a pop can and fell down the hole by the water."

Taylor narrows her eyes at the road. "At the dam? You saw somebody fall?"

"Yes."

"Where people were sitting, on that wall?"

"No, the other side. The water side."

Taylor takes a breath to find her patience. "That man out on the lake, riding around on that boat thing?"

"No," Turtle says. "The man that fell in the hole by the water."

Taylor can make no sense of this. "It wasn't on TV?"

"No!"

They're both quiet. They pass a casino where a giant illuminated billboard advertises the idea of cashing your paycheck and turning it into slot-machine tokens.

Turtle asks, "How will he get out?"

"Honey, I really don't know what you mean. You saw somebody fall down a hole by the dam. But not into the water?"

"Not the water. The big hole. He didn't cry."

Taylor realizes what she could mean, and rejects the possibility, but for the half second between those two thoughts her heart drops. There was a round spillway where the water could bypass the dam during floods. "You don't mean that spillway, do you? The big hole between the water and the parking lot?"

"Yes." Turtle's black eyes are luminous. "I don't think he can get out."

"There was a big high fence around that." Taylor has slowed to about fifteen miles an hour. She ignores the line of traffic behind her, although the drivers are making noise, impatient to get to Las Vegas and throw away their money.

"Turtle, are you telling me the absolute truth?"

Before she can manage an answer, Taylor U-turns the Dodge, furious at herself. She'll never ask Turtle that question again.

* * *

Hoover's guardian angels are in the dark now. The place is abandoned. They bang on the locked museum doors and Taylor cups her hands to see inside, but it is deserted. A huge blueprint of the dam shows elevators, maintenance towers, and on each side a long spillway looping like a stretched intestine under the dam to the river below. Taylor's own gut feels tight. "They've gone home," she tells Turtle, who won't stop banging the door. "Come on. Show me where he fell."

Turtle is willing to substitute one course of action for another. The legs of her shorts whip against each other as they cross to the Arizona side, where she dripped a trail of ice cream an hour before. "There," she says, pointing down.

Taylor examines the throat of the spillway: a rectangular concrete funnel, maybe fifty feet across, whose lower end narrows into a large round hole.

Dots of car lights twist down the mountain, looking lonely. Out over the lake, bats dip and flutter after mosquitoes. Taylor looks at the dark gullet. "Head first, or feet first?"

Turtle ponders this. "He was walking on there." Her finger projects a line down the retaining wall between lake and spillway. "He picked up a pop can. Then he fell down. Sideways first." Her hand burrows into her shorts pocket, frightened of its own revelations.

Taylor squeezes the other hand. "Don't worry. He's one lucky sucker that you've got such sharp eyes. Did you see him go all the way into the hole?"

Turtle nods.

Taylor feels weak-kneed, as she did looking over the parapet wall. The hardest thing about motherhood, she thinks, is that you can never again be the baby of your family, not even for ten seconds. She tries to sound steady. "Should we yell? Think he might hear us?"

Turtle nods.

Taylor screams: "Anybody in there? Hey!" They listen to the passive response of two million tons of concrete.

Taylor leans farther over the rail and makes a splay-fingered megaphone with her hands, to show Turtle this is fun, and will work. "Hey! Youuu! Hello down there, can you hear me? Heyy! Got two dimes for a nickel? Whooo! Hello!"

From far away over the lake comes the high buzz of a motorboat. Nothing else. Turtle cries without making a sound.

She feels for her mother's fingers, the one sure thing. They are standing in the dark. Taylor makes the round moon of flashlight go all over the policeman in the chair but he doesn't wake up. Behind the metal house are machines with long animal necks, and they are sleeping too.

"Hey, mister," Taylor says, louder. The light slides up his brown shirt and brights out a square name badge. Then his eyes. He wakes up and goes for his gun.

"What the fuck?"

"Excuse me, Mister Decker, but don't shoot us, okay? My daughter here is six and we're real defenseless."

Turtle makes herself feel her mother's hand. The man gets up and switches on a world of light. A motor sings and cries in the metal house. "What the hell you after?"

"We'd like to report an emergency, okay? Somebody fell into the dam. Into the spillway."

Mister Decker stares while all his dreams run away.

"He had on a dark shirt, and a green bandana around his head." Taylor looks down, and Turtle touches her hair.

"And long hair. Dark brown."

"Intoxicated?"

"We don't know. It's not somebody we know, we're just reporting it."

Mister Decker fixes his crotch. "When?"

"Around sunset."

"And you decided to come tell me about it in the middle of the night."

"There's nobody at the museum. It took us forever to find anybody."

"It's fucking Easter Sunday tomorrow. You want a parade?"

"Well, I'm sorry you got stuck on a dog shift, but we're trying to report a human life in danger here."

"Sumbitch."

Taylor clicks her flashlight on and off. "You ever think about a new line of work?"

Mister Decker goes into the shed and makes a phone call. When he comes back out he asks, "Any more I.D. on this guy? How old?"

Taylor asks Turtle, "How old was he?"

Turtle looks inside her forehead. "Big."

"Like, a big kid? Or my age? Or older than me."

"Bigger than a kid. Maybe like you."

Mister Decker's whole body slumps suddenly, like a sack with nothing in it. "Are you telling me you personally didn't see the incident occur?"

"My daughter saw the incident occur."

"*She* saw it." He looks. "You believe in Santa Claus, honey?"

Turtle finds her mother with the front of her face and doesn't say. Inside her mother she feels the air rising up.

"Sir, you're intimidating your witness here. She saw what she says she saw. My daughter doesn't miss much. When your boss gets here she could tell him how hilarious you looked when we found you up here snoring on your shift. So you want to take some happy pills and try acting a little nicer to us, or what?"

Hugo Alvarez, Decker's boss, looks them over. His office is the kind of no-frills arrangement that goes out of its way to prove the Park Service isn't wasting taxpayers' money. Taylor makes herself sit still in the orange plastic chair while Mr. Alvarez takes down the facts. "Your daughter doesn't look a thing like you," he notes.

She's used to this. Strangers stare at the two of them with that inquiring-minds-want-to-know look, wondering if maybe they've seen that child on a milk carton somewhere. "She's adopted," Taylor says flatly.

"Mexican-American?"

"Indian. Cherokee."

Mr. Alvarez writes this down on his notepad; apparently it's one of the facts.

"The guy might be banged up," Taylor points out. "Could we speed this up at all?"

Mr. Alvarez has a dark fringe around his bald head, and the eyes of an indifferent hound. He states with no apparent emotion, "There's an eight-foot security fence around the spillway."

"We don't know how he got over the fence," Taylor says, trying to match his tone. The fluorescent lights seem abusive at this hour, and she squints, trying to remember the hillside near the dam. "Maybe he came the other way, down the mountain. Or off the lake."

"We have security personnel watching that area like hawks."

"No offense, but we spent the better part of this night looking for one of your hawks."

"It's a holiday weekend."

"Happy Easter," Taylor says. "Let's go hunt some eggs."

Alvarez sighs. "I know you mean well, miss, but it doesn't sound very probable. Somebody else would have seen it. We can't justify calling out a rescue on this unless we have a witness."

"We have a witness. My daughter is the witness."

Alvarez rubs his nose with his pen and decides not to add anything to his log of facts.

"She's never told a lie in her life," Taylor adds.

"Frankly," he says, "I haven't heard her say anything."

"She doesn't talk much. If you leave out all the bullshit in life, there's not that much left to say, is there?"

Alvarez looks at Decker again and carefully winds his watch. Taylor gets up and walks to the door and back, reining in a real need to kick a chair leg with her cowboy boot. "Do you want *me* to lie? Do you want me to say I saw it too? If you write that down on your report, then can you call a rescue party?"

"Just tell me what happened. Just the truth."

"Just the truth is: a man fell down the spillway of your wonderful dam, today, right around sunset. My daughter saw him go in, and it would give her a better impression of the human race if you'd act like you give a damn. Because if he dies in there he's going to be just truly dead."

* * *

On Sunday, after a few hours of cramped nightmares on the seat of the Dodge, Taylor and Turtle find the head grounds janitor in the employee parking lot coming onto his shift. Taylor likes the looks of his truck: a '59 Ford, cherry. Maybe he'll be the one to listen. She works in the automotive business and has noticed that people who take care of old things usually have some patience.

"Down the spillway?" he asks. "Can't be. We got a fence around that. I saw a guy go right over the top once, down there." Taylor shudders, thinking of that long free-fall. "Middle of the day," he says. "Accident. Your suicides, they mostly hop off at night. Scrambled eggs in the morning."

Taylor is woozy from lack of sleep and could live without the scrambled-egg report. "This guy was about my age. Long hair. He had on overalls and, what else? A bandana."

"A green bandana?" The janitor's face comes on like someone threw a switch behind it. "Tied around his head, like this? And hair like this?" He chops his hand to his shoulder.

Taylor and Turtle nod.

"Oh, hell, that's Lucky Buster." He heads for the spillway.

They follow him. "You *know* this guy?" Taylor asks.

"Retarded guy. Oh, hell. I can't believe this. When?"

"Last night. You know him?"

"He's been hanging around here a couple weeks. I can't believe this. He was driving me crazy. He's a little kid in his mind, you know what I mean? He has this thing about litter."

Taylor yells, "Wait up!" Turtle is dragging on her fingers like a water skier. "What thing about litter?"

"He's nuts. Two or three times I caught him climbing around places a damn mountain goat should not be climbing around. Trying to pick up soda cans, would you believe. Oh, hell. Lucky Buster."

He stops at the spillway and they all look down, at nothing. The janitor is trying hard to catch his breath. "Oh, hell."

At ten o'clock Monday morning, six volunteers from the North Las Vegas Spelunking Club, plus one paramedic with rock-climbing experience, emerge from the spillway on the Arizona side. It took all night to assemble this team, and they have been down in the hole for hours more. Taylor and Turtle are front row in the crowd that is pushing quilt-cheeked against the security fence. Guards shout through bullhorns for the crowd to disperse, attracting more new arrivals.

The rescuers look like miners, blacked with grit. The rope that connects them waist to waist went down at dawn in yellow coils, but now is coming up black. Only the clinking buckles of their climbing gear catch the sun.

The stretcher comes out of the hole as a long, stiff oval, like a loaf shoved from the oven. Lucky Buster is wrapped in rubber rescue blankets and strapped down tightly from forehead to ankles with black canvas straps, so he bulges in sections. He can't stop blinking his eyes. That crowd on the fence is the brightest thing he has ever seen.

THE TRUE STORIES

TEN O'CLOCK IN KENTUCKY: THE sun has barely started thinking about Arizona. She can't call yet. Alice has been cleaning out her kitchen cabinets since dawn. She saw something on the early-morning news that disturbed her and she needs to talk to Taylor. Time zones are a mean trick, she feels, surely invented by someone whose family all lived under one roof.

Cardboard boxes crowd the linoleum floor like little barges bristling with their cargo: pots and pans, Mason jars, oven mitts, steak knives, more stuff than Alice can imagine she ever needed. The mood she's in, she's ready to turn out the cookstove. She doubts Harland would notice if she stopped cooking altogether. When she met him he was heating up unopened cans of Campbell's soup in a big pot of water every night. It amazed her to see the cans rolling around like logs in the boiling water. "Don't they bust?" she asked him, and he shyly put his hand on hers and allowed as how sometimes they did. His idea of a home-cooked meal is when you open the can first and pour it in a saucepan. Alice has been wasting her talents.

With aggressive strokes of her cleaning rag she reaches back into a high cabinet, feeling her Bermuda shorts slide up her thighs where the veins have turned a helpless blue. She's exposing herself to no one at the moment, but still feels embarrassed that her circulatory system has to start showing this way. Getting old is just a matter of getting easier to see through, until all your failing insides are in plain view and everyone's business. Even the ads aimed at old people are embarrassing: bathroom talk. You're expected to pull yourself inside-out like a sleeve and go public with your hemorrhoids.

It's hard for Alice to picture the portion of her life that still lies ahead. Her friend Lee Shanks saw a religious call-in show about turning your life around through Creative Imaging, and Lee has been trying ever since to image a new Honda Accord. But when Alice closes her eyes she sees, at the moment, Mason jars. She knows that no woman with varicose veins and a brain in her head would walk away from a decent husband, but she's going to anyway. Aloneness is her inheritance, like the deep heartline that breaks into match sticks across her palm. The Stamper women might sometimes think they're getting somewhere, nailing themselves down to kin, but some mystery always cuts them loose from people in the long run. Her mother used to tromp around the farm with her eyes on the sky as if some sign up there said: FREEDOM AND HAPPINESS THIS WAY, AT THE END OF THE LONELY ROAD.

Alice never wanted to be like her. She married young and misguided but with every intention of staying with her first husband, Foster Greer. She met him in a juke joint at the edge of the woods by the Old Miss slaughter pen, and on that very first night he danced her out to the parking lot and told her he was going to take her away from that smell. Between the hog farm and the slaughter pen Alice had lived her whole life within a perimeter of stench, and didn't know what he meant. It amazed her to discover that air, on its own, was empty of odor. She breathed through her nose again and again like an addict high on a new drug, and in the narrow parting of a highway cut through cypress swamps they drove all the way to New Orleans before breakfast. Even now Alice can feel in her skin the memory of that crazy adventure: speeding through the alligator bayous at midnight, feeling alive and lucky, as if there were only one man and one woman on earth this night and they were the ones chosen.

As a husband, though, Foster wore his adventures thin. He made a career of what he called "fresh starts," which meant getting fired from one house-framing job after another and consoling himself with Old Grand-Dad. Anything that's worth doing, he told Alice, is worth starting over right in a new town. And then he told her she was too much fun, as if it were her fault he could never settle down. He made Alice promise she would never try anything cute like getting pregnant, and she didn't, for nearly ten years. It wasn't so easy in those days; it was an endeavor. When it finally did happen, she'd known Foster long enough to know a good trade when she saw one, him for a baby. He had given her fresh air, but that's not such a gift that you have to stay grateful your whole life long. When he moved on from Pittman, Alice and the baby stayed.

She'd believed that motherhood done fiercely and well would end her family's jinx of solitude; Alice threw herself into belief in her daughter as frankly as Minerva had devoted herself to hogs. But kids don't stay with you if you do it right. It's one job where, the better you are, the more surely you won't be needed in the long run. She looks at the clock again: seven-thirty in Tucson. She picks up the phone and dials.

A baritone voice says, "Yo."

That would be Jax. Alice feels ridiculous. What she saw on TV was not about Taylor and Turtle. They are probably still in bed. "Oh, well, hi," she says. "It's me, Alice."

"Hey, pretty Alice. How's your life?"

"It'll do," she says. She never knows what she ought to say to Jax. She hasn't met him and finds him hard to picture. For one thing, he plays in a rock and roll band. He comes from New Orleans, and according to Taylor he is tall and lanky and wears a little gold earring, but his voice sounds like Clark Gable in Gone With the Wind.

"Your daughter has fled the premises," Jax reports. "She took the second generation and went to see the Grand Canyon. How do you like that?"

"Then it's true!" Alice shouts, startling herself.

Jax isn't rattled. "True blue. They abandoned me here to talk things over with the door hinges." He adds, "Then what's true?"

Alice is completely confused. If something had happened to them, Jax would know. "Nothing," she says. "Some darn thing I saw on TV. Harland had the news on and they had somebody falling over the Hoover Dam, and I could have swore there was Taylor Greer talking to the camera, just for a second."

"If Taylor fell off the Hoover Dam, she wouldn't be talking to the camera," Jax points out.

"Well, no, she wouldn't, so I got worried that it was Turtle that had fell off."

"Couldn't be," Jax says in his gentleman's drawl. "She would never let Turtle fall off anything larger than a washing machine. And if she did, she'd be on the phone to you before the kid hit bottom."

Alice is disturbed by the image but feels fairly sure Jax is right. "I kept hoping they'd show it again, but Harland's gone over to Home Shopping now and there's no coming back from that."

"Could be they're at the Hoover Dam," Jax says thoughtfully. "She doesn't always keep me up to date."

"They both did go, then? She took Turtle out of school?"

"School is out for Easter break. They thought they'd go have a religious experience with sedimentary rock."

"You should have gone with them. That ought to be something, that Grand Canyon."

"Oh, believe me, I wanted to. But my band got a gig in a bar called the Filth Encounter, and you can't miss something like that."

Alice finds herself calming down, listening to Jax. He always sounds so relaxed she wonders sometimes about his vital signs. "Well, that's good they went," she says mournfully. "That little girl's already way ahead of me. I've never even got down to see the new Toyota plant at Georgetown yet."

"Is everything okay?" Jax asks.

Alice touches her eyes. Half the time he comes across like he was raised on Venus, but his voice is wonderfully deep and slow, something she could use around the house. "Well, not really," she says. "I'm a mess. Just crazy enough to think I was seeing my own daughter on TV." She pauses, wondering how she can confess her troubles to someone she's never met. It's midmorning in an empty kitchen: the territory of lonely-hearts call-in shows and radio preachers for the desperate. She tells him, "I guess I'm leaving Harland."

"Hey, that happens. You never did like him much."

"I did so. At first." She drops her voice. "Not to live with, but I thought he'd improve. Under the influence of good cooking."

"You can't rehabilitate a man who collects light bulbs."

"No, it's headlights."

"Headlights. Is that actually true?"

"Off old cars. Any old car parts really, as long as they don't make any noise. You should see my living room. I feel like I've died and gone to the junkyard."

"Well, come live with us. Taylor leaves all her car parts at work. We need you, Alice. Taylor hates to cook, and I'm criminal at it."

"There's no hanging crimes you can do in the kitchen," Alice says. "I give a man extra points just for trying."

"Your daughter doesn't give a man extra points just for anything."

Alice has to laugh. "That's a fact."

"She says I cook like a caveman."

"Well, forever more." Alice laughs harder. Clark Gable with a gold earring and stooped shoulders and a club. "What does that mean?"

"No finesse, apparently."

"Well, I couldn't move in with Taylor. I've told her that fifty times. I'd be in your way." Alice has never lived in a city and knows she couldn't. What could she ever say to people who pay money to go hear a band called the Irritated Babies? Alice doesn't even drive a car, although few people know this, since she walks with an attitude of preferring the exercise.

"I don't think Taylor loves me anymore," Jax says. "I think she's got her eye on Danny, our garbage man."

"Oh, go on."

"You haven't seen this guy. He can lift four Glad Bags in each hand."

"Well, I'm sure you've got your good points too. Does she treat you decent?"

"She does."

"You're in good shape, then. Don't worry, you'd know. If Taylor don't like somebody, she'll paint the barn with it."

Jax laughs. "She does wish you'd come visit," he says.

"I will." Alice has tears in her eyes.

"I do too," he says, "I wish you would come. I need to meet this Alice. When Taylor says she wants you to live with us, I'm thinking to myself, this is ultra. Everybody else I know is in a twelve-step program to get over their dysfunctional childhoods."

"Well, it's my fault that she don't give men the extra points. I think I turned her against men. Not on purpose. It's kind of a hex. My mama ran that hog farm by herself for fifty years, and that's what started it."

"You have a hog farm in your maternal line? I'm envious. I wish I'd spent my childhood rocked in the bosom of swine."

"Well, it wasn't all that wonderful. My mother was a Stamper. She was too big and had too much on her mind to answer to 'Mother,' so I called her Minerva, just the same as the neighbors and the creditors and the traveling slaughter hands did. She'd always say, 'Mister, if you ain't brung it with you, you won't find it here.' And that was the truth. She had hogs by the score but nothing much to offer her fellow man, other than ham."

"Well," says Jax. "Ham is something."

"No, but she'd never let a man get close enough to see the whites of her eyes. And look at me, just the same, chasing off husbands like that Elizabeth Taylor. I've been thinking I raised Taylor to stand too far on her own side of the plank. She adopted the baby before she had a boyfriend of any kind, and it seemed like that just proved out the family trend. I think we could go on for thirteen generations without no men coming around to speak of. Just maybe to do some plumbing once in a while."

"Is this the Surgeon General's warning?"

"Oh, Jax, honey, I don't know what I'm saying. I'm a lonely old woman cleaning my kitchen cupboards to entertain myself. You kids are happy and I'm just full of beans."

"No, you stand by your stories. Whatever gets you through."

"I better let you go. Tell Taylor to send pictures of the baby. The last one I have is the one from Christmas and she's looking at that Santa Claus like he's Lee Harvey Oswald. I could live with something better than that setting on my TV."

"Message registered. She'll be back Sunday. I'll tell her you called, Alice."

"Okay, hon. Thanks."

She's sad when Jax hangs up, but relieved that Taylor and Turtle aren't dead or in trouble. She hates television, and not just because her husband has left her for one; she hates it on principle. It's like the boy who cried wolf, spreading crazy ideas faster than you can find out what's really up. If people won't talk to each other, they shouldn't count on strangers in suits and makeup to give them the straight dope.

She crosses the kitchen, stepping high over boxes of spatulas and nested mixing bowls. It looks like an estate sale, and really Alice does feel as though someone has died. She just can't think who. Out in the den, the voice of a perky young woman is talking up some kitchen gadget that will mix bread dough and slice onions and even make milk shakes. "Don't lose this chance, call now," the woman says meaningfully, and in her mind Alice dares Harland to go ahead and order it for their anniversary. She will make him an onion milk shake and hit the road.

4

LUCKY BUSTER LIVES

LUCKY AND TURTLE ARE ASLEEP in the backseat: Taylor can make out their separate snores, soprano and bass. She scrapes the dial of the car radio across miles of West Arizona static and clicks it off again. Suspended before her in the rearview mirror is an oblong view of Lucky's head rolled back on the seat, and now that it's safe to stare, she does. His long, clean hair falls like a girl's across his face, but his pale throat shows sandpaper stubble and a big Adam's apple. He's thirty-eight years old; they are a woman, man, and child in this car, like any family on the highway headed out on an errand of hope or dread. But Taylor can't see him as a man. The idea unsettles her.

From the moment of his rescue he has begged them not to tell his mother what happened. Angie Buster runs a diner in Sand Dune, Arizona, and over the phone sounded tired. Lucky has no idea that she has spoken with Taylor, or that she watched his body come out of the hole again and again on the TV news. Computer graphics turned the Hoover Dam inside-out for America, showing a red toy image of Lucky moving jerkily down into the spillway and lodging there like the protagonist of a dark-humored video game. Only Lucky and Turtle, perpetrators of the miracle, still believe they've witnessed a secret.

It was Turtle's idea to drive him home once the doctors had bandaged his sprained ankle and held him for observation. Turtle is a TV heroine now, so police officers and even doctors pay attention to her. One reporter said that Turtle's and Lucky's destinies were linked now; that according to Chinese belief, if you save someone's life you're responsible for that person forever. Taylor wonders if he was making this up. Why would you owe them more than what you'd already provided? It sounds like the slightly off-base logic you sometimes get in a fortune cookie.

She turns the car south on Arizona 93 and picks up a signal on the radio. An oldies station, they're calling it, though it's playing the Beatles. If Beatles are oldie now, where does that leave Perry Como, she wonders, and all those girl groups with their broken-heart songs and bulletproof hair? As nearly as she remembers, Taylor was in kindergarten when the Beatles first hit it big, but they persisted into her adolescence, shedding the missionary suits and skinny ties in favor of LSD and little round sunglasses. She can't identify the song but it's one of their later ones, with that odd sound they developed toward the end—as if their voices are coming from inside a metal pipe.

What did he think about for a day and a half down there? Taylor can't bring herself to imagine. Now, with his fingernails scrubbed, his red checked shirt cleaned and respectfully pressed in the hospital laundry, what he's been through seems impossible. The doctors presumed he never lost consciousness, unless he slept. From the looks of him now, he didn't, or not much.

She came so close to driving away that night. Worn down by the uniforms and beard stubble and patronizing looks, it would have been such a small thing to get back in the car and go on to Nevada. She shivers.

The Beatles give up the ghost and Elton John takes over, his honky-tonk piano chords bouncing into "Crocodile Rock." This one Taylor remembers from dances on the bleached wood floor of the Pittman High gym, with some boy or other who never could live up to her sense of celebration on those occasions. They were always too busy trying to jam a hand between two of your buttons somewhere. The song is about that exact war, and it excited the girls as much as the boys to hear it because you knew how Suzy felt when she wore her dresses—as the song says— tight. Like something no boy could ever touch. Taylor liked Elton John, his oversized glasses and preposterous shoes, laughing at himself—such a far cry from other rock stars with long limp hair and closed eyes and heads rolled back to the sounds of their own acid chords, going for the crucifixion look.

Music is all different now: Jax belongs to neither breed, the Jesuses or the Elton Johns. Now they don't just laugh at themselves but also their audience and the universe in general. Jax's wide-eyed, skinny band members wear black jeans and shirts made of torn newspapers. Irascible Babies, pleading ignorance, just wishing they could suckle forever at the breast of a pulsing sound wave.

Jax is a problem in Taylor's life, though she would never say that aloud. She feels disloyal for thinking it, even. He's the first boyfriend she's ever had who is actually funnier than he thinks he is. He is nice to Turtle to the point that it's nearly embarrassing. Jax is so laid-back it took Taylor months to figure out what was going on here: that he's crazy in love with her. Possibly that's the problem. Jax's adoration is like the gift of a huge, scuffling white rabbit held up at arm's length for her to take. Or a European vacation. Something you can never give back.

She turns southwest at the little noncity of Kingman, back toward the Colorado River or what's left of it after all those dams, a tributary robbed blind and fighting hard to make the border. Mountains rise low and purple behind the river like doctor's-office art. She'll follow the river south through Lake Havasu City, where some rich person, she has heard, actually bought the London Bridge and shipped it over block by block to stand lonely in the desert. Eventually they'll reach Sand Dune, where Angie Buster awaits her son. Taylor can call Jax from there and tell him about the new twist on their vacation.

She's not keeping close track of the radio: now it's Otis Redding singing "Dock of the Bay." This one always chokes her up. You can picture poor Otis looking out over the water, the terrible sadness in his voice suggesting he already knows he's going to end up frozen in a Wisconsin lake while the fans wait and wait for his plane to come in, for the concert to begin.

You can't think too much about luck, good or bad. Taylor has decided this before, and at this moment renews her vow. Lucky Buster is lucky to be alive and unlucky to have been born with the small wits that led him to disaster in the first place. Or lucky, too, for small wits, that allow him so little inspection of the big picture. In the ambulance on the way to the hospital, he wanted to go to McDonald's.

Over the phone, Angie Buster confided that Lucky had run away many times before. She asked Taylor not to repeat this to the doctors, fearing that it might interfere somehow with Lucky's insurance. "He's not really running away," Angie explained, "he just don't have a real good understanding of where home ends and the rest of the world takes up."

Taylor agreed that was sometimes a tough call.

Sand Dune is not sandy so much as dusty. Everything Taylor can see in the Parker Strip is covered with dust: battle-scarred regiments of mobile-home parks, cellophane flags whipping from the boat docks, and out in the river the duckish, bobbing boats with yellow bathtub rings on their bellies. A fine silt clings even to the surface of the Colorado, proof that this river has had all the fight knocked out of it.

The town is a congregation of swayback tile roofs and front yards blighted with the kind of short, trashy palm trees that harbor worlds of sparrows. Portions of dilapidated stucco wall stand along the road like billboards, crowded with a square-lettered style of graffiti. There's no chance of losing her way here: the approach to Angie's Diner is festooned with yellow ribbons and a bedsheet banner stating: HAPPY EASTER LUCKY BUSTER. Taylor pulls in at the motor lodge Angie told her to look for, the Casa Suerte, next door to the diner.

"Wake up, kiddos," she says gently. She's afraid Lucky might bolt, but he doesn't. He and Turtle both rub their eyes, equally children. "We're here," she says, and helps Turtle out of the car. She's uncertain how to handle Lucky. He takes off in no particular hurry across the courtyard of the Casa Suerte toward the diner. At the building's front entry is a shrine to the Virgin of Guadalupe, who is studded all over with yellow stick-on bows as if she's been visited with some kind of pox. On the other side of the door a colorless bulldog is ensconced on a padded chair, panting in the air-conditioning. He stands up and barks twice. A big woman in Lycra shorts and a tight yellow T-shirt appears, arms open, to envelop Lucky like a starfish.

"Get in here!" she shouts at Taylor, scooping a hefty arm through the air. Taylor has Turtle in hand and was hanging back to give them their reunion, but apparently this is routine. Some women have swarmed out to make a brief fuss over Lucky, while an old man stands picking the bows off the Virgin, putting them in a plastic sack to save for next time.

Angie's Diner is draped with paper streamers and banners welcoming Lucky home. "Get in here," Angie repeats, once they are inside. "This photographer here wants to take the little girl's picture that saved my son's life. Is this her?"

"This is Turtle," Taylor says. Turtle's grip on her fingers is jeopardizing the blood circulation.

"Oh, Lord," Angie says, swamping Taylor with a hug. "I about lost my mind this time. Once he got kidnapped down to the border by some mules, and that was bad but I think this was worst. Sit, let me get you some pie. Did you all eat lunch yet? Red, get over here!"

The counter is crowded with porcelain knickknacks, and Angie is so busty and energetic in her yellow T-shirt it seems likely she'll knock something over. A freckled man with a camera introduces himself as "Red from the paper." He hands Taylor a copy of the *Sand Dune Mercury* and attempts to remove Turtle from her other hand.

"It's okay, I'll be right here," Taylor promises Turtle's upturned eyes. She rubs the feeling back into her fingers and stares distractedly at the paper while Red poses Lucky and Turtle in front of the salad bar. She's stunned when the banner headline eventually registers:

LUCKY BUSTER SAVED BY PERVERSERING TUSCON PAIR.

She has to read it twice to get the intention of *perversering*. "Wow," she says.

"The papers picked it up all over the state," Angie informs her. "Would you sit down and let me get you something to eat? You kids must be starved."

Taylor follows Angie to a table near the dust-frosted window pane. Angie's hair is dyed such a dark black that she has a slightly purple scalp, like some of Jax's backup singers. She turns around suddenly and tells Taylor in a quieter voice, "I owe you for this. You just don't know, that boy means the whole world to me."

Taylor is startled by the tears in Angie's eyes and can only think to say, "Thank you." For no physical reason Taylor can work out, Angie reminds her of her own mother. It must be nothing more than the force of her love. Angie goes to retrieve Turtle and Lucky from the photographer and deliver them both to the table. Lucky looks ecstatic, and surprisingly so does Turtle.

"Everybody's real proud of you," Taylor tells her.

"I know. I saved my friend Buster." She swings her feet against the legs of her chair. Lucky reaches out and strokes Turtle's shoulder twice. Taylor thinks of the reporter's fortune-cookie prediction that Turtle's life has been changed forever.

Angie doesn't take any orders, she just brings food. Lucky leans so eagerly over his mashed potatoes that Taylor has to look away. This must be what people dislike about the retarded: they get straight down to the animal business of life, revealing it for what it is. Taylor admits to herself how hungry she is.

Angie brings over a customer named Collie Bluestone. "He's a real good rooster fighter," Angie says by way of introduction.

"No," he says modestly, sitting down. "I don't fight them. I sew them up afterward."

Taylor is intrigued by the man's mystifying profession and the scar on his neck. He's handsome in the same way Jax is, thin and knuckly. On men it works, it can be sexy. "I used to go to cockfights," she tells him. "Well, once I did. In somebody's barn, in Kentucky. On a blind date."

Collie makes an odd noise, a sort of a hiss, but he is smiling so it's apparently not a threat. "I hope your date turned out better than the chicken's."

"Not a whole lot better, but thanks. It's not too legal back there. Is it legal here? Or just kind of a hobby?"

"The fights aren't up here," he says. "They're down by the Crit reservation. That's where I live. I just come up here ever so often to check on Angie."

Taylor speculates on the relationship of Angie Buster and Collie Blue-stone, and wonders briefly if Collie is Angie's chicken supplier, but decides not to ask. Turtle is eating as if she hadn't been fed since the change of seasons. Taylor is positive they had breakfast. "What kind of Indian is Crit?" she asks Collie. "I never heard of them."

Collie makes the same noise again. "C-R-I-T, it stands for Colorado River Indian Tribes, which there aren't none. It's a fake tribe made out of whoever got left out when they carved up the territory. It's like if they called everybody in a prison 'the Leavenworth family.' "

"Oh. Sorry I asked."

"Well, everybody's got to live someplace, right? There's some Hopi, Navajo, Mojave."

"And everybody gets along okay?"

"We marry each other, but we don't get along."

Angie arrives again with more food and men. She introduces the men but Taylor doesn't catch their names, only their hands to shake as they sit down. One of them wears a dog-colored cowboy hat and keeps putting his arm around Angie's waist. "Did you see that London Bridge up at Lake Havasu?" he asks.

Lucky pipes up suddenly with his cover story. "Mom, I accidentally walked on the railroad tracks to Havasu."

Angie and all the men throw their mouths open and laugh. Lucky joins in, enjoying his own joke, since that's what it turned out to be. Angie wipes her eyes and it gets very quiet.

"We didn't stop this morning to look at the bridge," Taylor says. "I've heard about it, though. Some guy really did buy it and bring it over here?"

Lucky quietly sings, "London bridges falling down."

"Some fat cat," says the man in the cowboy hat. "And here's the thing. After he bought it, he decided he had to get it cleaned. He said it cost more to clean it than to buy it."

"I had a jacket like that one time," Taylor says, feeling a certain pressure to keep the conversation going.

"Set down," cowboy hat tells Angie. Ordering people around seems to

be the m.o. of Angie's Diner. "Tell them about the time Lucky run off with
the Hell's Angels."

"He didn't run off with them, either." Angie crosses her arms and
doesn't sit.

"I want to hear about the mules that kidnapped him in Mexico." Taylor
looks uneasily at Lucky, after she's said this, but he is beaming. This is his
element. The window illuminates his face, raising the color of his eyes to a
gas-flame blue.

"Oh, honey, that was unbelievable," Angie says. "They told him they was
going to shoot him." Taylor tries to imagine stubborn four-legged animals
with guns, until Angie explains that mules are men who have something to
do with drug running. "If you're anywheres near Mexico and someone shoots
you for no apparent reason," she says knowledgeably, "they're a mule."

Taylor is relieved to be home in one piece. She and Jax sit up in bed with
his tape of They Might Be Giants turned down low, so they'll hear when
Turtle has fallen asleep in the next room. Turtle talks herself to sleep
nearly every night in a quiet language no one can understand. Over the
years, Taylor and Alice have had many long-distance phone calls about
motherhood. Alice told her not to worry when Turtle was three and still
didn't talk, or later, when she did talk but would say only the names of
vegetables in long, strange lists. Alice still says there's nothing to worry
about, and she has always been right before. She says Turtle is talking over
the day with her personal angels.

They hear Turtle sigh and begin to hum a low, tedious song. Then they
hear the clunk of her comfort object, a flashlight she calls Mary, which she
has slept with since the day she found it years ago in Taylor's employer's
truck.

"I missed you," Taylor tells Jax. "Compared to what I've been through
lately, you seem normal."

He kisses her hair, which smells like a thunderstorm, and her shoulder,
which smells like beach rocks. He tells her, "Sex will get you through
times with no money better than money will get you through times with
no sex."

"The thing I really missed was your jokes."

"I missed your cognitive skills," he says. "And your syntax. Honestly, that's all. Not your body. I *despise* your body." He drawls on purpose, sounding more southern than he needs to, though he can't match the hard-soft angular music of her Kentucky hills.

"Well, that's sure a load off my mind," she says, laughing, shuddering her dark hair off her shoulders without self-consciousness. She's the first woman he's ever known who doesn't give a damn how she looks, or is completely happy with the way she looks, which amounts to the same thing. Usually women are aware of complex formulas regarding how long the legs should be in relation to the waist in relation to the eyelashes—a mathematics indecipherable to men but strangely crucial to women. Taylor apparently never took the class. He wishes he could have been there when she was born, to watch the whole process of Taylor. He lies across the bed with his head in her lap, but when he realizes she's looking at his profile, turns his face away. Although he rarely sees it himself, he knows his profile is unusual and even startles people: there's no indentation at all between his forehead and the bridge of his nose. Taylor says he looks like an Egyptian Pharaoh, which is exactly what she would say, with no apologies for never having seen any actual Egyptian art. Taylor behaves as if what she believes, and what she is, should be enough for anyone.

She's not the first woman on earth to insist on his good looks; that's not why he is in love with her. Jax has broad shoulders and hands that apparently suggest possibilities. He's proud that he can reach an octave and a half on a piano like Franz Liszt; his one gift is largeness. When his band performs, women tend to give him articles of their clothing with telephone numbers inked on the elastic.

"You think she's asleep?"

Taylor shakes her head. "Not yet. She's having trouble relaxing. I learned a lot about her breathing on this trip."

"You're picking up certain character traits from your friend Lou Ann."

Lou Ann Ruiz, who is like a second mother to Turtle, tends toward an obsession with health and safety. But to her credit, Jax allows, Lou Ann is making bold changes in her life: she recently got a job at an exercise salon called Fat Chance and now wears Lycra outfits in color combinations that seem dangerous, like the poisonous frogs that inhabit the Amazon.

"Is now a good time to tell you about the phone calls?"

"What phone calls?" Taylor asks, through a heartfelt yawn.

"The approximately four thousand calls that have come in since you achieved national prominence on Monday."

"Oh, right."

"You think I'm kidding." Jax gets out of bed and rifles through the mess of music and lyrics on his desk. Sometimes, in his nightmares, everything on this desk sings at once. He comes back with a legal pad and his horn-rimmed glasses, and reads.

"Lou Ann: wants to know if you took Dramamine for Turtle because she threw up that time in the car. Lou Ann again: to tell you never mind, it was *her* son that threw up in the car."

"Lou Ann often called me before I was famous." Taylor presses her mouth against her kneecap. Sometimes when she's concentrating on something else she seems to be kissing her own knees, or the backs of her hands. Jax has tried it out in private, to see how it feels to love oneself unconsciously.

"Okay," he says, "I'm skipping all the Lou Anns." He runs his finger down the page. "Charla Rand from the *Phoenix Gazette*. Marsh Levin from the *Arizona Daily Star*. Larry Rice, photographer from the *Star*. Helga Carter from the *Fresno Bee*."

"The what? I don't believe this. What do they want?"

"The story of the year. A suspense-movie plot with endearing characters, a famous tourist landmark and a happy ending."

"Shit. Is that all of them?"

"Almost. There are five more pages."

"Skip over the *Queen Bee News* exetera."

"Check. Skip the *Queen Bee News* and the Lou Anns." He turns a couple of pages and then flips back. "Oh, your mother. She called before I'd started writing everything down. She thought she saw you on the news."

"In *Kentucky?* That can't be."

"Well, basketball season's over."

"Lord, it must have scared the bejesus out of her."

"Don't worry, I'm very good in crisis situations. I told her she was hallucinating. Then after I heard, I called her back and told her you and Turtle pulled through without a scratch."

"It's not like *we* fell down any holes."

"She won't completely believe that till she hears from you."

Taylor smiles. "I'll call her in the morning."

"She wants a new picture of Turtle. Her theory is that in the one you sent Santa Claus looks like Sirhan Sirhan."

"No, like Lee Harvey Oswald."

He looks at her, takes off his glasses and throws the notepad on the floor. "How did you know that?"

"I lived with her twenty years. I know what she'd say."

"You two ought to be in the *National Enquirer.* TELEPATHIC MOTHER-DAUGHTER DUO RECEIVE MESSAGES THROUGH FILLINGS."

"We're just close."

"*Perversering* mother-daughter duo."

"Would you please shut up? You're jealous of everything, even my mother."

"Did you and Turtle really persevere perversely?"

"I'm going to be sorry I let you keep a scrapbook."

"It's great material. Oh, and another news flash also: She's leaving her husband."

Taylor stares at Jax. "Who? My mother is leaving Harland? Where's she going? Is she coming here?"

"You didn't get the message through your fillings?"

"She's *leaving* him? Where's she going?"

"I don't know." He closes his eyes. "Not here. She sounded a little sad."

"I have to call her right now."

She shoves his head off her lap, but Jax catches her around the waist and pulls her back onto the bed. "It's two in the morning there, sweet thing. Let her sleep."

"Damn it. I *hate* time zones. Why can't they just make it the same time everywhere at once?"

"Because if they did, somewhere on earth some poor musicians would have to sleep at night and go to work in daylight."

Taylor relaxes a little against Jax, who puts his arms around her. He spreads his hands across the bony marimba of her ribs, wishing for the music they hold. "Are you in love with our garbage man?" he asks.

"Danny! Oh, pew, his truck smells like compost city."

"Uh huh. So you're saying you *would* be in love with him, if his truck smelled better."

"Jax, why do you do this?"

"I'm thinking you'll leave me, now that you're famous."

"A world-famous employee of a car-parts store."

"You're the manager. Don't sell yourself short. You don't need me."

She strokes his kneecap, which is angular and hard as a box terrapin. "Jax, honey, I never did," she says.

"I know."

"Or Danny, or Bruce Springsteen, or the man in the moon. It's nothing personal."

"I know. It's because of your mother's guiding myth."

"What's that?"

"That the women in your family need men only as a remedy for minor plumbing irritations."

"Well, maybe that's true. And I'm here in your bed anyway, how about that," she says. It is, technically, his bed; she got rid of hers in a yard sale when she and Turtle moved into Jax's tiny house at the edge of town. She tips her head back until it rests against his chin. "So will you shut up about my leaving you, and is that all the big news you have for this evening?"

"I'll show you big news," he says, delicately biting the nape of her neck. He lifts her breasts, which fit perfectly into his hands, though he knows this is no promise that he gets to keep them. A million things you can't have will fit in a human hand. He lets her go, gently. "No, that's not all. There's something else, but we can talk about it tomorrow."

Taylor's pulse jumps. "What?"

"Really, you do not want to hear about it now."

"Don't tell me what I want."

"Okay. Oprah Winfrey called."

She laughs, relieved. "Did she? I've been neglecting her and I feel awful about it."

"It's not a joke. Oprah Winfrey called. Not *Oprah,* but one of her producers, or researchers or something. They're doing a show called 'Children Who Have Saved Lives.' "

"Would you please save the hooha for your screaming fans?" She settles back against his chest.

"I agree with you, it's one of the weirder things I've heard of. They want you and Turtle to come to Chicago."

It dawns on Taylor that Jax is not making up Oprah Winfrey. "Why would we want to go to Chicago?"

"It's a happening town. You could show Turtle the Museum of Science and Industry. Since she got short-sheeted on the Grand Canyon."

"What would I say on national TV?"

"Most of the time you strike me as having no shortage. What would you *like* to say on national TV?"

"Would they let me say *anything?*"

"Well, it's not Geraldo."

"I'm serious. Could I say what I wanted to, do you think?"

"She'd probably want you to stick to the general theme of children who have saved lives."

"That's a very weird subject," Taylor points out. "How many could there be?"

"The Chinese say if you save somebody's life you're responsible for them forever."

"Somebody else told me that! I thought he was making it up. Do you think Turtle's life is changed forever?"

"Could be," Jax admits. "Not necessarily for the worse."

"I liked her the way she was."

They are quiet for a long time with their eyes looking down, listening.

Taylor says quietly, "You know what I keep going back to? Nobody believed her. They took one look at this skinny Indian kid and said, 'Well, ma'am, we don't actually have a witness.' "

"But you believed her. And Lucky Buster lives."

"I had to, Jax, I'm her mother. That part is nothing."

They both listen again. Turtle has stopped conversing with the angels.

5

THE SECRET OF TV

TAYLOR IS GETTING A LONG, hard look at someone's bald spot. He has reclined his seat to a point where he's closer than a dinner plate, maybe twelve inches from her face. The top of his head is covered with fine, almost invisible fur that lies flattened in a complicated pattern, like a little prairie swept by a tornado. It reminds Taylor of a theory Jax once told her about, that humans evolved from some sort of water ape and spent the dawn of civilization in a swamp. Streamlined hair patterns are supposed to be the proof, but Taylor wonders as she stares, Does that mean we moved through the water headfirst? Could be. Kids move through the world that way, running into things with the tops of their heads. This man has a scar up there, no doubt forgotten through the decades until now that it's lost its cover.

The pilot comes on the intercom again. He's a chatty one; right after takeoff he introduced himself as "your captain," and Turtle's eyes grew wide. She asked Taylor if he only had one hand. Now, after mulling it over the whole afternoon, it dawns on Taylor that the only captain Turtle knows about so far is Captain Hook. She may never get on a plane again without envisioning a pirate at the helm.

Captain Hook now explains they are passing over the Mississippi River, and that if he can do anything to make the passengers more comfortable they should just let him know. Frankly, although she doubts the captain can help her out here, Taylor doesn't feel comfortable being intimate with a stranger's hair loss. She doesn't even know the top of Jax's head this well. She's looked at it, but not for three and a half hours.

Turtle is finally sleeping. She seems to be coming down with a cold, and really needed a nap, but was so excited she sat for hours with her face pressed hard against the window. When the window turned icy cold, even when there was nothing to see but a vast, frosted field of clouds spread over a continent, rutted evenly as if it had been plowed, Turtle still stared. Everybody else on the plane is behaving as though they are simply sitting in chairs a little too close together, but Turtle is a child in a winged tin box seven miles above Planet Earth.

Taylor hasn't flown before either, and for the first few hours she felt the same excitement. Especially when they were taking off, and before, buckling up, watching the stewardess show how to put on a yellow oxygen mask without messing up your hair. And before that, leaving the airport: walking behind Turtle down the sloping hallway to the door of the plane, stepping across from solid ground to something unknown, furtively checking the rivets around the door, but what can you do? She has no choice but to follow her daughter into this new life she's claimed from a fortune cookie.

Chicago is tall on one side of the freeway, open sky on the other, because of the lake. Taylor never thought of Chicago as a beach town, but there they are, hundreds of people in swimsuits throwing Frisbees into the wind. It's the first week of June. She and Turtle are cruising down the freeway in a long white limousine with smoked-glass windows and baby blue velvet upholstery. As they speed away from the airport, people in other cars turn their heads to try and get a look inside this vehicle of mystery. The driver calls them both "Miss," as if they are the types to travel everywhere by limo.

It occurs to Taylor that this would be quite the line of work, driving Oprah Winfrey guests around: some would be royalty and some would be famous murderers or men with a wife in every state, and if you're only the driver you'd never know which was which. You'd have to play it safe and treat them all politely.

"This is the best-planned city in the nation," the driver explains. Turtle is glued to the window, still. "It all burned down in the great fire of October 8, 1871. Everything went. Two hundred million dollars of property damage. So they had the opportunity of starting it over from the ground up."

"I've heard of that fire," Taylor says. "I heard it was started by a cow."

"No, that is not true, that is a myth. The Great Chicago Fire was not started by a cow." He hesitates a little, and Taylor realizes she's blown their cover; bringing up the subject of livestock has put them more on the criminal than the royalty side of the fence.

"Well, it makes a good story," she says. She doesn't care if he thinks she and Turtle are serial killers. He still has to take them to their hotel.

For all this city's famous planning, the traffic is horrible. As soon as they turn away from the lake toward the tall glass buildings, they are mired in a flock of honking cars. The driver has evidently finished with the glories of his city. Once in a while as they sit there he hits the horn with his fist.

Turtle sneezes. She's got a cold, there's no getting around it. Taylor hands her a tissue out of her pocket. "How're you feeling, Toots?"

"Fine," she says, blowing her nose carefully, still looking out the window. Turtle almost never complains. Taylor is well aware of how unusual this is. If all you knew about kids came from watching the sitcoms, she thinks, you would never guess there were children on earth like Turtle.

"Mom, look." She pulls on Taylor's finger and points at a City of Chicago garbage truck, which is stalled next to them in the traffic jam. A fancy gold seal painted on the side gives it an air of magnificence. The driver smiles down at them from his perch on high. Then he raises one eyebrow and winks.

"Why'd he do that?"

"He thinks you're cute," Taylor says, "and he likes my legs. Also he probably thinks we're rich."

"But we're not, are we?"

"Nope, we're not."

"He gets to drive a better truck than Danny's."

"Definitely."

Taylor is wearing a skirt—something she's not accustomed to, but Lou Ann insisted on loaning her a nice beige suit for Oprah Winfrey. She claimed it was against some regulation to wear jeans on television. Jax got a good laugh out of that, but to his credit, he is nicer to Lou Ann than most guys would be.

Taylor gets a nervous stomach when she thinks about the taping tomorrow morning. She suspects these shows are just a way of making a spectacle out of bad things that happen to people. But Turtle really wanted to do it. She'd never understood before that actual people could appear on television. She seems to have a vague idea they will meet the Ninja Turtles.

The garbage guy is still looking. He has curly hair and a terrific smile. Taylor crosses her legs and raises her hand just a little. If he can really see in, he'll take it as a wave.

He does. He makes a small motion with his chin, indicating that she and Turtle should abandon their limo in favor of his garbage truck. Taylor gives it some thought, but decides to go ahead with Oprah.

"It's an adorable outfit," the wardrobe woman tells Taylor, "but I'm just suggesting something a little more feminine. We have this little jumper from wardrobe, see? The color would look absolutely super on the set."

Lou Ann can have the last laugh now. Oprah Winfrey's people don't want Turtle to wear her overalls on television. The overalls are brand new, bright green, perfectly decent. "That dress is ten sizes too big for Turtle," Taylor says.

"Doesn't matter. We just pin it in back, see? Nobody sees the back. That's the secret of TV—you only have to worry about what shows up front, your back can be a mess. And we'll put this bow in her hair, okay, sweetheart? She'll look super."

"She'll look younger," Taylor says. "If that's what you're going for. She'll look like a baby doll that saved somebody's life."

The woman crosses her arms and frowns. Her short, black hair looks wet and oiled, like a sea otter. The comb rakes through it stay perfectly in place. "It's going to be difficult," she says. "We'd have to run her mike wire up from the back."

"You can manage," Taylor says, knowing this can't be the problem. Men wear pants on television every day of the week. The other guests are not being harassed about wardrobe concerns. Taylor met them all in the hotel lobby this morning while they waited for the limos. There's a Cub Scout who flagged down help when his scoutmaster collapsed on their tenderfoot survival hike; a fourth-grader who saved her sister from a pit-bull attack by hitting it with a dog dish and the whole Barbie Dream Date ensemble, including the convertible; and an eleven-year-old who drove the car home when her baby-sitter passed out from multiple bee stings in a city park. Taylor feels, frankly, that the eleven-year-old showed bad judgment all around, and the other two probably just acted without thinking. Turtle is the youngest and has the best story. She doesn't see why they need to blow it out of proportion by dressing her up like Barbie's baby sister.

The small green room where they are waiting is crowded and tense. Turtle fidgets, and the wardrobe woman hovers, her raised eyebrows still pushing the question.

"What do you want to wear?" Taylor asks Turtle.

Turtle hugs herself. "This," she says.

Taylor smiles at the sea-otter woman. "Looks like she's made up her mind."

The woman pushes the purple jumper against Turtle's front, looking at Taylor. "I really think, look, don't you? It's so much more of a visual."

"My daughter said no, thank you." Turtle recoils from the bunched fabric, and Taylor narrows her eyes at the woman, who seems nevertheless to be holding her ground. A makeup man comes over at a trot. He's wearing the laced-up, tassely loafers that people call "boating shoes," even though most of them will never lay leather to a boat. Taylor wonders why everyone here seems dressed for some kind of sport—the secretaries in leggings, the camera crew in running shoes, all bustling around frowning, with nothing the least bit sporty on their agendas. It's as if they're expecting at any minute a sudden announcement: Vacation starts *now*.

"You have wonderful cheekbones, dear," the makeup man tells Taylor, and he lobs her in the face with a powder puff.

6

THIEVES

OF CHILDREN

Annawake Fourkiller looks up from her law briefs, startled. "Could you turn that up?"

The secretary, Jinny, automatically reaches to turn down the volume on the little TV at the end of her desk.

"No, up, please." Annawake stares with her head cocked. Her black hair is cropped so close to the nap it stands up like an exotic pelt, and her broad mouth has the complicated curves of a foreign punctuation mark, making it anyone's guess whether she's smiling or not. Jinny shrinks behind her glasses, wondering if Annawake is making a joke and she's not getting it. "It's just Oprah Winfrey," she says.

"I know. I want to hear this."

Jinny shrugs. "Okay." She stretches one blue-jeaned leg out behind her for balance as she reaches across hills of papers for the volume knob, then slumps back down to her typewriter. Mr.

Turnbo is out of the office for the afternoon so it's just the two of them, and Jinny is unsure of her relationship with Annawake. Jinny has worked here longer—she started as Franklin Turnbo's secretary-receptionist when she graduated from high school last year; Annawake only finished law school out in Phoenix a month ago, and has come back home to Oklahoma to intern here on an Indian Lawyer Training grant. Mr. Turnbo has never minded if Jinny's little TV talked quietly on the desk, as long as she gets everything typed. She's not wrapped up in the soaps, she just likes Oprah and Sally Jessy and sometimes *General Hospital*. Annawake doesn't say she minds, either, but she makes faces at Sally Jessy and calls her the blonde Puerto Rican, which makes Jinny feel guilty for perming her hair. For trying to look *yonega,* as her grandma says.

Through the front window she sees a line of dusty cars and pickup trucks pulling out of the parking lot of Cherokee Nation headquarters, heading back up the highway toward Kenwood and Locust Grove; the afternoon session of Tribal Court is over. Mr. Turnbo will be back soon and she's still behind on her work, but that's not Oprah Winfrey's fault.

"That little kid in the overalls?" Annawake asks. She is staring with her chin on her hand. "I heard somebody say she was adopted."

"Yeah. Before the first commercial Oprah introduced them as being somebody and her adopted daughter Turtle."

"Cherokee," Annawake says. "I'll bet you a Coke."

"Uhn-uh," Jinny says, "Navajo, I bet. They're from Arizona. She looks exactly like my brother's girlfriend's little girl, out in Albuquerque."

"Where in Arizona, did they say?"

"Tucson."

Annawake eyes the TV as if it had just called her a name. Jinny finds Annawake completely fascinating: she dresses like she doesn't give a hoot, in jeans and moccasins and white shirts from J. C. Penney's men's department, and she totes around a backpack held together by gray duct tape instead of a briefcase, but she has that fashion-model mouth with a deep indentation in the center of her upper lip that's hard to stop staring at. Men must want to kiss her every minute, Jinny thinks. When the perky music comes up and Oprah fades out to another commercial, Annawake takes off her glasses and rubs her eyes. "Tired," she says. "You too?"

"Yeah. Grandma's mad at my brother Woody for quitting school. Nobody's been getting much sleep at our house, except Woody. He took his bed out in the yard."

"Robert Grass didn't call yet?"

"Robert Grass! That turkey. Not since the drive-in two weeks ago."

"He will," Annawake says. "My brother Dellon knows him from the construction site over on Muskogee highway. He said Robert Grass is talking *osda* about his new girlfriend."

"Maybe she's nobody I know."

"If she's not you, you would have heard about it. Tahlequah's not that big."

"That's the truth. The whole *Nation's* not that big. Somebody all the way over to Salisaw told Grandma she'd seen me in a truck with the weediest Grass ever to come up."

Annawake smiles. "There's no getting away from the people that love you." She slides her glasses back on and takes the pencil from behind her ear to mark up the page she's reading. Jinny thinks: *You don't even know. Nobody would gossip about you, they all adore you too much, plus you have no noticeable habits other than working.* She blows a puff of air through her bangs and flips to a new page of the Arkansas River Gravel Claim. Why anyone cares this much about river gravel is beyond Jinny Redcrow.

"This Oprah show is about kids that saved people's lives," she offers Annawake as an afterthought, wondering if there's a legal angle she has missed. Annawake and Mr. Turnbo are always speaking to each other in a language Jinny types but can't read.

"Mmm-hm," Annawake says, not looking up. She's ignoring the sexy-sounding commercial and doing the smile-frown thing she does when she is reading. Annawake is known for being a super brain. Jinny went to Tahlequah High School seven years after her, and the teachers were still talking about Annawake Fourkiller like some comet that only hits Oklahoma once per century. Once at a stomp dance the chief gave her as an example of a good life path. He didn't embarrass the family by singling out her name, though of course everybody knows who he meant. But Annawake acts like *she* hasn't figured it out yet. She lives with one of her sisters-in-law in a bad little house on Blue Springs Street, and she ducks her head into the files when the good-looking guys come in making noise about their land-use papers, and she's even nice enough to ask about stupid Robert Grass. The only real problem with her is her hair is strange. She used to have long Pocahontas hair—Jinny has seen pictures in the yearbook: valedictorian, jock, president of Cherokee Pride club, nick-named "Wide Awake Annawake"—but she cut it all off when she went away to law school. Now it's spiky and short like Jinny's little brothers', more Sinead O'Connor than Cherokee Pride. She doesn't see how Annawake can go pointing her finger at Sally Jessy Raphael.

"Can I put Arkansas River on the floor?" Annawake asks suddenly. Oprah is back, and Annawake is scooting some papers around to make room for herself on the edge of Jinny's desk.

"You can put Arkansas River in the river," Jinny says. Annawake laughs, and Jinny feels guilty for thinking bad-hair thoughts. Actually, Jinny thinks, if she had Annawake's bone structure she'd cut her hair off too, or do *something* different.

"So what's the story on that little kid?"

There are four kids: a show-off boy in a scout uniform who keeps pat-ting the hand of his huge father; two tall, skinny white girls in braces who could be sisters; and the Indian girl in overalls.

"That white girl with her is the mom. The adopted mom."

The mother is young-looking and pretty, dressed in a nice beige suit but swinging her crossed leg like it's not her business to act like Nancy Rea-gan. She is telling the story of how her little girl saw a man fall down a hole in the Hoover Dam.

Annawake makes a face of pain. "Give me a break. She made up that Hoover Dam to get on the show."

"No, that was on the news. You were out there in Phoenix when it hap-pened, didn't you see it on TV?"

"Really? Maybe. I can't think of it if I did. In law school I missed all the news that was legally uncomplicated."

"Oprah has people that check your story," Jinny says, a little defensive. She spends almost every afternoon with Oprah, and feels she can be trusted.

"You think it's true?"

Jinny shrugs. "Listen. You can tell." The woman explains that she herself didn't see the man fall down the hole, only Turtle did. For two whole days no one else believed it, but she did, and they kept trying to get help.

"*National Enquirer* for sure," Annawake says. "She read it in the grocery store."

Oprah is talking to the mother now, whose name is something Taylor. "I can see there's a wonderful bond between you and your daughter. Can't you see it?" Oprah turns around, her loose rayon jacket swirling, and the studio audience says Yes, they can. She asks, "You adopted her when she was how old, two?"

"Probably she was three," the mother says. "We don't know for sure. She was abused and hadn't been growing right before I got her. It was kind of an unusual situation. Somebody just gave her to me."

"*Gave her to you?*"

"Left her in my car."

Oprah makes one of her funny big-eyed faces at the camera. "You all hear that?" she asks in a deeper, down-home voice. "*Check your car* before you drive out of the parking lot."

Annawake looks at Jinny with raised eyebrows, and asks the TV set, "Where?"

"I'd just stopped for a cup of coffee," the mother says, and seems a little surprised when the audience laughs. *No way is she making this story up,* Jinny thinks. "I was on a trip across the country. I'd just left home and was headed out West. The funny part about it is, all the time I was growing up in Kentucky my main goal was to not get pregnant. All my girlfriends had these babies up to their ears."

"But that wasn't going to happen to you," says Oprah.

"No, ma'am."

"And your first day out, somebody gives you a baby."

"Second day out," she says, and the audience laughs again. With Annawake watching, Jinny feels slightly embarrassed about the low laugh threshold of Oprah's studio audience.

"You could have walked away. Why did you take her?" Oprah asks in a caring way.

"Seeing as how it's against the law," Annawake adds.

"Which law?" Jinny asks, surprised.

"Indian Child Welfare Act. You can't adopt an Indian kid without tribal permission."

Franklin Turnbo has come in and hung up his jacket. Annawake motions him over, still concentrating on the black-and-white screen. The three of them watch the mother push her hair out of her eyes, thinking. She seems unaware that she's on TV—unlike the Cub Scout, who keeps bobbing on the edge of his chair and raising his hand as if he knows the answer.

"I felt like I *had* to take her," the mother finally answers. "This woman just plunked her down on the seat of my car and looked at me and said, 'Take her.' I said, 'Where do you want me to take her?' I thought she needed a ride somewhere."

Finally the audience is completely quiet.

"Take who?" Franklin Turnbo asks.

"That Cherokee kid," Annawake says, nodding at the screen. The mother looks down at the little girl and then back at Oprah. "The woman told me Turtle's mother was dead, and that somebody had been hurting Turtle. She was the dead mother's sister, and it looked like somebody'd been hurting her too. Then she got in this truck with no lights, and drove off. It was the middle of the night. At the time I felt like there was nothing else in the world I could do but take the baby. I'd been driving forty-eight hours. I guess my judgment was impaired."

The audience laughs, uneasily. The little girl is staring at Oprah and clutching a fistful of her mother's skirt. The mother carefully moves the child's hand into one of hers. "The next summer I went back and legally adopted her."

"Can't be," says Annawake. "Not legally."

Oprah asks, "Where did all this happen?"

"Oklahoma, Indian country. Turtle's Cherokee."

Annawake bangs the desk like a judge, bringing the court to order.

The sky has gone dishwater gray. There could be rain on this west wind, Annawake thinks. But it's Third Saturday, stomp-dance night, and old people love to tell you that rain always holds back till the dancing is over. They're mostly right. She parks her truck, gathers up her bouquet of blue and white papers from the office, and wonders briefly what ought to be done about the aluminum siding that is buckling on the north side of the house. With two free fingers she forks up the handlebars of a tricycle from the front walk and parks it out of harm's way on the porch.

"*Siyo*," she says, latching the screen door to keep kids in and dogs out. Her brother and sister-in-law are kneeling on the kitchen floor and return her greeting without looking up. They must be on speaking terms this week: they're hammering the legs back onto the old pine dining table, and it's not easy to take on a project like that without communicating.

Annawake watches the two of them, united for once as they both concentrate on keeping the table leg on straight while Dellon drives the nail. His thick braid swings like a bell rope as he hammers, and their heads almost touch. "Got her?" he asks, and Millie nods, her crinkled perm softly brushing Dellon's shining black crown. They were married less than a year and have been divorced for five, but it hasn't interfered with their rate of producing children. When the table leg is secure, Millie rolls sideways and takes hold of the lip of the sink. Annawake takes her other hand and pulls her up.

"Seems like you take one month longer with every baby," Dellon says, and Annawake laughs because it's true: the first was premature, the second right on time, the third one three weeks late, and this one seems to have staked Millie's ample territory for its homestead.

"Don't say that out loud, he'll hear you." Millie leans over her stomach and tells it, "You're coming out of there this weekend, you hear? If you go any longer past due you're walking home from the hospital yourself."

Annawake gets a soda out of the refrigerator and sits in a chair, moccasins together, facing the upside-down table. "Is this thing going to live?"

"It'll never walk again," Dellon says, squatting on his heels. He shrugs his braid back over the great round loaf of his shoulder and gives the table leg a couple of trial knocks with the hammer. He grins up at his little sister. "You scalp the cowboys today?"

"I did my best."

"Don't make fun of Annawake's job, Dell," Millie says, turning her back on them, running water into a big aluminum kettle. The sun shining through her shocked hair reveals the perfect globe of her skull.

"I never make fun of Annawake. She'd beat me up."

"Dad, let's go." Baby Dellon, who is almost six and hates to be called Baby Dellon, runs into the kitchen with a football helmet on.

Dellon stands up and puts a hammerlock on Annawake's neck from behind. "When you getting married, beautiful?" he asks.

"When Gabe says he'll come to my wedding." She feels Dellon's body slump against her back, and she realizes she said what she did just to feel that slack sadness in another person. She's the only one who will still say their brother Gabriel's name.

"Leave her alone," Millie says, shifting her heavy kettle onto the stove. "Getting married's not what it's cranked up to be. What time you bringing Baby Dellon back?"

"Tomorrow noon, if we're not too hungover."

"I'm going to kill you one of these days."

"I'm not Baby Dellon, I'm Batman," says Baby Dellon, and they are out the door.

"I'm going to kill him one of these days."

"He's a good dad," Annawake says, setting the table back on its feet, wondering if it might give itself a dignified shake and walk off, like a turtle. "He won't be drinking at a stomp dance. He wouldn't even get into the stomp grounds if he was."

Millie laughs. "Did you ever hear what happened on our first date?"

"You went to a stomp dance."

"That's how Dellon tells it. If I told you the real story he'd shoot me." Millie leans against the counter, smiling. Her bunched print skirt hangs down from her waist like a dust ruffle on a bed. She brushes crimped wires of hair from her eyes, and Annawake knows she's going to tell the story.

"We were up in the mountains and it was hot, and Dellon wanted to have a beer. I knew there was the dance that night so I wasn't going to drink, but he did anyway. We had a fight, and later on we both went to the dance, but not together. I was in the inside circle wearing the turtle shells, so here comes Dellon, dancing right in the next circle, trying to get my eye. Next thing I hear him say, 'Uh-oh, here comes the fuzz.' Ledger tapped him on the shoulder and he had to leave. He'd just had one beer, but Ledger knew. He can spot it a mile away."

"Tell me about it. I lived through most of my teenage years under Uncle Ledger's eagle eye."

"But you had nothing to worry about, you were Miss Perfect," Millie says, wagging her stirring spoon at Annawake.

"Well, of course. I never had a chance." Annawake knocks back her soda.

"You had to make up for your wild brothers," Millie says, grinning. "I should have known right there and then not to marry him."

A Mason jar on the counter at Millie's elbow is crammed with daisies and wild phlox the kids have picked by the road somewhere; Annawake reaches for the jar and sets it in the exact center of the table. "I think he wishes you'd trust him more with the kids."

"I trust him. But you still have to tell him what to do."

Millie's youngest, Annie, all big dark eyes and belly, stands naked in the doorway. Annawake jumps up from her chair. "Whoah, let's get a diaper on you, baby doll, before we get puddles."

"It's okay, I decided to get her started on potty training today. Figured it's easier to let her run around that way. Put her out in the yard every hour, like a pup."

"Millie!"

"I'm kidding. Annie, go show Annawake your potty."

Annie disappears.

"You're not going back to the office, are you? On Third Saturday?"

Annawake sighs. "I'm thinking about it. There's this wild goose I'm chasing down. An illegal adoption."

"Forget it. Whatever it is will keep."

"I don't know."

Annie reappears in the door with a stuffed bear twice her size. "Pa-pa," she says.

"You better learn the difference between a teddy bear and a potty seat," Millie says. "Your time's about up as baby of the family."

Annie drops the bear on its head and climbs onto Annawake's lap.

Annawake laces her fingers together over the child's naked belly, which has the rubbery firmness of a hard-boiled egg. "Dellon hates it when I bring up Gabe," she tells Millie's back.

"I don't think Dell was ever as close to him as you are. You're his twin. Dell was half grown before you two were born."

"They're still brothers."

"Mm," she says. She dumps a package of macaroni into the pot of boiling water. "But now he's got his own kids to worry about."

"What difference does that make?"

Millie rocks her body to the table and carefully sits down. "None, that's not what it is. He hates it when you bring up Gabe, because he's the oldest and he thinks he should have done something to keep the family from getting torn up."

Annawake looks at Millie's tired face. The skin under her eyes looks bruised, the way it gets with every pregnancy. The things people go through for love. "It's not his fault, what happened."

"Not yours, either, Annawake, and look at you. I think it's great you went to law school and everything. But you don't ever stop."

The egg of Annie slides through Annawake's hold and vanishes again.

"I'm not blaming myself for Gabe."

"If you say so. Seems to me like all of you do. Like you're all married to him, some way."

They both listen to the small, steady sounds of children in other parts of the house. Annie comes back to the kitchen again, this time dragging her white potty seat. "Bear," she says.

"What would you do," Annawake asks Millie, "if you found out somebody was trying to take a Cherokee kid out of the Nation?"

"It's a whole different thing, asking me that now. You were little when they took Gabriel. I'm not little."

"That's what I mean. If it happened right now, what would you do?"

Millie pulls a bedraggled daisy out of the Mason jar and twirls its stem between her thumb and fingers. "It can't happen now. That's what we've got people like you for, isn't it? To watch out for the kids."

Annawake feels the weight of this confidence exactly as if Millie had lovingly sat down upon her chest.

* * *

Tahlequah is a town that might as well roll up its sidewalks at sunset. Annawake knows what night life there is—the stray dogs stealthily marking streetside oaks, and the bootleg liquor houses where music from parked cars stakes an otherworldly claim on the night air. She's walked these streets after dark since high school, pacing the length of her loneliness, Annawake the perfectly admired untouchable. Tonight she has nearly finished her circular route home. Her restlessness had no destination until just now, when she thought of a shoebox of old things she stashed in Millie's carport shed years ago, before she left for Phoenix. The box seemed empty at the time; the only thing of any value at all was the gold locket her mother used to wear for luck. But tonight she could use the company of family secrets. She turns up Blue Spring Street, finding her way by moonlight.

The back shed has a metal door that complains when she scrapes it open. She snaps the chain of the overhead bulb at the same moment a thin slice of white cat, an antishadow, slips past her legs. "Hi, little ugly," she tells it. The cat skits away and turns its head far sideways like a bird to look at Annawake. It's been hanging around for a week or two—Millie even put out a can of tuna for it, and now the can is empty but the cat has nothing to show for it, still just ears and bones. Annawake feels guilty for getting its hopes up. In the pocket of her backpack she finds half a hard peanut candy bar degenerating to sand. "Come on," she says, holding out the candy on her flat palm. The cat watches her with its head oddly tipped; it might be blind in one eye. It makes no move to come to her, but when she sets the candy bar on the doorsill the cat makes a predatory leap, holding the candy down with its paws, making cracking sounds as it jerks its tiny head up and down, laboring over the peanuts. It's pitiful food for a carnivore. With one finger Annawake tentatively strokes its back. The cat allows this, but its little back is nothing. A hammock of fur slung between shoulder blades.

She finds her shoebox wedged under a pile of Millie's baby equipment waiting to make its comeback. Annawake sits cross-legged on the floor with the box on her lap, sorting its treasures with her slender fingers. She finds the locket and works the catch gently to open it. Inside is a photograph of her mother and father in front of the old brick Cherokee County courthouse on the day they married. Her mother's hair is blowing across her eyes, and she looks worried. She's already carrying the beginnings of a boy whose name will be Soldier, who will die before he's old enough to fight back.

Annawake closes the locket and tucks it into her pocket. She doesn't want to jinx it, but she seriously doubts its power. Her mother was wearing it the day she met her husband and thereafter believed in it so thoroughly she wouldn't go anywhere important—not to a baptism or a funeral or even the landlord's to borrow another month—without it. It's difficult, though, for Annawake to picture the more luckless version of that life.

She wishes her mother had left her something that held more promise for blessing her decisions: a beaded medicine pouch with oak leaves inside, or ash from a ceremonial fire. But there's no chance; all the ceremony is on her father's side of the family. Her mother would have called anything of that nature a piece of junk. Annawake smiles a little, hearing her mother's profound Okie accent say *"a pace of ju-unk."* Bonnie Fourkiller was a die-trying acculturated Cherokee, like most of her generation, who chose the Indian Baptist Church over stomp dances and never wore moccasins in her life. She owned one pair of nylons at a time, throughout her lifetime, each folded carefully into the same piece of tissue paper that had harbored all its forebears.

Annawake leafs through other mementoes in the box. A photo of Redbird, her dog, taken in front of their house in Kenwood. Several other shots of her Uncle Ledger's shantyboat on Tenkiller Lake, where she and her four brothers lived out most summers until they were old enough for more productive employment. She finds a picture of herself and Gabe on the wide porch of the shantyboat, wearing baggy cut-off jeans and dumb-kid smiles, and there goes all their ragged laundry strung from the porch posts to the willow trees. The lard buckets were strung up high on poles, out of reach of the notorious thieving armies of raccoons that ran the riverbanks at night. Uncle Ledger claimed the raccoons would steal anything, even a child, but Annawake could never see the point in that. Children were the one thing you could always have plenty of. She'd had no idea.

She and Gabriel passed the months on Ledger's shantyboat with their hearts in their throats, dreading the end of summer. Gabe, her roommate in the before-life, who followed her out the birth door and right through childhood. Sweet Gabe, who was stolen from the family and can't find his way home. She holds the photo as close as her eyes will focus, and drinks the frightening liquor of memory: an A-frame of twins leaning on themselves, elbows around each other's necks. When Annawake runs she can feel the stitch in her side where the invisible wound closed over, the place where they tore him out. How would it have been to go through high school with Gabe? To walk into adulthood? To have had that permanent date, instead of being the Only. The perfect lonely heart. Two hearts, they became, separated by the Texas Panhandle and a great plain of want.

She turns the photos facedown and glances through other things. Letters from her brothers and Uncle Ledger, a photo of someone's new baby. And the family inheritance: a very old book of medicine incantations written by her grandfather in the curly Cherokee alphabet Annawake wishes she could read. She still speaks Cherokee in her dreams sometimes, but never learned to write it. By the time she was six, they only taught English in school.

With her fingertips she delicately unfolds another old document and is surprised to recognize a fragile, creased magazine ad, black and white, showing a smiling young woman wearing a halo of flowers and holding up a soft drink under the sign outside their town. WELCOME TO HEAVEN, the sign in the ad declared, so everybody in America could laugh at the notion of finding heaven in eastern Oklahoma, she supposes. The ad is older than Annawake—the woman was a friend of her mother's, Sugar Hornbuckle. The picture made her famous for a time.

The cat is back at the door, staring in.

"No, you go on now. I'm not a reliable source."

She puts the photographs away. She should have taken these things to school with her. In that air-conditioned universe of mute law books she was terrified that she might someday fail to recognize her own life. You can't just go through life feeding cats, pretending you're not one of the needy yourself. Annawake has spent years becoming schooled in injustices and knows every one by name, but is still afraid she could forget the face.

7

A WORLD OF

FREE BREAKFAST

THE WORDS ON THE PAGE in front of Franklin Turnbo have disappeared. He stares at the front door of his office and sees a little forest of African violets there, leafy and leggy and growing out of their pots, heading for the light as if they intend to walk once they get out there. A bright yellow eye blinks in the center of each purple flower. The front office space where Jinny and Annawake work is overgrown with plants as healthy as children: a huge rubber tree slouches at ceiling level like a too-tall girl, and something with small leaves spreads itself flat-handed against the storefront window. Jinny brings them in and tends them, Franklin supposes. He feels sure he's never seen the plants before this moment, although he could have been hanging his hat and coat on the rubber tree for months, for all he knows. As usual, the place is being taken over benignly by women, without his notice.

The front door jingles and Pollie Turnbo brushes past the violets. She comes into her husband's office cubicle and sets a basket on his desk. "I made bean bread, it's still warm," she says, breathless as if she herself were fresh from the oven.

Franklin never makes it home for dinner on Monday nights, though their ritual is that he pretends he'll try, and she pretends she just happened to be passing by his office with food in hand. He stands up to kiss Pollie. Her hair is coming loose at the back of her neck and her eyes are bright, in a hurry. She looks like the African violets. Franklin wishes Pollie would stay and talk, but she won't.

"I have to get out there and keep the boys from running under cars," she says, as if the boys had a plan to do that.

He looks into the basket after she's gone. Bean bread, pork chops, much more than he can eat. Pollie misses him these days; he is working too much, and it's her way to try to make up for every loss with food. She still cooks all the old-fashioned things that take more time than most women have had for decades. She learned from her mother, a full-blooded Cherokee, who grew up around Kenwood and never learned English. Franklin's mother is full-blood too, but his father is white, and Franklin grew up in Muskogee. His mother served time in the kitchen only at Christmas and when it was her turn for the PTA bake sales. Franklin never gave two thoughts to being Cherokee until he began to study Native American Law—like many his age, he's a born-again Indian. He laughs at this. Annawake would like him better if he had that title on a little plaque on his desk.

Thinking of Annawake brings the return of his dread. He leans out his door and asks her to come into his office. Franklin already knows what she is going to do, but has to make the show of talking her out of it.

"Would you like something to eat? Pollie makes this bread."

Annawake shakes her head. "Thanks, Jinny just brought me a Big Mac, and like a fool I ate it. I should have waited."

"No baby at your house yet?"

Annawake smiles and shakes her head. "We think it's waiting for a new administration."

She breaks off a slice of bean bread anyway, and Franklin uses the silence to wrestle his doubts. The AILTP is paying her to work in his office and learn from him, but he feels like an ungenuine article—a new car put together from the parts of a lot of old ones and given a fresh coat of paint. A born-again Indian lawyer. Annawake learned about truth from her old uncle, who, Franklin has heard, comes from a medicine family and lives on a houseboat on Tenkiller and shoots squirrel with a blowgun.

Franklin opens his mouth for a long time before talking, and then starts slowly, the way he would get into ice water if he had to.

"This case you've opened. You have to have something on a birth parent," he tells her.

Annawake slaps crumbs off her hands and leans forward, her eyes alive. "Okay, but look. In the case of Mississippi Band of Choctaw *versus* Holyfield, the mother voluntarily gave her children to the white couple. The children had never even lived on the reservation. And the Supreme Court *still* voided that adoption." Annawake apparently has learned enough white-lawyer ways to leap into ice water without flinching.

"And how does that apply here? In that case, both birth parents were known and involved."

She lifts her chin a little. Annawake always enunciates her words as if she can taste each one and there is nothing else left to eat. "The birth mother gave the children up, but her choice was overruled."

"Meaning?"

"It shows the spirit of the law. The Indian Child Welfare Act is supposed to protect the interests of the Indian community in keeping its children. It's not supposed to be defeatable by the actions of individual tribe members."

Franklin waits until there is a question, and Annawake finds it. "So why do we need a birth parent?"

"The Supreme Court recognized that the tribal court had exclusive jurisdiction over that adoption, you're right," he says, correcting her as tactfully as a knife touching up a pencil point. The Holyfield decision was handed down just weeks ago, and Annawake appears to have memorized it. "But if I'm remembering it right, that birth mother was domiciled on the Choctaw reservation, making the child a tribe member. In this case, we have no idea whether this child falls under our jurisdiction. You don't have a domiciled parent or an enrolled parent because you don't have a parent."

"I have a mystery parent. Two of them. The transfer of custody was witnessed by a notary in Oklahoma City, who had no business with this kind of placement. The parents are listed as Steven and Hope Two-Two, allegedly Cherokees but not enrolled, also not enrolled Social Security–paying citizens of the U.S.A."

Franklin's eyebrows rise. "You found all that?"

"It was Jinny Redcrow's big moment. She got to call up Oprah Winfrey on official business. The researchers were pretty helpful with i.d. and background. And the United States government is always eager to be of assistance, naturally."

He doesn't smile. "You still don't have anything that makes it officially our business."

Annawake touches her fingertips together, making a little fish basket of her hands, and looks into it. Sometimes she mentions her spirit guide, a thing Franklin Turnbo can only half understand. She is so quick she seems guided by racehorses or the fox that runs ahead of the dogs.

"You heard the mother on TV, right? Her story was that on her way out to Arizona she picked up this baby, who is obviously Native American, in Cherokee territory, from the sister of its dead mother. But in the official records we have consent-to-adoption forms filed by two living parents with invented names. I'd say it's incumbent on the mother to prove it's *not* our business."

"You seem angry," he says.

She looks surprised, then says, "Well, yeah. Maybe. All the housewives watching TV last Friday saw that our kids can be picked up as souvenirs."

"Like your brother was."

Her eyes don't register any change. She says only, "I'm asking you if we could make a case for vacating an improperly conducted adoption."

"And then what?"

"And then we could work with Cherokee Nation Child Welfare Services to find a proper placement."

"Are you getting ahead of yourself?"

"Okay, or to evaluate the existing placement, first. But that should all be the tribe's decision. That baby should never have been taken out."

Franklin Turnbo leans back in his chair and sighs like a punctured air mattress. Annawake respectfully waits for him to run out of air.

"Annawake, I admire your energy. I wish I had it. But we have child-welfare problems filed in this office that could keep us all busy till I personally am old and gray. And then there are the land-use disputes and civil rights cases and the divorces and the drunks and the disorderlies. And all the people trying to hold on to what little there is left."

Annawake makes a basket with her hands again, and waits for the question.

"You've gone to school, and now you've come back to fight for your tribe. Who's going to do this work if you're riding your white horse around, gathering up lost children?"

"Don't you think there's a hole in somebody's heart because that child is gone? Did you *ever* hear of a Cherokee child that nobody cared about?"

"But somebody cares about her now, too. That mother who found her."

Annawake's eyes register a cloud of doubt, but she asks, "Finders keepers? Is that fair?"

"Not for wallets. Maybe for kids."

"You and I could have been lost children. I very nearly was. What would you be, without the tribe?"

Franklin, avoiding her eyes, looks out his office window, which reveals the highway to Muskogee. Along with the sound of tanker trucks there is the crazy music of a meadowlark on a telephone wire. Franklin has a powerful, physical memory of the time he ran out of gas on I-40 at age nineteen, a mixed-up kid playing hooky from university, driving home to see his mother. He coasted into a Chevron station laughing at his good luck. It took him a minute to realize the place was boarded up, the nozzles padlocked to the pumps. All around him were fields of oil derricks, and he was on empty. But the fields were so beautiful, and a meadowlark above him on the wire was singing its head off, and Franklin still couldn't stop laughing at his good luck.

She asks, "What did you mean when you said, trying to hang on to what little there is left? You think we're that pitiful?"

Franklin is embarrassed, and reaches for his meadowlark: the memory, at least, of right-mindedness. "I used to feel about this place the way you do," he says. "That the Nation is spiritually indestructible, because the birds in the woods don't care who owns the title to the land. And you're right, belonging to this tribe gave me a reason to stop chasing girls and show up for Judicial Process classes. But I've been a lawyer so long now I mainly just see how people fight and things get used up."

Annawake stares at him, and Franklin wishes she were less beautiful. A treacherous thought, for many different reasons. "It's such a terrible long shot," he says. "There may be nothing at all, no relatives, no proof."

"I know," Annawake says gently, the same way Pollie would, the way women talk to men: I know, honey. Relax.

"You'll probably lose what you put into it," he tells her. "I want to give you free rein, but it's also my business to look after the investments of time in this office."

"The Native American Law conference starts on the fifteenth, so I have to be in Tucson anyway, to give my paper. That's where she lives, Tucson. I can just go by and talk to the mother, see what her story is. No big investment."

"No matter what her story is, a lot of hearts are involved."

"I know," Annawake says again, but this is one thing Franklin doesn't believe she can truly know. She isn't a mother.

"Can you tell me why you're sure this is the best thing?"

She presses her curved lips together, thinking. "In law school I slept in the library pretty often. There was a couch in the women's lounge. After I pass my bar exams they're probably going to put up a plaque there. The Annawake Fourkiller Couch."

Franklin smiles. He finds he can picture it.

"People thought my life was so bleak. And I guess it was, so far from home, hearing the ambulances run by all night to the hospital, somebody cracked up or beat up or old and dumped out by their family, and laws jumping up and down in my head. But I always dreamed about the water in Tenkiller. All those perch down there you could catch, any time, you know? A world of free breakfast, waiting to help get you into another day. I've never been without that. Have you?"

"No," he admits. Whether or not he knew it, he was always Cherokee.

The fish were down there, for him as much as for Annawake.

"Who's going to tell that little girl who she is?"

Franklin wants to say, "She will have other things," but he can't know this for certain. Franklin wears a Seiko watch and looks as Cherokee as Will Rogers or Elvis Presley or the eighty thousand mixed-blood members of his Nation, yet he knows he isn't white because he can't think of one single generalization about white people that he knows to be true. He can think of half a dozen about Cherokees: They're good to their mothers. They know what's planted in their yards. They give money to their relatives, whether or not they're going to use it wisely. He rotates his chair a little. On his desk is an ugly little duck-shaped paper-clip holder his kids gave him as a present. He told Annawake once that it was his spirit guide. She didn't laugh.

"Okay," he says finally, "I trust your judgment on where to go with this."

Annawake's mouth moves into its most irresistible presentation, the strange upside-down grin. Her eyes are laughing, not at him, but at something. Crazy chances. "Thanks, boss," she says, standing up, touching his desk. "While I'm in Arizona I'll see if I can find me a big white horse."

8

A MORE

PERFECT UNION

TAYLOR SITS ON THE FRONT porch steps, hugging her knees, glowering at the indifferent apricot tree. It's an old knotty thing planted long ago when the house was new, and rarely bears anymore. But this summer it has hit on some prolific internal cycle to bring the neighborhood a bonanza of apricots—and birds.

"If they'd all get together and eat the fruit off one side of the tree, I wouldn't grudge them," she tells Lou Ann. "But they just peck a little hole in each one and wreck it."

Lou Ann looks mournful in spite of her outfit of lime-green Lycra. In ten minutes she has to go lead the Saturday-morning Phenomenal Abdominals class at Fat Chance. She's come over to Taylor's porch to wait for her ride. "I thought Jax was going to make a scarecrow," she says.

"He did." Taylor points at a cardboard cutout of a great horned owl in the top of the tree. It has realistic eyes and a good deal of feather detail, but is hard to recognize because of all the finches perched on it.

"Poor Turtle," says Lou Ann, sadly.

"This kills me. Have you ever seen her make a fuss before over something to eat, *ever,* before this? And now all of a sudden she loves apricots. But she won't eat one if it's got a hole pecked in it."

"I don't blame her, Taylor. Who wants to eat after a bird? There's probably bird diseases."

Cicadas scream brightly from the thorn scrub around the house. It's a shimmering day, headed for a hundred degrees. Taylor picks up a rock and throws it through the center of the apricot tree, raising a small commotion of brown feathers. They immediately settle again. The birds turn their heads sideways, wet beaks shining, bead eyes fixed on Taylor. Then they return to the duty of gorging themselves.

"Granny Logan used to say she was going to take my school picture and set it out in the cornfield to scare the crows."

"Your Granny Logan ought to be shot," Taylor suggests.

"Too late, she's dead." Lou Ann puts her hands behind her neck and knocks off a few quick sit-ups on the floor of the porch. Her curtain of bobbed blond hair flaps against the lime-colored sweatband. "I should get Cameron ... to come over here and ... stand under the tree," she puffs between sit-ups. "That'd scare them off."

Cameron John is Lou Ann's recurring boyfriend, and it's a fact that he is scary in several ways. He has dreadlocks down to his waist, for example, and a Doberman pinscher with gold earrings in one of its ears. But Taylor expects the birds would perceive Cameron's true nature and flock to him like St. Francis of Assisi. She can picture his dreadlocks covered with sparrows. She tosses another rock just as her neighbor, Mr. Gundelsberger, comes out of his house across the way. The rock lands near his feet. He stops short with his heels together, looks at the rock in an exaggerated way, then pulls his handkerchief out of the pocket of his gray flannel pants and waves it over his head.

"Peace," he shouts at Taylor. "No more the war."

"It's a war against the birds, Mr. G.," Taylor says. "They're winning."

He comes over and stands directly under the tree, shading his eyes and peering up into the branches. "Ach," he says. "What you need is a rahdio in the tree."

"A rodeo?" Lou Ann asks, incredulous. Her ex-husband was a rodeo rider. She could picture him roping birds, he was that small-minded.

"No, a *rahdio*." Mr. Gundelsberger holds his fist against his ear with one finger pointed up. "Transistor."

"A radio!" Lou Ann and Taylor say at the same time. Taylor asks, "Really?"

"Rock and roll," Mr. Gundelsberger says, nodding firmly. "You try it, you will see. Rock and roll will keep da birds off da peach."

Lou Ann grabs her bag and sprints down the stone steps in her waffle-soled cross trainers. She waves at Taylor as she and Mr. Gundelsberger pull out of the drive in his Volvo. He often gives her a ride downtown, since his jeweler's shop is only two blocks from Fat Chance.

Mr. G. moved in just a few months ago. His daughter, a locally famous artist who goes by the name of Gundi, has for years owned this whole little colony of falling-down stone houses in the desert at the edge of town. In bygone days it was a ranch; the gravel drive that leads uphill from the main road is still marked with an iron archway that reads RANCHO COPO. The first time Jax brought her out here, they sat on his roof and he told Taylor a wild tale about fertility rites and naming the ranch Copo to get the cows to copulate. Since then she's discovered it means "Ranch of the Snowflake," which frankly makes less sense than cow copulation. But it's an enviable place to live. Taylor heard of it even before she met Jax. People get on waiting lists to move out here, once they've been approved by Gundi.

Gundi lives in the big hilltop house, where she displays her huge abstract paintings on the stone walls of what was once the ranch hands' dining hall. All the other houses are small and strange: some have no heating or cooling; one has an outdoor bathroom. Jax's is tiny but has a weird stone tower on its southern end. The places rent for almost nothing. Taylor has noticed that a lot of the people who live here are musicians, or have Ph.D.s in odd things.

Before Rancho Copo, Taylor and Turtle lived downtown in a more conventional rundown house with Lou Ann and her baby. Lou Ann took them in when they first arrived in Tucson, and Taylor still feels a debt. She

wouldn't move in with Jax until Gundi had also approved Lou Ann as
Rancho Copo material.

Taylor goes in the house and rummages through the studio Jax has created in his bell tower. He says the acoustics are Christian. There isn't a lot
of floor space, but the shelves on the four narrow walls go all the way up.
She drags the ladder from wall to wall, certain that in all this mess of elec-
tronics he must have a transistor radio, but she can't find one. She brings
down a portable tape player instead, and one of Jax's demo tapes. She's
decided to try out the Irascible Babies on a new audience.

Annawake bumps up the long gravel drive in her rented car until she's
stopped by the sight of a woman in a tree. She can't be sure from the legs
that it's the same woman she saw on Oprah Winfrey, but the address
seems right so she parks and gets out. The ground is covered with spoiled
fruits and hard pits that hurt the soles of her feet through her moccasins.
She shouts into the branches, "Hello, I'm looking for Taylor Greer."

"You've found her, and she's up a tree." Taylor is using a rope to attach a
boom box to an upper limb. "You just stay right there. To tell you the
truth I prefer the ground."

A thunderous bass line begins to pound through the leaves. Annawake
watches the woman's sneakers step down the cross-hatched ladder of
limbs, then hang for a second, then drop. At ground level she's a few
inches shorter than Annawake and maybe a few years younger, with long
brown hair and unsuspicious eyes. She slaps the thighs of her jeans a few
times, looks at the palm of her right hand, and extends it.

"Annawake Fourkiller," Annawake says, shaking Taylor's hand. "I'm
from Oklahoma, in town for a professional meeting. You've got some
pretty country out here."

Taylor smiles at the mountains, which at this hour of the morning look
genuinely purple. "Isn't it? Before I came here I didn't expect so many
trees. The only difference between here and anywhere else is that here
everything's got thorns."

"Tough life in the desert, I guess. Be prickly or be eaten."

Taylor has to raise her voice now to compete with Jax, who is singing loudly from the treetops. "You want to talk? Come in and I'll shut the door so we can hear ourselves think."

Annawake follows Taylor inside, through a narrow stone hallway that barely accommodates an upright piano, which they squeeze past into the kitchen. The walls there are cool slant faces of slate. Annawake sits at a wooden table, whose legs are painted four different colors; she thinks of Millie and Dell fixing the table at home, and the new baby ruling the roost now. Taylor is putting water on for coffee.

"So, what did you kill four of, if I may ask?"

Annawake smiles. This is the woman she saw on TV—she recognizes the confidence. "It's a pretty common Cherokee surname."

"Yeah? Is there a story?"

"The story is, when my great-great-grandfather first encountered English-speaking people, that's the name he got. He had four kids, so he'd carved four notches in his rifle barrel—it was something they did back then. Out of pride, I guess, or maybe to help remind them how much game to bring home every day. But the white guys took it to mean he'd shot four men." Annawake glances at Taylor. "I guess Grandpa never set them straight."

Taylor smiles, catching the slender, almost dangerous thing that has passed between them. She clatters coffee mugs and pours black grounds into the filter. "Your accent makes me homesick. I know it's Okie, but to me it doesn't sound that far off from Kentucky."

"I was just thinking that," Annawake says. "You sound like home to me. Almost. There's a difference but I can't name it."

Taylor stands by the stove and for a while neither woman speaks. Taylor takes in Annawake's appearance: her black brush of hair all seems to radiate out from a single point, the widow's peak in her forehead. Her skin is a beautiful pottery color you want to touch, like Turtle's. She's wearing a maroon cotton shirt with blue satin ribbons stitched on the yoke and shoulder seams. Taylor fiddles with the gas burner. They listen to a long guitar riff and Jax's voice coming from outside:

"Big boys ... play games. Their toys ... follow me home. Big boys play games, big bang, you're gone ..."

Annawake raises an eyebrow.

"That's my boyfriend's band." Taylor looks out the window. "Hey, it's working. No birds."

"Is this some kind of experiment?"

Taylor laughs. "You must think I'm cracked. I'm trying to keep the birds out of the apricot tree. My little girl likes apricots more than anything living or dead, and she's the kind of kid that just doesn't ask for much. I've been going out of my head trying to think how to get the birds out of the fruit."

"My grandma planted mulberry trees next to her peach trees. The birds liked the mulberries better. They'd sit in the mulberry and laugh, thinking they were getting away with something good, and leave all the peaches for us."

"No kidding," Taylor says. "Wish I'd thought of that twenty years ago."

"Your daughter. That's Turtle, the apricot lover?"

"That's right."

After another long minute of quiet, the teakettle begins to rattle. Taylor lifts it and pours hissing water into the coffee grounds. "She's not here at the moment. She'll be real surprised when she comes back and sees those birds gone." Taylor smiles down at the counter in a way that surprises Annawake because it is almost timid. Private. It passes, and Taylor looks back at Annawake. "Jax took her and a neighbor kid to see these two new rhinoceroses they got in at the zoo. He and Turtle are trying to write a song about endangered species."

"What's the story of that name?"

"What, Turtle? Well, not as good as yours. It's just a nickname more or less, because of her personality. Turtle is ... well, she holds on. From the time she was little she'd just grab me and not let go. In Kentucky where I grew up, people used to say if a snapping turtle gets hold of you it won't let go till it thunders. Do you take cream or anything?"

"Black, please."

"That's the story," she says, serving Annawake and sitting down opposite. "There's not much about us that hasn't been in the papers already. To tell you the truth, I think we're storied out. No offense, but we're hoping to just get back to normal."

Annawake shakes her head slightly.

"You're a reporter, right? I just assumed you saw us on TV. You said you're here for some kind of a journalist convention?"

Annawake holds her coffee mug in both hands and takes a sip. "I'm sorry, I've misled you," she says carefully, one phrase at a time. "I did see you on television, but I'm not a reporter. I'm an attorney. I'm in town for a Native American Law conference."

"A lawyer? I never would have guessed a lawyer."

"Well, thanks, I guess. I work in an office that does a lot of work for the Cherokee Nation. That's what I want to talk with you about. Turtle's adoption might not be valid."

Taylor's cup stops an inch from her lips, and for nearly half a minute she does not appear to breathe. Then she puts down the cup. "I've been through all this already. The social worker said I needed adoption papers, so I went to Oklahoma City and I got papers. If you want to see, I'll go get them."

"I've already looked at the records. That's the problem, it wasn't done right. There's a law that gives tribes the final say over custody of our own children. It's called the Indian Child Welfare Act. Congress passed it in 1978 because so many Indian kids were being separated from their families and put into non-Indian homes."

"I don't understand what that has to do with me."

"It's nothing against you personally, but the law is crucial. What we've been through is a wholesale removal."

"Well, that's the past."

"This is not General Custer. I'm talking about as recently as the seventies, when you and I were in high school. A third of all our kids were still being taken from their families and adopted into white homes. One out of *three*."

Taylor's eyes are strangely enlarged. "My home doesn't have anything to do with your tragedy," she says. She gets up and stands at the window, looking out.

"I don't mean to scare you," Annawake says quietly. "But I want you to have some background on the problem. We need to make sure our laws are respected."

Taylor turns around and faces Annawake, her hair wheeling. "I didn't take Turtle from any family, she was dumped on me. *Dumped.* She'd already lost her family, and she'd been hurt in ways I can't even start to tell you without crying. Sexual ways. Your people let her fall through the crack and she was in bad trouble. She couldn't talk, she didn't walk, she had the personality of—I don't know what. A bruised apple. Nobody wanted her." Taylor's hands are shaking. She crosses her arms in front of her chest and slumps forward a little in the manner of a woman heavily pregnant.

Annawake sits still.

"And now that she's a cute little adorable child and gets famous and goes on television, now you want her back."

"This has nothing to do with Turtle being on television. Except that it brought her to our attention." Annawake looks away and thinks about her tone. Lawyer words will not win any cases in this kitchen. She is not so far from Oklahoma. "Please don't panic. I'm only telling you that your adoption papers may not be valid because you didn't get approval from the tribe. You need that. It might be a good idea to get it."

"And what if they won't give it?"

Annawake can't think of the right answer to that question.

Taylor demands, "How can you possibly think this is in Turtle's best interest?"

"How can you think it's good for a tribe to lose its children!" Annawake is startled by her own anger—she has shot without aiming first. Taylor is shaking her head back and forth, back and forth.

"I'm sorry, I can't understand you. Turtle is my daughter. If you walked in here and asked me to cut off my hand for a good cause, I might think about it. But you don't get Turtle."

"There's the child's best interest and the tribe's best interest, and I'm trying to think of both things."

"Horseshit." Taylor turns away, facing the window.

Annawake speaks gently to her back. "Turtle is Cherokee. She needs to know that."

"She knows it."

"Does she know what it means? Do *you?* I'll bet she sees Indians on TV and thinks: *How.* Bows and arrows. That isn't what we are. We have a written language as subtle as Chinese. We had the first free public school system in the world, did you know that? We have a constitution and laws."

"Fine," Taylor says, her eyes wandering over the front yard but catching on nothing. *We have a constitution too,* she thinks, *and it is supposed to prevent terrible unfairness,* but all she can remember is a string of words she memorized in eighth grade. "We the people," she says out loud. She walks over to the sink and picks up a soup ladle, then puts it back down. The voice outside sings, "*I can't feel it. You know they're stealing it from me.*"

Annawake feels an afterimage of her niece's egg belly under her hands. "I'm sure you're a good mother," she says. "I can tell that."

"How can you tell? You march in here, you ..." Taylor falters, waving a hand in the air. "You don't know the first thing about us."

"You're right, I'm assuming. You seem to care about her a lot. But she needs her tribe, too. There are a lot of things she'll need growing up that you can't give her."

"Like what?"

"Where she comes from, who she is. Big things. And little things, like milk, for instance. I'll bet she won't drink milk."

Taylor picks up the ladle again and bangs it against the metal sink, hard, then puts it down again. "You've got some Goddamn balls, telling me who my kid is. I'd like to know where you were three years ago when she was on death's front stoop."

"I was in law school, trying to learn how to make things better for my nation."

"We the people, creating a more perfect union."

Annawake offers no response.

"This here is my nation and I'm asking you to leave it."

Annawake stands up. "I'm sorry this hasn't been a more friendly meeting of minds. I hoped it would be. I'd still like to see Turtle." She leaves her card on the table, a small white rectangle embossed with red letters and the seal of the Cherokee Nation. "I think it would be good for her to talk about her heritage."

Taylor says nothing.

"Okay. Well, I'm in town till Monday. I'd like to meet her. Should I come back tomorrow maybe? After dinner?"

Taylor closes her eyes.

"Thanks for the coffee."

Taylor walks to the front door, holds it open, and watches the visitor pick her way through the fallen fruit in the yard. Annawake finds the keys in her pocket and stands for a second with her hand on the car door.

Taylor shouts, "She loves milk. We buy it by the gallon."

Annawake's rental is a low-slung blue Chrysler that gives her some trouble backing out. It wobbles and crunches its way down the rutted drive, headed back toward town.

Taylor stands on the porch, arms crossed, witnessing the retreat. The words "a more friendly meeting of minds" are smacking like angry pent-up bees against the inside of her head.

High overhead in the apricot branches the taped music has reached its end, and gone quiet. One by one the birds emerge from the desert and come back to claim their tree.

9

THE PIGS

IN HEAVEN

UNCLE LEDGER WOULD SAY, "ONCE you have ridden a horse, you should know what a horse is." So it bothers Annawake that when she stands for the second time in front of the little rock house where Turtle stays she sees things she could swear were not there before. An odd stone tower at the end of the pitched roof, for instance, the kind of thing the white people in storybooks would hold prisoners in, or crazy aunts.

Of course, last time she was nervous. And watching a woman up a tree. Now there is only a skinny man in black jeans sitting on the porch steps. He's staring at his hands, which seem to be dozing on his knees, a pair of colossal, torpid spiders.

"Hi," Annawake tries. She stands with her own hands in her pockets, waiting for some kind of offer. "I'm Annawake," she adds.

"Oh, believe me, I know that." He seems to be rousing himself from his thoughts, very slowly, with a lot of effort, as if coming out of hibernation. "Where are my manners?" he says finally in a voice deep with despair, or the South. "Sit down here on this dirty old porch."

The stone step is broad and slumped like the gateway to some ancient wonder of the world. When she sits, it bleeds coolness into her thighs, a feeling of dampness. "Are you the musician?"

"Jax," he says, nodding a couple of times, as if barely convinced that this is his actual name.

"I heard your work yesterday. From that tree."

"It terrified the birds, I hear. I think I've found my market." Jax picks up a green apricot the size of a golf ball and flings it toward the cardboard owl in the treetops. It misses by a generous margin.

"Maybe. I liked your music all right," she says. She throws an apricot and hits the owl with a loud pop, causing it to shudder and list on its branch.

"Jesus," he says. Jax throws again, this time aiming for the trunk, and nicks the side. Annawake follows quickly, hitting the spot where his shot bounced off.

He looks at her sideways. With his dark brows and glint of gold earring, he resembles a pirate. "Is this one of those visitations? Are you about to reveal the meaning of my life?"

Annawake doesn't feel she ought to laugh. "I used to be kind of good at this throwing game we have, *sgwalesdi*. It's just a coincidence, I'm not that good at everything."

"If you are, I don't want to hear about it."

"I don't know the meaning of your life."

"Good. Because I'm not ready to hear it. Takes the fun away, you know? Like when you're reading a good book and somebody says, 'Oh, that's a great one, did he get hit by the train yet?' "

Annawake smiles. She's noticed that the house is truly run-down by social-service standards, worse than some things she's seen in the Cherokee Nation, and accepts that this could be used to her advantage. Toward the west, the desert rises up to meet the splintered rock peaks of the Tucson Mountains. Annawake shades her eyes to look at the descending sun. It's an effort for her not to shove the conversation forward. "I can see why you'd want to live out here," she says. "Out of the city."

"Oh, well, that's a very sad story. I got kicked out of the city of Tucson. They have an ordinance against Irascible Babies."

"Who?"

"My band. We all used to live together in a chicken house, downtown. But by some estimates we were too loud."

"Why would they have a chicken house downtown?"

"It wasn't, anymore. They'd closed it down because of the smell. I'm telling you, it's a very intolerant town."

This boyfriend is nothing that Annawake planned on. She's surprised to find him so serene and obliging, though she knows she may be mistaken. He may simply be in a coma. "Jacks is short for Jackson?"

"No, with an X." He makes a cross with his marvelously long index fingers. "Short for nothing. My mother was one of the best-known alcoholics in the French Quarter of New Orleans. I was named after a venerated brand of beer."

"You're named after Jax Beer?"

He nods morosely. "Somewhere in this world I have a sister named Hurricane. I'm telling you the God's honest truth."

"You don't know where she is?"

"Mother nor sister. If they are even on this earth."

"Damn. I used to think all you needed was white skin to have an easy life," Annawake says.

"I used to wish I was an Indian. I shaved my head one time and wore beads and made everybody call me Soaring Elk."

Annawake looks at him, and this time she does laugh. "You're not a Soaring Elk."

Jax studies his sneakers. "I could use a more meaningful name, though, don't you think? Something athletic. Maybe Red Ball Jets."

For a minute they regard their four shoes lined up on the step. Jax's trashed-out hightops look oversized and tragic, whereas Annawake's moccasins are perfect: stitched suede, the burnished red of iron-oxide soils in Oklahoma.

"Cool moccasins," Jax observes. "They look brand new."

"They are. I have to buy them out here. Nobody in Oklahoma wears moccasins anymore."

"No?"

She shakes her head. "The ones they sell to tourists at the Cherokee Heritage Center are made by this hippie in Albuquerque."

Jax sighs. "What is this world coming to?"

Suddenly, noticeably, the failing sunlight turns golden and benevolent. The cacti lit from behind glow with halos of golden fur, and Jax's and Annawake's faces and limbs seem similarly blessed. After a minute the light changes again, to flat dusk.

"They're gone, aren't they?" Annawake finally asks.

"Yep."

"How gone?"

Jax ponders the question. "She packed all Turtle's clothes. All of her books. She picked about two hundred green apricots and laid them out on the shelf behind the backseat hoping they'd ripen. When they pulled out of here it looked like the Joads."

Annawake has to think awhile to place the Joads, and then remembers *The Grapes of Wrath,* from high school English. White people fleeing the dust bowl of Oklahoma, ending up as fruit pickers in California. They think they had it bad. The Cherokees got marched out of their homelands *into* Oklahoma.

"No forwarding address, I guess."

Jax smiles.

"She manages an automotive place downtown, right? For a woman named Mattie, who must be a friend because she couldn't come to the phone when I called. You're lucky to have a mechanic in the family."

"Good work, Sherlock, only, A, even if Taylor were a mechanic she'd probably tell me to fix my own car. And B, she's not one. It used to be mainly a tire store, but Taylor hates tires so when they branched into auto parts Mattie let her take over the muffler and fanbelt side of the enterprise."

"I guess she had vacation time saved up."

"Nobody down there exactly punches a clock," Jax says. "It's a nice out-fit. Kind of sixties Amish. They take in strays."

"Like Turtle?"

"Like Central American refugees. Could I remind you that you are the engineer of my recent wrecked life? Is this an official interrogation?"

"I'm sorry. No. I can get the information some other way, if you'd like me to go now and leave you alone."

"Left alone is exactly what I have been," Jax says. He's quiet long enough for Annawake to hear air moving around them.

"Mattie loves Taylor like a son," he says suddenly. "So you're going to end up talking to the air compressors down there. Don't waste your time."

"But you can't tell me where she's gone, I don't suppose."

"You suppose correctly."

They both watch as the sun touches the mountains. The horizon is softly indented as if the landscape had been worn down right there, like the low spot in the center of an old marble step, by the repeated tread of sunset. The red ball collapses, then silently hemorrhages into the surrounding clouds.

"I may get phone calls now and again, to let me know they're all right. But there is no forwarding address."

"Well, thanks for being honest," Annawake says.

Jax laces his fingers behind his head and cracks some junction of his bones with a resounding pop. "I do a lot of wicked things to my body, but I never perjure it."

"Wise choice," she says. "Only we're not in court."

"So are they really in trouble? Is this going to be a James Dean kind of situation where the Cherokee Nation chases them down to the riverbank and shines the lights in their eyes and finally they surrender?"

Annawake says, "No."

"Could I have that in writing?"

"You haven't told me anything, but you've been very nice about it, so I'll be honest with you. The Cherokee Nation isn't pursuing this case, I am. The thing is full of holes. I don't know how we can prove Turtle is Cherokee, unless some relatives come forward on the Nation. And even if that happens, I'm not positive the tribe's Child Welfare Department would take her from Taylor. Or even if they *should*."

"What does the law say?"

"The law says we can take her. There have been kids who were with adoptive parents five, ten years, that the Indian Child Welfare Act has brought back to their tribe, because the adoptions were illegal."

"Wow. That's radioactive."

"It's hard for someone outside of our culture to understand, I guess. To see anything more sacred than Mom and Dad and little red baby makes three."

"What do you see?"

Annawake hesitates. "First choice? I'd rather have seen her go into a Cherokee home, with relatives, that's always the best thing. But we can't always get first choice. And now that she's been taken out, it's way complicated. My boss thinks I'm on the warpath. Annawake Crazy Horse."

"Are you?"

"Well, sure. Taylor should have gotten permission from the tribe. And Turtle should have connections with her people. She should know ..." Annawake pauses, corrects her aim. "There are ways of letting her know about who she is. My position is essentially neutral. I have information Taylor could use."

"Neutral snootral. You know that thing they say about getting between a mother bear and her cub? Annie dear, *you* might think you're just out picking blueberries, but that's highly irrelevant to Mama Bear."

"I accept your point."

A small breeze seems to come right up out of the ground, stirring the tree branches in every direction. Voices drift down from the large stone house on the hill, fragments of laughter, and a chorus of bird chatter rises from the mesquite thicket. Annawake listens to the bird music, identifying some of its individual parts: the monotonous croon of a dove, a woodpecker's laugh, and stitched through it all, the intermittent shriek of crickets. She stops listening so closely then, preferring the whole song to any of its solo voices.

Jax slaps his knee abruptly. "Damn this," he says.

"I agree."

"You don't know the half of it, listen. Taylor is the woman my mama used to tell me to save myself for. I swear, I kind of wish I had. You ever feel that way about a person?"

"Not one person, no," Annawake says. She doesn't have to think about it.

"Well, then, maybe you can't understand what I'm going through. If I went in and played it on the piano, you'd understand. You'd say, This Jax, boy, I think he going to lie down here and die if that woman stays away past the fourth of July."

The clouds in the western sky are still lit brightly on their undersides like the yellowy-silver bellies of fish, but overhead some stars are out. "There you go," Jax tells Annawake. "That's Venus, the goddess of love. Don't ask me why she comes out at eight o'clock when people are still washing their supper dishes."

"Prime time," Annawake says. Listening to Jax encourages free association.

"You bet."

"You know the thing that first really got my attention about this case?"

Jax says, "The sheer awesome height of Hoover Dam."

"No, I missed that part of the show, believe it or not. What got me interested is that her story doesn't square up. On TV she said Turtle was a foundling, more or less. That some Cherokee woman handed her this kid in a coffee shop. But the records show two parents who voluntarily gave Turtle up."

"Did anyone ever tell you that you, personally, are beautiful beyond the speed of light?"

She stares at Jax for a minute, then laughs. "In those words, no."

"Just wondering. Could I kiss you?"

"Is this a diversionary tactic?"

"Yes, more or less. Although I'd probably have a good time."

"Your heart's not in it, Jax. Nice try, though."

"Thank you."

"So apparently, from what I've found out, the story of the foundling in the coffee shop is the true one. Strange but true. They fixed up that adoption, didn't they?"

"Righty-o."

"Why?"

"Well, you know. You need papers in this big old world. Some social worker here in Tucson figured out that legalwise Taylor's goose was cooked, finding the birth parents was hopeless. So she put her onto some official in Okie City that apparently is not obsessed with the long arm of the law. Taylor went back there with two friends that posed as Turtle's parents."

"So Steven and Hope Two Two are a fraud."

Jax runs a hand through his ragged hair. "You'd already figured that out, don't play Little Bo Peep. But you'll never find Steven and Hope; they were Guatemalans without papers and they've disappeared into America the beautiful. And the guy that approved the adoption, he was old, Taylor says. He's probably retired. There couldn't be a whole lot of brownie points involved in nailing him now."

She understands suddenly what Jax is doing, and admires it: he is neither obliging nor comatose, he's protecting the people he loves. He has learned much more from her than she from him. She feels some lawyerly chagrin. "I'm not necessarily looking to nail people," she says.

"You're a good shot, Ms. Fourkiller. Maybe you should just make sure you're not loaded."

"I want to do the best thing for the most people."

"She loves Turtle, that's one thing you should know. She would jump off Hoover Dam herself for that kid, headfirst. Me, the great Jax, she *enjoys*, but Turtle she loves. She didn't exactly have to meditate before she walked out of here. It was no contest." He looks at her, his eyes luminous and hard, and then back at the mountains. For the first time Annawake notices his strange profile: a perfectly straight line from his forehead to the end of his nose. She finds it beautiful and disturbing. She clamps her hands tightly between her knees, shivering a little. The temperature has dropped unbelievably, as it will when the desert loses the sun.

Jax stands up and goes inside and stays for quite a while. She's uncertain whether this signifies the end of the interview. She hears a few dramatic nose blows, and then she can hear him singing quietly: "Be careful what you take, Anna Wake, be careful what you break." She decides that if he starts playing the piano she will leave, but he comes back out with his fingers hooked into the mouths of two slim brown bottles of beer.

"Here," he says. "Let's have a party. Kennedy and Khrushchev drink to a better world." He sits beside her, very close, and she can feel his body heat through her jeans. Strangely, she feels comforted rather than threatened, as if Jax were one of her brothers. Possibly it's because she has only heard her brothers, and no other man before now, confess to her his absolute love for some other woman.

Jax leans back on one elbow and begins pointing out constellations: Ursa Major, which Annawake has known since she could walk, and the Pleiades.

"The what?"

"Pleiades. Seven sisters."

She takes a long pull on her beer and squints at the sky. "You people must have better eyes than we do. In Cherokee there are only six. The Six Bad Boys. *Anitsutsa.*"

"*Anitsutsa?*"

"Yeah. Or *disihgwa*, the pigs. The Six Pigs in Heaven."

"Excuse me but you're making this up."

"No. There's a story about these six boys that wouldn't do their work. Wouldn't work in the corn, wouldn't fix their mothers' roofs, wouldn't do the ceremony chores—there's always stuff to be done at the ceremonial grounds, getting firewood and repairing shelters and things like that. They weren't what you'd call civic-minded."

"And they got turned into pigs."

"Now wait, don't jump ahead. It's their fault, they turned themselves into pigs. See, all they wanted to do, ever, was play ball and have fun. All day long. So their mothers got fed up. They got together one day and gathered up all the boys' *sgwalesdi* balls. It's a little leather ball about like this." Annawake holds up a green apricot. "With hair inside. Animal hair, human, whatever. And they put all the balls in the stewpot. They cooked them."

"Yum, yum," says Jax.

She throws the apricot, carefully aiming at nothing. "Okay. So the boys come home for lunch after playing around all morning, and their mothers say, 'Here's your soup!' They plop those soggy old cooked balls down on their plates. So the boys get mad. They say, 'Forget it, only a pig would eat this,' and they rush down to the ceremonial grounds and start running around and around the ball court, asking the spirits to listen, yelling that their mothers are treating them like pigs. And the spirits listened, I guess.

They figured, 'Well, a mother knows best,' and they turned the boys into pigs. They ran faster and faster till they were just a blur. Their little hooves left the ground and they rose up into the sky, and there they are."

"Holy crow," Jax says. "Your mom tell you that, when you wouldn't make your bed?"

"My Uncle Ledger," she says. "There's a lot of different versions of all the stories, according to what mood you're in. But you're right, that's the general idea. The Pigs, and also Uktena, this big snake with horns—those are the Cherokee boogeymen. I was always very civic-minded when I lived with my uncle."

"So that's your guiding myth. Do right by your people or you'll be a pig in heaven."

Annawake thinks this over. "Yes. I had a hundred and one childhood myths, and they all added up more or less to 'Do right by your people.' Is that so bad?"

"Myths are myths. They're good if they work for you, and bad if they don't."

"What are yours?"

"Oh, you know, I heard the usual American thing. If you're industrious and have clean thoughts you will grow up to be vice president of Motorola."

"Do right by yourself."

Jax finishes the last half of his beer in one swallow. She watches his Adam's apple with amazement. "You think Taylor's being selfish," he states.

Annawake hesitates. There are so many answers to that question. "Selfish is a loaded word," she says. "I've been off the reservation, I know the story. There's this kind of moral argument for doing what's best for yourself."

Jax puts his hands together under his chin and rolls his eyes toward heaven. "Honor the temple, for the Lord hast housed thy soul within. Buy that temple a foot massage and a Rolex watch."

"I think it would be hard to do anything else. Your culture is one long advertisement for how to treat yourself to the life you really deserve. Whether you actually deserve it or not."

"True," he says. "We all ought to be turned into pigs."

Annawake's mouth forms a tight, upside-down smile. "Some of my best friends are white people."

Jax goes limp, as if he's been shot.

"We just have different values," she says. "Some people say religion is finding yourself, and some people say it's losing yourself in a crowd."

Jax revives. "You can do that? Lose yourself?"

"Oh, sure. At the dances."

"Dancing?"

"Not like *American Bandstand,* not recreational dancing, it's ceremonial. A group thing. It's church, for us."

"I say po-tay-toes, and you say po-tah-toes." Jax lies flat on his back and balances his empty bottle on his stomach. It tilts a little when he breathes or talks. "And never the Twain shall meet, because he's dead." He laughs crazily and the bottle rolls off and clinks down the stone steps, but doesn't break. He sits up. "You're being kind of *anisnitsa* yourself, you know."

"Anti-*what?*"

"Anisnitsa. Isn't that what you said, for pig?"

"*Sihgwa.*"

"Whatever. You're being one. In your own fashion."

"I'm trying to see both sides."

"You can't," Jax says. "And Taylor can't. It's impossible. Your definitions of 'good' are not in the same dictionary. There is no point of intersection in this dialogue."

"Surely you don't think it's *good* for the tribe to lose its children? Or for Turtle to lose us? She's entitled to her legacy."

"Her legacy at the moment may be green apricots for dinner."

"What a thought. Did they have someplace to go?"

Jax doesn't answer.

"It's not a trick question."

"Well, then, yes. The answer is yes. Right now they are someplace."

"Please tell her I'm sorry if I'm the cause of this."

"*If* you're the cause of this?"

"You have to believe this much, the last thing I want is to put Turtle through more dislocation."

Jax reaches down carefully and sets the beer bottle on its head. "Dislocation," he says.

"You're the only connection between Turtle and me at this point, and," she waits for him to meet her eyes, "and I need that connection."

"Don't look at me, Mama Bear," says Jax. "I'm just picking blueberries."

IO

THE HORSES

"Turtle, drink your milk."

Turtle's plate is a boneyard of grilled-cheese sandwich crusts. She picks up her full glass and drinks, holding a steady sidelong eye on Taylor. As soon as Taylor looks away, she sets down her glass.

Angie Buster's diner is deserted. At four o'clock Angie declared that not even the starving Armenians would come out for a meal in this weather, and she went home to take a nap. Taylor and Turtle and Pinky the bulldog sit near the front window watching long knives of rain attack the ground at a hard slant. The first storm of the summer has blown in from Mexico, arousing the dust and dampening the Virgin of Guadalupe outside, causing her yellow bows to drop off one by one. Lucky is missing in action again. Angie isn't worried; it has only been half a day, and she says she can feel in her bones when it's going to be a long one. Her bones say this one isn't.

Angie owns not only the diner, it turns out, but also the adjacent Casa Suerte motor inn, which Taylor understood as "Casa

Sweater" over the phone. According to Angie, *suerte* means "good luck"; she bought it ten years ago when the state finally persuaded Lucky's father to catch up on his child support. The idea of this place as someone's good fortune depresses Taylor. The low brick units of the motor inn surround a doubtful patch of grass, an empty swimming pool, and one palm tree that escaped the short, trashy stage only to find itself leggy and ridiculous above the telephone wires. Each unit has a single metal chair outside its door, suggesting a concept of neighborliness, but the place seems short on neighbors. Taylor has seen only one other person around, an old woman with frightened-looking hair. She is grateful to have somewhere to hide out while she considers their next move, but being here is only slightly better than being nowhere.

"So what do you want to do now?" she asks Turtle.

"Go home."

"I know. But we can't. We're on vacation for a while."

Turtle bites her lips between her teeth, then releases them. She picks up her fork and idly begins poking things with it: her plate, the tablecloth, her hair. The bulldog watches with mild interest. Taylor frowns unconsciously, fearing slightly for Turtle's eyes, but she bites down on the impulse to tell her to put the fork down. Turtle will only go so far, she's found. Not to the point of self-damage.

From their table Taylor can see the glossy slabs of laminated newspaper hanging in the entrance to the diner: articles from the *Phoenix Republic*, the *San Francisco Chronicle*, even the *Washington Post*, all concerning the great adventure of Lucky and Turtle. It's no comfort to Taylor that people in San Francisco and Washington, D.C., are aware of Angie's diner.

"Let's watch TV," Turtle suggests.

"Sure, we can go watch TV. Pinky will cook and wait tables if the starving Armenians come in. Right, Pink?"

The dog wags its rear end with its ghost of bobbed tail, and Turtle smiles, her first all day. Taylor feels relieved for that, at least, as they shove the door open and run across the wet courtyard.

* * *

Sideways rain stings Turtle's eyes and arms. She tried to see in the pool as they hurried by but there is no blue in there, only a big mud-color shape of a thumbprint growing on the bottom. Lucky Buster said he could swim, before, and now Lucky Buster is gone. Her mother is trying to fit the key in the door of their room. The scaredy white-hair woman comes toward them holding a little roof of newspaper over her head.

"Have you seen the horses?" she wants to know.

"No," Taylor says. The key is on a wood card like Popsicle sticks. When it slips out of Taylor's hand it goes away on the water down the sidewalk.

"Well, they were here," the woman says. "Can you give me a present?"

Turtle catches the float-away key and gives it back. "What kind of present?" Taylor asks. She tries to make the lock open, but her hands are shaky like they were the day Turtle and Jax and Dwayne Ray came home from the rhinoceros zoo and they had to put everything in a suitcase.

"The horses! Didn't you see them?"

"I'm sorry," Taylor says.

Turtle doesn't want to see a horse's clomping feet. Everyone here is afraid. Turtle feels the old place coming, with him and no light and you can't get air.

"Oh, you're sorry. I'm sure you are." The woman runs away with her feet in flip-flops splatting the ground with little steps. The door gives in and they fall inside, where the room smells safe and nose-stinging like clean bathrooms. She finds Taylor's cold hand and knows they will stay right here.

Turtle clicks on the television and stands a few inches from the screen, punching the channel button, sorting through the brazen images. She settles on a documentary about repairing a cathedral, and climbs onto the bed. Taylor isn't sure what the appeal is, but she accepts Turtle's choice. The narrator is describing the chemicals they have to use on the ancient walls; meanwhile, a man in a little wooden swing moves up and down the high steeple in his system of ropes, like a spider, but not so graceful. A male spider with a bucket seat and chemicals.

"Where do you think Lucky Buster is now?" Turtle asks.

Taylor has stripped down to her bra and begins pulling off Turtle's wet clothes. "Oh, I think he's at a friend's house chewing banana bubble gum and eating all kinds of junk Angie won't let him have."

"Like me and Jax do when you're at work?"

"Ha, ha." Gently she pushes a dry shirt over Turtle's damp head, which smells like baby shampoo, and pulls her arms through the holes.

The cooler unit in the window thumps doggedly, overworked but useless in the damp heat. Taylor is suddenly irritated with the prickly weight of her hair; it reminds her of Jax breathing on her neck. She yanks it over her shoulder and begins corralling it into a braid.

"Why do we have to have this vacation?" Turtle asks.

Taylor feels gooseflesh rise on the skin of her bare arms. "Well, because we can't be hanging around at home right now."

"Why?"

Taylor examines the end of her rope of hair, trying to look unconcerned. It would be so simple to lie: Jax decided to paint the whole house purple. "Do you remember when I took you to Oklahoma that time to get your adoption papers?"

Turtle nods, and Taylor doesn't doubt that she remembers. Sometimes she will mention events from years ago. Taylor finds it miraculous and disturbing that Turtle can find words for things she witnessed before she could talk.

"We had to go on that trip because the social workers said we needed those papers so you could stay with me. And this is something like that. We need to go on another trip, to make sure we can stay together."

"A trip to where?"

"Well, that's the part I don't know yet. Someplace lucky. Where do you think we should go?"

"Sesame Street."

"Good idea," Taylor says.

Now the television is showing the paintings inside the church. There is a sad, long-faced Jesus made up of small squares and triangles, as if he were glass, and had been smashed and reassembled. Taylor rolls over on her stomach and nuzzles Turtle's neck. Her spirit is revived by the exact unchanging smell of Turtle: shampoo, sweat, and something nutty and sweet, like peanut butter. She blows against her brown cheek, making a loud noise, then gives her a kiss. "This church is getting depressing," she says. "Could we watch something with a little more story line?"

Turtle gets up and changes the station to a movie.

"Thanks, pal."

The movie is about a big, tough, angry wife who is trying to ruin the life of her rabbity husband, who ran off with a rich romance writer. Nothing about the movie seems realistic to Taylor, but Turtle asks her not to talk to the TV, so she tries. They both like the mean wife the best. She does spectacularly horrible things, and they laugh. Taylor also likes the Indian actor who plays the rich lady's smug, smart-alecky butler. The lady keeps snapping, "Garcia, take care of it this instant!" and Garcia keeps rolling his eyes and walking away.

In the last few days Taylor has been noticing images of Indians everywhere: the Indian-chief profile on a Pontiac. The innocent-looking girl on the corn-oil margarine. The hook-nosed cartoon mascot of the Cleveland Indians, who played in Tucson. Taylor wonders what Annawake meant when she said Turtle should be in touch with her Indian side. Maybe that doesn't mean feathers, but if not, then what? Taylor is supposedly part Indian herself; Alice used to talk about some Cherokee great-grandmother way in the back of the closet, but everybody and his brother has one of those, even Elvis Presley did. Where do you draw the line? Maybe being an Indian isn't any one thing, any more than being white is one thing. What mascot would they use for a team called the Cleveland White People?

The movie has become a commercial without Taylor's notice: she realizes now that the dancing women lifting drinks from a tray have nothing to do with Garcia the Indian butler. Taylor doesn't care for her own train of thought. She could end up like the woman outside, running around in the rain, asking people, "Have you seen the Indians?"

Just as Angie's bones predicted, Lucky returned with the end of the rainstorm. He was at his friend Otis's, working on model trains. "Next time use your brain and call me, will you, Otis?" she scolds when he drops Lucky off at the diner.

"My phone went out," Otis says.

"My butt," Angie replies.

Otis is very old and bald, with bad posture and big splay feet in white sneakers. She orders him inside for a piece of pie, and he obeys. Like everyone else around, he seems to turn into a child in the presence of Angie. Taylor marvels at this talent of hers, like one of the superpowers a cartoon character could possess: the hypersonic mother-ray.

Taylor is helping Angie put away the soggy yellow bows from the Virgin of Guadalupe. The storm has left them floating in a puddle around her feet like bedraggled water lilies. "Do you put these up every time he disappears?"

"Well, it's kind of a signal to the town, to be on the lookout," Angie says. "So if anybody sees him wandering they'll send him on home."

Angie pronounces "wandering" like "wondering," and before her meaning dawns on Taylor, she is stumped on what it is that Lucky would be wondering about. He seems to have little room for doubt in his life. She can see him inside now, talking excitedly to Turtle. Turtle looks rapt. Taylor envies Lucky's assurance, and Turtle's state of grace: to be able to see neither forward nor backward right now, to see Lucky as a friend, just that. Not an instrument of fate.

The phone rings and Angie goes in to get it, but returns immediately. "It's for you."

Taylor's heart thumps hard when she picks up the receiver; she can't think what news there might be that isn't bad.

"Are we not the species of critical thinkers?" the telephone inquires.

"Jax!"

"Oh, big surprise. Nobody else on Planet Earth knows where you are."

"I hope. Have you heard from her? Did she come back?"

"She walks in beauty like the night." He pauses. "Are you jealous?"

"No. What did she say?"

"That the Seven Sisters are actually the Six Pigs in Heaven."

"The what?"

"Seven Sisters, the constellation. They're actually six juvenile males who got turned into pigs because of being selfish and not community-minded."

"I swear I never can follow you, Jax. What did she say really?"

"That she's really on your side."

"Right. What else?"

"She says she's on the warpath. Can you picture that woman galloping over the hill on an Appaloosa? Too divine."

Taylor can picture it. She looks out the window and sees Otis filling up his car at the minimart across the street. "Does she know I've left town?"

"Yes. And her aim is true. She can hit a cardboard owl between the eyes at fifty paces."

"Meaning what, Jax?"

"This woman is smarter than your average box of rocks. Before she came here she'd already talked to people down at Mattie's, and she'd figured out everything about the fake adoption. She might figure out where you are—returned to the scene. First she'll try Oprah, then Lucky Buster."

"You really think that? Is she still in Arizona?"

"No. She flew back to Oklahoma this morning."

"How can you be sure?"

"I can't, as a matter of fact. She could be over eating kugel with Mr. Gundelsberger at this moment."

"Shoot, Jax, I'm scared. We've got to get out of here. But I don't know where. I can't even go home, Mama's moving out on Harland. Turtle wants to go to Sesame Street."

Jax laughs. "Good idea."

"I think we've had enough of TV land." Taylor rolls her head from side to side, relaxing her neck, trying to stave off panic. Turtle is watching from the corner of the diner. "How's everything back at the ranch? How's Lou Ann? And Mr. G.?"

"Lou Ann is Lou Ann. Mr. G. is a troubled individual. He has to leave his shades down at all hours so he won't see his voluptuous daughter exploring the desert in her natural state."

"Gundi's started her nature walks again? She's amazing. I'd be scared of getting snakebit in a personal area."

"Gundi has no personal areas. She's painting a series of nude self-portraits with different cactus configurations."

"Well, be nice to her anyway. She's your landlady."

"Landperson, please. Don't worry, she's not going to kick me out. I'm one of her favorite boys this week. This morning she was taking a very special interest in the cactus configurations outside my studio window. Turtle would have gotten an education."

"Well, pay the rent anyway, it's due this week, okay? Being handsome will only carry you so far in life."

"Would you say that I'm actually handsome? I mean, in those words?"

"Listen, Jax, do you feed Turtle junk food when I'm at work?"

"We experiment. Peanut butter and green bean sandwiches. Nothing hard core."

"She misses you."

"I miss you both. I'm radioactive with despair."

Taylor knows he wants her to say she loves him, but she can't. Not under pressure. It feels a little empty and desperate to her, like when husbands send wives into the store to pick out their own birthday gifts.

"Well, look," he says finally. "Don't even tell me where you're going next, because maybe Miss Jaxkiller will come back and seduce me, and I'll tell all."

"I'm thinking we'll head north," Taylor says. "I'm so nervous right now I can't think right. I'll call you from somewhere outside the state."

"Have you slept with another man yet?"

"Jax! Good Lord, it's only been forty-eight hours."

"So you're saying you need more time."

"Thanks for calling. You're really making my day here."

"I'm sorry. It's just, this is harder than it looks. You pack up your unripe fruit and drive out of here and you're gone."

"We didn't leave *you*, Jax."

"I know."

"We'll be back. This will be all right."

"Make me believe."

"You'll see." Taylor hangs up, wishing she had Angie's power to make the entire world sit down for milk and cookies.

* * *

"For an adventure you have to have rations," Taylor insists. She's in the grocery, trying to get Turtle interested in food. She made the mistake of panicking, hurrying Turtle away from Lucky and into the car after Jax's phone call, and now Turtle has gone deep inside herself. In situations where other children have tantrums, Turtle does some strange opposite of tantrum.

"Look, these pears are three pounds for a dollar. You can tell they're ripe because they smell like pear. We'll eat these until the apricots turn ripe."

Turtle sits backward in the shopping basket with her eyes fixed on Taylor's shirt buttons. This is the Turtle of years ago; for months after Taylor found her, Turtle gazed out at the world from what seemed like an empty house. But all through those mute seasons Taylor talked and talked to Turtle, and she does it again now, to keep her fear at bay. People in the store look at her and then look closely, for ten seconds too long, at this child too big to be sitting in a shopping basket. Taylor doesn't care.

"Okay, listen up because I'm going to give you a valuable lesson on how to pick the best checkout clerk when you're in a hurry. Okay? As a general rule I say go for the oldest. Somebody that went to school in the days when you still learned arithmetic."

"I know arithmetic," Turtle points out quietly, without expression. "I know how to add."

"That's true," Taylor says, trying not to leap at this. "But that's because you come from a privileged home. I taught you how to add when you were four years old. Right? What's three plus seven?"

Turtle recedes again, giving no hint that she has heard. Exactly as in the old days before she spoke, Turtle seems to be concentrating hard on some taste at the back of her mouth. Or a secret sound, a tuning fork struck inside her head.

Taylor considers the checkout options: three female teenagers with identical sticky-looking hairdos, and a middle-aged Hispanic man with a huge mustache. Taylor heads her cart toward the mustache. While they wait she scans the tabloids by the register, half expecting to see news of herself and Turtle on the run. She was right about the cashier: their line moves twice as fast as the others and promptly the store has expelled them into the parking lot. When she loads in the groceries and slams the trunk, apricots go flying.

"Those damn things!" she says, and Turtle's mouth hints at a smile. Taylor lifts her with some effort out of the basket and sets her down beside the car. She stands motionless, a stuffed child skin, while Taylor returns the cart. Taylor has been swearing at the apricots since they left Tucson, and Turtle has found it funny: the fruits roll around noisily on the shelf behind the backseat and bobble forward like a gang of little ducks at every hard stop. There are green apricots in the ashtray, on the seat, on the floor. Taylor is pretty sure they were a bad idea. Instead of turning yellow, most of them seem to be hardening and shrinking like little mummy heads.

She lifts Turtle into the front seat and she scoots across and buckles up mechanically, letting Taylor in after her. "Will you look at this?" Taylor reaches down and fishes an apricot from under the clutch. Pretending to be furious, she throws it hard out the window, then ducks her head when it hits another car. Turtle giggles, and Taylor sees then that she is back, there is someone home behind her eyes. "So what we're going to do now," she says calmly, touching the tears out of her own eyes, "is we have to look for a sign. Something to tell us where to go."

"There," Turtle says, pointing at a billboard.

"That says to go buy snakeskin boots at Robby's Western Wear Outlet. You think we should buy snakeskin boots?"

"No!" Turtle says, pulling her head back hard against the seat, tucking her chin down and shaking her whole body with the negative.

"Okay, look for something else."

"There," Turtle says after a minute, pointing at an envelope stuck under the windshield wiper.

"Shoot, how can they give you a ticket in the parking lot of a damn grocery store?" Taylor opens the door at a stop sign and reaches around to grab it. "I'm sorry to set a bad moral example for you, Turtle, but if this is a ticket I'm throwing it away. I didn't do anything wrong, plus they'll never find us anyway." She hands it to Turtle and accelerates.

Turtle takes a very long time to tear open the envelope.

"What's it say? 'Citation' starts with C-I-T, it means a ticket."

"It says: Dear Cad Die ..."

"Dear cad die?"

"C-A-D-D-I-E."

"Caddie. Let me see that."

"I can read it," Turtle says. "It's not too long."

"Okay." Taylor concentrates on being patient and not hitting pedestrians. People in Sand Dune don't seem in tune with the concept of traffic lights.

"Dear Caddie. I am sorry I did-n't see you at miggets ..."

"Miggets?" Taylor glances over at Turtle, who is holding the paper very close to her face. "That's okay, keep going."

"At miggets like I pro, pro-my-sed."

"Like I promised."

"Like I promised. Here is the S 50."

"S 50?" To Taylor it sounds like a fighter plane.

"The S is crossed out."

"A line through it?" Taylor considers. "Here is the 50? Oh, a dollar sign, here is the *fifty dollars*? Look in the envelope, is there anything else in there?"

Turtle looks. "Yes." She hands over two twenties and a ten.

"What else does it say? Is there a name at the bottom?" Taylor can't wait any longer, and reaches for the note:

Dear Caddie, I'm sorry I didn't see you at Midget's like I promised. Here's the $50. Now we're even and I'll beat the pants off you next time, right, Toots? Love, Hoops.

It reminds Taylor of the mysterious ads in the newspaper's personal section: "Hoops, I'll never forget the fried clams at B.B.O.G., Your Toots." It stands to reason that the kind of person who would waste money on those ads would leave fifty dollars on the wrong car.

"Who's Caddie?" Turtle wants to know.

"Somebody else with a big white car. Some guy named Hoops owed her money, and didn't want to face her in person."

"Why did he give it to us?"

"Because we're lucky."

"Was that the sign telling us where to go?" Turtle asks.

"I guess. It's a sign our luck has turned. Money's walking to us on its own two feet. I guess we ought to go to Las Vegas."

"What's Las Vegas?"

"A place where people go to try their luck."

Turtle considers this. "Try to do what with it?"

"Try to get more money with it," Taylor says.

"Do we want more money?"

"It's not so much we want it. We just have to have it."

"Why?"

"Why?" Taylor frowns and tilts the rearview mirror to get the setting sun out of her eyes. "Good question. Because nobody around here will give us anything, except by accident. Food or gas or what all we need. We've got to buy it with money."

"Even if we really need something, they won't give it to us?"

"Nope. There's no free lunch."

"But they'll give us money in Las Vegas?"

"That's the tale they tell."

Even a joke has some weight and takes up space, and when introduced into a vacuum, acquires its own gravity. Taylor is thinking about her high school physics teacher, Hughes Walter, and what he might say about her present situation. To amuse herself on long drives she often puts together improbable combinations of the people she's met in her life, and imagines what they would say to each other: Her mother and Angie Buster. Lou Ann's mean, prudish grandmother and Jax. Better yet: Jax and the woman looking for the horses.

They are driving toward Las Vegas because it's the only suggestion any-one has made so far, besides Sesame Street, and when introduced into a vacuum the idea acquired gravity. They're approaching the Hoover Dam now. Maybe it's what Jax said, that they've been drawn back to the scene of the crime. Whether she is the one who made off with the goods, or was robbed, she doesn't know yet. Taylor would just as soon skip the dam, but the only way out of this corner of the state is to cross the Hoover or get wet. Turtle is sitting up, looking excited.

"We're going to see those angels again," she says, her first words in more than thirty miles.

"Yep."

"Can we stop?"

"And do what?"

"Go see that hole."

Taylor is quiet.

"Can we?"

"Why do you want to do that?"

"I want to throw something at it."

"You do? What for?"

Turtle looks out the window and speaks so quietly Taylor can barely hear. "Because I hate it."

Taylor feels her face go hot, then cold, as her blood strangely reverses its tide. Turtle understands everything that has happened. There is no state of grace.

"Yeah, okay. We can do that."

Taylor parks the car very near the spillway. Since the dramatic rescue, they've added a new fence on the mountainside and pinkish floodlights in the parking lot. It feels bright as day when they get out, but deserted and wrongly colored, like some other planet with a fading sun. They both stand with their hands in their pockets, looking down.

"What can we throw?" Turtle asks.

Taylor thinks. "We have some empty pop cans in the car. But I hate to throw trash. It doesn't seem right."

"Rocks?" Turtle suggests, but the parking lot has been resurfaced and there aren't any rocks. The Hoover Dam people have really gone all out.

"Green apricots!" Taylor says suddenly, and Turtle laughs out loud, a chuck-willow watery giggle. They clamber into the backseat and scoop up armloads of the mummified fruits.

"This one's for Lucky Buster," Taylor shouts, casting the first one, and they hear it: ponk, ponk, ricocheting down the bottomless tunnel.

"Here's for Boy Scouts that have saved lives, and that stupid purple dress they tried to make you wear on TV. And for Annawake Fourkiller wherever she is." Handfuls of fruit rain down the hole.

"Lucky, Lucky, Lucky, Lucky," Turtle chants, throwing her missiles slowly like precious ammunition. While the two of them, mother and child, stand shouting down the hole, a fine rain begins to fall on the desert.

*   *   *

Afterward, Turtle seems spent. She lies across the front seat with her head on Taylor's right thigh and her tennis shoes wagging idly together and apart near the passenger door. The low greenish lights of the dashboard are reflected in her eyes as she looks out at the empty space of her own thoughts. Beside her face Turtle cradles Mary, her square utility flashlight. It's the type that people take deer hunting, large and dark green, said to float if dropped in water. She never turns it on; Turtle doesn't even particularly care whether it has batteries, but she needs it, this much is clear. To Taylor it seems as incomprehensible as needing to sleep with a shoebox, and just as unpleasant—sometimes in the night she hears its hollow corners clunk against Turtle's skull. But anyone who's tried to take Mary away has found that Turtle is capable of a high-pitched animal scream.

Taylor squints through the windshield wipers. She's driving toward the blaze of lights she knows has to be Las Vegas, but she can barely see the sides of the road. The storm moving north from Mexico has caught up to them again.

Turtle shifts in her lap and looks up at Taylor. "Am I going to have to go away from you?"

Taylor takes a slow breath. "How could that happen? You're my Turtle, right?"

The wipers slap, slap. "I'm your Turtle, right."

Taylor takes a hand off the wheel to stroke Turtle's cheek. "And once a turtle bites you, it doesn't let go, does it?"

"Not till it thunders."

Turtle seems cramped, and arches her back, pushing herself around with her feet. When she finally settles, she has crawled out of her seat belt and curled most of her body into Taylor's lap with her head against Mary. With one hand she reaches up and clenches a fist around the end of Taylor's braided hair, exactly as she used to do in the days before she had any other language. Outside, the blind rain comes down and Taylor and Turtle flinch when the hooves of thunder trample the roof of the car.

SUMMER

AY

SOMEONE THE SIZE

OF GOD

Cash Stillwater looks up from his work and sees a splash of white birds like water thrown at the sky. They stay up there diving in circles through the long evening light, changing shape all together as they fly narrow-bodied against the sun and then wheel away, turning their bright triangular backs.

Cash had only glanced up to rest his eyes but there were the birds, shining outside his window. His eyes fill with tears he can't understand as he follows their northward path to the dark backdrop of the Tetons, then back again to some place he can't see behind the Jackson Hole fire station. They make their circle again and again, flaunting their animal joy. He counts the birds without knowing it, sorting the shifting group into rows of odd and even, like beads. In the daytime Cash works at a health-food store putting tourists' slender purchases into paper bags, but in the evenings he makes bead jewelry. His lady friend Rose

Levesque, who works at the Cheyenne Trading Post, takes in the things he's made, pretending to the owner that she did it herself. Cash learned beadwork without really knowing it, simply because his mother and sisters, and then his daughters, were doing it at the kitchen table all his life. Before his wife died and the family went to pieces and he drove his truck to Wyoming, he raised up two girls on the Cherokee Nation. He never imagined after they were grown he would have to do another delicate thing with his hands, this time to pay the rent. But since he started putting beads on his needle each night, his eye never stops counting rows: pine trees on the mountainsides, boards in a fence, kernels on the ear of corn as he drops it into the kettle. He can't stop the habit, it satisfies the ache in the back of his brain, as if it might fill in his life's terrible gaps. His mind is lining things up, making jewelry for someone the size of God.

Rose walks in his door without knocking and announces loudly, "Nineteen silver quills down the hatch, did I tell you?" She plumps herself down at his kitchen table.

"Down whose hatch?" Cash wants to know, watching his needle. The backs of his hands remind him of paper burning in the fireplace, the moment the taut membrane goes slack into a thousand wrinkles, just before it withers to ash and air. He wonders if you get used to waking up old.

"Willie Levesque's big old, ugly, hungover hatch, that's whose." Rose lights a cigarette and drags on it with an inward sigh. Willie is Rose's oldest boy, who is half her age, nineteen, and twice as big. "I had them in an aspirin bottle in the kitchen. In the *kitchen,* for God's sake, it's not like they were in the medicine cabinet."

Cash glances at Rose, who is peevishly brushing ash off her blouse. Because she is shorter and heavier than she feels she ought to be, she clacks through her entire life in scuffed high heels, worn with tight jeans and shiny blouses buttoned a little too low. You can tell at thirty paces she's trying too hard.

"Didn't he look what he was taking?" he asks her.

"No. He said they went down funny, though. Like fillings." Cash works his needle and Rose smokes inside another comma of silence, then says, "The *silver* ones, wouldn't you know. Twenty dollars' worth. I'm about ready to take it out of his hide. Why couldn't he have eat up some fake turquoise?"

Rose brings Cash the supplies for making jewelry, pretending she is taking them home herself, but her boss, Mr. Crittenden, holds her accountable for every bead. In the morning he puts on his jeweler's glasses and counts the beads in every piece she's brought in, to make sure they're all there. It must be hard work, this business of mistrust.

"Those quills ought to pass on through without much trouble," he tells Rose. "My girls used to swallow pennies and all kinds of things, you'd be surprised. They always turned up. You could tell Willie to give them back when he's done."

"Maybe I'll do that," Rose says. "Hand them over to Mr. Crittenden in a little paper sack." Cash can tell she is smiling; he knows Rose's voice, its plump amusement and thinned-out resentments, because so often he is looking at something else while she speaks to him.

He met her, or rather saw her first, in the window of the Trading Post. He made a habit of pecking on the glass and winking at her each day on his way to work, which apparently won her heart, since she says she feels like a plastic dummy up there on display. Mr. Crittenden makes her sit at a little antique schoolroom desk in the bay-window storefront, where tourists can behold a genuine Indian hunched over her beadwork, squinting in the bad glare. Presumably they will be impressed or moved by pity to come inside.

Rose's beadwork is unimpressive, close up. She's nothing close to a full-blooded Indian, that's her excuse, but she could learn the more complicated patterns Cash does, if she cared to. It's a skill you acquire, like tuning an engine. The things you have to be an Indian to know, in Cash's experience—how to stretch two chickens and a ham over sixty relatives, for example—are items of no interest in the tourist trade.

He gets up to take his bread out of the oven and start dinner. Cash has discovered cooking in his old age, since moving away from his sisters and aunts, and according to Rose he acts like he invented the concept. She doesn't seem to mind eating what he cooks, though—she's here more nights than she's not. While she smokes at the kitchen table, Cash unpacks the things he brought home from the Health Corral, lining them up: six crimson bell peppers, five white potatoes, six orange carrots. He imagines putting all these colors on a needle, and wishes his life were really as bright as this instant.

"Looky here, girl," he says, waving a bell pepper at Rose.

"Cash, you watch out," she says. The pepper is deformed, with something like testicles. Cash gets to bring home produce that is too organic even for the health-food crowd. In his tiny apartment behind this tourist town's back, Cash feeds on stews of bell peppers with genitals and carrots with arms and legs.

He spreads newspapers on the table and sits to peel his potatoes. He feels comforted by the slip-slip-slip of his peeler and the potatoes piling up like clean dry stones. "Somebody come in the store today and told me how to get rich," he says.

"Well, from what I hear you've gotten rich fifty times over, except for the money part," Rose says.

"No, now listen. In the store we sell these shampoos they make with ho-hoba. It's this natural business the girls want now. A fellow come in today and says he's all set up down in Arizona to grow ho-hoba beans on his farm. They'll just grow in the dirt desert, they don't need nothing but a poor patch of ground and some sunshine. I'll bet you can buy you a piece of that land for nothing."

"Why would somebody sell it for nothing if they could get rich growing shampoo beans on it?"

"It takes five years before the plants start to bear, that's the hitch. Young people don't have that much patience."

"And old people don't have that much time."

"I've got my whole retirement ahead of me. And I know how to make things grow. It could work out good."

"Like the silver foxes did," Rose says, slicing him carelessly. In January, before the tourist jobs opened up, Cash skinned foxes. With frozen fingers he tore the delicate membranes that held pelt to flesh, earning his own pair to breed. It seems like a dream to him now, that he believed he could find or borrow a farm of his own. He was thinking he was still on the Nation, where relatives will always move over to give you a place at the table.

"Johnny Cash Stillwater," Rose says, shaking her head, blowing smoke in a great upward plume like a whale. She speaks to him as if she's known him her whole life long instead of two months. "I don't think you've ever gotten over being your mama's favorite."

Cash only lets Rose hurt him this way because he knows she is right. As a young man he turned his name around in honor of his mother's favorite singer. Now he's working as a fifty-nine-year-old bag boy at the Health Corral; his immediate superior there is an eighteen-year-old named Tracey who pops the rubber bands on her braces while she runs the register. And still Cash acts like luck is on his side, he's just one step away from being a cowboy.

Rose says suddenly, "They're going to shoot a bunch of pigeons that's come into town."

"Who is?"

"I don't know. A fellow from town council, Tom Blanny, came in the Trading Post today and told Mr. Crittenden about it."

Cash knows Tom Blanny; he comes into the Health Corral to buy cigarettes made of lettuce leaves or God knows what, for people who wish they didn't smoke.

"Tom said they're causing a problem because they don't belong here and they get pesty. They flock together too much and fly around and roost in people's trees."

Cash looks up, surprised. "I saw those birds tonight. I could see them out this window right here." His heart beats a little hard, as if Rose had discovered still another secret she could use to hurt him. But her concern is Town Council men and information, not an unnamable resentment against some shining creatures whose togetherness is so perfect it makes you lonely. Cash attends to peeling his potatoes.

"Tom says they could crowd out the natural birds if they last out the winter. A pigeon isn't a natural bird, it's lived in cities so long, it's like a weed bird."

"Well, aren't they natural anywhere?" He knows that in Jackson Hole people are very big on natural.

"New York City," she says, laughing. Rose has been around. "There's nothing left there for them to crowd out," she says.

Slip-slip-slip goes the peeler. Cash doesn't feel like saying anything else.

"What's eating on you, Cash? You thinking about going back to Oklahoma?"

"Naw."

"What's the weather like there now?"

"Hot, like it ought to be in summer. This place never heats up good.
We're going to be snowed under here again before you know it. I wasn't
cut out for six feet of snow."

"Nobody is, really. Even up in Idaho." Rose fluffs her hair. "You'd think
they'd be used to it by now, but I remember when I was a kid, people
going just crazy in the wintertime. Wives shooting their husbands, prop-
ping them up on a mop handle, and shooting them again."

Cash is quiet, leaving Rose to muse over murdered husbands.

"Well, go on back, then," she says. "If the weather's not suiting you
good."

They have had this argument before. It isn't even an argument, Cash
realizes, but Rose's way of finding out his plans without appearing to care
too much. "Nothing to go back for," he says. "My family's all dead."

"Your daughter's not."

"Might as well be."

"Well then, what about your other daughter, the one that died—how
about her baby?"

When Cash first knew Rose, she made herself so comfortable in his bed
that he felt safe telling her family stories. Now he regrets it. "She's gone,"
he says.

"A baby ain't made with disappearing ink, Cash."

"You read about it in the papers ever day," he tells her, but he knows
this is a lie. A mother might drive her car into the river on purpose, but
still there will be a basket of outstretched hands underneath her children,
or should be. It's the one thought in Cash's mind that never lights and
folds its wings.

"I waited my whole life away down there in the Nation," he tells Rose.
"Where nobody is nothing but poor. When my wife died, seem like I'd
been waiting out something that wasn't coming. At least in Jackson Hole
people have something."

"You and me don't have any of it."

"No, but we're right next door to it," he says, standing up to throw vegetables into hot water. "Maybe some of it will fall off the tree."

At one o'clock exactly, Rose whips off the patterned headscarf she has to wear in the window and scoops little cascades of clicking beads back into their plastic vials, careful to let none escape onto the plank floor. Mr. Crittenden allows Rose to go to lunch with Cash if they go late, after what he imagines to be the noontime rush. The truth is there is no rush, just a slow, steady dribble. Jackson Hole has a hundred Indian trading posts, and most of them have better gimmicks than a tired mother of teenagers in the front window ruining her eyes.

Rose wants to walk across town to the Sizzler for the salad bar, but Cash warns against it; a storm is cooking in the south. They stay close by at McDonald's just in case, taking the shortcut through the little flowered strip park on Main. While Rose talks and Cash doesn't listen, his mind counts pansies and ageratum: yellow, yellow, purple, purple, a beautiful, cast-off beaded belt of flowers stretched along the highway collecting dirt.

"Foof," Rose says. "I don't see how it has any business being this muggy." While they wait for traffic she reaches back to adjust something in the heel of her shoe. Rose is thirty-eight, the age his daughter Alma would be now if she had lived, and Cash realizes he treats Rose more like a daughter than a lady friend, cautioning about getting caught in the rain, clucking his tongue over the escapades of her boys. He wonders what she sees in him. Cash at least doesn't drink, or eat beads, but he knows he's getting old in a way that's hard to live with. It was a purely crazy thing for him to want to move up here two years ago. Oklahoma Cherokees never leave Oklahoma. Most don't even move two hickory trees away from the house where they were born.

In line at McDonald's, he notices men looking at Rose. Not a lot, not for long, but they look. Cash they don't even see; he is an old Indian man no one would remember having just walked by. Not just because of three generations of tragedy in his family—even without cancer and suicide and a lost grandchild, those generations would have come to pass; he would have gotten old.

"Just french fries and a chef salad today, hon, I'm on a diet," Rose says, flirting with the teenager at the register.

Cash misses his wife with a blank pain in his chest, and he misses his sisters and cousins, who have known him since he was a strong, good-looking boy. Everyone back there remembers, or if they are too young, they've been told. The old ones get to hang on the sweet, perfect past. Cash was the best at climbing trees; his sister Letty won the story bees. The woman who married Letty's husband's brother, a beauty named Sugar, was spotted one time drinking a root beer and had her picture in *Life* magazine. They all know. Now she has thin hair and a humped back but she's still Sugar, she gets to walk around Heaven, Oklahoma, with every-body thinking she's pretty and special. Which she is. That's the trouble with moving away from family, he realizes. You lose your youth entirely, you have only the small tired baggage that is carried within the body.

It shouldn't matter so much to Cash. He still has most of what he started with: a talent for schemes and friendship, and all of his hair. No one can ever hold a thing against Cash, except his restlessness. For thirty years, whenever Cash started talking like a white man, his wife would put extra food on his plate and turn her back tenderly and a little abruptly. After she got sick, Cash came untethered somehow, decided they needed to ride horses and see the Rocky Mountains. She died the year after they claimed she was cured: the doctor found no more cancer in her, and she only wanted to sit down and breathe out slowly and watch her grandbaby grow, but Cash danced her around the kitchen and swore he would show her the world. She told him television was a bad influence. Probably she was right. Like those white birds he's been seeing outside the window, it flashes its wings and promises whatever you want, even before you knew you wanted it.

Rose has nabbed a spot for them in the crowded restaurant and clears a huge mess from the table; the previous people were probably foreigners who didn't know the McDonald's custom of dumping your own burger wrappers. "It's party time in Jackson, ain't it?" Rose asks over the din, plumping down in her chair.

Cash nods. For nine months he trudged out on sidewalks dangerous with glassy shards of ice, the dirty snow piled deep and hopeless as a whole winter's worth of laundry. Now, for five or six weeks, the laundry is done. The streets swarm with people who will take their sunny raft trips and green-meadow pictures and spend the rest of their lives claiming Jackson Hole as one of the places they know.

The couple at the next table are speaking some language. The woman has on little green cloth slippers that you'd think would have fallen apart long before they made it halfway to anywhere from overseas. Cash knows these women; they come into the store and go crazy over anything herbal, then they march straight over to the Trading Post and buy Cash's earrings, Rose tells him, three pairs at a time. The Indian look is evidently big in Europe, where they don't have any Indians. They ask Rose personal questions, thinking she is something exotic. The Americans are different, they edge around Rose in the store, not looking, as if her clothes were terribly stained and she didn't know. Sometimes they'll come close and snap a picture. Cash has witnessed this, and he has to hand it to her for the way she sits still, holding her tongue for once. The customers pile up their purchases by the register, dropping in one minute what it takes Cash three weeks to earn.

"That guy mopping the floor has one cute butt," Rose states, fluffing her layers of dyed-black hair. "I feel like dropping a spoon or something just to see him pick it up."

"Rose, you have to decide if I'm your boyfriend or your daddy. I can't do both."

She flashes her eyes at him. "You know how much I love you, honey."

Cash doesn't add anything to that. He is grateful that McDonald's doesn't give out spoons.

"Just think," she says, "we could be in Paris, France or Hong Kong. They have McDonald's in every country in the world."

"That's what I hear," Cash says, but he doesn't feel like he's in Paris, France, he feels like he's in McDonald's.

"You seem depressed," Rose observes, and Cash wonders if that's what he is, after all. He thinks of the way you press dough down with your fist: take a big, round hopeful swelling and punch the rise right out of it. Yes, he thinks. Depressed.

* * *

Cash is off work at last. For the last ten minutes of his shift a couple stood in line arguing over whether or not to buy some expensive peaches. Cash stood silently by, wishing they would take their marriage someplace else, but Tracey rolled her eyes in a way that could not be missed, and still the couple paid no attention. The man's T-shirt said THINK ONLY OF SURFING. It amazes Cash what people will advertise, as if convictions mean so little they can put on a new one each morning after a shower.

The birds come every day now, mysteriously increasing their numbers overnight. Cash can see them right now as he walks down Main toward the Trading Post to pick up Rose. She has repeated to him the theory that pigeons are migrating here from Salt Lake City, to escape the falcons that are nesting on the ledges of tall buildings there. The balance of nature is upside-down, Cash thinks: the predators are moving to the cities and city birds taking over the land where the buffalo roam. He finds he mistrusts the pigeons. One minute they flash their silver underwings all together, all one color, and the next, their white backs, changing from moment to moment like a card trick.

This evening Mr. Crittenden wants to talk with him, a fact Cash dreads. He finally noticed that the beadwork Rose does in the store is nothing near the quality of what she brings in. Rose hedged, fearing she'd lose her job, but finally confessed it was made by her Cherokee friend. Mr. Crittenden wasn't angry, it turns out, but wants to meet Cash to ask about his methods. Cash has been in the store more than fifty times, but Mr. Crittenden never wanted to meet him before now.

"Foof, it's muggy," says Rose when he walks into the store. "I wish that rain would get here and get over with. It's not the heat gets me, it's the humanity."

Cash smiles. "That's the whole truth."

"Mr. Big Shot stepped out. He'll be back in a minute."

The cluster of tin bells over the door jingles behind Cash, but it's a customer, a tall, thin man wearing sandals and gray-speckled socks. He nods at Rose, who is at the register.

"Take a look around," she tells him with a broad smile Cash understands, and dislikes. "Does it look like that storm is coming in? We need some rain. We haven't had rain in a long time." Cash grins. He likes Rose better now because she is speaking to Cash in code, saying, "This one is going to look at everything in the entire store, and then buy some post-cards." When she asks, "You folks drive a long ways?" she's predicting a big buy. "Front case is all marked down, rock bottom" means "All the jew-elry in Jackson won't help this homely soul."

Cash stands near the window, looking out. He doesn't see the white birds but he knows they're up there still, moving in their rich, lazy wheel above it all, showing off, taking their freedom for granted. They aren't real birds like the ones he hunted in childhood, whose eggs he shimmied trees to snatch, birds who catch insects and build nests and feed their young. These are tourist birds. Like his own restless dreams that circle with no place to land.

The man in sandals leaves finally, without even buying a postcard. "Yep, long drought," Cash says, and Rose laughs. The tin bells jingle again, and they look up to see the white cockaded head of Mr. Crittenden. They stop talking, but the quiet that has come in with him is heavier than an absence of talk. He acknowledges Cash, then stands for a minute with his hands resting on the glass jewelry case, his thin elbows angled out. He always wears a white shirt and black bolo tie. Rose is curious about whether he is married; Cash says, just look at the pressed shirts he wears to work, but Rose maintains he could afford to send them to the laundry, which is true. She's heard a rumor that he owns his own airport some-where, and another rumor that he has cancer. Neither of them believes the cancer story. If he planned on dying anytime soon, why would he spend so much of his time counting beads?

He nods at Cash again, and with a tight throat Cash follows him into the office, a small room crammed with ledgers and anthropology books and strange pets. Mr. Crittenden has seven or eight shrieking birds back there, and a python in a jewelry case half filled with dry sand. Rose warned Cash about the snake; she has to come in here to get her pay-checks under its cool eye. The air chokes him with bird smells and loneli-ness. Mr. Crittenden gets down two large books that smell of dust. When he opens them, their insides are slick as white glass.

"This is very old beadwork," he tells Cash. He slowly turns the pages of black-and-white photographs. "Do you recognize the patterns?"

Cash does, some of them, but is afraid to admit to much, so he only nods or shakes his head at the photographs. While Mr. Crittenden turns the pages, a nervous gray bird in a cage near the window makes clicking sounds and picks at its neck as if it has a skin disease. Occasionally it raises its head and screams, and then the rest of the room rings with whistles and the scratch of dry feet on thin metal bars. Cash holds his air inside him for as long as he can between breaths.

"This whole world of knowledge is being lost," Mr. Crittenden says, touching the page of his book as if he can feel the patterns. He leans his white head into the space between them, his blue eyes feverish, pink-edged.

"Are the men the artists in your tribe?" he asks.

Cash tries not to smile. "No, the women just let me pick it up a little."

"Do your daughters know how to do this kind of work?"

"They do it," Cash tells him, and it's true, they did, before Alma landed upside-down in the river and Sue landed in the hospital for the third or fourth time with a broken cheekbone and a few other presents from her boyfriend. But even before all the sadness, they didn't do beadwork in the picture-perfect way Mr. Crittenden surely imagines. Cash's daughters and nieces have perms and belong to Weight Watchers. If they make up a pair of earrings from time to time, it happens while they're on the phone with each other, laughing their deep smokers' laughs, criticizing their husbands' friends. Cash was never entirely in on the conversation, but still, that is the world he's sad to have lost.

Mr. Crittenden sees Cash staring at the window. "That's a gray-tailed cockatoo. They used to be terrible pests in Australia. Wheat farmers shot them by the thousands. Now there aren't a great many of her kind left."

But Cash had been thinking how sad it was there was not even a plant on the windowsill in here. Not one green thing that can sit in the sun and be quiet.

The humidity rises all week. Friday afternoon feels weighted and endless, like the end of a life. By six, Cash feels desperate. He is back at the Trading Post again, waiting for Rose to finish up. Maybe they will go to a movie. Something to take his mind away from here for two hours. But Mr.

Crittenden still hasn't come in to lock up and dole out his beads.

"When was he in last?"

Rose thinks. "Didn't he come at lunchtime?"

"No, we just went."

"That's right."

Cash stands in the bay window, looking up at the birds he despises, wheeling in a tight, anxious circle. Tonight they seem to be looking for something—their own lost wishes. New York City, maybe. He smiles to himself.

"His door's open," Rose says.

"Maybe we should close it up and go."

"Maybe we should go find where he keeps all the money."

"Rose, I swear. Just close the door. I don't know how you listen to them parakeets all day, they would drive me insane." He watches the gathering storm. *Man, you're already crazy, no driving needed,* he thinks, just as Rose shouts: a tremulous, rising "Whooo?"

Cash's shoulders tighten and he turns. "What is it?"

"He's in here."

Cash wonders instantly if Mr. Crittenden has been listening to their talk, to Rose's gossip. Her joke about taking his money! He tries to remember what other wild thing she might have said that could lose her job for her.

"Cash," Rose says, her face white, her voice once again a rising note, and then he understands what it is. Mr. Crittenden has not heard a thing.

Cash stays up late working on a beaded belt. He is tired, but can't imagine sleeping. He and Rose spent a long time repeating the details to each other, as if they'd been shipwrecked in some new place where only this event existed: the police said suicide, no question, he'd taken prescription sleeping pills and left his account books organized. There is a wife, it turns out; she lives in Rock Springs and probably had nothing to do with his shirts. Her instructions over the phone were to keep the store open for the rest of the season, if possible. A management company in town will see that Rose gets paid. Cash doubts that she will have the nerve to go back. The whole time the police were there she clutched her bosom and breathed as if she'd run a mile in those high heels.

Cash wants to know things Rose hadn't even considered: who will come get the animals, for example? He doesn't favor the idea of her working under the same roof as a starving snake. And how long was Mr. Crittenden dead in there? He can't get his mind's eye to stop staring at Mr. Crittenden blue at the mouth and fingertips, frozen in his last slump while three men turned him through the doors like furniture and carried him out of the store. Did he kill himself in the middle of the night, or at dawn? Cash wanted every single how and what, in order to muffle the sound of "Why?"

Rose has taken the Valium the doctor gave her and gone to untroubled sleep in Cash's bed, leaving Cash alone with the bare light bulb and the wall calendar from Wickiup Hauling. The month of July shows families on a yellow river raft. They have cameras and bright-colored clothes and expressions of surprise, each mouth like a slack little rip in the face: they're coming into white water. He recognizes his own innocence, before he came up here. Now he knows enough about shining promises to wonder who sat by the river all day slapping mosquitoes to get this picture, and what he got paid for it. His knuckles ache because of the changing weather, and twice tonight he has lost plastic beads into the orange linoleum, which is curled up and cracked in places as if volcanoes planned to erupt from under his floor. "Let them go," he whispers aloud, but the habit of holding on to every small, bright bit of color is hard to forget.

When he finally goes to bed he still doesn't rest, but has a dream about his dead wife. She is standing in the kitchen of their little crooked house in the woods, cutting up a hen for soup.

"How come you won't turn around and face me?" he asks.

"You turned loose of family," she says. "I have to turn my back on you."

"Why even talk to me, then?" he asks.

"I'm cooking for you, aren't I?"

"Yes. But I'm afraid you hate me."

"Why would I cook for you, then?"

"I don't know," he says.

"Pay attention to who takes care of you."

She stirs the huge pot on the stove. Turning in the bubbling surface,

Cash can see a dry tuft of Mr. Crittenden's white hair. His wife is very large. There is no roof on the kitchen, only a forest clearing and legs like trees. Her head looks like carved stone against the sky, a head he can't precisely recognize. It could as easily be his mother, or his daughter. "There's a hundred ways to love someone," her voice tells Cash. "All that matters is that you stay here in the same room."

He wakes with his chest so full it might burst. He wonders whether he has had a heart attack, or is simply dying of loneliness. "I have to go back," he tells Rose, not caring that she is asleep, and will not hear.

The summer rains in the Rockies come all the way up from Mexico. Or so Cash has often told himself, in an effort to make himself believe he's leading an exciting life. But Mexico or no, the rain is terrible for tourism, the Health Corral has been empty all day. Tracey sits at the checkout counter reading the gossip magazines, asking Cash whether he believes a woman could actually give birth to triplets with three different fathers. Cash thinks of his own wild daughters, and doesn't doubt it.

Rose wasn't afraid to go back to work. At lunchtime she reported it was the same over there, no business. She claims the news has gotten around and nobody wants to come into a store where a man took his life. Cash knows better: people around here would come in hunting bargains, hoping for a suicide sale. It's the weather causing the slowdown. Vacationers expect perfect happiness, perfect weather, and if they don't meet it here they'll drive on toward Missoula or wherever else they imagine they will find it. Young people, like Rose, one eye always on the road out of town.

When Cash hears the first shots, he feels strangely exhilarated. He'd thought maybe they would call off the bird shoot because of the rain, but the boom of gunfire comes again, rattling the plate-glass store front. He leaves his post at the checkout and presses himself near the window, waiting. "They're shooting those pigeons today," he tells Tracey.

"I read about that in the paper. That's gross, isn't it? They can't just let some poor little birds alone?"

"They're weed birds," Cash says. "They want to live here but they can't. That's why they keep going around and around up there."

He feels another boom, and the subtle aftershock. His whole body vibrates with the plate glass. Suddenly the birds are there in the sky, not circling in their perfect wheel but scattered in every direction by twos and threes, turning in flighty panic. On their own. He thinks of the place a world away from here where he climbed trees with no greater longing in his chest than to find a nest full of eggs. Cash can see his own face in the plate glass, empty with relief, as the shot birds fold their wings and vanish one by one, finding the ground at last.

THE TWILIGHT ZONE

OF HUMANITY

ALL THREE GENERATIONS OF ALICE'S family have been lifted into the air for the first time this summer: first Turtle and Taylor flew to Chicago and back, and now the first leg of Alice's own flight is coming in for a landing. Alice feels this shows an unusual degree of togetherness. Her plane scoots under the clouds, revealing the Mississippi River and St. Louis far below. A huge metal arch on the riverbank stands higher than any building, put there for no purpose Alice can envision. As useful as spitting off a bridge, but people do such things, to prove they were here on earth for a time. The descending plane sweeps over the largest graveyard Alice has seen so far. Her neighbor in the window seat has spent the flight hunched in silence, and now remarks: "Well, that's some welcome."

"I can see the point of it," Alice says, determined to disagree cordially with this cheerless woman. "If you have to make so much noise, you'd just as well pester the dead as the living."

"We won't have far to be carried if we don't make it," the woman says dryly. She has a surprisingly small head, and auburn hair that looks artificial, and for the whole trip from Lexington she has been wearing an aggrieved little face as if her shoes are on the wrong feet. Alice is dismayed. She'd expected everyone else on the plane to be experienced travelers from big cities slouched back in their seats, snapping open their papers to the Money section. But here she is as usual, bearing up those around her. To change the subject from graveyards she asks, "Is St. Louie the end of the road for you?"

The woman nods faintly, as if the effort might be incompatible with her hairstyle.

"I stay on till the next stop, Las Vegas," Alice reports. "I've got a daughter and a little grandbaby out there that have fell on hard times."

The woman perks up slightly. "She divorcing?"

"Oh, no," Alice says, "my daughter's never been married. She found the little girl in her car one time and adopted her. She's independent as a hog on ice."

The woman turns back to the window and its outstanding display of graves.

"Somebody just left the baby in her car and said 'So long, sucker!' What could she do?" Alice reaches for the pictures in her purse. "It turned out all right, though; that little girl is a pistol. Whoever left her off had no eye for good material."

Alice flatters herself that she knows how to get a conversation going, but for this woman it's the subject of divorce and graveyards or nothing; she snaps the window shade down and closes her eyes. Alice leaves the pictures of Turtle in her wallet, dreading the picture in her mind's eye: an old woman talking to herself. She offers a peppermint LifeSaver to the man across the aisle but it's the same story over there, he barely shakes his head. They are a planeload of people ignoring each other. Alice has spent her life in small towns and is new to this form of politeness, in which people sit for all practical purposes on top of one another in a public place and behave like upholstery.

She can't remember when she was ever around so many people at one time that she didn't know. They look strange: one is shrunken-looking with overblown masses of curly hair; another is hulky and bald, the head too big for the body; another has the troublesome artificial look girls get from earrings, glasses, a glint of braces, too many metal things around the face. It's as if these people were all produced by different manufacturers who couldn't agree on a basic design. Alice saves this up to tell Taylor when she gets to Las Vegas. Whenever she used to mention to Harland anything more than life's broadest details, he thought she was cracked. But Taylor will know what she means.

Alice takes off her glasses and lays her hands on her face, feeling her eyes like worried, wet marbles under the lids. Taylor in trouble is not something Alice knows how to think about. Everything she's done before now, however crazy-quilted it might have seemed, always ended up with the corners square. The first time Taylor took a step, she walked right out the door of the Pittman P.O. Alice was at the counter buying stamps and asking the postmistress, Renata Hay, when her baby was due; Taylor was eleven months old and hung on the hem of Alice's coat until she felt she'd grown a heavy tail back there. Suddenly a grand round of applause went up among the old men waiting for their Social Security checks, and Alice turned in time to see her baby headed out into the street. Old Yancey Todd held the door for her like a gentleman.

Some people would say a headfirst child like that was bound to wind up headfirst in the mop bucket. Alice doesn't think so. In her heart, she knows her daughter would have looked both ways before she went out to play in East Main. Or Yancey would have flagged down the cars. When you're given a brilliant child, you polish her and let her shine. The universe makes allowances. When Taylor called from a phone booth in Las Vegas with her soul broken in twenty pieces, Alice felt deeply betrayed. The universe has let them down.

The seat-belt sign dings on, and Alice opens her eyes. A stewardess is coming slowly down the aisle taking people's plastic cups away, like a patient mother removing toys her babies might try to swallow. Alice watches, marveling at the outfit: under her navy blazer she wears a buttoned white shirt and a paisley silk tie with, even, a fine gold chain fastened across it. How long it must have taken her to get it all just right, in spite of her busy life. Alice is a passenger in need of comfort and she takes some from this: the touching effort some people put into just getting dressed in the morning, believing a little gold chain fastened over a silk tie will somehow make a difference.

Taylor and Alice tower over Turtle, holding on to each other with heads together and legs apart, leaning like a crooked teepee. They stand that way for a long time in the airport while people walk around them without looking, desiring only to make their connections. Alice's empty white sweater sleeves hang from her shoulders. Turtle pushes her head against Taylor and holds the hem of her shirt, since there isn't anything else. She met her Grandma Alice once before but that time nobody was crying.

"Mama, I haven't been like this, I swear," Taylor says. "I didn't fall to pieces till just this minute."

Alice rubs her back in a circle. "You go ahead and fall apart. That's what I'm here for." Turtle watches the hand with big knuckles move up and down her mother's back, and waits for something to fall. After a while they move apart. Taylor tries to carry everything Alice has.

"What'd you put in this suitcase?" she asks. "Rocks? Harland's headlights?"

"I'll Harland's headlights you," Alice says, laughing, smacking Taylor on the bottom.

She comes down to Turtle with a hug. She smells like chewing gum and Kleenex and sweaters. Turtle thinks: this is the telephone Grandma. She is nice and this is how she looks.

"Turtle, you can carry this carry-on bag for Grandma, okay?" Taylor stoops to put the strap over Turtle's shoulder. "I can't believe how strong you are. Look, Mom, doesn't she walk like a queen? I swear I didn't teach her that. It's a natural talent, she has perfect posture."

Turtle leans against the weight of the bag and puts each heel and toe on the long blue line in the carpet.

Alice blows her nose again. "Did you all eat? I'm starved. I had roasted peanuts for lunch."

"We had apricots for lunch," Turtle says, and her mother starts crying again. It's the crying that looks like laughing from the back, but isn't. The most bad thing would be if her mother goes away and the bad place comes. Turtle wishes she could put the words she said back in her mouth and eat them. They would taste bright and sour, like dimes. She feels the door of her back teeth closing. There are forty or a hundred people in the airport so she makes sure to follow the blue jean legs and the white grandma sandals. Their heads are big and too far away like dinosaurs. The talking comes out like round bubbles. When they go outside the sun hurts a little, as much as water hurts when it runs out hot on your hands.

"Turtle, Turtle, Turtle," someone is saying. "It's okay, Mama, I told you about." All the cars are shiny animals under water. They can't get air.

Somewhere else in the old place was that shine of angels or stars too close, the underwater, shoes on the floor and no light and a man's voice across your mouth and you can't get air. A woman crying.

A woman turned on a flashlight and moved her arms that were like fish arms, and her mouth opened and closed.

"We can eat at the coffee shop," her mother's voice is saying. The bubbles break open and Turtle hears each one of those words come out. So much time has passed that it might be another day, or the same day but dark. It isn't dark. They are in the car, moving. The front seat is far away. A boy on a bicycle goes by, the gold bicycle lifting its front wheel off the sidewalk again and again like a scared horse. The boy has a yellow shirt and blond hair in his eyes, laughing, not afraid. His feet move faster than he is going. Turtle kneels on the seat and looks back, watching this one boy and bicycle that look the right way, until they are gone. She sits down again.

"The good news is you can get a hotel room in this town for eleven dollars a night. If you stay in a junky place with a casino downstairs. I guess they figure on getting your money by other means."

"They done got yours," Grandma says.

"A hundred and ten dollars. I could shoot myself."

Turtle sees her hands, and thinks: *These are my hands.*

"That's if you would have stopped when you got to the top. That's not what you started out with."

"No, we started with fifty."

"So that's all you lost, really."

"Why didn't I stop?"

"Because you were speculating. If you could get a hundred and ten out of fifty, why couldn't you make a thousand out of a hundred and ten."

"Stupid."

"Stupid as every other soul in this town, honey. Look at those neon lights, and tell me who you think is paying the electric bill."

"We were feeling lucky."

"That's who's paying it. Mister and Missus I was feeling lucky."

"We found the fifty dollars on the car windshield. Turtle found it." She looks back in the driving mirror and smiles. Her face around her eyes is red and white. "It felt like maybe that money was charmed." She laughs the way that means nothing is really funny: tssh, pushing out air, shaking her head. "I still can't believe a person could put two hundred quarters in a slot machine one right after another and not win *anything.*"

Grandma laughs. "You've got a hair of your daddy in you. Foster was a gambler."

Turtle says, "Mama, do you have a daddy?" But they don't hear, the words only walked inside her ears. The back-teeth door is still closed. When her six-year molars came in, they felt like a pocketful of small rocks squeaking and rubbing.

"A better one than me, I hope."

"Lord, no, he wasn't worth a toot as a gambler. If there was a storm coming in he'd bet you it was going to stay dry, just to put spice in his day. One time he bet a man he could outrun his dog."

"What kind of a dog was it?"

"I don't know, but it left Foster at the starting post. If the dog had lapped up as much Old Grand-Dad as Foster had, Foster might of had a chance."

Turtle opens her mouth wide and says, "Mama, do you have an old granddad?" In the front seat they both laugh out loud. True laughing, not pushed air. They have heads on their bodies, laughing mouths, and hands; they look the right way again. Turtle has hands also. She lies down and hugs herself.

"Look at us. Three crazy girls in the city of lonely hearts." Taylor squeezes Alice's hand on top of the table. The hotel is called the Delta Queen Casino, and the coffee shop is decorated in a con-artist theme: on the wall are large framed photos of Clark Gable as Rhett in *Gone With the Wind*, and Paul Newman in *The Sting*. The red plastic chairs look like someone got them in a bad trade. The background music is a chorus of high steady dings, the sound of coins in slot machines, which reach Taylor like repeated small slaps in the face. She can't believe she was a fool just like every other fool. The one thing she's always hoped for is to stand out of the crowd. She grits her teeth at the TV screen over the bar, which is blinking out colorful letters and numbers so that the people who don't want to waste any time can play video Keno while they eat.

Alice is making conversation with Turtle. "Do you hate it when old ladies make a big fuss and tell you you've grown two feet?"

Turtle shakes her head.

"Well, you have." She bends her gray head close to Turtle's and speaks seriously, without condescension. "You're a big long-legged *girl* now, not a baby anymore." Taylor watches the cards of her own childhood played out at the table. Alice always knows what you need. Being near her mother makes Taylor aware of all her inside parts, cradled soft things like the livers in supermarket chickens.

"Taylor says you know how to write your name." Alice fishes in her huge purse for a pen, and turns a napkin on the table in front of Turtle. "Can you show me?"

Turtle shakes her head again.

"Doesn't matter. You still know how, right? If you need to sign a check or something, then we know we can count on you. No sense wasting a signature on a napkin."

She leaves the pen on the table. From the casino someone's voice shouts out "*Ho*-ly," followed by the chattering rain of quarters into the jackpot bucket. Taylor is afraid she's going to cry again and send Turtle into a tail-spin, so she keeps her face behind the plastic menu. "What do you want for dinner, Turtle?" she asks. "A glass of milk and what else?"

Turtle shrugs. Taylor can see the gesture without even looking.

"Grilled cheese?"

"Okay."

Taylor looks over the top of the daily special and tells Alice, "You get kind of hypnotized, sitting there listening to the quarters ding. Then you start thinking, 'It's been this long, my number's got to be *almost* up.' And then you put your hand in your pocket and pull out a gum wrapper."

Alice holds on to her hand.

At a table nearby, a wife and husband are having a fight. They have on matching outfits, jeans and fringed shirts that cowboys might wear, or people in a cowboy-related industry. The woman has colorless flippy hair molded together with hairspray so that it all comes along when she turns her head. The man looks very old. "Five hundred dollars," he keeps say-ing, again and again, like the talking change machines out in the casino that will turn your paper cash into silver dollars. The woman says differ-ent things each time, including "Like hell" and "You don't know your butt-hole from the road to China." Suddenly she stands up and starts hitting him on the side of the head with her purse. Her stiff hair wags excitedly. The man bends his head down and accepts the blows as if he has known all this time they were coming, like pie for dessert. Taylor is relieved that Turtle has her back to this event.

"I don't know what I would have done if you hadn't said you'd drop everything and come," she tells Alice. "I swear I was at the end of my tree."

"Well, it was good timing," Alice says. "I'd run out of marriage and I needed a project. Have you heard any more about," she moves her eyes slowly toward Turtle and back.

"It's okay to talk about it, Mama. Turtle knows. I called Jax last night and he said there was nothing new."

They both look at Turtle, who has put the menu very close to her face and is quietly reciting the names of different foods.

The woman who was hitting her husband sits down for a breather. She drags heavily on her cigarette, as if her only possible oxygen must come through that less than ideal source.

"This is the twilight zone of humanity," Taylor announces. "That's what Jax would say right now: 'We have arrived at the twilight zone of humanity. Let us bow our heads in a moment of silent prayer.'"

"I believe he's making you turn cynical," Alice says. She adds, "That waitress over there has been staring at us like a stuck pig."

"I know. I hope she's getting her eyes full."

Turtle twists in her seat to look at the staring waitress.

"How's that Jax treating you, anyway?" Alice asks.

"Oh, he treats me good. Too good. I don't deserve him."

"You hush. You know better than that."

Taylor smiles. With her left hand, the one that isn't holding Alice's, she puts down the menu and rubs the bone behind her left ear. "Yeah, I know better."

"I picture him as looking exactly like that." Alice points to the photo of Rhett Butler.

Taylor laughs out loud. "Oh, that's Jax to perfection. If you leave out the hair, the face, the body and the mustache."

"Well, that's how he talks, anyway. Like a southern gentleman. Except for some of the wild things he comes up with. He's real entertaining over the phone."

"I'm glad you think so. He keeps asking me if I'm truly in love with our garbage man. He's a lot more insecure than Rhett Butler."

"If you're having trouble sticking with him, that's my fault. I didn't bring you up with men as a consideration. I think single runs in our family."

"It's nothing you did wrong, Mama, I never missed having a dad. Plus I don't think your theory holds water. My friend Lou Ann grew up without her dad, and she feels like if she doesn't have a man in the house she's not worth taking up shelf space."

"Well, you're solid gold, honey, don't let that slip your mind. You deserve the King of France."

"Maybe that's my problem then. Jax is definitely not the King of France."

The staring waitress walks toward them. When she gets to the table she stands staring while three glasses of ice water sweat it out in her hands. She is tanned and blonde, her hair in a tight ponytail, almost aggressively pretty; the jawbones and cheekbones push up hard under her skin as if something in her might burst. Finally she says, "Oprah Winfrey, right?"

Alice makes a surprised smile with raised eyebrows and her tongue against her lips. Taylor waits a second before saying, "Is that the whole question?"

"I saw you on Oprah Winfrey, right? The show where the Barbie Dream Convertible was used to save a young girl's life? I have it on tape. It's you, right?"

"Kind of."

She thunks down the glasses of water with conviction. "I knew it! When you came in I saw you sit down over here in my station and I'm like, 'It's them, it's them!' and the other girls go, 'You're nuts,' but it is. I knew it was."

She extracts a pencil and pad from the pocket of her low-cut uniform, a short, red showboat outfit with frills. She stands gazing at them some more. Up close, Taylor decides, she looks slightly apart from the mainstream of the human race; she has hair of an unnatural color, pure yellow, and little curled bangs, and blue eye makeup that exceeds the size of her actual eyes. Her figure is the kind you notice even if you're not all that interested in women's great figures.

"I think we're ready to order now," Taylor says.

"Okay."

"A glass of milk, two Cokes, three grilled cheeses."

The waitress doesn't write anything.

Taylor asks, "You have that Oprah Winfrey show on *tape?* That's amazing."

"I have probably the largest personal collection of Barbie-related items in the entire world. There's this Barbie Hall of Fame Museum down in Palo Alto, California, right? And I've been there ten times so I know everything they have, all the original ones that cost, like, one thousand dollars to buy, in the original box. I don't have those. But I've got videotapes and stuff they don't have in Palo Alto. I'm like, why not? You know? Didn't they even think of it? I have autographs, even. That kid that hit the dog with the Dream Convertible and saved a young girl's life, is she a friend of yours?"

"No," Taylor says.

"After I saw that show I got the idea of an ensemble called the Barbie Rescue Team, with an ambulance, where she's dressed up as a paramedic, you know? A little white skirt with a tiny slit, and an emergency bag with those blood-pressure things? It could come with a teeny bulldog to inflict the wounds. I wrote Mattel about it, I'm like, 'Guys, this would be so cute,' but I haven't seen them come out with it yet."

Taylor and Alice look at each other. Turtle rubs her nose. The waitress blinks, exactly twice. "So a milk, two Cokes, three grilled cheese, anything else?"

"No, I changed my order," says Alice. "I want the turkey open-face special. I've gotten hungrier while we were setting here waiting to order."

"Sorry!" the waitress says, and heads for the kitchen fast on her red wedgie heels.

"Well, shut my mouth," Alice says. "I had no idea I belonged to such a world-famous family."

"Mama, that's not normal. Nobody ever recognizes us from that show. Do they, Turtle?"

Turtle shakes her head.

"The waiters here are just weird. The one this morning was a comedian; he kept telling us knock-knock jokes about the Manson family."

"Well," Alice says, "why else would somebody live here? They're looking for a career as nightclub acts, and hashing tables till they get the big break."

"Yeah, but this one takes the prize. She's accepted Barbie as her personal savior."

Alice spits out her ice water on her lap, and Taylor feels like something special again. She still can make Alice laugh.

13 ☾

THE CHURCH

OF RISK AND HOPE

CHECKOUT TIME AT THE DELTA Queen Casino is eleven o'clock; at 11:17, Alice is having a difference of opinion with the manager. "All we want is to grab a bite of lunch and we'll be out of your hair in a jiffy," she explains. Huck Finn and Tom Sawyer, pictured from some old movie, grin from the wall behind the desk.

The manager has fat, pale hands decorated with long black hairs, and a gold watch that looks painful on his wrist. "You're welcome to stay in your room another hour, ladies, but I'm going to have to charge you the full day's rate."

"For seventeen minutes. Because people are banging down your door to get in here and you're turning them away," Alice says, staring him down. The place looks deserted, maybe even shut down on account of hygienic difficulties. The brown edges of coffee stains on the manager's desk blotter remind Alice of a map of the world that Columbus might have used. The front door has cardboard taped where some panes of glass should be, causing the sign to read oddly: "A QUEEN SINO HOTEL." The casino shows no sign of life at this hour. Apparently the Las Vegas lifestyle involves gambling till dawn, then remaining passed out through the heat of the day. Only a few lone hangers-on sit stubbornly at their video poker machines.

"Okay," Alice declares, looking him in the eye, "we're gone. Our room's empty. We left the key up there in the ashtray and walked out at ten fifty-nine." She crosses her arms, daring him to jog upstairs and see if she's telling the truth. His craggy eyebrows are collecting sweat under her gaze. He belongs to that species of men who are so spherical in the trunk you have to wonder what holds their pants up. There's no chance in this world Alice is going to lose her gamble. After they pay, Taylor can run up, pack their things, and come down by the fire exit.

"I'll meet you at the pancake house across the street," Alice whispers to Taylor as she takes Turtle and heads for the front door. Taylor reads her mind perfectly. They are Tom Sawyer and Huck Finn.

"Vegas ain't what it used to be," Alice tells Turtle as they wait outside to cross the street. "I was here before, I drove out here one time with your mama's wild daddy. But it's all different with these video games. People dragging downstairs in house slippers and sitting at a machine all day. Back then it was pigs in clover."

"What's pigs in clover?"

"Rich people that don't know how to behave. Ladies in high heels smoking, and gentlemen drinking too much and pinching their bottoms." The pedestrian light blinks WALK, a woman in leather shorts on a motorcycle runs the red light, and then they cross. Turtle is holding Alice's hand in a way that reminds her of an arthritis flare-up.

In truth, Alice thinks Las Vegas was far more interesting the last time. She remembers people crowded around a green felt table, each one bringing a different story and a different need to that smoky room, joined together in a moment of risk and hope. In a way it was like church, with more interesting clothes.

Now there is hardly a green felt table to be seen; Las Vegas is just a giant video arcade. Blackjack, poker, whatever you want, you play it on a machine. Last night they went down to Caesar's Palace just for fun, and in the giant casino five hundred people sat expressionless and completely alone, slumped at their machines, dropping in tokens. From what Alice can see, Americans now prefer to lose their money in private.

The Queen Bee's House of Pancakes is sunny and clean, at least, and puts her in a better mood. Each table has three different kinds of honey in a cloverleaf-shaped container, and the busy-bee waitresses wear antennae headbands with bobbling yellow balls on long springs. Alice and Turtle sit at a booth by the window, where Turtle's head is crowned with light. Alice writes words on her napkin for Turtle to read, discovering that she is confident with three-letter words, and likes rhymes. Turtle ducks her head and giggles at the sentence, "I let my pet get wet." Her skin is brown velvet against her white T-shirt, and her soft bangs divide on her forehead when she shakes her head, making long upside-down Vs.

"What a con job," Taylor declares, out of breath, suddenly sliding into the booth beside Turtle. "I had to set off the fire alarm to get out the back door. That guy's going to put our picture up in the lobby." Taylor sits back, closes her eyes and tilts her head against the high seatback. Her long hair slides behind her shoulders like a curtain drawn open. She exhales loudly, sounding happy. "Mama, it's hot as fire out there already. We're going to roast, driving out of here." She's wearing a pale pink T-shirt, Alice notes— a color Taylor used to make a point of hating. She always had to wear outspoken things, red, purple, orange, sometimes all at once. Alice realizes something important about her daughter at this moment: that she's genuinely a mother. She has changed in this way that motherhood changes you, so that you forget you ever had time for small things like despising the color pink.

Alice is filled with satisfaction, sitting with her daughter and granddaughter in a booth where three varieties of honey glow in the sun. Taylor's skin is much lighter than Turtle's but her hair is nearly as dark, and they share something physical, a beautiful way of holding still when they're not moving. Alice reminds herself that it's not in the blood, they've learned this from each other.

"Oh, my God!" Taylor almost shouts suddenly, staring, but Alice can't see what she's seeing.

"What?"

"America's number-one teenage fashion doll."

It's the waitress from last night, sitting on a stool at the counter. Her red uniform looks slept-in, and her makeup looks as if she's given birth to a child since it was applied. "Good Lord," Alice whispers. Turtle is trying to see too. Taylor waves, with limited enthusiasm.

"We ought to invite her to join us, don't you think?" Alice asks. Clearly the child is in some kind of fix.

Taylor rolls her eyes. "And hear more about the one point two million pairs of shoes that have been sold for Barbie's personal use?"

Alice hesitates, but is overcome by mothering drives. "But look at her."

"Okay, sure." Taylor motions her over, and she appears instantly, with bright eyes and a smile sunk into her desperate face.

"Set down, hon," Alice says. "No offense, but you look like you've been drug through a knothole."

"No, I lost my job at the Delta Queen." She scoots in and reaches for a paper napkin to blow her nose, then delicately works at her eyes. Alice finds a mirror in her purse, which is a mistake. The poor child takes a look and starts bawling.

The pancake house waitress appears just then with their paper place mats and a pot of coffee. Her antennae bob quietly over her gray curls as she stands for a moment appraising her chances of getting them to place an order. She looks at Alice's eyes and says, "I'll come back."

Turtle stares at their new friend, the disheveled waitress. Taylor looks down, studying her place mat, a line-drawing map of the Southwest noting features of interest and Queen Bee's Houses of Pancakes in four states. They all seem to radiate out from Salt Lake City, the mother hive.

"I'm Alice," Alice says finally, pouring everyone coffee. "I'm the mother and grandmother of these two famous girls."

The waitress rallies quickly. "I'm Barbie. No last name, I had it legally changed. I sign it like this, with the little trademark sign after it." She picks up Alice's ballpoint pen and writes a cheerfully looped, upward-slanting "Barbie TM" on Turtle's napkin, directly beneath "I let my pet get wet."

"Well, that's real unique," says Alice.

"I was born in 1959, exactly the same year that the first Barbie was developed and marketed by Mattel. Don't you think that's like too coincidental? The woman that invented her named the doll after her own daughter Barbara, and guess what. My name at birth was Barbara." She looks wide-eyed around the table and blinks. Her eyelashes have remained amazingly long in spite of the disaster that's occurred on the rest of her face.

"How'd you get fired?" Taylor inquires, trying for common ground.

"The manager said I spent too much time talking to you guys. He said I was ignoring the other people in my quadrant. That's what he says, *your quadrant*, okay, like he's the designer of the space module."

"Well, that couple near us was having a bad fight," Alice says helpfully. "I don't think they wanted to be served."

"I know." Barbie makes her mouth into a specific pout. "The poopy old manager says some stupid thing to me every single day. And the other waitrons don't help, they take his side. They say I tell people too much about my hobby. This is, like, so stressful for me, that choice of words. Barbie is not a hobby, do you understand what I mean?"

Alice, Taylor, and Turtle say nothing, but she has their complete attention.

"This is a *career* for me, okay? I've changed my name, and I have worked so hard getting the wardrobe, I have thirteen complete ensembles and a lot of the mix-and-match parts. To fit me, I mean, that I can wear. They have to be made special, or you can put things together from St. Vincent de Paul's and the Goodwill, but it's extremely creative. I study the originals very carefully. I think somebody ought to appreciate a person's career goals, don't you?"

Alice says, "Were you thinking maybe you could be Barbie in a night-club act?"

Barbie dips a fresh napkin into her water glass and goes at her eyes again. "I haven't totally thought out all the details, but something like that. I did the Barbie birthday party at a shopping center in Bakersfield. I was only nineteen at the time and they paid me two hundred dollars. But there's only so many opportunities in Bakersfield, so I thought being a waitron at, like, a casino in Las Vegas, you know? You're bound to meet somebody in high places. Life is full of surprises, right?"

Alice thinks of the sad outfit at the Delta Queen and can't imagine the depths of this poor girl's delusion. She is ready to adopt her on the spot. Their waitress sneaks back tentatively on her crepe soles, and looks relieved when they all order the breakfast special.

"There's a very exciting development coming out this fall," Barbie says, looking back and forth between Taylor and Turtle. "Mattel is launching its new line of ethnic Barbies. Hispanic and African-American."

Alice realizes with an indignant shock that Barbie has been scrutinizing their skin color. Taylor is stirring her coffee and seems not to have noticed. "Here, Turtle, you can color your placemat," Taylor suggests.

"I saw pictures of them," Barbie continues, leaning forward confessionally. "I have access to some very exclusive advance information on this. They appear to be identical to the original model except I think maybe they used plastic from darker dye lots. Also the hair is very special."

"Turtle has a Rastafarian Barbie," Taylor says. "Talk about special hair. She has blond dreadlocks."

Barbie goes blank. "I thought I knew every model on the market."

"This one isn't on the market. It's been rolling under the bed too long with the dust bunnies."

Alice turns to Barbie. "Hon, what you need is a cold washcloth and ten minutes in the ladies' room. Why don't you take my hankie and put yourself together before the pancakes come."

"Oh, thank you so much," Barbie says, taking Alice's handkerchief and rising as if there's a book on her head.

Taylor puts up her hand, knowing what's coming. "Mama, I know I wasn't nice, but she's a kook." She glances at Turtle, who is using Alice's ballpoint carefully to blacken the entire state of Nevada.

"A kook in need of kindness."

"She's thirty years old!"

"Well, you will be too here in a minute. And I guess you've never been caught with your head stuck out on a limb."

Taylor drinks her coffee. "I don't see what we can do for her."

"What are we going to do for any of us?" Alice asks. "Get out of here, to start with. This town feels like poison. Everybody's so busy looking out for number one they'll run over you in the crosswalk. We ought to head for California or Yellowstone Park. Someplace wholesome."

"You think we should offer her a ride out of town?"

"I do. If she's ready to give up on meeting a movie star producer in the Delta Queen."

"That's a big If, Mama. We'd have to try to deprogram her like they did those Moonies."

"If she stops being perky for ten seconds, we'll know we're making headway."

"What's Moonies?" Turtle asks. "Moon people?"

"No, earth people," Taylor says. "People that got stuck thinking too much about one thing."

"Oh," Turtle responds. "Like Barbie."

The pancakes arrive, along with Barbie, surprisingly repaired except for the crumpled uniform. They eat in silence. Alice wonders how much makeup this woman carries on her person at any given time. She decides to let Taylor make the move, if she wants to take on an extra passenger. It's her car, after all, and her life that's gone to hell in a handbasket.

"Drink your milk, please, Turtle," Taylor says.

Turtle's dark eyes go to her grandmother's, then back to Taylor. She picks up the big white glass like some unwanted child of her own.

After several minutes Taylor asks, "So um, what are your plans now?"

"I could really use a shower," Barbie says. "Sheesh. But here's the thing, I live in the Delta Queen, and I'm just like totally not interested in going back in there at this moment in time."

"I meant, for the longer term."

"You mean later today? Or tomorrow? Holy smokes, I don't know. Get another job, I guess."

"Do you have any other prospects? Because if you ask me, this whole city looks like more of the same."

Barbie looks out the window and narrows her eyes, momentarily making a face unlike any ever seen on a teenage fashion doll. "Shit," she says, "I hate this town."

Taylor cuts Turtle's pancakes into small triangles, and smiles at her mother.

* * *

After breakfast they find the car where Taylor has hidden it, in the alley behind the Delta Queen.

"I'll just run upstairs and get my stuff and be down in ten seconds," Barbie says.

"Don't tell the manager you're with us," Alice warns.

"I'm not telling him poop," she replies.

"Mama, this is crazy," Taylor says when she's gone. "We don't know one thing about her except she's an obvious nut case. She could be a serial killer."

"You reckon she'll stab us with her eyebrow pencil?"

Taylor smiles, though she's trying to be serious. "The next town, that's all, Mama. I know you're the world's number-one soft heart, but you've been in Pittman all these years, and the world's changed. Don't you watch 'America's Most Wanted'? It's not safe to pick up hitchhikers."

"We're kind of responsible, though," Alice says. "She got fired for talking to us."

"I'm sure she talks to everybody about Barbie till their ears drop off."

"Yeah, but you and Turtle were a special case. She'd seen you on an Oprah Winfrey show devoted almost entirely to Barbie." Alice blinks her eyes twice.

"Mama, you kill me. I can't fight with you." She looks at her little mother, ready to hit the road in her white shell blouse and lavender pants.

"Well, what else are we going to do, just run off and leave her flat?"

"*Flat* she's in no danger of," Taylor says.

Alice is puzzled for a minute, then laughs. "You think those are real?"

"I dare you to ask."

They both watch the back door of the Delta Queen. Turtle is already in the center of the backseat, her usual post, prepared for whatever comes next.

"Are we going to fit all thirteen of her mix-and-match ensembles into the car?" Taylor asks.

"We'll see."

"It's just to the state line, right? Maybe she'll have better luck in Lake Tahoe. Maybe Ken lives there."

"We'll see," Alice repeats.

Barbie takes more than ten seconds, but less than half an hour. She appears, dressed in a traveling ensemble that includes white gloves and a hat. The rest of her outfits fill only two suitcases and a hatbox, and fit easily into the Dodge's huge trunk. While Taylor reorganizes their things in the back of the car, Barbie clutches her square black purse possessively and seems nervous. She yawns and stretches in the way people really don't do in real life. "I am so tired!" she exclaims. "Can I take a snooze in the backseat?"

Turtle nods, her whole body moving with her head, and moves far to one side of the seat to let Barbie lie down. Alice gets in front and heaves the door shut. It weighs about as much as she does. Taylor seems relaxed in the driver's seat, even without a specific destination.

From a highway overpass Alice gets a glimpse of the desert that lies around them. "Mercy, look what we've got to drive through now," she says. "A whole lot of nothing."

Taylor nods. "I think that's why Las Vegas is the way it is. It's kind of like the only trash can for a hundred miles, so all the garbage winds up in it."

"Imagine if you really lived here. I mean born and raised." They've left the city and are speeding through the suburbs now, row after row of square brick houses with yards that aren't even trying. No flowers, barely a bush. At the corner of a deathly quiet intersection, two tough little sunburnt girls have set up a lemonade stand. They aren't having a great day. A series of descending prices have been marked out on their cardboard sign. Now it says, LEMONADE: WHATEVER YOU CAN PAY.

"Look at that," Taylor says. "Socialism has arrived at the outskirts of Las Vegas."

Alice replies, "Lord, let us pray that it's so."

14

FIAT

"WE ARE COMING TO THE FINISH LINE of the human race," Jax says in the key of D, trying it out. "If you want to see who wins, then don't be in first place." Not very satisfying, but he writes it down anyway on the back of an envelope, which happens to be a telephone bill he hasn't had time to open yet.

Jax is writing the song in Gundi's Fiat. The car doesn't have a steering column at the moment, and is parked in what the neighborhood kids call the Retarded Desert, since this piece of land lies between Rancho Copo and a former halfway house for retarded adults. Jax has already written a song called "The Retarded Desert," so he isn't concerned about that right now. Like many musicians and other people who have tried out singing in different locales, he feels his voice expresses its best qualities inside a small car. Jax doesn't have a car of any size, so he borrows Gundi's. The windows have to be rolled up for acoustical reasons, and since it's July, Jax is sweating a good deal. His skin reminds him of porpoises. He rolls down the window for a breather. Above his house he can see a hawk with white underwings, riding air currents. It has been there for hours. The sparrows in the apricot tree have achieved perfect stillness, waiting for death, each one hoping to outlast its small feathered neighbor.

Turtle should be here now. She likes to sit in Gundi's Fiat with him in all seasons except summer, and often contributes verses. Jax feels that children below the age of, say, driving are more lyrical than adults.

He misses Taylor too, badly. She's been gone twelve days, with no homecoming party in sight. Taylor's and Jax's arrangement, sex-wise, is indefinite: Taylor said if Jax felt like being with someone else, that was okay with her, because it was going to be a long haul. "It's not like we're married," Taylor told him, and Jax felt the small green tree that had been growing up in the center of their bed suddenly chopped back to the root. He doesn't feel fine about Taylor's being with someone else. He wants her to get his name tattooed on her person, or have his baby. Or both. Jax would like his own baby. He and Turtle could take it to the park, where they go to observe duck habits. He would wear one of those corduroy zipper cocoons with the baby wiggling inside, waiting for metamorphosis. He likes the idea of himself as father moth.

Someone is coming toward him in a hurry through the Retarded Desert; it's Gundi, his landlady and owner of the Fiat. She has clothes on today. She moves fearlessly among her intimate friends, the cacti, and waves a small green slip of paper toward him. He doesn't get out of the car, but puts down his portable keyboard and sits with his elbow out the window, like a driver waiting for a long line of traffic to pass.

"A registered letter for you, Jax," Gundi says in her purple silk voice with its foreign, deeply emphasized r's. She hands him the green slip, but he is still listening to the dark carved valleys of her r's: "A registered letter for you." If his name were Robert, the sentence would have been musically perfect.

"This is a letter?" he asks eventually.

She laughs, a purple silk laugh. "You have to sign that. Come, Bill is waiting. He says he can't give the letter to anyone but you. It must be very important."

Jax totes his keyboard and follows her "vurry im*pohr*tant" back over Gundi's invisible path of safety through the desert. She moves snakishly, her blonde hair strumming the ridges of her shoulder blades. She's wearing leather sandals of the type worn by practitioners of yoga and pacifism, though the rest of her outfit is more aggressive: something in the line of a black brassiere, he can't get the full picture from behind, and a skirt made up of many long, satisfactorily transparent scarves.

Bill the mailman stands patiently in his blue shorts on the entry patio of Gundi's stone house. He has left a large pile of letters and catalogs in the little grotto by her door, where all residents of Rancho Copo come to collect their mail. The stone grotto was formerly a shrine, but Gundi removed the Virgin long ago and put in one of her own sculptures, a bright-colored dancing dog with a parrot in its mouth.

"Mr. Jax Thibodeaux?" the mailman asks.

"I am he." If Jax had a hat on, he could take it off and bow.

"Can you show some form of identification?"

Gundi says, "Oh, yes, of course, this is Jax," waving lazily to make everything agreeable, and the letter is left in Jax's hand. Gundi kisses Bill, who is not particularly young, on the cheek before he goes. Being European in origin, Gundi kisses everyone, probably even the exterminators who show up from time to time to rid her foundations of termites.

"Well, Jax, *come in,* you have to share your mystery."

The letter is from Oklahoma, on stationery belonging to the Cherokee Nation. Jax doesn't care to read the letter in front of Gundi's black brassiere, but he follows her into the cave of her entry hall, and then into the light of her sun-struck studio. The rest of the odd little houses of Rancho Copo are falling down by degrees, but Gundi has done a lot of remodeling here in the main house. The windows across the west wall reach all the way to the high ceiling, framing a dramatic view of the mountains.

"Sit here," she commands, pointing to the turquoise cushions of the long window seat. Jax puts down his keyboard and sits at one end of the window seat, his back resting against the deep windowsill, his legs stretched out on the turquoise cushions. He holds the letter at arm's length, looks at Gundi, and drops it on the knees of his jeans.

"It's bad news, I'll share that much of my mystery without further ado." He crosses his arms.

Gundi rests her weight on one sandal, a little uncertainly. "Then I will leave you and go make a pot of raspberry tea. When I come back you have to tell me what is so important and terrible that you have to prove with identification you're Mr. Jax Thibodeaux." She pronounces it correctly, "Tee-ba-doe," the first person in years to do so, but Jax tries not to be too grateful; it may just be an accident on Gundi's part, a result of being foreign-born.

When she's gone, he slits one end of the envelope and sees the same seal on the letter inside, Cherokee Nation, an eight-pointed star inside a wreath of leaves.

Dear Jax,

I'm glad I met you in Tucson. I feel you're a person with careful thoughts and a kind spirit. I want to tell you frankly that I'm worried about Turtle. I've spoken with Andy Rainbelt, a social psychiatrist who works with Cherokee children, and he authorized me to write on behalf of our Social Welfare Department. It's premature to take legal action yet, he says, but it's extremely important for Taylor to be in contact with the Nation; there are things she needs to know. I trust you'll get this information to her.

It's difficult, I know, for non-Native people to understand the value of belonging to a tribe, but I know you care about problems Turtle will face on her own. I appeal to you on those grounds. Adopted Native kids always have problems in adolescence when they're raised without an Indian identity. They've gone to school with white kids, sat down to dinner every night with white parents and siblings, and created themselves in the image of the family mirror. If you ask them what they think about Indians, they'll recall Westerns on TV or doing Hiawatha as a school play. They think Indians are history.

If these kids could stay forever inside the protection of the adoptive family, they'd be fine. But when they reach high school there's enormous pressure against dating white peers. They hear ugly names connected with their racial identity. If you think this kind of prejudice among teenagers is a thing of the past, think again. What these kids find is that they have no sense of themselves as Native Americans, but live in a society that won't let them go on being white, either. Not past childhood.

My boss thinks I'm crazy to pursue this case, but I have to tell you some-

thing. I used to have a brother named Gabriel. We grew up wearing each other's jeans and keeping each other's secrets and taking turns when our uncle asked, "Who made this mischief?" Gabe was my ayehli, my other wing. When I was ten, our mother was hospitalized with alcoholism and other problems. Social workers disposed of our family: my older brothers went with Dad, who did construction in Adair County. I stayed with my Uncle Ledger. And Gabe was adopted by a family in Texas. No one has ever told me why it was done this way. I assume they thought my dad could handle grown, income-earning sons, but not Gabe and me. As for Gabe, probably the social workers knew a couple who wanted a little boy—something as simple as that. He wrote me letters on fringe-edged paper torn out of his ring-bound school notebooks. I still have them. Texas was hot and smelled like fish. His new parents told him not to say he was Indian at school, or they would treat him like a Mexican. He asked me, "Is it bad to be Mexican?"

They put him into the Mexican classrooms anyway; his parents were bigots of the most innocent kind, never realizing that skin color talks louder than any kid's words. He failed in school because the teachers spoke to him in Spanish, which he didn't understand. The Mexican kids beat him up because he didn't wear baggy black pants and walk with his hands in his pockets. When we were thirteen he wrote to tell me his new Mom had closed the bed-room door and sat on the foot of his bed and said quietly he was letting his new family down.

When he was fifteen, he was accessory to an armed robbery in Corpus Christi. Now I only know where he is when he's in prison.

You said, the night we met, that I was only capable of seeing one side of things. I've thought about that. I understand attachments between mothers and their children. But if you're right, if I have no choice here but to be a bird of prey, tearing flesh to keep my own alive, it's because I understand attach-ments. That's the kind of hawk I am—I've lost my other wing.

I wonder what you are giving Turtle now that she can keep. Soon she's going to hear from someone that she isn't white. Some boy will show her that third-grade joke, the Land O' Lakes Margarine squaw with a flap cut in her chest, the breasts drawn in behind the flap, and ask her, "Where does butter come from?" On the night of the junior prom, Turtle will need to understand why no white boy's parents are happy to take her picture on their son's arm.

What does she have that will see her through this into a peaceful woman-hood? As a citizen of Turtle's nation, as the sister of Gabriel Fourkiller, I want you to understand why she can't belong to you.

Yours sincerely,
Annawake Fourkiller

15

COMMUNION

"It's not such a hard name, Teebadoe," Gundi says. "It's Cajun, right? A bayou name." The turquoise cushions are on the floor around them, and Jax's head is in her lap. The raspberry tea is gone; they are past that stage of the consolation.

"My daddy was an alligator," Jax tells her, enjoying the pity. "He only bit once."

"What do people usually say, when they get your name wrong?"

"Thimble Dukes."

"And your girlfriend, what does she say?"

"She says, 'Jax, honey, get your butt in here please and pick up your socks.'" He rests his long hands on his face and rubs his eye sockets deeply.

Gundi strokes Jax's hair. "I'm very sorry for this strange disaster that has entered your life."

"I'm sorry too." Jax sits up, putting a few inches of turquoise cushion between himself and Gundi. She talks like a nineteenth-century romance novel with twentieth-century intentions. "I'm sorry Taylor and Turtle are living in a Dodge Corona. That part I know is a disaster. The rest I'm not sure about." He picks up his cup and cradles its warmth in his palms. They're drinking saki. Gundi believes in drinking warm things on warm days. The afternoon sun through the west windows is finally losing some of its hostility, but Jax's skin remains salty from his session in Gundi's Fiat. She commented on his taste, earlier, when she put a teacup in his hands and kissed his forehead.

"What if this Fourkiller is right?" he asks. "Just as an exercise in giving equal consideration to out-there points of view. What if the best thing for Turtle is to go back?"

"You mean go back permanently?"

"I think that's what *she* means."

"Isn't there another path?" Gundi asks. She says *pahth,* and moves her head in a large, lazy loop so that her light hair slides out of her eyes. Her earrings are made of beads that glitter like small metallic sparks. "The *I Ching* advises the moderate path," she says.

"Unfortunately, skin color doesn't come in 'moderate.' It comes in 'white' and 'other.' "

"I don't know about this. When I was a girl in Germany we read a little story in school about the Hopi, and I wanted to grow up to be an Indian. I think that's why I came here to Arizona, because of unconscious desires. I wanted my paintings to be touched by the primeval spirits of the land."

On the wall behind her, facing Jax, is a full-length portrait of nude Gundi with a saguaro. She stands in profile, her arms outstretched, so close to the cactus that her chin and other parts of her body appear to be recklessly touching its spines. The painting is more realistic than those in her previous series, which represented the moods of water. It will sell for more money, too.

"Do you think people like you and me can understand the value of belonging to a tribe?"

She looks at him, tilting her head. "Of course. We all long for connection."

"What do you want most in the world?" he asks.

"For my paintings to be extraordinary and great," she says without hesitation.

"And you write your name on every one."

"Well, I paint it on there. With a fine brush. Yes. Does that make me a bad person?"

"It makes you a solo flyer. Charles Lindbergh aiming for France. Not a group migration of geese."

"But I don't make paintings for myself, they are for other people. For the world. I want them to bring the world something more than its ordinary light."

"But you also want it known that Gundi made that light."

"Well, I want to get paid for my paintings, sure."

"Okay," Jax says, stretching his limbs. "Say I'm a genial millionaire and I will pay you a stellar salary to live on Rancho Copo and paint the great paintings, and donate them benevolently to the universe. Then you wouldn't sign them?"

"I think I would, still."

"Why?"

"Because I would want people to know this was the work of Gundi, and it didn't fall out of the sky."

"Gundi alone, apart from all other paintbrush-friendly members of the breed."

"Well, what about you, Jax? Would you perform your music with a ... with a grocery sack over your head?"

"I have, as a matter of fact. As a courtesy to my listening public."

She inclines her head again, smiling. Her beaded earrings struggle in the air like small hooked fish. "Would you like to take a bath?" she asks him. "I have a Japanese tub, four feet deep, you float in it."

"I don't float. I sink like a Cadillac."

Gundi laughs. "No, really, it's totally relaxing. I've used it almost every day since the workmen finished it." Jax can imagine Gundi kissing each one of these workmen on the day they departed. She stands up, and he finds himself once again following the irresistible gravity of a woman.

The room with the Japanese tub is the deep slick blue of a starless night, entirely tiled except for a tall window that opens onto a westward exposure of empty desert. Gundi sheds her clothes, which seemed only provisional anyway, so it isn't a big step. Jax follows her example while her back is turned, as she adjusts the steaming water. They sit on opposite sides, waiting for the deep, square hole between them to fill.

Jax with clothes on looks impossibly thin, but without them he is something else, articulated limbs, long and fine without excess. Exactly like his hands. Gundi glances at his legs stretched on the dark blue tile while she attends to the water. The gleaming faucet grows too hot to touch, and she winds her hair around it to protect her hands when she needs to adjust it. She is wearing only earrings and a fine gold chain around her left ankle.

"It's a lot of water," Jax says, looking out the window at dry mesquites and one lone saguaro, its arms raised in surprise or invocation. "Don't you feel guilty, with all those thirsty plants staring in at you?"

Gundi shrugs. "They are plants." She sits across from him, facing him with the full ammunition of her body, her back very straight. A square, steaming lake is rising between them. "We don't really belong in this desert, you and I," she says. "When we have used up all the water and have to leave, the plants and snakes will be happy to get rid of us."

"What about your unconscious Hopi desires?"

"Sometimes I feel I belong to this place. Other times I feel it is only tolerating me with a curled-up lip."

Jax curls his lip. "Did you see how much H_2O the blonde puts in that tub?" he asks in a cactus voice.

Gundi laughs. "You should write a song with all this angst."

"I think I was. Before you and Bill the Mailman impeded my progress."

They both watch the surface of the water, pummeled by the incoming stream but still glossy and intact.

Jax asks, "How do you claim your position as a citizen of the human race?"

"I don't know," she says apologetically. "Register to vote?"

"But how can you belong to a tribe, and be your own person, at the same time? You can't. If you're verifiably one, you're not the other."

"Can't you alternate? Be an individual most of the time, and merge with others once in a while?"

"That's how I see it," Jax says. "I'm a white boy, with no tribal aptitudes.

My natural state is solitary, and for recreation I turn to church or drugs or biting the heads off chickens or wherever one goes to experience sublime communion."

"The only people I know who experience sublime communion all the time are yogis and heroin addicts." Gundi tests the water with the ball of one foot. "Do you think it's possible to live without wanting to put your name on your paintings? To belong to a group so securely you don't need to rise above it?"

"As I understand it, that's the policy Turtle is being offered."

"It sounds very romantic," she says. "But when I went to the Navajo reservation to buy jewelry, I saw people living in falling-down mud houses with television antennas and bottles stacked by the door."

"And that's the whole story, poverty? Nothing else more important could be stacked behind those doors?"

Gundi is quiet. The clasp of her ankle bracelet winks in the slanted light.

"I think it was bad strategy for them to jump bail," Jax says.

"Bail? Taylor was arrested?"

"Not legally. Morally. She felt accused, and was too freaked out to stand trial, and now they're fugitives. It makes it look like she's in the wrong."

"Why did she go, then?"

"For the reason mothers throw themselves in front of traffic or gunfire to save their offspring. It's not an answerable question."

Gundi places both her feet on the surface of the water and looks at them for a long time. "I don't have children," she says finally. "I suppose I don't know that kind of love."

"I suppose I don't either. To put yourself second, every time, no questions asked? Sounds like holy communion."

Gundi turns off the water and eases herself, a pale crocodile, over the dark bank of tile. "You are supposed to be relaxing. Come into the water, I know a type of massage for bodies floating in the water."

Jax laughs. "The problem is, as I told you, I don't float."

"Of course you do. Every living human body floats."

"Theoretically it's possible that I'm dead," he says. "You decide." He slides onto the scalding water, inhaling slowly. He begins gradually to sink, first his feet and legs, then the rest of him. He empties his lungs and refills them just before his face slides under the surface.

"All right, you don't float," Gundi says, reaching under his arms and pulling him up, dripping and laughing. His hair lies close to his skull and his forehead is gleaming. "You're extremely dense, for a human."

"So I'm told," he says. Droplets of water collect in his eyelashes. Gundi lightly touches them with her fingertips, stroking downward from his face to his neck and then his chest. His nipples are hard. His mouth and hers exchange a gentle pressure and their tongues salute each other, blind sea creatures without armor, touching one another's soft surfaces with hopeful recognition.

Jax slides around behind her, holding her against him, burying his face against the nape of her neck. Her hair is a soft veil around her, still dry except for the ends, hundreds of small dark points like watercolor brushes, ready to paint the world with more than its ordinary light. Jax explores her strong, slick belly with his hands, thinking for the second time in a day of porpoises. But then he turns her around to him, cupping her jawbone gently in one hand and placing his other on the small of her back, yielding to the urge that humans have, alone among all animals, to copulate face to face. At least for the first time. At least with an unknown member of the tribe.

16

MAROONED

"SEX-MAD MOM, FIFTY-FIVE, elopes with daughter's prom date," Alice reports.

Barbie, who has already been laughing to the point of makeup damage, collapses in the backseat. Turtle asks, "What's a prongdate?"

"Mama, don't even get started on that one," Taylor warns.

Alice turns to the inner pages of her tabloid. "Here you go, an educational story from nature. The cassowary of Australia is a bird that has been known to kill humans. Eight feet tall, it attacks by leaping in the air and slashing its victim with razor-sharp toenails."

"Mama, that's not exactly educational," Taylor says, frowning into the freeway glare.

Alice reads on, carefully pronouncing all the syllables. "They are kept as pets and form a part of the economy of certain aboriginal cultures as payment for brides."

"What a deal," Taylor says. "I'll trade you my daughter for an eight-foot bird with razor-sharp toenails." Instantly the words "trade you my daughter" seize up in her stomach. She moves the rearview mirror to find Turtle, who has grown dangerously silent in her nest of stuffed toys and dog-eared books. Taylor has been having panic-stricken dreams of misplacing Turtle.

"I want to hear about the sex-mad mom," Barbie whines. "Practically that exact same thing happened to me when I was in eighth grade. My mom flirted with my boyfriend Ryan till he was like, 'Excuse me, I don't even want to come to your house.' I was so depressed I stopped using hair spray for three weeks."

Taylor snaps the mirror back into driving position. "Okay, read the sex-mad mom," she concedes, since it may be the only hope of fending off another Barbie story. This morning they have already heard about the new ecological Animal Lovin' Barbie, and the mystery of the transvestite Ken, who turned up factory-sealed in a Tampa toy store wearing a lace apron and miniskirt. They have also learned that a Barbie doll's measurements translated to the human figure are 36-18-33, which are Barbie's own measurements except she's still a few inches away from the 18. Taylor asked if Eco-Barbie was biodegradable.

"Here we go," Alice pipes up cheerfully, doing her best to keep the peace. She has been reading tabloids aloud since Tonopah. "What an adventure. Three men were marooned on their overturned charter boat off the coast of Florida and drifted without food for thirty-seven days before rescue."

Taylor shivers. "They must have been ready to eat each other."

"Oh, *gag* me," from the backseat.

"Taylor, hush," Alice says. "They probably played alphabet games."

"Right."

She reads ahead silently, and a worried expression clots her forehead. "Well, they didn't eat each other. But it's not very nice. They kind of ganged up on the one they didn't like. Oh, dear. They used him for bait."

The air in the car becomes quiet. The only sound is the sticky hiss of tires on the road, coming in through the vents. The women take in this sound as if their lives depended on it.

Alice says abruptly, "Francis the runaway pig on the lam in Canada. Francis the pig broke out of a slaughterhouse in Red Deer, Alberta, jumped a yard-high fence, sneaked through a sausage factory and pushed open the back door with his snout. The butcher chased but lost him." She skims ahead for the good parts. "... took up residence in a large park. Was once seen fighting off coyotes. Case became nationally known when Francis, grown lean and powerful, evaded professional trackers for six weeks.

Finally he was hit with a tranquilizer dart, but ran for miles and escaped into the bush. Schoolchildren across the nation contributed money to the butcher, asking that his life be spared. Psychologists explain the support for Francis by comparing him to Jesse James or Pretty Boy Floyd."

"Way to go, Francis," Taylor says.

"Who's for lunch?" asks Barbie.

"Francis the pig."

"Oh, gross, Taylor. Who *wants* lunch, I mean."

Taylor has the eerie feeling that the cracked brown desert moonscape outside the car will go on forever. That only the four of them are alive. She checks her watch and informs Barbie that it's only eleven o'clock.

"Well, tell that to my *tummy*. It's like, 'Feed me, okay, I'm starved.'"

Alice gives Taylor a meaningful glance over her newspaper. Taylor asks, "Turtle, do you have to pee?"

Turtle nods.

"Okay. Next exit we'll stop."

"Oh, shoot, it has a sad ending," Alice says. "He was finally installed in his own St. Francis Park. But one of the tranquilizer darts had pierced his intestines and he developed per-i-tone-something or other." Alice adjusts her glasses. "And died. Vets called it a strange twist of fate."

"Mama, this is depressing, all your stories have morbid endings. You're as bad as Lou Ann. She always thinks Dwayne Ray's going to catch perito-something or other at day care."

"They're not my stories," Alice says, raising the palm of her hand toward Taylor, as if taking a vow. "I'm just reading you the printed word."

Taylor wishes with all her might that someone else was in the driver's seat of this car. Even Jax. She's visited with a sudden memory of Jax standing with her in the grocery, leaning down to kiss the top of her head. A gesture that is all give and no take.

"Excuse me," Barbie says to Alice, leaning forward over the seat. "I'm in this awkward situation so I'll just go ahead and say it. I don't know your name. Taylor introduced you as her mom, but it's not like I can call you *Mom*."

"Alice Greer," Alice says.

"Greer?" Taylor asks.

"I never did like Harland's last name a bit. It never sat right."

"Are you newly divorced, Alice?" Barbie asks, sounding exactly like a talk-show host.

"Well, I didn't get the papers yet, but it's over with. All over but the shouting."

"Didn't sound to me like there was ever much shouting," Taylor says.

"Oh, no. It's just an expression. I don't know what it would take to get Harland to let out a holler. He wouldn't even fart out loud. There was days I'd walk by him in his chair in front of his everloving TV set and I'd think, 'Well, now, what if Harland was to die on me? I wouldn't even know it till the fumes started coming off him.' "

"Oh, *gag* me," says Barbie.

Don't tempt me, Taylor thinks. She eases into the right lane and takes an exit marked Gabbs. They have spent the morning climbing out of Death Valley, but escaping from that particular death comes only by degree, it seems. The territory still looks empty. Only the square-headed good samaritans of gas-station signs loom above the dead fields.

"We're like Francis Pig," Turtle announces suddenly. "We're runaways."

"That's right, we're heroes. But nobody's going to shoot us with tranquilizers," Alice promises.

"Or take up a collection to install us in our own park," Taylor adds.

"Do you think we could find a place with milk shakes? I would die totally for a shake right now."

Taylor is not too distressed by the idea of Barbie dying totally. Last night she hinted strongly that they should go their separate ways in the morning, but so far Barbie has absorbed hints with the sensitivity of a fire hydrant. And Alice does nothing to discourage her. They pull in at an interstate diner and Barbie leads the way across the parking lot. She's wearing a pink-and-yellow flounced miniskirt over a baby-blue leotard and tights, with a silver-studded pink fringed jacket and pink high-heeled cowboy boots. Her boots make deep scraping sounds on the asphalt and her short skirt swings like a bell.

The diner has gingham curtains at the windows and a surplus of artificial flowers; Barbie fits right in with her Western ensemble. Her purse is at odds, though: she has been clutching the same square black bag against herself like a stomach ache since they left the Delta Queen. She even took it with her into the bathroom when she showered, in their motel room in Tonopah. It looks heavy.

"What do you think she's got in there?" Taylor asks, once Barbie has downed two burgers and a strawberry shake and excused herself to visit the so-called little girls' room.

"Makeup," Alice says.

"Pennies," Turtle says. "I heard it jingle."

"All I can say is she eats enough for Ken too," Alice observes. "I'd like to know how she hangs on to her 36-18-33."

"She acts like that purse is her baby kangaroo," Taylor says. "Why would you have to take your purse to the bathroom every single time?"

"She has a relationship with the bathroom, don't she? Every time she eats something, up she has to get to the little girls'."

Taylor is relieved to feel that she and Alice are on the same side again, united in their mistrust of Barbie. Turtle takes the pen Alice offers and writes her name four times on her napkin: twice from left to right, and twice in reverse.

"I'd like to get a look in that purse. I bet she's on drugs."

"Makeup," Alice says confidently.

"Could be," Taylor concedes. "She has to fix herself up so much from crying. She seems nervous ever since we left Las Vegas. Maybe she's depressed that things didn't pan out at the Delta Queen."

"Well, she can't be that depressed," Alice points out. "She hasn't quit using hair spray yet."

"No, she hasn't. I think we've got our own personal Eco-Barbie hole in the ozone following us across Nevada. We'd better look out where we park it."

Behind Gundi's bed are tall windows standing open to let in the clear yellow scent of creosote bushes and whatever bird or long-legged animal might be passing by. Gundi props her head on one elbow. Lit from behind, her hair is like golden mosquito netting. To distract himself, Jax imagines a country where people sleep under such a thing, to protect themselves from tiny golden mosquitoes carrying a blissful golden strain of malaria. He sings with his eyes closed.

She strokes the center of his chest. "You have a problem, don't you?"

"I do." Jax opens his eyes briefly, then closes them again.

"Tell me."

"Do you want to know everybody's problems as much as you want to know mine?" he asks.

"No," she says. "I'm selective. You have interesting problems. Bill the mailman has hives." She waits. "Well?"

"My situation here is something like being Catholic, which I was at one time. It takes a lot of the fun out of the moment of sin when you know you're going to have to confess it later."

Gundi stares. "What we have been doing all week you have to confess to a priest?"

"No. To Taylor."

Gundi draws the sheet up to her shoulders. "Why?"

"Because I can't lie to her."

"You think she tells you everything?"

"She tells me everything. Believe me."

Gundi's eyes grow wider still. "You have to tell her the *whole* thing? Details?"

"Just the general plot line, I think. Boy meets girl in Japanese tub, et cetera."

Gundi sits up to light a cigarette. She shakes out the match with annoyance, inhales, and crosses her arms over her sarong of white sheet. "Well, maybe she won't ask."

"Yes, by George, that's it. Next time she asks me what I've been up to, this will be one of the tiny little boring things I'll just leave out: Rucker broke his E string during rehearsal, naturally she doesn't want to hear about that, and I mopped the bathroom floor, I had blistering sex with Gundi, I mopped the bathroom floor again."

"A lot of mopping you have been doing."

"Jax mops till he drops." Flat on his back, arms at his sides, he looks as if he may not float even on a mattress.

"Who does it hurt if you don't tell her?"

He sits up, facing Gundi. "Then I know something she doesn't. I've got this robin's egg in my hand. Sky blue, you see it?" He cups his hand and they both look at it and Gundi can see the blue egg plainly.

"Do I give it to her, or do I not?" Jax asks, watching his hand. "Maybe she'll cook it, maybe she will throw it at me, who knows?" He moves his hand carefully behind his back, palm upward, so slowly she can see the ropes of tendon in his wrist roll over one another.

"So I keep it in my hand, right here. And every day when I talk to Taylor, and when I lie in bed with Taylor, it's here in my hand, and I'm thinking, If I forget for one minute then we'll roll over on this thing, uh-oh, big mess. Until that happens, I'm holding it and I can feel the shell of it as thin as the shell on your teeth. I'm choosing what Taylor knows and what she doesn't. I have the power. I will be the nervous yet powerful guy in the know, and she will be the fool."

They both watch the trail of smoke from Gundi's cigarette. It broadens into the room like a genie.

"And if she's a fool," Jax says, "then how can I worship the ground she walks on?"

"Which at the moment you are doing?"

"Which at the moment I am doing. I'm being a bad boy, but bad boys can still confess and beg for penance."

Gundi blows smoke, dispersing the apparition. "You talk about Taylor as if she is the Notre Dame Cathedral."

"She is. And the Statue of Liberty and Abbey Road and the best burrito of your life. Didn't you know?"

"I don't think so." Gundi jabs out her cigarette in the china-red bowl by the bed and gets up.

"Hey, whoa, Miss Kitty. I broke the rules, didn't I?"

"What rules would those be?" Gundi throws open her lacquered armoire and begins putting on more clothes than she has been seen in anytime this year.

"Rules like, when you're in bed with somebody, even if it's just a roll in the snow, you tell the woman you're with that she is the Snow Queen of your Heart." He folds his hands primly over his penis. "I apologize."

"I don't need you to lie to me, Jax. We both know this is nothing."

Jax lies back with his hands behind his head, trying on the feeling of "this is nothing." He finds it surprisingly painless.

"Thank you, Jax. I need to paint now. Why don't you go mop some floors."

"Yes, ma'am," he says, making no immediate move from her bed.

"And, your rent is past due."

"Tyrant," he says, and steps out her bedroom window with his clothes in his hands.

17

TREASURE

IN THEIR MOTEL ROOM OUTSIDE Carson City, Barbie stands between the two double beds in her white silk pajamas, stubbornly brushing her hair one hundred strokes.

"We could rent another room if you want to pay for it," Taylor says. "Otherwise, we have to share." She is using a more patient voice than she would normally use with a person her own age. Like Lucky Buster, Barbie doesn't strike all the right chords as a true adult. Taylor wonders if this is some new national trend like a crop disease. Failure to mature. Taylor matured at age nine, she feels, on a day she remembers: a Saturday when Alice was cleaning for Mrs. Wickentot. One of the little Wickentot boys told his friend as they came in the house, "You don't have to talk to her, that's the cleaning lady's girl." Taylor presses her spine against the imitation wood headboard of the motel bed, still dressed in her T-shirt and jeans. She is thin and leggy like Barbie, but feels like a member of an entirely different species, one that wears canvas sneakers with holes in the toes instead of fluffy slippers with small heels.

"I'll share a bed with Turtle," Barbie says, and goes back to her hair-brushing project, frowning intensely.

The four of them have taken one room, as they did the night before in Tonopah, but the sleeping arrangements are awkward this time. The manager here claims he can't bring in an extra cot because of fire regulations, so they have to share two beds. Barbie feels the most appropriate thing is for herself to share with Turtle, and for Taylor and Alice to take the other bed, but Turtle will have none of it. She's sitting on Taylor's legs with a hank of Taylor's hair wound around one fist like the leash of a wayfaring dog.

"Don't worry, hon, I won't bite," Alice says, clicking off the bedside light and rolling to the far edge. "I'll probably be up most of the night anyway. I don't sleep that good since I went through the change of life."

Barbie sits, bangs her hairbrush down next to her black purse on the night table, and takes off her mules, leaving them crouched like Pekingese littermates on the carpet. Wordlessly she pulls up the covers.

"Goodnight," Taylor says. Turtle lets go of Taylor's hair and happily begins to get ready for bed.

Barbie reaches for her black purse, stuffs it under her pillow, and resettles her head with several irritated heaves. By the time Taylor and Turtle are curled under their own blanket, she is snoring demurely.

Taylor feels pressure on her shoulder and confuses it inside her dream of being chased in a strange landscape, a city where it rains and rains and streets rise suddenly into walls. In a corner against dark buildings, a cluster of horses look at her, muscles twitching inside the cloth of their damp shoulders. The pressure comes again, and she hears Alice whisper, "Shhh."

"What?" The horses, gone. Where is Turtle?

"Shhh. Come here. You've got to see this."

Taylor slowly reassembles her memory of this room. She carefully moves Turtle's hand, which feels like a rubber glove tightly packed with flour, from her own arm. "Christ, Mama, what?" she whispers.

She can see nothing but the small outline of Alice moving toward the bathroom. She follows, and Alice closes the door behind them. She clicks on

Turtle's flashlight and Taylor sees silver moons, silver edges and circles. Silver dollars. Hundreds of them, in the silk-lined cave of Barbie's black purse.

"Holy shit. Buried treasure."

"Shhh." Alice turns off the flashlight and they sit on the cold tile in total darkness.

"Mama, I told you it wasn't makeup."

"Where do you think a gal comes by about a thousand dollars in silver coin?"

Taylor grabs Alice, what turns out to be her arm in its pajama sleeve. "She stole it from the casino."

"We don't know that."

"Okay, where'd she get it?"

Alice speaks reluctantly. "I've been studying on that for a couple of hours. So far I haven't come up with a story I feel real positive about."

"No wonder she came out of that hotel like a bat out of hell!" Taylor squeaks in a high whisper, "Okay, everybody, I've got my Bank Robbin' Barbie ensemble on, let's go!"

"Hush!"

"Mama, what do we do?"

"Call the police, I reckon."

"No way. And get them on our case?"

"Taylor, the *police* aren't after you."

"No, but we'd have to identify ourselves. It would get in the news. Believe me, I know how that one goes. Me and Turtle and Francis the Pig are out of the hero business."

"Well, we can leave her here, then."

"Mama, you were the one that said we had to bring her. She's a pain in the butt, but still. We can't just dump her in the middle of Death Valley. That would be like those guys marooned on that fishing boat."

"It wouldn't be just dumping her, she's got *coins*. She wouldn't have no trouble getting her way in a phone booth."

Taylor smiles in the dark. "That hotel manager must be having a conniption. He was a creep. *You* lied to him, Mama. Right in front of your own grandchild."

Alice laughs. "I did lie. Like a rug."

"It's gambling money, anyway. It was wrongfully come by in the first place. It wasn't really his."

"Whose was it, then? And how come you're on her side now? Ten hours ago you were ready to dump her off at a rest stop with no facilities."

Taylor can't answer the question. She reaches out in the dark and, as if guided, her fingers touch cold silver. "That money belonged to the hard-luck cases of Vegas," she says. "Part of it's mine."

Even in the Carson City *laundromat* there are slot machines lined up on the wall to laugh at Taylor. "We've got to get out of this state," she says bitterly.

"Every laundromat's a gambling parlor," Alice says, making herself at home among the white-elephant appliances. "You drop your quarters in and hope maybe this time the spin cycle will work."

"We should have brought some extra change from you-know-who." Taylor glances at Turtle, who is building a tower of bright orange detergent empties. Barbie claimed her clothes were clean, and elected to sleep in. She asked if they would do just a couple of things for her, which turned out to be bikini underwear and a pair of purple Spandex pants.

"How do you think she's planning on spending her loot?" Alice asks, holding a pair of Turtle's jeans under her chin and pulling a pink sock out of each leg. She throws the socks in with the whites. "I notice she hasn't offered to pick up the tab for anything yet."

"Don't you think that'd be a little suspicious, Mama? Plunking down Long John Silver's booty bag on the check-in desk and counting out thirty dollars in coin?"

A heavy young woman comes into the laundry with a jumbo box of clothes and three brown-skinned, orange-haired children. The oldest sticks out his arms and begins barnstorming around the machines. He knocks over Turtle's tower and careers away, making burning-engine noises. Turtle begins rebuilding without a word.

"Maybe we should stop at a bank and let her trade in her change for paper money," Taylor suggests. "She's going to get a hernia hauling around all that precious metal."

Alice stares. "I'll swan, Taylor. You talk like you're still going to let her ride with us."

Taylor fiddles with the unrolling hem of one of Turtle's T-shirts. "I kind of respect her now. This robbery thing adds a whole new dimension to her personality."

"Well, it's your car. If you want to use it for transporting the criminal element." Alice begins sorting a dark load. "Have you given any thought to where we're going to end up? We can't just drive and read dumb newspapers till the cows come home."

"Mama, don't you think I know that?" Taylor feels her whole self shaken by this small, continuing antagonism with her mother. Her mouth turns down at the corners as she tears open a detergent box and shakes its green-smelling contents into the machine. "How am I supposed to know? I jumped in the car with Turtle because I was scared to death and it seemed like the safest way to go. That's all I can tell you. I got started rolling down this hill, but I don't know why or how far."

"Don't you sometimes think you ought to just go talk to this Six-shooter woman, see if she'll listen to reason?"

"Fourkiller. No, Mama, I don't. Because what if she won't?"

Alice leans her hip against the washer and looks kindly at her daughter. "I know, hon. No mother that ever loved her child is going to argue with you."

Taylor feels an ocean of relief. She busies her hands with clothes. "I don't know how far we should go. I was thinking California maybe, some little town where you and me and Turtle could find a place to rent. I'm smart enough to know how to keep us from starving, I can find work. And in two or three months this thing will pass over and we can go back home."

Alice holds Barbie's stretch pants against herself, and laughs. She has hardly an ounce of extra on her frame, but against that purple Spandex outline she looks like a stout tree trunk. Taylor holds them against her own body, which is lean but nothing close to Barbie's hourglass. She tosses the pants in with their jeans. "I'll have to cross off fashion model as a career option. I've put on weight since I got Turtle." She laughs at herself. "And I wasn't even pregnant. I don't know what it is. I guess just observing regular mealtimes for Turtle's benefit."

"Taylor, I can't believe my ears. Look at you, slim as a grass snake. You're perfect."

At the light, clattering sound of cardboard boxes, they both turn and see that the orange-haired boy has leveled Turtle's tower again. His mother pays no mind; her doughy breasts in a stretched T-shirt tremble with concentration as she loads one machine after another with crumpled jeans. As the boy zooms away, Turtle keeps her eye on him for a long time. Finally she starts again from the bottom.

"Well, Mama, perfect I may be, but I *have* put on weight. Hanging around Miss America in her leotards makes you notice yourself."

"Taylor, I never heard you run yourself down before. You'd just as well jump off a bridge than to start in like that." Alice closes a machine lid and sighs. "When I was in my thirties I had these little square hips left over from being pregnant and I just hated it. I kept thinking, 'All those years before, I had a perfect glamour-girl body, and I didn't spend one minute appreciating it because I thought my nose had a bump in it.' And now that I'm old, my shoulder hurts and I don't sleep good and my knuckles swell up, and I think, 'All those years in my thirties and forties I had a body where everything worked perfect. And I didn't spend one minute appreciating it because I thought I had square hips.'"

Taylor smiles. "I take your point."

Turtle has made a new tower, bright and precarious by the window, nearly as tall as she is. She stands beside it with her fingers tense at her sides, following the boy around the room with her eyes like a person with a fly swatter and a killing intention. He wheels around the end of a row of washers and starts toward her. Turtle waits till his fingertips are almost in reach of the tower before she scoops both arms wide and knocks it down herself, sending the boxes flying.

Jax's voice on the phone is empty of humor. The voice by itself scares Taylor, let alone what he is reading to her, a letter from Annawake Fourkiller. She can't concentrate at all.

"... premature to take any legal action yet," he says, and Taylor is distracted by her memories of confronting social workers before Turtle's adoption—confident young women in offices who wouldn't believe in a child named Turtle without a birth certificate, any more than they believed in fairies.

"What does she have that will see her through this into a peaceful womanhood?" Jax asks, but it isn't Jax asking, it's Annawake Fourkiller, who sat in the kitchen drinking coffee less than two weeks ago, when Taylor's world was still intact. Her mind fathoms random images of Turtle, the mean, dark eyes of that boy in the laundromat when Turtle sent boxes flying into his face.

Jax reads, "... she can't belong to you. Yours sincerely, Annawake Fourkiller."

Taylor is quiet for a long time, watching her mother and her daughter through the scratched glass of the telephone booth. They're working off steam in a playground across the highway while Taylor makes her call and Barbie attends to her cuticles. Turtle is in the swing, and Alice is trying to teach her how to pump. Turtle does the right moves, pulling back on the chains and kicking out her legs, but she does them at the wrong time and the swing goes nowhere. There are things the mind can learn but the body will only do when the time is right.

"What else, Jax? Is there anything more?" Taylor asks. Behind the phone booth is a gas station and, some distance away, a middle-aged man with longish hair leaning on his red sports car, apparently waiting to use the phone. Taylor doesn't care that he's waiting. Probably he stayed out all night gambling and is thinking up some excuse to tell his wife.

"Any more to the letter? No."

"I wish I could read it. I can't tell if I'm hearing it right. What does it mean?"

"I think this letter is about Gabriel Fourkiller, the boy who got lost."

"But the Social Welfare Department thing, that part about legal action. Does that mean I have to talk to the guy or else?"

"Taylor, sweetheart, I don't think so, but I don't know. You decide."

"I can't think straight."

Turtle has finally gotten herself going in an acute zigzag. Alice catches the chains and straightens her out a little. Tall pines shade the playground area, and the park beyond them is empty save for a heavenly field of green grass, probably the envy of every cow forced to graze in the state of Nevada.

"I took your suggestion, I'm working on the song about the Twilight Zone of Humanity," Jax says, trying for cheerful but sounding like he's trying.

"Jax, did you pay the rent yet?"

There is a pause. "In services rendered."

"What's that supposed to mean?"

"It means I have to tell you something."

Taylor watches Turtle jump out of the swing and run for the slide. She seems, physically, happy. "You know what, hang on, I'm going to go get Mama. I want you to read that letter to her. She'll know what it means."

"Taylor, I'm crazy in love with you," Jax says, but Taylor has dropped four more quarters in the slot and dashed across the highway, leaving the phone dangling.

Taylor sits in one of the swings; Barbie has gotten out of the car, stretched conspicuously, and ambled across the road to come and sit in the other swing. Turtle is collecting pop tops out of the dust and carefully bending the tab of each one into the ring of the next, making a chain. She says it's a necklace for Mary. Probably the most beloved utility flashlight of all times, Mary already possesses a baby bottle and some doll clothes, which naturally don't fit all that well. Taylor has offered to buy her a real doll, but Turtle is offended by the suggestion. She has accumulated yards of pop-top necklace by now and is dragging it behind her, looking like an escapee from a chain gang. Alice has been on the phone a long time.

Barbie's skirt has lost some of its flounce. Her poodle bangs flip up and down as she rocks in the swing. Taylor finds herself looking at this woman a lot, trying to find the hidden casino robber in the picture.

"What time is it? You guys are like, E.T. phone home on this vacation. Why does your mother have to talk to your boyfriend? If my mother ever talked that long to my boyfriend, then for sure I'd know she had the hots for him. No offense. I mean, Alice doesn't seem like the type."

Taylor sits quietly for a while under the rain of Barbie's chatter. Then she says, "I don't know how to bring this up, but Mama and Turtle and I are not on vacation, and you've got something besides blusher in your purse."

Barbie looks at the black pocketbook in her lap, as if it had suddenly been flung there from an asteroid belt, then back to Taylor. "How do you know what's in my purse?"

"We looked. We invaded your privacy when you were asleep last night."

"Snoops." Barbie kicks out her pink boots and drifts in the swing.

"I was just curious why you always had to take it to the bathroom with you. If you'd left it sitting in front of my nose, believe me, I wouldn't have had the slightest desire to look in your purse."

"So? Okay, so I've got money in there."

The man with the red sports car sits on the front fender and crosses his arms, impatient to make his call.

"Money from the casino," Taylor says.

"Yeah. From the silver-dollar machine. Stupid Wallace kept the key in the cash register. At the better establishments they keep all the machine keys in a safe."

Taylor is startled that Barbie makes no effort to lie. "Well, that's between you and Wallace," she says. "I personally don't care that you ripped him off, but I'm not interested in being chased by the police."

"Wally would never call the cops." Barbie narrows her eyes at the highway. "They'd check his gaming odds and send him directly do not pass go to San Quentin."

Taylor understands that where Barbie is concerned she has no idea what she's dealing with. But she finds she prefers this to her previous assumption, which was that Barbie had cotton candy for brains. "Well, here's *my* true confession," Taylor says. "I don't want the police around because Turtle and I are hiding from somebody. Not the police exactly. Somebody that might get custody of Turtle."

"Oh, your ex-husband? I've seen that on *America's Most Wanted*."

"No. It's complicated." Taylor wonders if child-custody disputes really do make it onto *America's Most Wanted*.

"Well, whatever," Barbie says. "Ask me no questions I'll tell you no lies."

Alice has come out of the phone booth. Taylor looks up and sees her standing by the road with her hands dangling at her sides and tears streaming down her face. She looks like she's been hit by something. Two cars in succession slow down to look.

"Could you stay here a minute and keep an eye on Turtle?" Taylor asks, setting off at a jog. By the time she's crossed the highway, Alice is in the car. Taylor gets in on the driver's side.

"I could take the bus from Reno," Alice says, staring forward, though her line of sight seems unable to pass through the windshield.

"Take the bus to where? We have the car."

"I can stay with my cousin Sugar. Somebody ought to go talk to them, Taylor. I understand why you ran when they yelled fire, but I think there's another way to handle this."

"Mama, I'm not giving up Turtle."

"I think all they're saying is they need to talk to you, to tell you there's another side to it." Alice speaks low, and Taylor feels shut out.

"I already talked to her. She wants to take Turtle."

"Maybe not. She's just touchy on the subject, on account of her brother." Alice looks out at the sky. "That poor little boy," she croons, hugging herself, as if she's had a dream.

"What little boy?"

"The one they took away."

"Jesus, Mama, whose side are you on here?"

Alice turns to Taylor and hugs her. "Yours. I'm with you and Turtle to the crack of doom, hon. You know that."

They sit rocking back and forth by the highway while Taylor holds on to Alice, trying to understand the bad news. Through the car window she can plainly see the man leaning on the red car, who suddenly brightens at the sight of a woman who must be his wife, coming from the service station. They hail each other with words in a strange language. Taylor is startled. This ordinary man in jeans, whose thoughts she believed she knew, opens his mouth and becomes a foreigner. It occurs to her that this one thing about people you can never understand well enough: how entirely inside themselves they are.

18

NATURAL SYSTEMS

ALONG THE HIGHWAY THE CORNFIELDS lie newly flayed, mile after mile, their green skin pulled back to reveal Oklahoma's flesh of orange velvet dirt. The uncultivated hills nearby show off a new summer wardrobe of wildflowers. The massed reds flecked with gold are Indian blanket; Cash recalls this name with pleasure, like a precious possession lost and retrieved. He fixes the radio on the sweet, torn voice of George Jones and breathes deeply of the air near home.

A woman in the Oklahoma Welcome Station told him that schoolkids take up collections of pennies to buy the wildflower seeds. Cash had thought wildflowers just grew. He considers this now as he drives, and decides maybe they just *tell* the kids they use their money for wildflowers. So the little ones can look out the car window and think they did all that with their pennies.

Cash hums along with George, who is gloating about putting a gold ring on the right left hand this time. He thinks briefly of Rose, back in Jackson Hole, admiring the rear ends of boys in

McDonald's; he wonders how quickly she'll forget about his tired, flat hind end altogether. He doesn't much care. He is headed back to the home he never should have left, and right now he feels the possibility of fresh love for his own life. When he stopped for the restroom at the welcome station, he gazed at the educational display of the seven different types of barbed-wire and felt he could leap over all seven in one bound.

As he nears the Arkansas River and Cherokee country, the fields give way to trees and there are more varieties of living things, it seems: scissortail birds snipping over the meadows catching bugs, and big-headed kingfishers sitting on high lines overlooking the river. He drives into the outskirts of Tahlequah, through the motel strip along the Muskogee Highway and then into the older, pretty part of town. The old brick courthouse and the seminary building and all the old oaks haven't changed. The main road leads him out again, into the woods.

At a bend in the road outside Locust Grove, Cash is moved by the sight of a little field with a heartbreaking hedgerow of wild pink roses and one small, sweet hickory in the center, left standing because the Cherokee man or woman who plowed that field wouldn't cut down a hickory. He keeps an eye out, afraid to miss one single sight as he makes his way. Crowds of black-eyed susans stand up to be counted, and five beagles sit side by side in someone's yard, reverent as a choir, blessing his overdue return.

Annawake is first aware of a rectangle of brightness framing the window shade, then the pile of quilts arguing on her bed: wild geese, double wedding ring, trip around the world, stitched by three different aunts who quarreled, when they were alive, about which pattern was best. And there is something under the quilts, a lump, stealing along like a mole beneath the garden. Annawake reaches behind her head, pulls herself to a half situp, and conks the lump with a pillow. It flattens and giggles. She pulls out a naked Annie.

"I found a rat in my bed. What am I going to do with this rat?" She covers Annie's face with kisses. When she exhausts her affectionate assault, Annie lies on her back next to Annawake and sucks her thumb with a contented, arrogant air.

"You got kicked out of Millie's bed, didn't you."

Annie nods.

"That's because there's another baby now. You've moved up in the world. Now you get to be a big sister. Doesn't that sound fun?"

Annie shakes her head.

"I don't blame you. Who needs it?" Annawake lies on her back too. They both look for a while at the ceiling, which is decorated with a few unwelcome suggestions of mildew. Before Annawake finished law school and moved back to Tahlequah, Millie doubled up the kids into the front room, mounted a convulsing stepladder and scrubbed this room to within an inch of its life. But there has been rain since then, and the roof is older than anyone living under it.

Dellon pokes his head in the door. "There she is. The escaped prisoner." He comes in with Annie's clothes, and Annie uses her sturdy legs to scoot herself under the quilts again.

"Hey, Dell," Annawake says. She sits up, clasping her arms around her blanketed knees. "Watch out, the prisoner's lawyer is present."

Dellon sits on the foot of the bed holding Annie's small red sneakers like baby birds in his large hands. Dellon's long hair is loose, his T-shirt looks like what grasshoppers do to crops, and his beefy shoulders seem slumped this morning with the weight of fatherhood. He narrows his eyes at Annawake. "Hey, that's my shirt. I've been looking for that one."

Annawake looks down innocently at the maroon flannel she's been sleeping in. "The color's good on me, don't you think?" She cocks her profile.

"Why don't you get a boyfriend, so you can steal *his* clothes?"

"Good idea. I knew there was some reason women sought out the company of men."

"Listen, I was supposed to have the kids out of here by ten o'clock. Millie has to take the baby over to Claremore for his shots or something."

"Christ, what time is it? Are you telling me I slept past ten o'clock?"

"Yeah, I think they're going to make it a national holiday. National Annawake Slept Past Ten O'clock Day."

"Look, I'll stay here with the kids. It's not even worth going into the office now."

"You're not going into the office? On a Saturday morning? Definitely a national holiday." He half stands and reaches behind the aged lace curtain to snap up the shade.

Annawake shades her eyes from the light. "Get out of here," she tells him affectionately. "Annie and I need our beauty sleep." She flips the pillow behind her head and lies back down. The lump of Annie wildly animates the double wedding rings in the region of Annawake's knees.

"Okay," Dellon says. "I'm taking Baby Dellon and Raymond over to my house. You've got this one." He stands up and gently swats Annie through the quilts with her red shoes. "The naked savage. Teach her some girl stuff, will you, like how to wear clothes?"

"See you later, Dell."

"Oh, listen. Did Millie tell you about the hog fry?"

Annawake sits up. "Another one? I'm going to get fat this summer. Who's this one for?"

"Cash Stillwater, just moved back from somewhere. It's down at Letty Hornbuckle's over in Heaven."

"Miss Letty, the one that used to run everybody's business in the grade-school cafeteria? I haven't seen her since I got breasts."

"You have breasts? Let me see."

Annawake makes a frightening face at her brother.

"So, you coming?"

"Cash Stillwater," she repeats. "I think I went to school with his son, who was it, Jesse Stillwater? Real tall?"

"No, Jesse is Cash and Letty's youngest brother. I think there was eleven or twelve of them. Cash had a daughter—remember that Alma, she drove herself into the river a few years ago?"

"Oh, yeah. Off that bridge."

"They're some kin to Johnetta Hornbuckle that drives the school bus. There's Johnetta and Quatie. She married Earl Mellowbug."

"Quatie." Annawake thinks. "That's right. Her mother was Mama's girl-friend. Remember her, the beauty queen? Mama kept that picture of her that was in a magazine. I still have that thing somewhere."

"I'll be back around six to pick you up. Unless you get a better date."

"We'll be here, Dell. You're the best I'm ever going to do."

Annawake smiles, watching the bear shape of her brother duck out through the doorway. Annie has made no progress with female apparel in the meantime, but has fallen back to sleep. Annawake smooths the layers of covers, remembering from her childhood the noisy aunts who made those three quilts: they lived in one house, and could never agree on anything in this world except that love is eternal.

On the stone floor of Jax's studio Lou Ann sits cross-legged, nervously tapping the toes of her athletic shoes while Jax frowns at his new amplifier rig. He picks up a yellow electrical cord and examines it closely. "Do you think this should be plugged into something?"

"Don't ask me. Do I look like Mozart?"

"No," Jax says. Today he doesn't have the energy even to laugh at Lou Ann.

"Dwayne Ray, honey, don't mess with Jax's stuff."

Dwayne Ray, a resolute child with disorganized mud-colored hair, is pulling an assortment of bamboo flutes out of a milk crate and laying them end to end.

"I'm making a space shovel," he explains.

"No problem," Jax says. "Take them out in the hall. You can line up the whole star fleet out there."

Dwayne Ray happily drags the crate out the door. In the hallway he begins to accompany his industry with Indy 500 sounds. Lou Ann simply stares at Jax. He finds a socket for the yellow plug and then glances up, feeling her eyes.

"Jax, you never let him *touch* those before. You would have cut his little pecker off if he'd tried to use your music stuff for toys."

Jax returns to his wires. "So, I'm feeling generous. Your male line has escaped dismemberment."

Lou Ann's blue eyes are wide. "Jax, honey, I miss her too, but you have got to get a grip."

He puts down his pliers and really looks at Lou Ann. The sun from the high east window lights her upturned face and her electric blue leggings and the bag of tangerines she brought over, and Jax wishes merely to weep. All this color and worry focused on his welfare, and it's going to waste. He sits down next to her.

"Do you know," he says, curling his long fingers through Lou Ann's, "all her earthly clothing fit into two drawers in the bureau. Can you believe God made a woman like that? And she saw fit to live with me?"

"Gosh, Jax, I could never be your girlfriend," Lou Ann says, sounding hurt. "I'd get disqualified just on the basis of shoes alone."

"I love you anyway. But you've got to let me wallow in my misery. This is not a situation that can be resolved through Welcome Wagon technology." He leans sideways and gives her a kiss of dismissal.

Lou Ann stands up and, with one last worried look, leaves him. She steps over the electrical cords as if they might be napping snakes. In the hall she collects Dwayne Ray and the flutes. Jax hears the sounds of their internal wooden emptiness as she piles them back into their crate. He stands up again, facing the window, realizing how clearly these days he can hear the emptiness inside things. He lets his hands walk around on the keyboard, which is powerless, its internal circles of current still interrupted somewhere by an imperceptible fault line. It makes no sound at all as his fingers modulate their laments in one key after another.

Jax feels entirely separate from his hands as he looks out the window. His eyes follow the golden, drawn-out shape of what he finally understands to be a coyote circling the trunk of a palo verde tree. His hands go still. The coyote's belly hangs low with incipient pups or with milk, it's impossible to tell which, because she keeps herself low in the brush.

Suddenly with violent effort she leaps into the tree and falls back, bouncing a little on her forelegs, with a nest of sticks in her mouth. A dove flies off in the same instant, startled as a heartbeat. The coyote crouches at the base of the tree and consumes the eggs in ugly, snapping gulps. She stands a moment licking her mouth, then creeps away.

Jax is crying. He feels deeply confused about whom he should blame for his losses. The predator seems to be doing only what she has to do. In natural systems there is no guilt or virtue, only success or failure, measured by survival and nothing more. Time is the judge. If you manage to pass on what you have to the next generation, then what you did was right.

19

CHEWING BONES

ALICE DIALS DIRECTORY ASSISTANCE FROM a motel room in Sacramento, in pursuit of Hornbuckles.

"You can't find a Robert? No, wait," she commands the operator, shifting the receiver to her better ear. "It's Roland, I think. Roland Hornbuckle. Look up that one." She waits, rolling her eyes across the room to Taylor, who returns a less irritated, more troubled version of her own expression. Alice has never gotten over the initial shock of seeing her own facial features plastered across another human being, with plans of their own.

"You worrying about Turtle?"

Taylor nods.

"What's her problem?"

"She found out you were leaving. She hates when anybody leaves her. I just went in there and found all our shoes and Barbie's slippers in the toilet. Now she's lying in the tub."

"I'll talk to her," Alice says. "I'll tell her it's just so I can try and make them let you and her stay together."

"I already told her that. It doesn't matter if you have a logical reason."

"Well, then, try Rocky Hornbuckle," Alice tells the operator. She whispers to Taylor, "Has she got her flashlight in there? I don't mean to worry you, but Harland's sister got killed listening to 'Jesus Loves You This Morning' on the radio in her bathtub."

"Oh, don't worry, there's no water. She just gets in with her clothes on and pulls a blanket over her head and says she's buried."

Alice says in a louder voice, "No? Okay, listen. Just give me every Hornbuckle you've got in Heaven, Oklahoma."

Taylor gets up to examine Barbie's slippers, which are drying out badly in front of the air-conditioner unit. "Boy, is she going to be pissed off when she sees these. They look like drowned guinea pigs."

"Where'd she go?"

"Who, Barbie? Out to get more Cheese Doritos, I think."

Alice begins writing hurriedly, trying to keep up. She hangs up and waves her list at Taylor. "Eight Hornbuckles with telephones. One of them's got to be Sugar, right? Maybe she remarried."

"Well, then, her name wouldn't be Hornbuckle anymore," Taylor points out.

"Isn't that the dumbest thing, how the wife ends up getting filed under the husband? The husband is not the most reliable thing for your friends to try and keep track of."

"Nobody holds a gun to your head, Mama," Taylor says. "Even if I married Jax, which I'm not going to, but what would I want with his stupid *name*? Just learning how to spell it is a big commitment."

"I'm going to call this whole list. One of them's got to know her, at least." Alice takes a deep breath and dials.

"I don't think *he* even ever spells it the same way twice."

Alice holds up her hand. "Ringing," she says. They both wait. After a moment they wait less breathlessly. Alice finally disconnects, then dials the next number on her list. "You've been picking on that boy all day long, Taylor," she says in a quiet voice, as if the ringing phone might otherwise hear her. "Either he's your boyfriend or he isn't, but don't just sit on the fence and run him down."

Taylor slumps in the swivel chair by the window and falls silent, twisting the chair slightly back and forth, while Alice tries two more numbers.

"I think they done dropped the bomb on Heaven, Oklahoma," she announces after getting no answer on number four. She scrutinizes her list, then glances up at Taylor, who is looking out the window with tears in her eyes.

"Hon, what is it? What I said about Jax?"

"I don't know if he is or he isn't. How can I have a boyfriend if I'm sleeping in motels and living in a car? No wonder Turtle wants to have a funeral for herself in the bathtub."

"This is going to pass," Alice says, beginning to dial again. "I know it's hard. But you and Turtle have a home back there waiting for you."

"Not waiting too hard," Taylor says without looking at Alice. "When I called last night he told me he'd gone to bed with the woman that collects our rent."

Alice's mouth falls open. She closes it, staring at Taylor, then suddenly blinks and says, "Hello? I'm a cousin of Sugar Hornbuckle's calling long distance, looking for her. She is? Good Lord. Yes, please."

Taylor looks up, her eyes still watery but changed, self-contained and inquiring.

"Don't give up the ship yet," Alice says. "We've found Sugar. It sounds like they're having a big old party in Heaven."

Sugar Hornbuckle hangs up the phone and goes cold at the sight of blue-lipped children, a host of them, running like a crowd of small ghosts stealing from the pantry. Letty shoos them off the peach pies and out of her kitchen, and Sugar blinks away what seemed like a bad omen.

"Who was that on the phone?" Letty asks.

Sugar backs up several stitches through her quilted thoughts. "Funniest thing. A cousin of mine I haven't seen since nineteen and forty-nine. She wants to come visit. She's got some business with the Nation but she didn't say what."

Letty's curiosity wakes up and knocks down the door. "Well, I wonder what that could be? She got some kind of a claim?"

"I doubt it. She's not from around here. We kind of grew up together down in Mississippi, as good as sisters. You ever been down South?"

"No. I heard it's hot."

Sugar laughs, wondering what could be hotter in summer than an Oklahoma woods.

"Could you give me a hand with these wild onions, hon?" Letty asks, not about to let her escape the kitchen yet with this thrilling news item. She crosses the kitchen to her freezer chest, walking like a bear; Letty is built square, with legs sticking out from the bottom of her dress that seem to be set two feet apart. She opens the freezer chest and bends over it, exposing the tops of her thick brown stockings rolled to her knees. A cloud of steam curls around her face and touches her hair with silver.

"Why'd you all go all the way down to Mississippi to get raised up?" Letty never leaves Heaven; as far as she is concerned, Mississippi might as well be India.

"It was the Depression," Sugar says. "Alice's mama had a hog farm."

"Hog farm? There's money in that, I guess."

"Oh, law, we never had three dollars at the same time. But we didn't have all that bad a time of it."

Letty grunts a little as she stoops deeply into the freezer. "Well, sure, you get by. I heard about them civil rights they had down there."

Sugar takes the frozen blocks Letty hands her, one by one, stacking them like cool firewood against her chest. She remembers helping Letty collect these wild onions in the spring, to be put away for a summer or fall hog fry. "It wasn't like they make it sound now. We were all more or less in the same boat, black and white. Or maybe we were just ignorant, but it seemed like we got along. My favorite thing in the world was going down to Jackson to see the maypoles and the State Fair. There'd be just hundreds of dark little children dressed up as angels, marching down the street, singing hymns. To this day, I swear that's the prettiest sight I ever saw."

"Mmhm." Letty is losing interest.

"Nobody had two bits, it was just like here. You didn't notice what you didn't have, because nobody was right there wagging it in your face."

"When's she coming?"

"She says just as soon as she can get here on the Greyhound bus."

Letty sighs. "Well, I'll bring over a pie, to say hello, soon as I help get Cash settled in."

Letty Hornbuckle is the nosiest person in three counties. Sugar knows why she'll bring over a pie—for the same reason she's been helping Cash: to snoop. She's probably been looking through all his things to see if he secretly got rich in Wyoming. Sugar helps Letty fill a pail and swish warm water over the freezer bags of wild onions. Letty will stir these into scrambled eggs, and Cash will declare he's never leaving home again. No, Letty can't possibly suspect her brother of having struck it rich. No Cherokee she's ever known would keep money a secret from relatives. Cash probably came back with the same nothing he bore away three years ago, and nobody will hold it against him. Especially not after all the funerals he went through. When they finish with the wild onions, Sugar slips quickly outside to find her husband and tell him about Alice.

The children she saw inside have joined a mob of others under Letty's big mulberry. She laughs at herself, her vision of ghosts. The children's hands and faces and soles are all inked blue from berries gulped and trampled.

Letty's yard is a small mowed clearing held in on every side by protective hickory woods. Sugar's husband, Roscoe, in the company of all the other old men, is standing watch over Letty's big iron washpot, which is settled like a hen on a white nest of coals. The fire adds more cruel heat to this hot day, quivering in the air around the men's boot leather and rising up into the arms of trees. Inside the enormous pot, a thousand thumb-sized pieces of what was yesterday a live fat hog swirl upward in the cracking oil. Sugar thinks: One more citizen of Heaven, making his contribution. Roscoe and his friends are studying the heat of the fire and the level of oil in the pot with the attitude men take on occasions like this, feeling the weight of their supervisory powers. Sugar smiles. A woman knows she can walk away from a pot to tend something else and the pot will go on boiling; if she couldn't, this world would end at once.

She stands alone under Letty's bent peach trees, wanting to be outside the crowd for a minute before it draws her back in. What will her cousin Alice make of this place? She can't imagine. Sugar looks fondly at the dark braids trailing down men's backs, the women's shoes lifted high in the uneven grass. Children are everywhere in sight. The ones too small to climb trees run low through the crowd, their smooth, dark heads passing under every hand. Sugar feels rocked in the bosom of family. All these people are related somehow to Roscoe and herself and her children. Probably she could pick out any two people in Cherokee County and track the human path that links their families. In fact, that's the favorite pastime of every old Cherokee, at gatherings of every kind. Even though she wasn't born here, Sugar has been a Hornbuckle long enough to do it as well as anyone: trace down Hornbuckles and Blackfeathers, Stones and Soaps and Swakes. She can remember, when she first moved here with her new husband, she felt she'd walked into an endless family reunion.

Her daughters, Quatie and Johnetta, are standing shoulder to shoulder in Letty's outdoor summer kitchen, Johnetta stirring the bean pot and Quatie working just as hard on some long tale she needs to tell. Quatie's husband's mother, Boma Mellowbug, is crossing the yard in a bright blue satin dress and a man's wool cap. She walks sideways like a crawdad, with her eyes on the sky. In Heaven it's a good thing to be related to Boma, because she sees things no one else does.

Earlier she saw Boma standing among the men, talking earnestly with Cash. Now she crosses to the grape arbor to talk to three boys and a girl that belonged to Bonnie Fourkiller, a dear friend of Sugar's now deceased. The girl has an odd haircut but still yet looks like Bonnie. Sugar can't remember any of these children's names except, strangely, the first baby boy who died—that was Soldier—and the youngest, Gabriel, who was taken off to Texas somehow, and killed, Sugar thinks, though she can't recall how. Today she can easily imagine those lost boys turning up here too, grown tall; she sees how their shoulders would fit into place between their brothers' and sister's.

The crowd is also missing Cash and Letty's mother, who died a few years back. She should be here ordering the children out of the pies and the old men away from idleness. In her last years she always organized gospel singing at the hog fries. For her whole life prior to that she went to the Locust Grove stomp dances, and wouldn't be persuaded to miss them for anything in this world, until her knees got bad; then she converted to Baptist. She said the kneeling and praying was trouble but still grieved her less than stomping. That was her way. So then they had to sing "Amazing Grace" and "Washed in the Blood" at every big occasion, with the Cherokee words, which were less appalling at least than the English. The obstinate practicality of old women pierces and fortifies these families like the steel rods buried in walls of powdery concrete. It astonishes Sugar that she's becoming one of these old women herself. She still feels pretty and young.

She jumps slightly, for Boma Mellowbug is standing beside her, reading her mind.

"Are you happy?" Boma asks, looking sideways at Sugar from under her wool cap and veil of white hair.

"I am, Boma. I haven't been sometimes, but now I am."

"Well, then, don't be tormented by the *kolon*. He's not always a bad thing."

Sugar looks up. "That bird?"

"That one flies over when somebody is going to die. You hear him call? He sounds like he's chewing bones."

A naked toddler wearing only red shoes moves from one group of adults to the next; none of them looks down, but each one honors the child's round head with a downstretched hand, as if it were a ripe melon that had rolled itself up from the field. Sugar stares at Boma, whose eyes are clear, light brown, and undisturbed. "I don't want anyone here to die," she tells her at last.

Boma blinks. "It's a big tribe. Somebody's always dying."

Sugar looks at the people gathered in this single green place and understands the price of love.

"All right then," she says. "Just so it's not one of the children."

"No," Boma says. "We're going to keep these children on."

20

THE WAR OF
THE BIRDS AND BEES

IN ALICE'S OPINION, HEAVEN HAS gone to pigs and whistles. She has no idea what promise the town held in days gone by, but on the morning someone named it Heaven there could not have been, for example, a mess of mean dogs holed up under the Post Office porch.

"Watch that one pup with the stump tail," Sugar says, dancing a little on the stairs and swinging her purse at the dogs. "His name's Choppers."

Alice can't pick Choppers out of the lineup of his yellow brothers and sisters; they are all leaping up as if they'd been caught by the mouth on fishing lines. The two larger dogs merely stare, considering whether the food value in this pair of old women is worth the bother. "Why wouldn't somebody rout them out?" Alice asks, framing the question as tactfully as possible as she skirts sideways up the steps with her hands on her pants legs, watching her blind side.

"Oh, honey, they live here," Sugar explains. She pushes open the screen door and introduces Alice to her daughter Quatie, postmistress of Heaven, before Alice has quite finished looking out for rear-guard attacks.

The Post Office sells cigarettes and notions and smells a good deal like tuna fish. Quatie has a Camel going and a sandwich in one hand, which she wipes before holding it out to Alice. "Pleased to meet you," she says, once she has licked her front teeth. Quatie has her father's broad, brown face but her mother's eyes, sloped faintly down at the outside corners, giving a touch of sadness to her smile.

"Our cousin from way back when," Sugar tells Quatie, raising her hands to show it's been more years than she can count.

Quatie rolls her eyes at Alice in a friendly way. "Mama talks about Mississippi like it was kingdom come."

"Well, sure I do," cries Sugar. "Me and Alice were the belles of the ball. This morning we decided we'd come on downtown and paint the town red."

Quatie winks. "Reckon that took about a quart."

"Pardon?" Alice asks, still nervous.

"Of paint."

"Oh. Well, I'm used to small towns. Small is nothing new to me." But Alice is being polite. She thinks, as they leave the P.O. and head up the road toward Sugar's house, that this place has problems beyond being small. It looks like everybody here has been out of work for the last forty years, and in fact Sugar says that's about right. In the past, she claims, the eastern end of the state was a reservation, and fairly prosperous. But the federal government cut up the land into small packets and gave one to each family; since the people here had no thoughts of land as something to be given or taken permanently, they were persuaded by clever investors to trade their allotment papers for a mule or a stove or, in one case Sugar knows of, a crate of peaches and a copy of *The Leatherstocking Tales*. Since then, most of eastern Oklahoma has been more or less looking for a job. Sugar came here freshly married to Roscoe in 1950; it seems to Alice that they've lived mainly off Sugar's local fame as the

"Welcome to Heaven" poster girl, though it wouldn't have paid any bills.

Roscoe dropped Sugar and Alice downtown on his way to repairing a pump for some relatives in Locust Grove; Alice happily agreed that they could walk back. She wanted to get her bearings. Now she has got more bearings than she cares for. They pass houses that Alice only hopes have seen better times; front yards where chickens run free and cars with no wheels enjoy the rich, rust pelt of eternal life. They stop to rest a minute at the spot where Main crosses what Sugar calls "the uphill road" (which, Alice thinks, must surely run downhill for someone), in the shade of big oak trees whose limbs dangle vines like Tarzan's jungle.

"How'd that husband work out?" asks Sugar, politely avoiding the more obvious question of why she is here. Alice wants to mention Turtle, but can't. She's not yet at home with Sugar. They haven't seen each other for a lifetime. The cousin she's just met is a thin, humpbacked woman in canvas shoes and a blue cotton dress that hangs empty in the bosom. Alice recalls mention of sons in and out of trouble, and in their last correspondence, ten years ago, an account of surgery for breast cancer, but Sugar still has a pretty smile and eyes you look at twice. She wears her snow-white hair the way she did as a girl, in an Andrews Sisters roll across the back, and she has an almost flirty way of talking that makes Alice think of the Andrews Sisters shaking their fingers, making round "o's" with their mouths: "No, no, no, don't you sit under the apple tree with anyone else but me-ee!"

"Harland is his name," Alice confesses. "The fellow I married. It didn't amount to much. I finally just couldn't stand the quiet."

"Oh, honey, don't I know. I think Roscoe used up his whole vocabulary when he asked me to marry him. All that's left now is 'Where's it at?' and 'When's dinner?' "

Alice breathes a little deeper. Sympathizing over the behavior of men is the baking soda of women's friendships, it seems, the thing that makes them bubble and rise.

They pick up their feet and walk on past a Shell station and a building covered with pockmarked yellow siding that advertises HEAVEN MACHINE TOOLS NEW & USED. Then they are beyond the pale of what Alice would call town. It's small all right, but even so she feels Quatie underestimated the amount of paint called for.

"Where did the name Heaven come from?" she asks Sugar.

"Well, that's for the blue hole. A great big water hole down in the crick where the kids love to go jump in and fish and all. Catch crawdads, that kind of stuff. The grown-ups like to go too, really. It's the best place around. They used to just call it 'The best place,' in Cherokee, and when they went to turn that into English somebody thought people was talking about Heaven. But they wasn't, they just meant the best place *around here.*"

"Isn't that the way," Alice says. She feels relieved to know that "Heaven" as a value judgment is only relative.

"How about your girl?" Sugar asks. "Where's she now?"

It stuns Alice to realize she has no earthly idea. And can't go into it with Sugar, which makes her sadder still. "She's living out in Tucson, Arizona. Taylor's my pride."

"Oh, sure, they are. When they don't give you no trouble, they're a blessing."

The road becomes a lane, passing under a tunnel of locust trees. A creek runs beside them in the thick woods; Alice can hear its satisfied rush. Birds sing loudly in the trees, and there seem to be dozens of terrapins in the road. The trucks that come along swerve to miss them, and they pull in their heads and sit like rocks, their small hearts surely pounding from another near miss. But somehow they must make it across, otherwise the roads would be lined with box turtle tragedies.

"Well, look, there's poke," Sugar says, suddenly animated. She pulls a wadded plastic bag from her purse and shakes it open as she steps sideways down the bank. There in the ditch she squats and picks handfuls of new green leaves. A truck passes, and Sugar waves. Alice doesn't know what to do with herself, and half turns her back, as if her cousin were going to the bathroom down there. She knows you can eat poke, has known it all her life. But she has also known for many years what people would say about her if they saw her collecting her salad greens from the roadside.

Sugar climbs carefully back up the bank, triumphant, her bulging sack the size of a lumpy basketball. "There used to be a world of poke right up behind our place, where they cleared the woods out under the power lines," she tells Alice as she falls into step beside her, catching her breath. "But a few year ago they started coming along and spraying something poison under those lines that kilt all the poke. Now, why do you think they'd do that?" she asks.

Alice doesn't say, "To kill the weeds, what do you think?" She says, "It's hot, isn't it?"

Sugar wipes her brow. "I was just thinking how hot it used to get, back in those summers when we were kids. The grown-ups would live on the porch, and not hardly move."

"It *was* hot," Alice says. "It was Mississippi."

"My mommy wouldn't want the baby on her lap because it was too hot. We'd take the babies on *our* laps because we were big britches, playing mommies. I guess we didn't feel the heat so much, any more than we knew the half of what it was to be mommy."

Ahead of them, a huge black snake parts the weeds and starts to slide into the road, thinks better of it, loops back over itself like a shoelace, and slips away into the bush.

Alice speaks abruptly from her thoughts: "Do you know anybody named Fourkiller?"

"Oh, honey, you can't hardly walk around here without stepping on a Fourkiller. There's Ledger Fourkiller, he's a chief, just the nicest man you'd ever meet. He does the ceremonies over at Locust Grove and lives on a shantyboat. He's lived down there on the lake since the second war, Roscoe says. He's got a landing built all out of old tires. It's a wonderful thing to see."

They walk in silence, until Sugar asks, "Do you remember the maypoles in Jackson?"

"Oh, sure. The kids in white shoes, walking circles. The boys would go one way and the girls the other."

Sugar touches her hair. "The State Fair," she says. "Them parades. I never will forget. And remember that carnival?"

"The cow with a human face!" Alice cries.

"Rubber man! The hypnotist!"

"The Siamese calves, two bodies eight legs!"

"You wanted your money back on that one," Sugar says, "because it turned out to be dead and stuffed."

"I got it, too," Alice points out.

"You had spunk, I'll say that."

"Well, think about it. Dead and stuffed, they could have just sewed two regular ones together."

"I've been thinking about that for forty years, Alice."

"That dead calf?"

"No. You. Telling the man you wanted your nickel back. I wisht I'd had more of that. I feel like I didn't show my girls what I was made out of."

Alice is surprised to hear this admiration from her lively cousin. "Seems like they turned out all right."

"Oh, sure. The boys are a peck of trouble, but the girls, they're fine. You didn't meet Johnetta yet. She'll come over after she gets the bus drove. She's something, she's the type to get her money back." Sugar laughs. "She would have climbed over the rope to *see* if it was two cows sewed together."

Alice has on her jogging shoes, and she is used to getting where she needs to go, but she has to shorten her stride for Sugar, who seems to get winded easily. "You could get a big bowl of soup for five cents," Alice argues. "You couldn't just throw away a nickel."

"No. Still can't."

The two women walk through the shade, their elbows occasionally touching. Whenever they pass a little house and yard mowed out of the woods, Sugar waves at the people on the porch. They are liable to be of any age. a grandmother plucking greens from a bucket, or a man in his twenties with black, greased hands, kneeling over an engine as if he's about to deliver a baby out of it. And kids, by the score. They all wave back, calling Sugar by name. She has already introduced Alice to dozens of people, who seem to know already about Alice. Their names stilt and lean in her head like pictures from an old-time children's book: Pathkiller, Grass, Deal, Still-water, Doublehead. Often she can't tell first names from last, or where the grandmother's name let off and the children's began. The young man with the engine is Able Swimmer. All of them seem to be related to Sugar through marriage or some catastrophe, or frequently both. Sugar is telling her right now, for instance, "Flossie Deal and I were at the courthouse in Tahlequah the day her son fell off the hotel they was building and busted his insides. Her other boy married Quatie's husband's sister."

Sugar slows her pace even more as they head uphill, and sighs a little.

"I loved that State Fair. Seems like ever time we went and sat in them bleachers, there wouldn't be a cloud in the sky."

"They had two fairs. First the State Fair, and after that the Black State Fair."

"Really? I never knew it was divided up."

Alice recalls that she used to find her beloved cousin sometimes naïve and in need of protection. "We only went to the second one. We liked it best, there was more music to it."

"There was. And the church floats."

"People dressed to beat the band, with hats and all. I liked all the hats."

"Remember those children that dressed like angels?"

Alice thinks. "No. I remember women dressed like bluebirds, in blue high-heeled oxfords. And I remember when they'd turn on those street-lights that were like light bulbs under fluted pie plates, and we'd dance in the street."

"Don't you remember those children? They'd sing 'When the Saints Go Marching In.' I just loved that."

Sugar and Alice pass by a dwelling that looks slightly more prosperous than most, though less interesting: a yellow brick rectangle set in a huge, flat lawn with nothing planted in it. A riding mower preens in the carport. "That's Les and June Courcy's, they're white," Sugar says, with neither favor nor disapproval, as if she'd simply said, "There goes a white rooster across the road." The two women walk on.

The land is steep. Everywhere Alice looks she sees long, dark loaves of hill cut with forested hollows. Around the houses, almost everyone has a goat to keep down the underbrush, although once in a while a front yard will sport an old orange mower alongside the satellite dish.

As they crest the hill, they're faced suddenly with a long mowed field surrounded by white fences, exactly like the horse farms Alice has seen in Kentucky. A brass sign on the white gate says HIDEAWAY FARMS. The shining asphalt drive trails proudly up the knoll to a stone house trimmed in white. The brass knocker on the front door is huge, as if to suggest you ought to be a fairly good-sized person to bother those within. Alice asks, "What's that place, racehorses?"

"Ostriches," Sugar replies.

Alice laughs at her cousin's sense of humor. "They get a good price for the meat?" she asks.

"No, the feathers. For ladies' hats and things."

Alice stares, but Sugar is not smiling. In fact, she looks irritated. "Ostriches?" Alice asks. "An ostrich farm?"

"That's what I'm a-telling you."

"Who ever heard of the like?"

"I never did," Sugar admits, "before this fellow name of Green come in from New Mexico or New Hampshire, one of the newer states, and says you can get rich on raising ostriches. He's been trying to get the state government in on it. The thing is, though, you have to be rich to *start* with, to raise ostriches. They cost you around twenty thousand dollar for a pair, just to set up housekeeping."

"Lord," Alice states. "Every feather on their hide must be worth a thousand."

"That's about it. The fellow was trying to sell the eggs for a hundred dollar, telling people around here they could hatch them out and get into the business that way." Sugar starts to giggle. She holds her fist in front of her mouth. "Roscoe's friend Cash, that just moved back here from Wyoming, told the man he'd buy one if Mr. Green would promise to set on it himself."

Alice feels intensely curious. She has never seen an ostrich, and combs the ridge for the sight of sassy tail feathers and a long pink neck, but she sees only velvet grass. "I don't reckon they're out today," she says at last, disappointed.

"Oh, you see them, some days," Sugar insists. "The kids like to pester them to pieces, to try and get them to run. Or spit, I heard they'll spit if they're mad. I don't know that a bird could spit, but they're an odd bird. They don't bury their heads, that's just a tale. Mr. Green says he's going to shoot the kids with rock salt, and that's *not* a tale, he'll do it. He said out loud in the grocery he'd like to see Boma Mellowbug drop dead tomorrow."

"Who?"

"Boma Mellowbug." Sugar nods at a great ramshackle house nested into the woods just over the fence from Hideaway Farms. The house itself is small, composed of wooden shingles, but it has many things tacked onto it to increase the living quarters, such as a school bus, very rusted. Alice can see chairs and a stovepipe inside the bus, and so many plants growing in there that their leaves jam against the windows and windshield like greenhouse plants. Horse trailers and refrigerators are parked in the yard among the huckleberry bushes. A trio of hens step primly around the splayed, spotted legs of a dead-looking beagle.

"What's the man got against Boma?" Alice asks, though she can guess. The white fence between the two properties could be the Iron Curtain. It's not clear to Alice, though, which country she'd want as her own, if she had to choose.

"Well, mostly he hates her bees. She's got bees living in her roof. He says they're going to kill his birds, but they wouldn't. They're good bees if you love them, and Boma does. A bird wouldn't know enough to hate a bee, I don't think. Do you?"

Alice has already decided that Heaven is a hard stone's throw beyond her ken. "I wouldn't know," she says, which is the truth. Nothing in her life has prepared her to make a judgment on a war between bees and ostriches. As they walk slowly past Boma's mailbox, which has been fashioned from a length of drainpipe and a wire egg basket, Alice hears the faint, distant thrum of the hive. She makes up her mind that for as long as her mission takes, on this stretch of Heaven's road at least, it would be a good idea to love Boma's bees.

FALL
SGƆS

21

SKID ROAD

TAYLOR TURNS THE HANDI-VAN UP Yesler Way, climbing the long hill above the waterfront. The streets are lined with dapple-trunked sycamores. From between the buildings come sliced glimpses of cold-looking water. A blind passenger in the seat behind her is telling Taylor about how she is forgetting the colors. She has lost all of them now but blue. "I *think* I recall blue," the woman says, "but I haven't seen it for forty years, so I have no idea how far off track I might really be."

Taylor stops carefully at a light. This morning she made a hard stop at a railroad crossing, and someone's seeing-eye dog slid all the way up the aisle from the back. She could hear the toenails scraping over the grooves in the rubber floor mat. After the van had come to a respectable standstill, the dog simply got up and walked back to the rear of the van, making Taylor feel terrible, the way people do when you step on their toes and they sigh but don't say a word.

"I never thought about that, that you might forget colors," Taylor says, trying to concentrate on her driving and also be friendly to the blind passenger, although this conversation is depressing her deeply. She recognizes the woman as a regular: Tuesdays and Fridays, for dialysis.

"Oh, you do, you forget," the woman insists. "It's not like forgetting somebody's name. It's more like you have in mind your idea of a certain color but it might drift, you know. The same way you can drift off the note a little bit when you're singing."

Taylor's radio comes on in a fit of static and demands to know her location.

"I just plussed at Pioneer Square and I'm ten-nineteen to Martin Luther King," she says. "I have two minuses at Swedish Hospital."

"Okay, Taylor, ten–twenty-seven after that," says the radio.

"Ten-four," she replies.

To get the job with Handi-Van, Taylor only needed a good driving record, a Washington State license, and three weeks of training, plus a course in CPR. The hardest part was learning to use the radio code, which she still feels is unnecessary. It doesn't actually save syllables, in Taylor's opinion; for instance, "ten–twenty-seven" is no easier to say than "return to base." It's probably less embarrassing to say "ten-twelve" than "I need a bathroom break," but the code doesn't keep any secrets, she has discovered. Yesterday the radio announced a 10-161, and all six of her passengers looked up and asked anxiously, "What's that?" Taylor had to read the code display on her sun visor to find out it meant an intersection obstructed by an injured animal. She could imagine every Handi-Van driver in the city looking up at the sun visor on that one.

On her way up Yesler, Taylor passes her own apartment, which resides in a long brown box of a building with twenty identical doors in the front, spaced every twenty feet or so like boxcars. The apartment is gloomy, with battle-scarred linoleum and precariously thin walls and neighbors on both sides who shout a lot in what sounds like Chinese; sometimes Taylor gets the feeling the two sets of neighbors are shouting at *each other,* using her apartment as a conduit for curses or strange instructions. But it's a roof over their heads, for now, and she's feeling more optimistic about finances. It took only about two-thirds of the $1,200 Alice gave her to pay the first month, get the lights on and move in. The rest she hid away inside a plastic cube on her night table that has family photos smiling on all six sides—Jax and Turtle back home in the Retarded Desert; Jax wearing his swimsuit and a paper bag over his head; a very old snapshot of Alice shelling out lima beans; that kind of thing. Taylor figures that's the last household object on earth a burglar would steal. Barbie is still with them, and was partly responsible for their winding up here; she insists the Pacific Northwest is on the verge of becoming very popular. She also agreed to use some of her loot to help cover expenses. For the time being, Barbie looks after Turtle in the daytime, and starting this week, Taylor is making eight dollars an hour.

She has decided she likes this city, which seems like Tucson's opposite, a place where no one will ever think to look for them. Bodies of water lie along every side, and snowy, triangular mountains crouch on the horizon, helping her to orient her mind's compass needle as she winds through unfamiliar city streets. Several times each day she has to drive the van across the lake on one of the floating bridges that bob like a long, narrow barge. Apparently they couldn't anchor them, as is usual with bridge construction, because the lakes are too silty and deep to sink concrete roots into. Taylor got this information and a world of other facts from Kevin, a fellow Handi-Van driver who has asked Taylor seven or eight times if she would like to go out with him. Kevin doesn't exactly float her boat; he's a pinkish young man whose jeans always appear brand new and never quite fit him. Kevin's main outside interest seems to be the pale mustache he is trying to grow. He talks in radio code even when he's off duty. In spite of all this, Taylor is about to relent. It's been so long since she had any fun she's afraid she'll forget how. The next time she talks to Jax, she wouldn't mind telling him she was dating someone. She makes her decision while she is helping the woman who has forgotten color find her way to the fire-engine-red door of the hospital: this Saturday, Taylor and Turtle will go somewhere with Kevin. If he didn't have Turtle in mind, that's his tough luck. He can go along with the idea, or he can turn himself around and 10-27.

Barbie and Turtle are out on the tiny patio behind the kitchen when Taylor gets home from work. Barbie has on a pink bikini and is lying on a bedspread, working on her tan. She looks like some kind of exotic bird tragically trapped in a rotten cage. Taylor slides open the stubborn glass door and drags out one of the falling-apart kitchen chairs, reminding herself to borrow a screwdriver and some screws from the garage at work. The late-afternoon light seems too weak to penetrate human skin, but it's the first time they've seen the sun in two rainy weeks, and Barbie claims she can't miss her window of opportunity. She says her tan is an important element of her personal identity. She has put Turtle to work cutting out gold foil stars and gluing them onto a short denim skirt Barbie found at a store called Second Hand Rose.

"That's going to fall apart the first time you wash it," Taylor observes.

Turtle stops cutting out stars. She lays the scissors carefully on the cracked concrete patio and comes over to sit on Taylor's lap.

"Oh, I know *that*." Barbie is lying facedown and her voice is muffled. "I just won't ever wash it. See, Taylor, this is costuming, it's not like regular clothes."

As far as Taylor can see, everything Barbie wears is a costume. "What happens if it gets dirty?"

Barbie turns over on her side, looking a little peeved. "I'm careful, okay?"

"Okay. It's your skirt."

"This is going to be the All American ensemble," Barbie says patiently. "It goes with a red-and-white-striped halter top and a lace petticoat. It's just come out, we saw it today when we were scouting out what's new in the Barbie section. I'm like, this is so perfect, but it's not going to be easy to get lace like that. That's going to be a challenge."

Taylor is tuning out; she's learned when to stop listening to Barbie. She knows she won't get a quiz later on the All American ensemble. Kevin, the computer whiz, would say that Barbie is all output and no interface. Taylor strokes Turtle's hair. She's wearing the same green overalls she wore on the Oprah Winfrey show, though they are a good deal the worse for a summer of wear, and, Taylor notices, they're short in the leg and tight around the middle. Her toes have grown an inch or two past the ends of her sneakers; Taylor was horrified to realize Turtle was doubling up her toes in there, without complaint. Now she's wearing Barbie's size-six yellow flip-flops. She'll have to have new clothes before she starts school in a week and a half. More costs. Taylor feels defeated. If only Barbie's wardrobe talents could be put to civilian use.

"What did you do today?" she asks Turtle. "Besides scouting out the toy store and cutting out stars?"

"Nothing."

Taylor doesn't consider Barbie the ideal baby-sitter, but she's obviously short on choices. She hopes school will begin before Turtle gets warped by the world of fashion design. "You want to go to the beach or something on Saturday?" she asks.

"Yes." Turtle leans back against Taylor's chest. She takes both Taylor's hands in hers and crosses them in front of her.

"I've decided to go out with Kevin," she tells Barbie.

"Who?" Barbie asks, with genuine interest.

"That rabbity guy from work. Just mainly so he'll quit asking."

"Oh, right, Taylor. Like going out with somebody is a real wonderful way to give him the message you're not interested."

"I see your point."

"Did you bring a newspaper?" Barbie asks.

"I forgot."

"Taylor! This is, like, the fiftieth time I've asked you. I wanted to look at the want ads."

"For a waitress job? But think about it, it's not worth it. You won't make as much as I'd have to pay for baby-sitting."

Turtle glances up at Taylor, her dark eyes showing a rim of white below the pupils and her mouth tucked like a made bed.

"Oh, I can make money all right," Barbie says. "And I don't mean waitress-ing, either. All I need is some job in an office with a color Xerox machine."

Taylor is afraid to ask for more details on this scheme, so she doesn't. But after a minute Barbie rolls over on her back and half sits up, so that the muscles form ridges in her narrow abdomen. She shades her eyes and looks at Taylor peculiarly.

"You want to know why I left Bakersfield?"

"You said there weren't enough career opportunities for Barbie look-alikes."

"Well, I lied," Barbie says flatly, her voice stripped of its usual friendly effort. "I was wanted for counterfeiting."

"Counterfeiting *money?*"

"What else can you counterfeit? Duh."

"How?"

"A color Xerox machine. It's so easy. Just come into the office a little early, lay out some twenties on the glass, copy them front and back, and blammo, you're ready to go shopping."

Taylor stares. "Are you kidding me?"

"Listen, I don't know why everybody in the world isn't doing this. My boss only found out because I left some messed-up bills in the trash once."

Taylor feels a little shaky. In these moments when Barbie's surface cracks, the feelings inside seem powerful and terrifying. Taylor wonders what it must have taken to turn someone's regular daughter into such a desperate, picture-perfect loner.

"Isn't that a federal crime?" she asks.

Barbie examines the end of her ponytail. "Oh, probably. I don't know."

"Are we going to start seeing your picture in the Post Office?"

"No way." She flips the ponytail behind her back and lies down again. "My boss won't press charges. I'd tell his wife what he tried to pull on me one day in his office."

Taylor glances down at Turtle, who unfortunately is taking everything in. "I don't think it's your boss you have to worry about. I think it's the U.S. Treasury Department."

"Well, don't you think they've got *criminals* to catch? I mean, it's not like I murdered somebody. I just stimulated the economy."

Taylor is never sure when to argue with Barbie, who behaves like a tourist from another solar system who only read a toy catalog before arriving here. You can't argue with someone like that about family values. But Taylor wishes Turtle weren't hearing this. The casino robbery seemed adventurous, like piracy or Robin Hood, but photocopying money sounds like a simple crime of greed.

Barbie, with her eyes carefully closed, presumably to get an even tan on her eyelids, feels around for the plastic glass near her elbow and rattles the ice cubes into her mouth.

"So why did you leave Bakersfield?" Taylor asks.

"They started putting up these signs in all the shopping malls, like 'Warning, warning!' I guess they started noticing the bills in their cash registers. Maybe when they tried to turn them in to the bank. I don't know. So I'm like, forget this! I have to leave town just to spend my money!"

Taylor doesn't know what to say. She would try to argue with Barbie, but she is bone-tired from driving the Handi-Van all day, strapping down wheelchairs and engaging in powerfully depressing conversations and enduring the superiority of seeing-eye dogs. She feels oppressed now by the ugly concrete patio. It's hardly big enough for a dog to turn around in, with a high brown fence separating it from the identical patios of the neighbors. She wonders if the color scheme of brown is some sort of international code for poverty. It would be more cheerful back here if she had a few plants, at least. A red geranium in a pot, or a tomato plant, something to use the free sunshine and give something back. But it will be weeks before they have even three extra dollars to spend on something like that. In the meantime, she thinks, who knows? Maybe Barbie has the right idea. Use the free sunshine yourself. Use whatever comes your way.

On Saturday, Kevin and Taylor and Turtle buy ice-cream cones in Pioneer Square to celebrate Taylor's first paycheck. Taylor is not in a party mood: the check was much smaller than she expected, after what fell out for taxes and Social Security. She's working full time, and has no idea how she's going to cover both rent and food, unless Barbie helps. She's not crazy about using Barbie's money, either, considering the source.

"Look, Turtle, lick the side toward you. Like this." Taylor licks the crown of her own pistachio cone to demonstrate. Turtle nods, but goes right on turning her ice cream cone upside-down to lick the opposite side. A growing dampness is spreading outward from her chin onto her T-shirt like a full, green beard. Kevin, inscrutable as a traffic cop in his mirrored aviator sunglasses, has been ignoring Turtle.

It's a hot day, but the sycamore trees, with their mottled brown-and-white trunks leaning like the necks of tired giraffes, seem to know it's almost fall. Their leaves are browning mournfully at the edges, starting to give up the ghost. Quite a few have already fallen. They curl together in piles like brown-paper lunch bags, and Turtle kicks up noisy crowds of them as the three cross through the little park under a wrought-iron gazebo. Listless men and women sit on the benches in every kind of clothing—some in grubby overcoats, some in thin cotton trousers—but still they seem alike, with weathered faces and matted hair, as if these clothing styles were all variations of the uniform of homelessness. Kevin leads Taylor away from the benches toward the street, past a parked car that must have come from somewhere less rainy because it is covered in a deep tan fur of dust. Someone has written WASH ME across the rear window. Kevin takes this opportunity to explain to Taylor that the eastern part of the state is a virtual desert.

"Mom, here," Turtle says, holding up the lumpy remains of her ice cream.

"What, don't you want the rest of it?"

"I don't like ice cream."

"Turtle, sure you do. It's good for you. It's got calcium and helps your bones grow. Who ever heard of a kid that didn't like ice cream?"

Turtle looks at her mother with sorrowful eyes.

"Okay, there's a garbage can." Taylor takes the sodden offering and throws it away.

They cross the street in the shadow of a huge totem pole that overlooks the park. Taylor thinks for the first time in several days of Annawake Fourkiller. She imagines being quizzed on which kind of Indians carved totem poles, which ones lived in teepees, which ones hunted buffalo, which ones taught the Pilgrims to put two fish in the bottom of the hole with each corn plant. She feels ashamed. She has no idea what she should be telling Turtle about her ancestors. These days she hardly has the energy to tell her to eat right and get to bed on time.

"Yesler Way used to be called Skid Road," Kevin explains. Taylor notes that the green ice cream on his mustache makes it more noticeable. "They changed the name recently. This was actually the original skid row. In the old logging days they skidded the logs down this hill to the waterfront, to load them onto the ships, and I guess it was kind of a natural congregating place for out-of-work loggers, looking for a handout." He laughs thinly. "As you can see, it still is."

Across the street from them, some formidable paintings of Jesus adorn the windows of a storefront soup kitchen. Turtle pulls Taylor forward stickily by the finger, up the hill toward the imagined beach.

"I can't believe this sun," Taylor declares. "Two days in a row, even. I was starting to go crazy with all the rain."

"They thought changing the name of the street might clean the place up," Kevin says. "It doesn't help that those projects are right on the other side of the hill."

Kevin doesn't know that Taylor lives in one of the so-called projects. Kevin lives with his parents. His eight dollars an hour minus taxes goes mostly for home-computer equipment, from what Taylor gathers.

To reach Kevin's car they cross through another small park with two more totem poles: a gigantic wooden dog and man, facing each other with outstretched arms. They might be tossing an imaginary ball, but they don't seem happy. Their open, painted mouths are enormous, as if they might swallow the world. Taylor's eyes slip toward a woman on a bench with two stunned-looking children beside her. The woman has swollen knuckles and a stained red blouse and she bluntly follows Taylor with her eyes. Taylor looks down, feeling exactly as if she were carrying something stolen in her hands.

In Kevin's sleek blue Camaro they continue the travelogue up Yesler. "That's the Smith Tower," he says, "the white building with the pointy top. That would be the oldest skyscraper west of the Mississippi."

"Would be?"

"Is, I mean."

Taylor says nothing. They pass a grocery-deli, the school that will soon require Turtle's attendance, and a lot of signs in Chinese, then turn onto Martin Luther King Way, where the frame houses have peaked roofs and little yards of leggy flowers. She knows these streets. A man on her route goes to Rogers Thriftway every other day for Coca-Cola Classic, microwave popcorn, and Depends. Kevin doesn't have to tell Taylor that just a few blocks away, closer to the lakeshore and farther from Skid Road, the property values skid upward rather drastically.

They take Rainier Avenue south into a neighborhood where Taylor can't read any of the signs. Thai and Chinese, according to Kevin. "You wouldn't want to live down here," he says from behind his mirrored lenses, "but they have great noodle soup at that Mekong place."

"We lucked out with this sun," Taylor says. "I don't know if I'll ever get used to how cloudy it is here. I was thinking I might get that disease the Eskimos get from not seeing the sun enough. Where they go insane and start eating up their shoes."

"Never heard of that one," Kevin says, running a hand through the side of his white-blond hair. "Now this is the place to live."

Taylor can't argue. The lakefront neighborhood is breath-taking: elaborate houses with cedar-shake roofs and gardens of bonsai and flowering trees in the yards, banked steeply down to the street. It seems like you might need a passport to come over here from the other side of the hill.

They get out of the car and cross a long grassy area to the lake. Turtle is excited. She didn't have a swimsuit, but Barbie, in a generous moment, sacrificed a piece of blue lamé she'd been saving for a Prom Date ensemble, and turned out a bikini with impressive speed. Taylor had argued against a bikini for a six-year-old, but Barbie ignored her. Turtle runs ahead of them now, her feet flapping duckishly in Barbie's thongs. She pulls off her T-shirt as she goes, revealing a bony brown torso and two puffy bands of shiny blue fabric. She looks like a Mardi Gras dropout. With Taylor in tow she climbs down the concrete steps into the lake and stands knee deep on the pebbly bottom looking up with knocking knees and joy on her face.

"You like that?"

Turtle breathes in through shivering teeth, and nods.

"It's not too cold? I'm going to pull you out when your lips get as blue as your swimsuit."

"Okay," Turtle agrees, hugging herself.

"Kevin and I will be right over there, and I'll be watching you, okay? Stay here where the other kids are. Don't go any deeper."

Turtle shakes her head vigorously.

Taylor retreats to the beach towel Kevin has spread in the sun, without ever taking her eye off Turtle. Kids of every color run around her, screaming and jumping off the steps, but Turtle is immobile except for her shivers, only watching.

"Doesn't she know how to play in the water?" Kevin asks.

"She always takes a minute to get her bearings."

"So, is she one of these adopted Koreans, or what?" Kevin pulls four different tubes of sunscreen and an apple from his backpack and bites into the apple.

"She's adopted, yeah." Taylor sees her own stunned face in his reflectors, stupefied by the rudeness of a person who would bring a single apple on an outing with other people. Her shock doesn't seem to penetrate the lenses to sink into Kevin.

"Well, don't knock it," he says. "At least those people are industrious."

Taylor wasn't about to knock it. She would like to change the subject, though.

"I went out with a Korean girl once," he says. "I repeat, once. She was the valedictorian of our high school class. Kind of pretty. But Christ, what a tragedy, that family. You should see where they lived. Mung Bean Row."

Taylor unpacks the sandwiches she brought to share. She seriously resents having spent fifty-five cents on a can of tuna for this guy, after she and Turtle ate peanut-butter sandwiches all week. "Don't you think it might be possible to be a decent person but still not get anywhere?" she asks.

"Oh, sure. Some people are just not born with all that much upstairs. But Christ, if you know how to turn on the water faucet you can clean yourself up, is what I always say."

Taylor's stomach feels tight, like the beginning of a twenty-four-hour flu. She passes it off as merely a growing hatred of Kevin and nerves about Turtle in the water. In her mind she calculates the number of seconds it would take her to bound across the grass and down the steps, if Turtle should slip under.

"You know what I mean," Kevin says, with his mouth full of apple. "With all the opportunities that are available, and somebody's still sitting around staring at his navel on a park bench, you've got to admit they must be that way partly out of personal choice."

He should have gone out with Barbie, Taylor thinks. *The two of them could jabber at each other all day without ever risking human conversation.* She watches Turtle climb slowly onto the lowest step and jump back into the water, landing stiff-legged, following the lead of two tiny girls whose swimsuits are nearly as strange as hers. Taylor wants to tell her to bend her knees when she lands.

"You like tuna salad?" she asks Kevin.

"Okay," Kevin says, wolfing down the sandwich without looking at it, then licking his fingers with an appearance of slight distaste. He wipes his hands on his cutoffs and carefully takes off his sunglasses in order to rub clear, glossy sunscreen that smells like dog shampoo onto his face. He uses a different tube, white stuff, for his arms and legs. Taylor watches with very mild amazement. He pulls off his shirt and hands Taylor still *another* tube, marked Number 28.

"A lot of it's just poor money-management skills," he says, lying belly down on the towel, crossing his arms under his chin. "Know what I mean? Could you be real careful with the sunscreen? Don't miss any spots. One time I missed a little triangle on the bottom part of my back and it was there for the entire summer and fall."

"Poor money-management skills?"

"Well, yeah. It's a matter of putting in the effort, and being careful what you spend, right? And just having the basic attitude of going out and getting what you want."

"If you can dream it," Taylor says, "you can be it." She toys with the tube of sunscreen in her hands, reaching a conclusion that makes her stomach feel better instantly.

"Basically, that's the American reality," Kevin says. He closes his eyes and looks as if he plans to sleep.

Taylor rubs dry hands over Kevin's sweaty back, taking her time, until he begins to snore softly. Then she opens the tube of sunscreen, applies it to one finger, and carefully writes across his back: WASH ME.

The apartment is dark when they get home. Taylor clicks on all the lights to try to make herself feel less dark inside. "I guess Barbie went out, huh?"

"She probably went to get some Cheese Doritos with her pocketbook money," Turtle says.

"That's a safe bet. You feel like a peanut-butter sandwich? We'll go to the grocery tomorrow, I promise. I've got a paycheck, babycakes! We can buy anything we want."

"Chocolate cookies!"

"Lamb chops!" Taylor says.

"What's that?"

"Lamb. You know, baby sheep."

"Does it hurt the lamb to chop it?"

Taylor closes the refrigerator door, reluctantly. There is hardly anything inside, but she doesn't want to lose the light. Turtle is standing in the doorway, her eyebrows raised in their permanent question mark.

"Yeah," Taylor says. "I'm afraid it does. I don't know that it *hurts* the animals a lot, but they do kill them, before we eat them. That's where meat comes from. Didn't I ever tell you that?"

Turtle shrugs. "I guess."

"So how about peanut butter and strawberry jam?"

"Do they kill the peanuts so we can eat them?"

"No." Taylor thinks about this. "Well, yeah. I guess. A peanut isn't an animal, though."

"No, it's a plant. It's a seed. If we eat it, it doesn't get to grow up."

"Turtle, this is too sad. We can't just give up on eating. Let me make you a sandwich."

"Mom, I'm not hungry."

"At least a glass of milk, then, okay? They didn't kill anything to get milk, they just drained it out of a happy old mama cow."

"Mom, my tummy hurts."

"Okay, sweetheart. Go get ready for bed, if you want. I'll read you a book."

"We read all the books already."

"Back to the library tomorrow then. Promise."

Turtle leaves the kitchen. Taylor's stomach has begun hurting again, too. The sky outside the kitchen window is the shade of dark blue a blind person might imagine.

Turtle is back in the doorway, big-eyed. "Mom, why's it so clean in here?"

Taylor tries to understand. She follows Turtle into the living room. "I'll be darned, Barbie finally got in the mood to pick up all her stuff."

They are both quiet for a minute, not wanting to look any farther. Then Turtle goes to the door of Barbie's room.

"She cleaned up her room, too," Turtle says. "She took the sheets and everything."

"Damn it!" Taylor says. She sits on the broken brown sofa and tries hard not to cry. Those sheets were Taylor's; she brought them all the way from Tucson.

"Did she leave a note, Turtle?"

For a long time there is only the sound of Turtle opening and closing dresser drawers. She comes back to the living room. "No note," she says. "Remember when we found that note on our car? That said I'm sorry I didn't see you at Migget's and here's fifty dollars?"

Taylor begins to laugh or cry, she's not sure which. "Yeah," she says. "Barbie should have left us a note like that, don't you think?"

Turtle sits next to Taylor on the sofa, but stares into the darkness. "Mom, did I make her mad?"

Taylor pulls Turtle onto her lap. "Turtle, you had nothing to do with this. Look at me now, okay?" She strokes Turtle's hair and gently turns her head toward her. "Look at my eyes. Can you look at me? Don't go away."

With a great effort Turtle pulls her focus out of the darkness and fixes it on Taylor's face.

"That's it. Stay right here with me, and listen. Barbie liked you. She's just a nut case. She's the kind of person that can only think about herself, and she just decided she had to move on. We always knew that, remember? We decided we'd give her a ride that time in Las Vegas, but we always knew she wasn't going to come with us the whole way. Remember?"

Turtle nods.

Taylor rocks back and forth with Turtle in her arms. "Don't worry, you know I'm not going to leave you alone. You'll stay with me. Tomorrow's

Sunday, I don't have to go to work. And maybe on Monday they'll let you ride the van with me. You can help me drive, okay?"

"I don't know how to drive."

"I know, but we'll think of something." Taylor has no earthly idea what they'll think of. She knows it's against every regulation of the Handi-Van company to bring family members on board.

"Before you know it you're going to be starting first grade," she says.

"Mom, remember Lucky Buster?"

"I sure do."

"I saved him, right?"

"You saved his life."

"Will we ever see him again?"

"I don't see why not. Sure."

Turtle relaxes her hold on Taylor just a little.

"You think we should get ready for bed? I think it's past my bedtime too," Taylor says. She exhales deeply when Turtle finally releases her and goes into their room.

Taylor gets up and turns out all the lights. She doesn't want to look in Barbie's room, but she has to, to make herself believe. Sure enough, even the double bed is stripped down to the ugly blue-striped mattress. At least now she and Turtle can have separate rooms, Taylor thinks—she'll move in here and let Turtle have the room with the twin beds for herself. She will meet friends in school, and invite them over. They will be a normal American family. Taylor is less optimistic about her own possibilities for sharing the double bed. She misses Jax.

By the time she goes in to kiss Turtle goodnight, Turtle is in her in-between sleeptalking stage.

"Buster has to go home, Mom, this one in the water."

"Goodnight, Turtle. Sleep tight."

"My tummy hurts. Do those trees real or the dog was talking. Is it raining?"

"Yeah," Taylor says softly. "It's starting to rain again."

She undresses and climbs into the other twin bed. She'll have to figure out how to get new sheets for the double bed before she can move into the other bedroom. There is a lot more than too much to think about. She never imagined it would be this much of a problem to lose Barbie from her life. She should have known better. You don't adopt a wild animal and count it as family. Before Taylor turns off the light, she reaches over to her nightstand to take a look at Jax in his paper-bag ensemble.

The photo cube is gone.

22

WELCOME TO

HEAVEN

"WELL, TAYLOR, YOU'VE BROUGHT YOUR pigs to a pretty market. How'd you lose your telephone?"

"Not the phone, Mama, the electricity. They couldn't shut the phone off because I didn't even have one yet. This number where you just called me back is a pay phone."

"Oh," Alice says, shifting the receiver. She's about decided her bad ear hears better than the good one. "Well, what's this other number I've got written down here?"

"That's the Handi-Van number. What I'm trying to tell you is you can't call me there anymore because I had to quit."

Alice is confused. It doesn't help that Sugar keeps coming in and out of the living room to ask questions. And this living room is crowded with enough furniture for two or three households. When Alice first peered into Sugar's huge china cabinet, she expected to see fancy dishes or Jesus stuff, but it isn't, it's Indian things of every kind. Old carvings, arrowheads, tacky little ceramic Indian boys. At least no headlamps.

"You quit that handicap job?" Alice asks, when it sinks in, what Taylor has just told her. "After you got trained in artificial retrucidation and everything?"

"Yeah, I had to, because Barbie left. There was nobody to take care of Turtle during my shift. I asked if I could take the week off, just till school started, but I was still on probation so they said they had to let me go."

"Well, that don't seem right."

"I know. It's okay. I just got hired as a cashier at Penney's. At least now after school Turtle can come here and hang out in Ladies' Wear till I get off work." Taylor laughs. "Until somebody gets wise and figures out that Turtle isn't going to buy any designer jeans."

A tall, thin girl with very long hair tromps through the front door and shouts, "Grandma!"

Sugar comes running. "What in the world?"

"Mama says you're not supposed to dance if you're on your period. I think that's an old wives' tale."

"Well, honey, it's all old wives' tales, if you think about it. I don't have your shackles done yet, anyway. Come here, I'll show you how far I've got."

The girl slumps on the couch. Alice is having a hard time concentrating. "Well," she tells Taylor, "you've been wanting to get shed of that Barbie since the day we run into her."

"I know. But I kind of needed her."

Sugar comes back carrying what looks like two masses of terrapin shells. They rattle heavily when she sits down with them on the couch next to her granddaughter.

"What's your new job like?" Alice asks.

"Above minimum wage, at least. Barely. It will come to around six hundred a month, I think, after what they take out. That's going to pay our rent and buy about three jars of peanut butter, but it's not going to get the utilities turned back on. I've got to figure out something else pretty soon. But at least I got a discount on school clothes for Turtle. She's starting first grade, Mama. Can you believe it?"

"You bought school clothes for Turtle instead of paying the electric bill?"

"Mama, I had to. I didn't want kids making fun of her. She looked like something off the streets."

"So I guess it's better to *be* out in the street than to *look* like something off the streets."

Taylor is quiet, and Alice feels terrible, understanding that what she just said is no joke. It's the truth. They are both stunned. A good deal of quiet static washes over the line before either one of them is willing to talk again.

"We're not living in the streets," Taylor finally says. "*Yet.* Mama, I feel bad enough, you don't have to tell me I've messed up."

"I'm sorry, Taylor. I hate to see you like this. Why don't you just come on down here and get it over with?"

"Mama, we don't even have gas money. And I'm not asking you to send any, either, because I know you left me all you had."

"What happened to that? The twelve hundred?"

"It's hard to explain. It's gone. It took most of it to get us moved into an apartment, because you have to pay a deposit and everything."

Alice senses that what Taylor just told her isn't completely true. But she lets it go. Trust only grows out of trusting.

"Have you met with that Annawake Fourkiller yet?" Taylor asks, her voice changed.

"I'm seeing her tomorrow. I'm so nervous I'm chasing my tail." Alice glances at Sugar and the girl, who are hunched together on the couch with the bright Oklahoma morning blazing in the window over their heads. Alice lowers her voice. "I didn't tell anybody yet, you know, what this is all about. I thought they'd make me spill the beans right off, but seems like people are willing to bide their time down here. They're all talking about me, seems like. Maybe they've all got their own explanations so they don't need mine."

"How'd you track down Miss Fourkiller?"

"There wasn't nothing to it. She just lives over here at Tahlequah, a little bit down the road. Everybody here knows everybody. I just called her up."

"What did she say?"

"Nothing. Just thanks for coming. She wants to buy me lunch and talk things over. She said she's been real worried about you and Turtle."

"I'll bet."

The girl gets up from the couch and goes. "Bye, Grandma," she calls, over the shriek of the screen-door hinge.

"Well, she could be," Alice says. "I'm not taking her side, but she sounded like she could be real worried."

"Don't tell her where we are, okay?"

"Taylor, honey, all you've given me is a phone number of a pay phone. For all I know you're at the North Pole."

"If we were, maybe Santa Claus would pull some strings and get our lights turned back on."

Alice feels the familiar deep frustration of loving someone by telephone. She wants to hug Taylor more than anything, and can't. So much voice and so little touch seems unnatural, like it could turn your skin inside out if you're not careful.

"Well, anyway, good luck when you talk to her, Mama. I better hang up on you now before you buy the phone company."

"Don't worry about it. I'm just putting it on Sugar's bill. She said we could work it out later on."

"Okay, Mama. Bye."

Alice waits. "Bye," she says, and then, "I love you," but the clear space at the other end of the line that held Taylor has already closed.

She sits slumped in the chair, feeling paralyzed. She feels the faces of Sugar's many grandchildren smiling at her from their frames on the wall. The ones who finished high school—mostly girls—Sugar has hung in the top row; below them, like a row of straight teeth, are the handsome, smiling, tricky-looking boys.

Sugar looks up. "Alice, honey, you look like you just run over your dog. How's that girl of yours?"

"She's all right. Having trouble making her payments."

"Isn't that the way," Sugar says, sounding as if this were an old joke. "Come over here and I'll show you what I'm making for Reena."

Alice sits next to Sugar and has a look: terrapin shells with holes drilled in them, and gravel rattling inside. "It's her shackles for the stomp dance," Sugar says. "The young girls wear them on their legs. She thinks it's the cat's meow. Most of the kids would just as soon go to the powwows, where they can drink beer, but Reena's real interested in the stomp dance."

Alice takes one of the shackles in her hands. It's surprisingly heavy. The fist-sized shells are sewn with leather thongs to the cut-off top of a cowboy boot, to make a sort of bumpy legging. The whole thing laces up the front with strips of gingham.

"Don't she get tired with all that weight on her legs?" Alice asks, not really seeing the point.

"Well, she'll have to practice. They wrap towels around their legs before they put them on, so they won't blister. These are training shackles, four shells on each one. As she gets better at it we'll add more, till she gets up to thirteen."

Alice hears the cough of a reluctant lawn mower starting up, then dying. "Why thirteen?"

Sugar thinks. "I don't know. Maybe Roscoe would know. That's just the number." She stands and looks outside, shading her eyes. "There's one of the grandkids come to cut my grass. I can't tell which one. You want some hot coffee?"

"No thanks," Alice says. "I'm jumpy enough already."

Sugar looks at her. "You are. Let's go take a walk down to the blue hole. You need to look at some water."

Alice is amazed by her cousin. Sugar is bent over with arthritis and doesn't move fast, but she never seems to stop moving. Today she is wearing a flowered apron that looks like a seed catalog, and cotton slippers instead of tennis shoes. She told Alice at breakfast she always knows when there's a storm coming in, because she can't get her shoes on.

Alice follows her out the door and down a worn path through the yard, to where a tall boy in huge unlaced sneakers is fiddling with the mower. He stands up and bends his head down for Sugar's kiss. A tiny blue butterfly lands on her shoulder.

"That means I'm gonna get a new apron," Sugar says, turning her head and pursing her lips to look at the butterfly before it darts away. Sugar's laugh is a wonderful, rising giggle.

She and Alice traipse down the hill past the outdoor kitchen, a wood stove with a pile of kindling beside it for cooking and canning when it's too hot indoors. "We planted this mulberry tree when we moved here," she tells Alice. "First thing Roscoe said we had to do."

"He likes mulberries?"

"No, he likes peaches. The birds like the mulberries better, so they'll leave the peaches to us. These here are Indian peaches, they call them. Blood red in the center." Sugar stops and looks at the dark mulberries scattered on the ground. "I wonder why chickens don't eat them."

"Maybe they'd rather have peaches," Alice says.

Sugar laughs. "No, a chicken's not that smart. Here's the fire pit where we have the hog fry."

"You fry hogs?"

"Oh, yeah. Cut him up first. For a special occasion. We had one here for me and Roscoe's anniversary, I'm sorry you missed that. Quatie organized it, she's the social director. We ate up the whole hog. Everybody came, all the kids and the grandkids and the husbands and the cousins. The only ones that didn't come was the ones that's dead." Sugar laughs.

Alice tries to imagine what it would take to get her family collected in one yard. "They come from far away?" she asks.

"I guess the furtherest anybody come was from Tahlequah. My kids all live right here." She points through the woods. "See them trailer houses? That one's Johnetta's, that's Quatie's, the two boys is on the other side of the road, they moved back in together since they both got divorced." She pauses and bites her lip. "No, one's divorced and the other one, his wife died. So they've got the kids up there. They's all right around."

"Why don't they move away?"

"Well, because they'd just end up coming back anyway, because this is where the family is. Why move away just to turn around and come back? Too much trouble."

"I never heard of a family that stuck together that much."

"Listen, in the old days they didn't even go across the yard. They just added onto the house. When you married, the daughter and the husband just built another room onto her folks' house. Roscoe says the houses just got longer and longer till there wasn't no place to sweep your dirt out. I think trailer houses was a right good invention."

Their trail has joined up with an old road, two mud tracks running through deep woods. Every mud puddle is surrounded by a prayer group of small blue butterflies. Alice is fascinated by their twitching wings. She wonders if the butterflies are all related to one another too. "How much of a piece of land have you got here?" she asks Sugar.

"It was Roscoe's mama's homestead land, sixty acres. Every one of them got sixty acres, back in the allotments. Most of them sold it or give it away or got it stole out from under them some way. I don't know why she didn't, probably didn't get no offers. So we ended up here. When the kids each one got big, we told them to find a place to set a trailer house and go ahead. They have to pay taxes. We don't. I don't know why, I guess because it's homestead land. Oh, look, there's poke."

Alice spies the purple-veined shoots clustered in a sunny spot beside the road.

"We'll have to be sure and pick those on our way back," Sugar says. "Roscoe told me there was a lot of them here. He come down here the other day looking for the eggs. We got one hen that's real bad about stealing the nest."

"That looks like a tobacco plant growing there," Alice says, pointing.

"Probably is. You might find marijuana, too." Sugar giggles.

The forest opens before them onto a grassy park with a long bank sloping down to the creek. Where the water is deep it stands a cool, turquoise blue. A steep limestone cliff pocked with caves rises behind the creek, and above the cliff, a wooded hill. Alice and Sugar stand a long time looking.

"I'll bet there's crawdads right in there." Sugar points to the shallows.

Alice feels herself relax, looking at the water. Bright orange dragonflies zip low and dive and stab their tails at their own reflections, then light in the rushes, transforming all that energy into perfect stillness. The sunlight reflected upward from the water lights the undersides of Sugar's and Alice's faces and the broad hickory leaves above them, as if they're all on a stage. "I can see why you'd call it Heaven," she says.

"Oh, this isn't the good one yet. This one they call the mushrat hole. I guess they used to trap a lot of mushrat and mink down here. Heaven's on down the trail a little bit," Sugar says, and she strikes out again downstream.

* * *

When Alice arrives in Heaven at last, a little breathless, she instantly begins to worry about boys cracking their skulls. Sugar is right, this blue hole is clearer, much larger and deeper, and the limestone cliff is alive with children leaping like frogs into the water. Sugar stands without a trace of worry on her face, watching small boys, most of whom are presumably her descendants, dive off twenty- and thirty-foot rocks. Some of the kids are barely past toddler age; they have more trouble climbing up the bank than jumping off. Alice is astonished. "Don't you worry about them?" she asks.

"Nobody's ever got drowned here," Sugar says. "They do sometimes up in the river, but not here."

The kids have noticed the two women; they wave their arms in wide arcs, shouting, "Hi, Grandma!" Sugar waves back, not very energetically, Alice thinks, as if it is no big deal to her to be acknowledged publicly by grandsons. Several older children stand knee-deep in water farther down the bank, fishing, and they, too, wave at Sugar. One boy crosses the creek and makes his way toward them carrying a heavy string of fish. He lays the fish on the grass in front of Sugar, just exactly the way Alice's old cat used to bring birds to lay at her doorstep. Alice can't get over what she is seeing: adolescent boys being polite. Even more than polite, they are demonstrating love.

Sugar makes over the fish. "Where'd you get all these? You must have been down here since Friday."

"No," he says, embarrassed. He is a stocky, long-haired teenager with broad shoulders and a gold razor blade on a chain hanging on his bare chest.

"What kind of fish are they?" Alice asks.

"The purple ones are perch," he tells her politely. "These are goggle-eyes. They go under rocks. The ones with the pink fins are chub." He turns back to Sugar, animated. "We caught a snapping turtle in the mud. Leon poked a stick at it and it bit it and wouldn't turn loose. We just pulled it right out of the water. Those things are *stout*."

"They'll give you a stout bite, too, if you don't leave them be."

"I'll clean these and bring them up later, Grandma."

"Okay, Stand. Bring me some watercress, too. I see some growing down there by them red rocks."

"Okay." Stand walks away with his catch.

Sugar hobbles over to a pair of decrepit aluminum folding chairs that are leaning against a tree and shakes them open, setting them in the shade. "That Stand likes to get drunk, but he's a good boy. He loves to hunt. He brings me something every week. 'Grandma, I brung you this,' he'll say. He don't stay home. Junior is always taking him somewhere and dumping him off and then about three o'clock he'll go after him, he'll have something. Squirrel, or anything green, you know."

"He's your older son's boy?"

"No, not exactly, he's Quatie's, but she already had six or seven when he was born, so Junior adopted him. You know how people do. Share the kids around."

Alice doesn't exactly know, but she can gather.

"I wish he wouldn't drink, though. I swear he's the spit image of Roscoe, when I first met him."

"You must have fell hard for Roscoe," Alice says. "You wrote me you'd met him at the railroad yard, and then the next thing I know you'd run off and married him."

"Well, I was mad because you run off and got married first. And anyway I was sick of factory work."

"I'll tell you, Foster Greer wasn't anything to be jealous of. You've been a whole lot luckier in love than I ever was."

The two women sit still, watching slim brown bodies slip through air into water as if they were made for nothing more than this single amphibious act. Sugar sighs.

"He had shoulders just like that. Roscoe did. From carrying the ties."

"Railroad ties? That's a job."

"Mm-hmm. He used to cut ties and posts. Later on when we got married and come on back up here he cut cookstove wood. Just cut it right out of these woods around here. He'd sell it for fifty cents a rick. Now you get twenty-five dollars a rick."

"Isn't that something, what we used to pay for things?"

"Oh, Lordy! Remember when we worked in that mattress factory for fifteen cents a day?"

Alice laughs. "That was fun, though. More fun than you'd guess."

"No, what was fun was when we'd go to beer joints, or sneak in to watch them wrestling matches they organized in the barns."

"Oh, I liked those!" Alice says. "Those matches they have now on TV are just plain stupid. Like a costume party of grown-up men. I liked those tough-looking boys in the baggy shorts."

"You had a crush on that one, what was his name?"

"Rough and Tumble Ludwig. I did not." Both women cover their mouths and laugh.

"You know what I really loved?" Alice asks suddenly. "When we'd go out to the colored church with that girl Arnetta from the mattress factory."

"Your mama tanned our hides on that one," Sugar says.

"I didn't even care. I kept on going, even after you all left the farm. They sang gospel on Wednesday nights, and there was one woman in particular that always spoke in tongues."

"I've seen that, the speaking in tongues and the carrying on," Sugar says. "I wasn't much impressed."

"This one was different," Alice says, though she knows she can't explain it to Sugar. She leans back, closing her eyes and remembering, feeling the light from the creek playing on her face. That woman could be counted on. Her eyes would go soft and faraway, not agitated, and she would lay her hand on the head of a child, whoever happened to be near, because nobody was afraid, and she would speak out in a slow, meaty voice: "Belbagged oh Lessemenee! Yemett algeddy boolando!" And you would understand what she meant. *Yes, sister,* they would all cry. No one doubted she was receiving the spirit. In the years since, Alice, too, has seen the ones who shake and scream and roll their eyes back as if snakebit, but she has always doubted the sincerity of this. Anybody can get worked up, if they have the intention. It's *peacefulness* that is hard to come by on purpose.

Annawake stirs her coffee. Through the café window she can see Boma Mellowbug's bottle tree, with hundreds of glass bottles stuck onto the ends of its limbs. It's a little thin at the top where no one can reach, but once in a while someone from the volunteer fire department will bring a ladder and move some bottles to the upper branches to even things out.

She reaches for the cream pitcher and knocks over the sugar bowl at the same instant she sees the woman who must be the grandmother. She's wearing running shoes and polyester pants and a bright, African sort of shirt, and she is trying not to look lost. Annawake taps on the window and waves. The woman raises her head like a startled animal and changes her course, heading across the street toward the café. Annawake tries to spoon the sugar she has spilled back into the bowl. By the time Alice gets there, Annawake has created a crater in the small white mountain in the center of the table.

"I spilled the sugar," she says.

"Sugar's cheap," Alice says. "You could do worse things."

Annawake is caught off guard, forgiven before they even start. "Sit down, please," she says. She takes off her reading glasses and stands up to shake Alice's hand just as Alice is moving to sit down. They both bend awkwardly to accommodate the difference, and Alice laughs.

"I'm sorry. I'm nervous as a barn cat," she says, sliding into the booth across from Annawake.

"Me too," Annawake confesses. "How long have you been in Heaven? You finding your way around all three blocks of it?"

"I can't complain. Sugar's looking after me. My cousin. I mentioned her on the phone, didn't I?"

Annawake feels wary. She'd said Sugar Hornbuckle on the phone, but she hadn't said *cousin*. "So you and your daughter have ties here in the Nation?"

"Oh, no. Sugar and me grew up together down South. But I never knew Roscoe till he hollered howdy at me two days ago in the bus station."

"Oh," Annawake says, and they look each other in the eye.

Alice exhales slowly. "Well. I had all this stuff to say, that I was practicing on my way over here. I was supposed to start out being real high and mighty, but that's never been my long suit."

Annawake smiles. She has seen so many people show up for court armored in suits and lies. But this bright-eyed little old lady turns out for Greer vs. Fourkiller in an African-print dashiki from Wal-Mart, and an attitude to match. "I think I know what you were going to say," Annawake tells her. "Can I give it a shot?"

"Go ahead."

"Miss Fourkiller, you've got no business butting into our lives this way. You might think you know what's best for our little girl, because she's Indian and you are too, but that's just one little tiny part of what she is. You weren't there while she was growing up, and it's too late to be claiming her now, because she's already a person in our family."

Alice frowns. "I'll swan."

"Coffee, hon?" the waitress asks as she fills Alice's cup. She's a very short, very broad woman with blunt-cut black hair and a face as round and flat as a plate. "I don't think I know you. I'm Earlene."

"Earlene, this is Alice Greer," Annawake says. "She's come to town on some business."

"Uh-oh," Earlene says, noticing the sugar volcano.

"I made a little mess," Annawake admits.

"You know what that means. Means somebody's a-gettin' a new sweetheart." Earlene looks at the two women, beaming. "Which one, you reckon? I know Annawake's on the market. How about you, you married, hon?" she asks Alice.

"Not so's you'd notice," Alice replies. Earlene laughs so hard her bosom heaves and the coffee slides dangerously in the glass pot.

"I'll bring back a rag directly and get that up," she says. "I'm sorry if it takes me awhile to get back to you. I'm the only one here today. You all want the soup of the day? It's beef barley, it's real good."

"That would be fine," Alice says, and Annawake nods. Their water glasses vibrate with Earlene's footsteps as she makes her way back to the kitchen.

"There's one thing you left out," Alice says. "In my speech."

"What's that?" Annawake blows into her coffee.

Alice looks out the window when she speaks. "She was abused."

"I know. I'm sorry."

"Sorry?" Alice takes her straight on now. "That's not enough. You don't know what that child goes through. She's still not over it. Whenever she feels like she's done something wrong, or if she thinks Taylor's leaving, she just ... I don't know what you'd call it. It's like her body's still there but her mind gets disconnected some way. It's awful to watch."

"It must be," Annawake says.

"What I think," Alice says, folding her paper napkin, "is that you people had your chance, and now it's Taylor's turn. And she's doing a good job."

For the first time Annawake feels a stirring of animosity. "When you say 'you people,' who do you mean exactly? Indians in general, or just the Cherokee Nation?"

"I don't know. I just can't see how a thing like that could happen to a little baby girl."

"I don't know why it happens *here*, because we love our children more than money. And there are almost always enough good-hearted people in a family to fill in for the hardship cases."

"Everybody loves kids, that's nothing new under the sun," Alice states. "Except the ones that don't."

"I don't think you understand what I mean." Annawake's jaw tenses with this familiar frustration: explaining her culture to someone who believes America is all one country. She thinks about what she wants to say, and sees in her mind *family,* a color, a notion as fluid as *river.* She tells Alice, "I used to work at the Indian hospital at Claremore, checking people in. Sometimes it would be years before we'd get straight who a kid's mother was, because one aunt or another would bring him in. Maybe the mother was too young, so another family member raised him. It's not a big deal who's the exact mother."

Alice blinks, taking this in. "So with all this love going around, how does it happen that somebody walks up to my daughter's parked car one night and gives a baby away?"

Annawake watches two girls passing by outside on the street, Flossie Deal's granddaughters, she thinks. They are walking fast, with earnest, bobbing heads, the way only adolescent girls can move. Annawake also had speeches in her head, and she too has forgotten them, or lost her introductions. "God knows why," she says. "What's happened to us is that our chain of caretaking got interrupted. My mom's generation." Annawake feels her stomach harden. "Federal law put them in boarding school. Cut off their hair, taught them English, taught them to love Jesus, and made them spend their entire childhoods in a dormitory. They got to see their people maybe twice a year. Family has always been our highest value, but that generation of kids never learned how to be in a family. The past got broken off."

"Well, that's a shame," Alice says.

"Yeah. The ones my age are the casualties. We have to look farther back than our parents, sometimes, to find out how to behave." Annawake feels unsteady. "The woman who gave Turtle to your daughter, I think I could probably tell you her sad alcoholic one-bad-man-after-another story. She gave Turtle up because she had no idea how to save a baby from repeating that life. But I also know that baby fell out of a family that loved her, and she's missed."

Alice's expression changes. "You know that for sure? There's relatives here that want her back?"

Annawake touches the pad of her index finger into the sugar on the table, making a perfect circle, deciding how much to tell. "Yes," she says finally. "I could have told you, before I knew anything about the specifics of this case, that somebody here was missing that child. And it turns out I'm right. I found out just recently as a matter of fact, more or less by accident. At a hog fry. People talk about things here, and it comes around."

"Well," Alice says, glancing around, nervous again.

"It doesn't really change anything. The law is still the law, Turtle's adoption is invalid, whether relatives come forward or not. Our job is to figure out what's the next step."

"Does Turtle have any say-so in all this?"

"Sure she does. And I'm sure she would say she wants to stay with Taylor. I understand that." Annawake begins pushing the sugar into another shape, making a point on the bottom of the circle. "We're not going to decide anything today. The best we can hope for is just to get acquainted."

Alice takes the offensive. "What happened to your mama, after the boarding school?"

Annawake stares at the heart shape she has drawn in sugar on the table, wondering what in the world it is doing there. "Bonnie Fourkiller," she says. "Tried hard to be an all-American girl, but she had none of the assets and all the liabilities. Pregnant at sixteen with my brother Soldier, who they tell me was born blue and died pretty quick. She married a Kenwood kid with less talent for making money than she had for conceiving boys. Three more brothers, then me and my twin, Gabe. What I remember is Dad always somewhere tracking down work, and Mama begging us for mercy and drinking seven days a week. Lysol on Sunday mornings, so she wouldn't smell like liquor in church."

"Lord," Alice says.

"She was institutionalized at the age of thirty-five. But I was lucky, I had lots of people looking after me. My dad and brothers, and mainly my Uncle Ledger. He's a medicine man. Not a doctor. Kind of a minister. Have you heard of the stomp dances?"

"I've seen those turtle shells. Looks like that would be a chore, to dance with all that on your legs."

Annawake laughs. "It's work, but it's not a chore. I did that. But Uncle Ledger decided I would be the one of us who'd learn the white world. My brothers could do their reckless things, but I had to learn to listen to my head, every time. He made me speak English, and he pushed me to do well in school. He thought we needed an ambassador."

"The ambassador? That's what you are? Whatever you told my daughter Taylor scared her to death. She's a mess, all uprooted, and now she can't even make her payments."

"It didn't cross my mind that she would pack up and move."

"Well, she did. Last time I talked to her she didn't sound like herself. She's depressed. It's awful what happens when people run out of money. They start thinking they're no good."

"See that guy over there?" Annawake points across the street to the hardware store where Abe Charley is standing out front in his horsehide suit, talking to Cash Stillwater.

Alice leans, to look. "What's that, a cowskin he's got on?"

"Horsehide. There's a rendering plant over toward Leech where you can get horse leftovers pretty cheap. Abe made that suit himself. He's pretty proud of it."

"Taylor's boyfriend wears some odd getups, from what he's told me. But to tell you the truth, not as bad as that horsehide. Taylor just bought new school clothes for Turtle instead of paying her bills. She was scared to death of Turtle looking poor at school. You know how it is."

"Luckily I don't. I mean, growing up here, you don't have to bother much with pretending you're not poor."

Alice is tracking Abe Charley's flamboyant hide as he crosses the street.

Annawake refines the point on her sugar heart. "People say Indians are ungrateful welfare recipients, but what they really mean is we don't act embarrassed enough about being helped out. The young people like me, the radicals, we'll say it's because we had everything stolen from us and we deserve the scraps we're getting back. And that's true, but it's not the point. The old people around here, they're not thinking about Wounded Knee, they're just accepting what comes their way. For us, it's the most natural thing in the world to ask for help if we need it."

Alice has finally gotten her fingers into the sheet of sugar that is spreading across the table. She draws a pig, then puts a fence around it. "I was noticing that about my cousin Sugar," she says. "We were walking along and she saw some poke growing down in the ditch, and she just went right down there and got it. Didn't care who drove by and saw. I was thinking, 'Now, I'll eat poke if I have to, but I'd hate for anybody to see I was that hard up.'"

Annawake smiles, remembering summers of gathering greens with her uncle.

Alice puts another fence around the pig.

"Your cousin Sugar was my mother's best friend," Annawake says. "Ask her sometime if she remembers Bonnie Fourkiller."

"You had that brother that got sent away, didn't you?"

Annawake is startled to feel tears in her eyes. "How did you know that?"

"It was in that letter you wrote Jax. He read it over the phone."

Annawake wipes her nose with her napkin. "My other brothers are still around here, and a slew of nieces and nephews. My dad is still living, he's over in Adair now. What about you? Do you have other kids besides Taylor?"

"Nobody but Taylor. No son, no daddy, and no husband to speak of."

"None to speak of?"

"Well, I had me one, Harland, but he never talked. It was like trying to have a conversation with a ironing board. He just wanted to watch TV all the time. That's what ruint him, really, I think. TV does all the talking for you, and after a while you forget how to hold up your end."

Annawake smiles. "Interesting theory."

"So I left him. I doubt he's noticed yet. Now it's just back to me and Taylor and Turtle. Seems like we're doomed to be a family with no men in it."

"Could be worse. You could have a family with no women in it, like I grew up in."

"Now that's true, that would be worse."

They fall quiet. The window gives their eyes a place to go when they need to take a rest from each other.

"If you don't mind my asking," Alice pipes up, "what's going on with that tree over there?"

"That's Boma Mellowbug's bottle tree," Annawake says. "Our little thing of beauty. Boma is, I guess you'd say, the town lunatic."

"I think maybe I saw her. In a dress and a ski hat?"

"That was Boma. You really have to be sure you don't run over her with your car. Sometimes she'll stand in the middle of the street and have a conversation with the oaks. But everybody's crazy about Boma."

"She did all that by herself?"

"No. She got it going. Back when I was little, she started sticking old empties down over the ends of the branches of that redbud. And pretty soon somebody else would come along and add another one, and then we all got into it, keeping our eyes peeled for something special. Once I found an old blue milk bottle in a ditch, and another time, one of those fancy glass cups they used to have up on the electric lines. I couldn't wait for Uncle Ledger to drive me over here in his truck so I could put my things on the tree."

"Well," Alice says, "it's different."

"Not for here. For here it's just kind of normal." She laughs. "One time in law school we were discussing the concept of so-called irresponsible dependents. That a ward of society can't be a true citizen. I wanted to stand up and tell the class about Boma and the bottle tree. That there's another way of looking at it."

"What's that?"

"Just that you could love your crazy people, even admire them, instead of resenting that they're not self-sufficient."

"Why didn't you?"

Annawake shrugs. "There are things I can't explain to white people. Words aren't enough."

"Well, that's it, isn't it?" Alice says. "If we could get it across, we wouldn't be sitting here right now."

Earlene comes back carrying two bowls of soup and grinning from ear to ear. "Oops," she says, "I forgot to get up that sugar." She lumbers briskly away singing, "Here comes the bride!"

Annawake stares at Alice, the woman from the family without men, and hatches the most reckless plan of her life.

23

SECRET BUSINESS

LETTY IS STANDING IN HER garden with a butcher knife when Annawake drives up. She looks formidable, but Annawake kills the engine anyway and makes her way through the bean patch. She waves Letty's pie plate in the air. "I'm returning this to you," she says.

Letty puts a hand on top of her dead husband's hat and squints at Annawake, frowning, until her face lights with recognition. "Annawake, I swear I wouldn't have knowed you, except you was here at the hog fry. With that hair all cut off."

"Well, Letty, I'm growing it back. I'll look presentable in a year or two."

"I reckon you will." Now Letty stares at her pie plate. "How'd you get hold of that?"

"I took some of your sweet potato pie home from that hog fry you had for Cash. We took it home to Millie, remember? It's her favorite."

"Well, she should have come. She missed a good one."

"She wanted to, but the baby was cranky from getting his shots."

"Oh, that's a shame."

"He got over it. Millie says thanks for the pie. She wasn't going to return the plate till she had a chance to catch her breath and cook something to send back in it. But that's not going to happen for about twelve more years, so I snuck out with it this morning. I figured you'd rather just have the plate."

Letty laughs. "That's how it is with kids, all right. They're all over you like a bad itch. I miss mine, though, now that they's done growed."

Annawake looks around for evidence that a person might need a butcher knife to stand out here in the garden. There is no danger she can see. "You look like you're hunting for another hog to kill."

"I would, if one run through here, and that's no lie. Or a ostrich. Did you hear about that ostrich feather Boma Mellowbug's got hold of?"

"No."

"She says it fell on her side of the fence. That Green fellow figures she climbed over and got it, and he wants it back. He says he'll take her to court over it. Cash saw her downtown yesterday, a-wearin' it in her hat."

Annawake is sorry to have missed that. "How's Cash settling in, anyway?" she asks.

"Oh, I guess he's all right. I think he broods. I got him fixing up my roof for me to improve his disposition."

"That must be why I saw him yesterday talking to Abe Charley at the hardware store. You know, he's got a secret admirer."

Annawake can see Letty's ears rise half an inch in her head. "Who are you thinking of?"

"There's a woman staying over at Sugar and Roscoe's place. She's some kind of relative of Sugar's."

"Oh, honey, I know all about that. I was standing right over there in my own kitchen the day the woman called on my telephone and told Sugar she had to come here in a big old hurry. She's got some secret business with the Nation. A big claim. I can't tell you no more about it. I really oughtn't to go into it even that much."

Annawake smiles. "Well, she's dying to meet Cash Stillwater, that's what I heard."

"We ought to tell him, don't you think?"

"Oh, I don't think so," Annawake says. "He'd just be embarrassed, I imagine."

"Probably. Far be it from me to go butt in. What's she like, the cousin?"

"Alice Greer is her name. She's nice-looking, divorced. She despises watching TV, that's the main thing I know about her. She said she likes a man that will talk to her."

"Well, goodness me, Cash will talk your ear plumb off. I ought to know that."

"I gather she's going to be in town for a while," Annawake says. "They'll run into each other one way or another, don't you think?"

"Oh, sure," Letty says. Her knife blade catches the sun and winks in Annawake's eyes. "One way or another."

Annawake decides not to ask again about the knife. She will drop off the plate and go, leaving Letty to her own devices.

24

WILDLIFE

MANAGEMENT

THE MAN WHO COLLECTS TAYLOR'S rent has pulled up in front of their apartment, just as she was about to leave to walk Turtle to school. His truck is loaded with strange things: large, long-handled nets, for example, and shipping crates. He gets out of the truck and steps snappily up the walk before Taylor can pretend she didn't see him.

"Hi," she says. "I was going to put it in the mail tomorrow."

"Well, they wanted me to get it from you today, if you don't mind. Since it's a week past due."

"Okay. Let me go in and get my checkbook."

The manager, a young man whose name she doesn't know, wears broad, flat-paned glasses that reflect the light, giving him a glassy-fronted appearance, like a storefront. Taylor actually feels a little sorry for him: what a hateful job. He once told her, apologetically, that his real job is in City Park Maintenance; he had to take on managing the apartments for extra cash after his wife had a baby. He has pale, uncommanding fuzz on his cheeks and seems too young to have all these worries.

She has just paid to get the electricity back on, so she dates the check for the middle of next week, after payday, and tries to think of something to say to distract him from looking at it too closely. "What's that on your truck?" she asks.

"Goose-catching stuff," he replies.

She tucks her checkbook into the back pocket of her jeans and returns her hand to Turtle's suspended grasp. "You catch geese?"

"We're having the big goose roundup today."

Taylor looks from his glassy face to the truck and back again, unsure of what one says in this exact situation.

"Canadian geese," he adds, to shed more light.

"Is that, like, a sport?"

"No, it's a citywide crisis," he says, hitching his brown Parks and Recreation jacket on his shoulders with the air of a man who considers himself something of a goose expert. "We've got these Canadian geese that come down here to the lakeshore," he explains knowledgeably, "while they're supposed to be on their way to somewhere else. Stopping for a little break, supposed to be. But everybody goes down there with their darling little child and a bag of day-old bread to feed the geese, and next thing you know, these birds have no intention of moving on. No intention whatsoever."

Turtle is tugging with a light pressure on Taylor's hand and looking at the toes of her new sneakers, which clearly want to head toward the schoolyard. But Taylor needs to be polite. This fellow may look nineteen, but his power over her life right now is infinite. "Well, I guess you wouldn't want every AWOL goose in Canada hanging out down by the docks."

"No, ma'am, you certainly do not. There's goose poop piled up to kingdom come down there. But our main interest is in protecting the welfare of these birds. It's poor wildlife management to allow a bird to live on handouts. A lot of these birds, and I'm not exaggerating this, ma'am, a lot of these birds have become too obese to fly."

Taylor clamps her teeth together so hard, to avoid smiling, she's afraid she's going to get a cramp. "Where are you taking them once you round them up?"

"Shipping them out to eastern Washington," he replies with satisfaction. "It's no party out there. Not a lot of rainfall. These geese will have to slim down and learn to fend for themselves, I'm telling you. Hard work will straighten out their bad habits pretty quick."

"What if they're just too lazy to learn better ways?" Taylor asks in a solemn voice. "You think they might just waddle on back west?"

"Oh, no, ma'am, there's no chance of them coming back here. No chance at all. Not where they're going. This trip is going to separate out the men from the boys, you might say."

"The sheep from the goats," Taylor says, nodding, a studied frown on her face.

"That's right," the manager says. He folds Taylor's check without a glance and places it carefully in his shirt pocket. "I have to be going now," he says.

"You certainly do," she says. "I sure hope you catch all the perpetrators."

Charged with Taylor's confidence, the manager practically sprints back to his truck and drives away in a hurry.

"I wish somebody'd give *us* some day-old bread," Taylor says to Turtle. "Don't you?"

She nods. "With strawberry jam."

The pair of them turn their toes out and pretend they are obese geese, waddling to school.

Late Saturday morning Taylor is headed south through steady rain toward the airport, wishing with all her might that she were flying somewhere too, instead of driving a man in a wheelchair to meet his plane. She's still on the Handi-Van roster as a substitute, and this morning she is filling in for Kevin. He isn't speaking to her but he let her drive his Saturday shift, since there was nobody else available, so he could go to a computer fair. Taylor feels uneasy about the baby-sitting she had to settle for; Turtle is with an elderly Chinese neighbor who wears a red wig and black stockings with brown plastic sandals. She sews uniforms for cheerleaders and baseball teams in her home, and seemed a safe enough bet. Unfortunately she doesn't speak English, so Taylor has no idea what she's being charged for the baby-sitting, and prays she'll come out ahead.

She has only one passenger at the moment, the man going to the airport. Taylor likes his looks: he's about her age, and has nice eyes that remind her a little of Jax. "You heading for someplace where the sun shines?" she asks him.

"Not likely," he says. "I work in the air traffic-control tower."

"You do?" She feels embarrassed; she had assumed he was just a passenger, not a working person. "What's that like? I heard that leads to heart attacks."

"Only if you let the planes run into each other. We try to discourage that."

"But how can you keep your eyes on everything at once? I think I'd be terrible at that job. I kind of freak out if the telephone and the doorbell both ring at the same time."

"We have radarscopes. You should come up to the control room sometime and see. Ask for Steven Kant."

She slows down to force a tailgater to pass. The windshield wipers are beating across the glass like a hypnotist's watch, instructing her to feel very, very sleepy. Taylor tries not to think about Turtle sitting in Mrs. Chin's dark apartment with no one to talk to, bearing mute witness to the flickering TV while Mrs. Chin's sewing machine plods through gaudy layers of satin. It would make Turtle's day if she could go see an air traffic control center. "Okay, I'll do that," Taylor says.

"Well, great."

The wide freeway is full of cars but empty of interest, merely blank and wet, the place where everyone on earth has surely been before. The air traffic controller doesn't seem to have anything more to say, which is too bad. In Taylor's opinion Steven Kant is probably the most upbeat passenger in the history of the Handi-Van corporation, and he's handsome, besides. "I'm Taylor, by the way," she tells him. "I don't usually drive this route. I guess you know that."

"No, I didn't. I don't usually go this route, either. My MG is in the shop."

"Oh, that's too bad."

"I don't mind the limo service once in a while." He catches her eye in the rearview mirror and smiles. "The service is friendly."

"Only the best. You just sit back there, sir, and pour yourself a glass of champagne."

"In my line of work they kind of frown on people showing up tipsy. But I'll take a rain check."

She looks in the mirror again, wondering if this is an invitation of some kind. She decides it is, but he's made it so gently that if she overlooks it neither one of them will feel bad. She supposes living in a wheelchair might train you in that kind of skill.

"You really drive an MG?"

"Yep. Convertible. Canary yellow, with wire wheels and hand controls and a very sporty wheelchair rack on the back."

"You got headers on that thing?"

"You bet. Headers and a glass pack."

"Whew. I'll bet she purrs."

"You know a lot about sports cars."

Taylor smiles. "Not a thing, really. I just used to sell them, a piece at a time."

Steven Kant laughs. "Sounds like a life of crime."

"No, nothing so profitable. A car-parts store." Taylor finds she can hardly remember working at Mattie's. She can picture herself in the store, joking with the men, among all those organized metal pieces of dream. But that saucy salesgirl seems to Taylor now like a confident older sister, rather than herself. Someone with her life well in hand.

"How about when your MG's fixed *you* can drive *me* someplace," she says. "Not to work, though. My other job is at the world's most hideous shopping mall."

"Okay. How about the locks?"

"The locks?"

"Yeah. Haven't you seen them before?"

"I've got about seven on my front door."

He laughs. "The locks between the sound and the lake, where the boats pass through. Really, you've never been there?"

"I'm new in town, sailor."

"Well, okay then, I'm going to show you the locks. And afterward I'll take you out for the freshest salmon of your life. What do you think, next Saturday?"

Taylor's stomach flips upstream when it hears about the salmon. Freshness is not the issue, either; right now she wouldn't be above taking home a salmon if she found one dead in the road. She's so tired of peanut butter she has stopped acting for Turtle's benefit like she cares about the murdered peanuts.

"Saturday would be good," she says, after pretending to think about it. "Only, I'm going to have to tell you right up front, I have a little girl that would love to come too. No husband or anything, but a kid. Would that be okay?"

"Two dates for the price of one," he says. "That's even better."

Taylor thinks: it won't be for the price of one. She eats too.

Jax has knocked over a nearly full bottle of beer into his synthesizer in the middle of "Dancing at the Zombie Zoo." He manages to play through to the last chords, touching the keys gingerly, not going for the demonstrative ending this time. He just hopes he won't get electrocuted. While they're fading on the final, he signals his lead guitarist for a break. Once the stage spots go off and they begin playing taped music through the house amps, Jax takes off his T-shirt and starts mopping the keyboard. He'll have to take the whole thing apart. He can't decide whether to start doing that now, before the beer has a chance to settle into the microprocessors, or wait until later. A young woman with terrible posture and limp, cherry-red hair hanging from exactly one half of her scalp is still dancing right in front of the stage. Or rather, she is doing shallow knee bends, bobbing in a slow rotation with her eyes closed. She has been drilling herself into the same spot for nearly an hour, annoying Jax for no particular reason. He picks up the beer bottle that committed its crime against music, and rolls it toward her, hoping it will fall off the stage and shatter her reverie. It merely clonks loudly and rolls past her. He takes his keyboard off its legs and kicks some amp cables out of the way to clear a space for it on the floor.

Rucker, the lead guitarist, crosses the stage and stands over him. "Man, you drowned it."

"Yeah. In beer, though, so it's happy. Do you know CPR?"

"No, man, I don't even *pay* my taxes."

"Rucker, you have no appreciable IQ."

"Jax, what do women see in you? The brunette working the bar sent you this note. She said it's urgent."

"Tell her I've got a disease, okay?" Jax takes a screwdriver out of his keyboard case and begins taking off the back plate.

"That's not funny."

"I'm only paid to entertain people with music here."

"What's wrong with you, some dog buried your bone? Did you see her? She's luminous."

"That's nice."

Rucker unfolds the note, which is inked on a cocktail napkin. "I'm reading this little love letter myself."

"I didn't know you could read." Jax kneels down with his head near the floor and peers inside his machine. It always amazes him: it can produce sounds exactly like a piano, a Hammond organ, a muted French horn, even breaking glass or a marble rolling down the inside of a pipe, and yet there is practically nothing inside. He remembers feeling this same astonishment the first time he took apart a TV.

"Who's Lou Ann?"

Jax looks up. "Let me see that."

"Lou Ann called," Rucker reads. "Super urgent emergency, call Taylor back at this number."

Jax swipes the napkin out of Rucker's hand and bounds off the stage, bumping into the bobbing half-bald dancer but still not waking her up. He makes a beeline for the pay phone between the bar and the kitchen. There's no hope of quiet, but he can't wait until he gets home. Taylor picks up on the first ring.

"Jax?"

"I'm going to die if I don't kiss your navel within one hour. Tell me you're calling from the Triple T Truck stop in south Tucson."

"I'm not. It kind of looks like the Triple T, though. I'm at a pay phone in the parking lot between a Kwik Mart and, I think, an open-air festival of drug users."

"Where's Turtle?"

"Asleep in the car. Hey, listen, you, I don't even know if I've forgiven you for screwing Gundi. Why would I let you kiss my navel?"

"Well, good, Taylor, you sound like yourself. You must be okay."

"I don't know if I am or not. I feel like I'm in hell. Do you have to pay rent and utilities in hell?"

"No. I think you make all the payments before you get there."

"Jax, my life's a mess."

"I wrote you another song. Listen."

"I don't know if I can listen to another broken-heart song."

"This one isn't as bad. Listen:

I made you happy,
I made you breakfast,
The only thing you ever made me was crazy.
I gave you flowers,
You gave me migraines,
Starting today you're going to give me the brushoff ..."

"Broken-heart song," Taylor diagnoses. "*Pissed-off* broken-heart song, which is worse. Jax, we've been over this. I didn't leave *you*, I left a situation."

"Would you mind writing that on the blackboard five hundred times?"

Her voice is quiet. "I miss you, Jax. Real bad. I get this aching in my throat sometimes and I'm not sure if you're real or not. It's been so long since I've seen you." Jax hears her blowing her nose, the most heart-warming sound he has heard in his life to date. He wishes he could program that nose blow into his synthesizer.

"I don't even have your picture anymore," she says. "Goddamn Barbie stole it."

"That's a crime against nature," says Jax. "She stole my photograph?"

"Well, there was money involved. It's kind of hard to explain."

"You had to *pay* someone to steal my photograph?"

A waitress with her blouse tied in a knot at the base of her rib cage passes Jax with a tray of dirty plates and gives him a look, running her eyes down his shirtless torso.

"I sacrificed my shirt to a medical emergency," he whispers.

She rolls her eyes as she wheels around and butts the kitchen door open with her hind end.

"I should have seen it coming," Taylor says. "That Barbie was petty larceny waiting to happen. I can't believe how bad I've screwed up here, Jax. Seems like I've made every wrong turn a person could make."

"You sound like a seven-car freeway pileup."

"I am. I didn't even tell you yet, I lost the van-driving job. I couldn't work out the baby-sitting. They kept me on the substitute board, but I don't get called much. Now I'm a cashier in a department store. Ladies Intimate Apparel, to be exact. Six dollars an hour."

"That's not so bad. Forty-eight dollars a day for selling undies. That's almost a thousand a month."

"Very good, math whiz, except it isn't. They take out some for taxes and Social Security and this mandatory insurance plan that I can't even use yet for six months. I'll get around seven hundred a month."

"Hey, that ought to melt away those unwanted pounds."

"I figured out a budget: our rent is three hundred and ninety, so if you figure in water and electricity and gas—we haven't turned on the heat yet, so I don't know what that will be—but say five hundred total, for rent and utilities. Then another fifty a month to keep the car going so I can get to work. If we can get by on a hundred a month for food, that should leave fifty dollars for emergencies. But Jax, we just keep getting behind. I had a car-insurance payment come due, and then today my register turned up forty-four dollars short, and they say they're going to take that out of my paycheck. I'm thinking, what paycheck?"

"That's robbery."

"No, it probably was my fault. I get distracted trying to keep an eye on Turtle in the store. They have this special aftercare program at her school for low-income, I guess that's me, but even that costs three dollars a day. Sixty a month. I don't have it."

"You're eating on twenty-five bucks a week?"

"Yeah. One dollar a meal for the two of us, plus Turtle's milk money that she has to take to school. We're not eating too high off the hog, as Mama would say."

"No, I'd say you were eating very low off the hog. I would say you are eating the hooves."

"Jax, poverty sucks."

"Can I quote you on that? Maybe a bumper sticker or something?"

"I know you're not rich either, but it was different there, with you and me to split the rent, and Lou Ann always around for baby-sitting."

"You should click your heels together and get your butt back home, Dorothy."

"Oh, I forgot to tell you the funny part. Now they're telling me I need to dress better for work. My supervisor says jeans and T-shirt is not acceptable attire for a cashier in Ladies' Wear. I wanted to tell her to shove her underwired bras and transfer me to Auto Repair. But if I lose this job we'll be living downtown on a bench, or in our car, and that's no joke. I swear I've considered shoplifting from the juniors department."

"Taylor, read my lips: Come home. I'll send you the money. I don't think this Annawake figure is going to come after you."

"You don't think so?"

"She seems more like the lurk-in-the-bushes and make-scary-noises type."

Taylor blows her nose again. "If I could get there on my own, Jax, I would. I feel tired all the time, like I could lie down and sleep a hundred years. But you can't be sending money. You don't have next month's rent."

"Don't be insulting. I could get it from Mattie."

"No!" Taylor cries.

"Well, Christ, keep your fingernails on. Mattie wouldn't mind."

"I mind," she says. "I'm going to make this work here. I have to. I'm not stupid, and I'm not lazy. I'm working so hard, Jax, but we never quite get caught up."

"It's not your fault, Taylor."

"Well, whose is it? I should be able to keep a roof over my own head. If I work at it."

"That's just a story. You're judging yourself by the great American cultural myth, but Horatio Alger is compost, honey. That standard no longer applies to reality."

"Right. Tell that to my landlord."

"What you need is a nice musician to take care of you."

"Now, there's a myth. Who did a musician ever take care of?"

"Not even his most beloved M1 synthesizer, at the moment. I just poured a beer down her front and left her gargling her final breaths on stage. We're on break right now."

"Well, guess what, I did meet this air traffic controller."

"Damn, I knew it. You're in love."

"No. But Turtle and I got to see the control room yesterday. It's this dark room full of little radar screens, with somebody in charge of each one. They sit there all day hunched over watching yellow blinking dots and drinking coffee and talking the pilots out of crashing into each other. What a life, huh? It looks kind of like a submarine."

"Is that what submarines look like? I always wondered."

"Well, I don't know. It seemed like it. It's called the Terminal Radar Approach Control. Turtle kept calling it the Terminal Roach Control. I'm not sure she had a real good understanding of the concepts."

"Don't be surprised if she did. Not much passes her by."

"That's true. It was kind of reassuring to see. At least somebody is in control of something in this world."

"Sounds like true love to me," Jax says miserably.

"Jax, I'm not in love with Steven Kant."

"Well, just make sure Steven Doesn't."

"That's great. You're telling me to be a nun, while you're finally getting the landlady interested in the plumbing."

Jax laughs, in spite of himself. "She's lost interest again, I promise you. Our toilet still defies the laws of hydrodynamics."

"Well, I'm sure glad to hear that. I wouldn't want to think she was showing you any special favors."

"You know what? I'm glad you're jealous. It makes me feel less remorseful about what I'm going to do to this Steven Can't when I locate his control tower."

"I'm not in love, Jax. He's nice, but he doesn't laugh at my jokes the way you do." She stops, but Jax knows from the quality of her silence to keep listening. She goes on. "I hate to say this, after what I just told you about making my own way, but he took Turtle and me to this nice restaurant in the airport, and I sat there thinking: everything on this menu costs more than our whole week's food budget. It was such a relief just to eat. Sometimes it's hard to separate that from love."

Jax can see through the bar to the stage, where his band is beginning to accumulate once again. Rucker and the drummer are standing over his synthesizer like forlorn relatives at a wake. The bobbing woman is still bobbing in a slow circle. Suddenly, as Jax watches, she keels like a mannequin and hits the floor with a somewhat frightening sound. Jax understands that he despises her because she is pitiful.

"I'm sending you two plane tickets home. Just tell me your address."

Taylor says nothing.

"I'm having trouble reading your lips."

"No. Don't send plane tickets. I can't just ditch the car here."

"This is not about your car."

"Jax, no."

"You damn proud little hillbilly."

She says nothing, and Jax holds his breath, afraid she'll hang up. Then her voice comes. "If that's what you want to call me, I don't care. I've hardly ever had a dime's worth of nickels but I always knew I could count on myself. If I bail out here, I won't even have that."

"You're breaking my heart," he tells Taylor.

"I'm breaking *mine,* Jax. I don't believe this is my life. I look in the mirror and I see a screwup."

Jax looks at the napkin in his hand that says, "Super urgent emergency, call Taylor." For once, Lou Ann hasn't exaggerated. He would give the world to know how to answer the call.

* * *

Something about the Seattle locks is reminiscent of the Hoover Dam. Taylor notices it right away, as they approach through a little park. The gate and entrance building have the same sturdy, antique look. Turtle has noticed too. "Remember those angels?" she asks.

"I sure do," Taylor says. "I was just thinking about those guys."

"What angels?" Steven asks.

"The guardian angels of the Hoover Dam," Taylor tells him. "They're sitting on this memorial for the people who died building it. Turtle and I were just there, not too long ago."

"You like public works, do you?" he ask Turtle.

"Uh-huh. I saw Lucky Buster fall down a big hole. We saved him, but then we had to run away from the Indians."

Steven laughs. "She's going to be a writer someday," he tells Taylor.

"Could be." Taylor squeezes Turtle's hand, a secret message. In her other hand she's holding Steven's umbrella, trying to give all three of them some protection from the drizzle. She feels a little self-conscious. It's the first time she has been on a date with two people whose heads reach about to her waist. She doesn't know whether to put her hand on Steven's chair, or just walk alongside. She was relieved when he popped open the umbrella and handed it to her.

They pass through the entry and Turtle runs a few feet ahead, for once excited, her black pigtails swinging like runaway jump ropes. She looks tall and impossibly thin in her new stretch kneepants and T-shirt and heavy white sneakers. It seems to Taylor as if something is pulling on Turtle's feet at night—she gets taller, but doesn't fill in. And her skin doesn't seem right. The worry surfaces at the front of Taylor's mind only at times like this, when she can watch Turtle with her full attention.

Inside the lock area, the three of them wait next to the rope, looking down into a long channel of water with a gate on either end. Despite the rain, there are jolly couples out boating: two sailboats already inside the lock, steadied by ropes, and a slender, aggressive-looking speedboat just now maneuvering itself in from the sound. A man in blue overalls directs the operation. Once everyone is secured, an alarm bell rings, the gate closes, and water rushes into the lock from underneath. The boats rise slowly on the crest of the engineered tide, from sea level to lake level. Taylor watches the voyagers bob like bathtub toys. "I guess around here you can't wait for a sunny day to go boating."

"You'd be waiting awhile," Steven says. "You should have seen it on the Fourth of July. Raining cats and dogs, and the traffic through here was still unbelievable. He had thirty or forty boats packed in at a time, like cars in a parking lot, all tied to each other."

"That sounds cozy."

"It was. There weren't three square feet of wasted space. You could have walked across, stepping from one deck to another. That guy is unbelievable," he says, pointing to the man in coveralls. "He can figure out how to pack forty boats in a quarter-block area, and then get them out again, without wasting an inch or a minute. He's got spatial skills that could get him into MIT."

"Is that so surprising? That a guy in overalls is brilliant?"

"Well, it's just ironic, considering what he gets paid."

"What do you think he gets paid?"

"I don't know, but I'm sure it's next to nothing."

Taylor already knew this, somehow. "I guess he should have gone to MIT," she says, feeling wounded, even though Steven has said nothing that could rightfully offend her.

The boats are nearly up to lake level now. The gate to the lake slowly opens and water rushes in, curling itself into eddies that make the boats rock from bow to stern. Steven leads Taylor and Turtle across the bridge to the other side.

"Now we get to see how the salmon do it," he says.

"Do what?" Turtle asks, looking at Taylor.

"Don't ask me. Ask him."

"Get from the ocean up into the lake," Steven says. "They live in the ocean all year, but then they have to swim back up into the rivers where they came from, to lay eggs."

"I've heard of that," Taylor says. "I heard they have to go back to the exact same place they were born."

"I don't know that they *have* to," Steven says. "Seems like they just always *want* to. Like all of us, I guess."

"Not me. I got out of Kentucky just as soon as I could get the tires of my car pointed rubber side down."

"And you'll never go back?"

"Oh, I might, I guess. You shouldn't forget who made you."

"How about you, Turtle, where were you born?" he asks.

"In a car," she says.

Steven looks at Taylor.

"It was a Plymouth," she tells him. "That's about all I know about it. She's adopted."

"I don't want to go back to live in a car," Turtle states.

Taylor thinks: Let's hope you don't have to.

They take the elevator down to the viewing area of the fish ladder. Steven explains that the fish have to swim up fourteen steps, against the strong current, to reach the lake. Through a thick window as high as a movie screen they see hundreds of grimacing, pale-bellied, pink-finned fish all headed the same way, working their bodies hard but barely moving forward. They look like birds trying to fly against a hurricane.

"Most of those are silver salmon," Steven says. "Those few you see that are bigger are king salmon."

They look beaten up, their fins bedraggled. "Poor things, why do they even come in here?" Taylor asks. "Seems like they'd be looking around for an easier way to go. A free ride in the locks, maybe."

"No, believe it or not, the strong gush of water flowing out at the bottom is what attracts them in here. The Corps of Engineers figured that out a few years back. They narrowed the channel to increase the flow, and a lot more fish came in. You know the really sad part?"

"What?"

"There are a couple of fat sea lions that like to hang around at the top, just licking their chops, waiting to meet these guys at the end of their hard day's work."

"That is so sad."

"Well, it's life, I guess. The law of the jungle."

The fish curve and buck and thrust themselves against the current, dying to get upstream and pass themselves on. Taylor stands flanked by Turtle and Steven. For a long time the three of them are very still before the glass, framed by greenish light and a wall of solid effort.

"I know how they feel," Steven says, his voice amused. "It's like getting into someplace that isn't wheelchair accessible."

I know how they feel, Taylor thinks, and it's not like getting into anywhere at all. It's working yourself for all you're worth to get ahead, and still going backward. She holds Turtle against her side so she won't look up and see her mother's tears.

25

PICKING

ALICE HAS A DATE. ANY minute now Cash Stillwater is going to pick her up and take her for a drive over to the huckleberry fields near Leech. She can't understand why, but there it is. Some out-and-out stranger has called her up and said, "Let's go pick berries."

Sugar insists he isn't a stranger—that Alice met Cash the day they were in town. She swears they spotted him opening the door for Pearl Grass coming out of the Sanitary Market, and went over to say hello. It must be so, she argues, because Roscoe's sister-in-law Letty claims Cash is sweet on Alice, and how could that be, if they hadn't met? Alice has to agree, it seems unlikely.

She is standing by the front window when his truck pulls up. His long legs come out first, in jeans and cowboy boots with curled-up toes, and then the rest of him. His face is flat and broad under the eyes, the dark skin creased rather than wrinkled. He wears gold-rimmed glasses that give him a kind, twinkling appearance. She has never laid eyes on this man in her life. But that's not to say she won't go for a ride with him, at least this one time. If someone is sweet on you without ever having met you, she reasons, you owe him that much.

She meets him at the door, gripping her purse for courage.

"You all set to go?" he asks. He seems to be looking her over just as thoroughly as she is eyeing him.

"Ready as I'll ever be," she states, looking down at her slacks and work-shirt. "Are these tennis shoes all right? If we're going to be in mud, I better borrow some boots from Roscoe. Sugar's wouldn't do me a bit of good, she wears a five. She always had the smallest feet of anybody."

"I don't expect we'll run into mud today, no. I think you'll do all right."

Alice follows him around to the passenger side of his truck, where he opens the door and gives her a hand up onto the running board. The truck is a wondrous, buttery copper color, though it seems about as old as anything with a motor could possibly be. The windshield is divided into two flat panes with a dark, puttied seam running down the center. Alice remembers Sugar's counseling, that Cash is a big talker, and she hurries to get some kind of conversation going. "You had this truck long?"

Cash starts it up. "All my life, near about. I keep putting new engines in her, and she keeps a-going. Wish I could do the same for myself." He pats his chest gently with his right hand, then reaches down to shift gears, which makes a sound like slamming the spoon drawer.

"They do that, now. Put new hearts and livers and stuff in people," Alice points out.

"I know. But that don't seem right, trading parts with dead folks just to keep yourself around, pestering the younguns. When you're wore out, I'd say that's a sure sign it's time to go."

"I agree," Alice says. She takes notice of some flower growing in the ditch that looks like a dandelion gone crazy, as big as a child's head.

"Ask me in ten year, though, and I might sing a different tune," Cash says, laughing.

"I know. It's hard to admit to being old, isn't it? I keep thinking, How'd this happen? Sixty-one! When I was young I looked at people this age and thought they must feel different inside. As different from me as a dog might feel, or a horse. I thought they would just naturally feel like they were wrinkled up and bent and way far along."

"It don't feel that way, though, does it?"

"No," Alice says, running a hand through her short hair. "It feels regular."

The trees crowd up against the road, each one a different shade of green. The oaks are the darkest. Their leaves angle downward and seem to absorb more light. Cash's truck rolls across a little bridge, and below them Alice can see a creek banked by a world of ferns, their spears all pointed straight up.

"You're kin to Sugar some way, is it?"

"We're cousins," Alice replies. "We grew up together, but we lost touch after I married."

"Well, it had to be Sugar's side you was related on, and not Roscoe's. If it was Roscoe's I'd of knowed you, because my sister Letty's the widowed wife of Roscoe's brother. Did you and your husband have a big family?"

"No, just my daughter. He didn't even quite stick around long enough to drive her home from the hospital." Alice laughs. "I had to get a nurse to drive us home. She was a great big woman with a Chevrolet as big as a barn. She said, 'I can drive home all the babies you want, Miz Greer.' I never will forget that. She made me wish I'd had twelve more, while I was at it."

"I wished that too. That we'd had more. We had the two girls, but then the doctor told my wife no more. Her blood was the wrong way, somehow. She had negative blood, is what he said. She always run to being peaked."

Alice feels embarrassed and amazed that within ten minutes of meeting one another they've gotten onto Cash Stillwater's dead wife's female problems. He doesn't seem bothered, though, only sad. She can feel sadness rising off him in waves, the way you feel heat from a child with a fever.

"Sugar tells me you've just moved back from someplace."

"Wyoming," he says.

They pass an old cemetery whose stone walls are covered with rose brambles, and then a white clapboard church set back in the woods. On a tree, a washed-out sign has been attached by a nail through its center, and rotated a quarter-turn clockwise. It crookedly advises: FLESTER DREADFUL-WATER FOR TRIBAL COUNCIL.

"Flester Dreadfulwater!" Alice says, hoping it's not impolite to laugh at someone's name who is no doubt some relative of someone related to Cash.

Apparently it isn't. "He lost the election," Cash says, smiling.

"Why'd you move to Wyoming?"

Cash stretches a little behind the wheel, though he never takes his eyes off the road. "I got restless after my wife died. I had this idea you can get ahead by being in a place where everbody's rich. That being close to good times is like *having* good times."

"My second husband was like that. He thought if he'd watched some loving on TV, he'd done had it." Alice instantly covers her eyes, feeling she has surely gone too far, but Cash only laughs.

"How long were you up there?" she asks, recovering. Riding through the woods with a talkative man is making her giddy.

"About two year," he says. "I despised it. Everbody rich, treating you like you was a backdoor dog. And not even happy with what they had. I did beadwork for a Indian jewelry store, and the owner one day up and took pills and killed himself clean dead. They say he was worth a million."

"Why'd he want to die, then?"

"I think he was depressed about the Indians being all gone." Cash points his thick hand at the windshield. "He should have come down here and had a look."

They pass a ragged little shack with a ragged little birdhouse on a post beside it, and Alice thinks: Then he would have taken the pills and shot himself too. But she knows that isn't entirely fair.

"They used to be a store up here," Cash says suddenly, as if he'd long forgotten this information himself. "A general store. I wonder what happened to that. We lived right down yander in them woods. We'd come up here for lard. You had to take a bucket. And me and mommy used to take fryers, we'd catch them and tie them up and walk to the store. And eggs."

"Oh, I remember carrying eggs," Alice cries. "That was just a criminal thing to do to a child. Make them carry eggs."

"Sounds like you know."

"Oh, yes. I was raised up on a hog farm in Mississippi. It wasn't just hogs, though. We raised a big garden, and we had chickens, and cows to milk. We'd sell sweet milk and cream. People would come in their wagons to get it."

"I miss that," Cash says. "Driving the mule. We had a mule team and a wagon."

"Well, sure," says Alice, feeling they've finally climbed onto safer ground. "Even up into the forties we still used horses or mules and the wagon. You'd see cars down in Jackson, but it wasn't the ordinary thing to have. We thought they were more for fun. For getting someplace, or hauling, you'd need the wagon and a team of mules."

"Wasn't that the time to be a kid?" Cash asks. "Our kids had to work out what to do with liquor and fast cars and fast movies and ever kind of thing. For us, the worst we could do was break a egg."

"Isn't that so," Alice agrees. "You know what seems funny to me, thinking about old times? We'd get excited over the least little thing. A man playing a fiddle and dancing a little wooden jigging doll with his foot. Even teenagers would stop and admire something like that. Now teenagers won't hardly stop and be entertained by a car accident. They've seen too much already."

"That's how I felt up at Jackson Hole. That's why I wanted to come back. Everbody acted like they'd done seen the show, and was just waiting to finish up the popcorn."

"Well, I met all Sugar's grandkids, and they seem interested in catching fish for their grandma. They're a nicer bunch than I'd ever in this world expect a teenager to be."

"Cherokee kids know the family, that's sure," Cash says. "They know the mother's birthday, the wedding anniversary, all that. We always have a big hog fry."

"You must enjoy your daughters."

"Well, we had a bad time of it in my family. My older daughter, Alma, is dead."

"Oh, I'm so sorry," Alice says, realizing she might have guessed this, from his stooped shoulders. She stops trying to talk for a while, since there is nothing to say about a lost child that can change one star in a father's lonely sky.

They pass clusters of little tin-roofed houses and trailer houses set near each other in clearings in the woods. Propane-gas tanks sit in the yards, and sometimes a wringer washer or a cookstove on the porch, or a weight-lifting bench in the driveway. There is really no predicting what you'll see here. One house seems to be hosting a family reunion: old folks sit around in lawn chairs, and six or seven kids are lined up straddling the silver propane tank as if it were a patient old pony.

"There's sassafras," Cash says, pointing at broad, mitten-shaped leaves sprouting among dark cedars in a hedgerow. "They use that in the medicine tea at the stomp dances."

"What's it do for you?"

"Oh, perks you up, mainly." Cash seems to be looking far down the road when he speaks. "My daddy, he knew all the wild roots to make ever kind of medicine. He tried to tell me what it's for, but I've done forgot about all of it. Back when I was a kid, I never did know people having operations for kidney and gallbladder and stuff, like they do now. Did you?"

"No," Alice says. "People didn't have so many operations. Mainly they got over it, or they died, one."

"When I had a bellyache he'd just get a flour sack, put ashes in that and put that on my side, and the pain would go away. People would always be coming to him, my dad. He died on New Year's day, nineteen and forty, and I didn't even know it for sixteen days. I was in boarding school."

"They didn't tell you?"

Cash doesn't answer for a while. Alice spies a black-and-white Appaloosa horse standing in the woods near the road, alone and apparently untethered; it raises its head as they pass by.

"I can't explain boarding school. The teachers were white, they didn't talk Cherokee, and seems like you got used to never knowing what was going on. You forgot about your family. We slept in a big dormitory, and after a few year, it was kindly like you got the feeling that's how kids got made. Just turned out in them lined-up beds like biscuits in a pan."

"That sounds awful. It sounds like a prison for children."

"It was, more or less. Half a day school, the other half-day work: sewing room, dining room, kitchen, laundry. Boys did the laundry. We didn't mix with girls. Except Sunday, when we had Sunday school, but sometime I couldn't go, I had to stay in the kitchen."

Alice tries to picture a herd of subdued little boys doing laundry and stirring pots. She can't. "Did you learn to cook, at least?"

"Not much. You know what got me through, though, after my daddy died? They had a big window on the west side of the dining room, and Miss Hay, she was the boss of the kitchen, she had a orange tree about two foot tall in a pot. She growed that from a seed. I watched it. There was two oranges on that tree when I left. They wasn't yellow yet, just green."

"Did you run away? I think I would have."

"I tried, a few times. But finally my mama said they needed me home, so they let me come on home. I just went up to seventh grade, that was all. I didn't learn too much English, even though they tried."

"Well, you sure speak it now," Alice says, surprised. Cash Stillwater talks more than any grown man she's met. She can't imagine how it would be if he spoke English any better.

"Oh, well, sure, you pick it up. We didn't talk Cherokee anymore at home after my girls started to get big."

"Why not?"

"I don't know. I talked to them when they were babies, and they knew it real good. But after a while it just all went blank. When they get up around four feet high and start mixing with the other kids, you know, in two weeks they can forget it. I feel like I done my girls wrong, some way. Like there was something they was waiting for me to tell them that I never could think of."

Alice feels his sadness again, and wishes she could lay a hand on top of his weathered brown paw on the gearshift. They've come out of the woods now into rolling, tall meadows of uncut timothy. At the head of a dirt road stands a hand-lettered sign: FIREWOOD. XMAS TREES. BLUEBERRYS HUCKLEBERRYS U PICK. As they turn in on the dirt track, a handful of quail run into the road and break into buzzing flight.

Alice feels excited, as if she has set sail for an unknown shore. She couldn't say why. The smallish bobbly heads of golden flowers are blowing in the wind, and the edges of the field are embroidered with tall white blossoms she remembers from childhood: Queen Anne's lace. They are as pretty as their name, but if you ever tried to take too close a look, they would sting your eye to tears.

It is nearly dusk when they get back to Sugar's with two full pails of huckleberries in the back of the truck. Alice ate some while they were picking, even though that's stealing, since you only pay for what you carry out. Cash teased her, warning that her blue tongue would give her away. She feels like a girl.

In Sugar's driveway, a banty rooster threatens to run under the wheels of the truck. Alice gasps a little.

"He'll run out of the way," Cash says. "If he don't, we'll make dumplings."

He turns off the key but the engine keeps chugging for a little while. Just like Cash, who can't seem to stop talking. "A week before Christmas, them roosters start crowing all night," he tells her. He reaches in his pocket and slips something into Alice's hand. It is dry and flat and sharp as a tooth. She examines it.

"An arrowhead? Where'd you get that?"

"Found it. While you was eating up all the berries."

"You take it home, then," she says, although she loves the feel of its ripply bite against her thumb, and doesn't want to give it up.

"No, you have it. I got about a hundred at home."

"You found that many?"

"No. Some I found, but most of them I made."

Alice turns the slim blade over in her hand. "How'd you learn to make arrowheads?"

"Well, it's a long story. I found my first one when I was five. A little white one about like that. It was broken, though, not much count. I got off my horse and picked it up, and then I picked up another piece of that same white flint, and later on I started knocking pieces off of it. I just kindly taught myself how. For a while I worked down there at Tahlequah making arrowheads for a tourist shop."

"I can't get over that. That's something."

"Oh, it isn't. We used to make ever kind of thing, when I was a kid.

We'd make blowguns out of river cane. Heat it over a fire, straighten it out. You blow a little arrow through there, it's good for killing a bird or a squirrel." Cash laughs. "Not that good, though. Now I use a rifle."

Alice wonders what it would be like to have a man go out and kill food for you. She opens the door and steps down from the truck before she can let herself think about it too long. Cash gets out too, and lifts one of the heavy pails out of the truck bed.

"There's a stomp dance coming up, Saturday week," he tells her.

"I know. Sugar's been talking about it."

"You planning on going?"

"I could."

"You want to plan on driving over there with me? I'd be happy to take you."

"All right," she says. "I'll see you."

Alice feels his eyes on her as she retreats to Sugar's front door. When she hears the truck kick up again, she turns and waves. His glasses twinkle as he pulls away with his arm trailing out the window.

Alice doesn't recall the sensation of romantic love; it has been so long she might not know it if it reared up and bit her. All she knows is that this man, Cash Stillwater, chose her. He saw her somewhere and picked her out. That single thought fills Alice with a combination of warmth and hope and indigestion that might very well be love.

26

OLD FLAME

ON THE NIGHT OF THE stomp dance, Cash comes to fetch Alice at a quarter to twelve. It had seemed to Alice a late hour to begin a date, but Sugar has assured her that the dances start late and run all night. "Cinderella wouldn't of had a chance with this crowd," Sugar tells her. "She'd of gone back all raggedy before anybody important even showed up."

Alice snaps on her pearl earrings and hopes for better luck. In Cash's truck, she teases about the hour as they drive through the woods. "I'm not so sure I know you well enough to stay out all night," she says.

"We'll have about two hundred chaperones," he says, a grin widening his broad face. "If I know my sister Letty, they'll all be keeping a pretty good eye on us."

Alice feels strangely excited by the idea that people are talking about herself and Cash.

"Can I ask you a question?" she asks.

"Shoot."

"I hope you don't mind my asking, but I'm sorry, I can't remember the first time we met."

He glances at her, and the dashboard lights glint on the curved lower rims of his glasses. "First time I seen *you* was on Sugar Hornbuckle's front stoop, the day we went berry picking."

"Well, how in the world?" Alice doesn't quite know how to go on.

"Did I think to call you up?" Cash asks.

"Yes."

"Letty told me." He looks at Alice again, bringing the truck to a complete, unnecessary stop at a quiet intersection on a thoroughly deserted road. Alice has her window rolled all the way down and can hear birds in the forest, fussing themselves into whatever activity it is birds perform at night. "She let me know you was interested," Cash says finally.

Alice is stupefied. "Well, I *would* have been, if I'd known you from the man in the moon, but I didn't. Sugar told me, she said Letty said ..." She can't finish.

Cash begins to laugh. He tips his straw cowboy hat far back on his head, smacks the top of the steering wheel with both his palms, and laughs some more. Alice merely stares.

"You have to know my sister Letty." He runs his index finger under his lower eyelids, behind his glasses. "Oh, law," he says. "If she had free run of this world, she'd like to get that Pope fellow fixed up with some nice widow woman."

Alice blushes deeply in the dark.

Cash reaches across and brushes Alice's cheek with the back of his hand before driving on. "And every once in a while," he says, "the old gal chases a pair of folks up the right stump."

A sign at the gate of the Ceremonial Grounds says: VISITORS WELCOME, NO DRINKING, NO ROWDINESS. Alice and Cash have fallen quiet. Several trucks are ahead of them and a station wagon behind, all rolling through the gate into a forest of small oaks. They pass a dozen or more open shelters with cedar-shake roofs and cookstoves inside, where women are gathered in thick, busy clumps. Above the roofs, the chimney pipes puff like smoking boys hiding out in the woods, giving away their location.

The dirt road ends at the edge of a clearing, and in its center Alice can see the round, raised altar made of swept ash, knee-high and eight feet across. The fire is already burning there, glowing inside a teepee of stout logs. At the edges of the fire a large log lies pointing in each of the four directions, giving it a serious, well-oriented look, like a compass. Cash has warned Alice that this fire is special. It's as old as the Cherokee people; someone carries off the embers in a bucket at the end of each ceremony and keeps them alive until the next monthly dance. Someone carried this fire over the Trail of Tears, he says, when they were driven out here from the east. Alice has only the faintest understanding of what that means, except that it's a long time to keep an old flame burning.

The altar is surrounded by a ring of bare earth some twenty yards across, and at its perimeter a circle of middle-aged oak trees stand graceful and straight-trunked, their upper limbs just touching. People are beginning to gather and settle on hewn log benches under the oaks, facing the fire. Cash gets out a pair of folding chairs and they settle down in front of the radiator grill. Alice can hear little overheated sighs and pops from the engine, and the buzz of a bee that has gotten tangled up there with the metal in an unlucky way.

"You reckon that's one of Boma's bees?" she asks Cash.

"Could be. We drove right by her place."

It was true. Alice saw her standing in her yard, wearing a fedora with a giant white ostrich feather cascading backward into a curl behind her left shoulder. It gave Boma a dashing look, like one of the three musketeers out checking the pressure on the propane tank. Alice feels a little guilty about the bee stuck here writhing on the radiator. "Sugar says Boma loves those bees," she says.

"Oh, she does. Bees are only going to stay living in your eaves if you have kind feelings toward them." He takes off his hat and gently swats the bee, putting it out of its noisy misery.

An old man ambles over to chat with Cash. He has a wonderfully round face and like every other man here wears a straw cowboy hat that has darkened and conformed itself to its master around the crown. Cash introduces him as Flat Bush, leaving Alice to wonder whether this is a first or last name, or both. The two men speak in Cherokee for a while. Alice is surprised that she can follow the general gist because of words like "Ace Hardware" and "distributor cap" that regularly spring up shiny and hard-edged from the strange soft music of the conversation.

People have begun to arrive now in a serious way, parking their trucks in a ring facing the fire, reminding Alice of a crew of friendly horses all tied nose in. She sneaks looks at the old women nested nearby in sag-seated lawn chairs. They all have on sprigged cotton dresses, dark stockings, dark shoes, and black or red sweaters. Their long white hair is pent up in the back with beaded clasps, and their arms are folded over their bosoms. Alice hopes she hasn't done anything wrong by wearing pants, or having short hair. But that's silly; no one has been anything but kind to her so far, or for that matter, looked at her twice. She listens in on the old women's conversation and it's the same over there, except that the hard, shiny words are "permapress" and "gallbladder" and "Crisco."

Roving bands of teenagers move through the woods from here to there: long-haired girls in jeans and Keds, and long-haired boys in jeans and complicated athletic shoes. Some of the boys are tough-looking, with black bandanas pushed high on their shiny foreheads and knotted in the back. They hail each other through the woods in English, but when they address the older people, their greetings are Cherokee. Even toddlers, when they run up to slap dark skirts with grubby hands, open their small mouths and let out strange little bitten-off Cherokee songs. Alice is fascinated. She thinks of the holy-roller churches in Mississippi, where people spoke in tongues, though of course in that case it was more or less every man for himself, whereas here they understand one another. She had no idea there was so much actual foreign language thriving right here under the red, white, and blue. The idea thrills her. She has always wished she had the nerve to travel to foreign lands. Whenever she suggested this to Harland, he reminded her that anything at all you could see in person you could see better on TV, because they let the cameras get right up close. She knew he was right, but always felt misunderstood, even so.

Suddenly there is a sense of quiet, although everyone is still talking.

The men are moving toward their trucks. Cash leans over to Alice as he gets up. "Ledger's just got here," he explains.

"Who?"

"Ledger Fourkiller. Our medicine chief. He's over by that standpipe."

Alice spots him: a small man in jeans and a hat and plaid flannel shirt, hardly one to stand out in the crowd. She doesn't know what she expected, surely not war paint, but still. "Where you going?" she asks Cash.

"Nowhere. Just to get my eagle feather."

The other men are doing the same: each producing a large brown feather from a glove compartment to tuck into a hatband. Alice would like to see Boma Mellowbug, but she doesn't. Instead, a woman with a walk like a she-bear is waddling over to Alice with two cups of coffee. She says something like "Siyo" to Cash. Cash introduces his sister Letty to Alice.

"Pleased to meet you," Alice says, though she actually feels just about every other known emotion besides "pleased." But she takes the coffee gratefully. The night has grown clear and chilly against her bare arms.

"You all looked cold. I thought you needed some hot coffee." She gives Cash some sort of look, but Alice has no idea what it means. Another woman, even shorter and broader than Letty, comes up behind them and reaches up high to clap Cash on the shoulder.

"This here's Alice," Letty tells the woman. "She's staying over at Hornbuckles'."

"My daddy's sister married a Hornbuckle," the woman tells Alice. "Did you know that?" she asks Letty.

"Well, now, sure I did. Leona Hornbuckle."

"No, not Leona. She was a Pigeon, before she married. I'm talking about Cordelia."

"Well, sure, Cordelia was your aunt. I knew that."

"She was a Grass. Cordelia Grass."

"Honey, I know it. I've got Grasses related to me through my oldest daughter."

"No, them's Adair Grasses. This is the Tahlequah Grasses."

Alice listens as the argument winds its way through Grasses, Goingsnakes, Fourkillers, and Tailbobs. At that point Cash touches his sister's arm and points to the fire circle. Both women give a little start and begin to move toward the fire. Cash leans down and touches Alice's hand. "I'm going to go smoke this pipe. I'll see you later on."

The benches have filled up entirely and the chief now stands by the fire. He's a man of slight build, maybe sixty, distinguished by the fact that a long, pale leather pouch hangs down from his belt. To Alice it looks like a bull's scrotum.

Sugar appears in the lawn chair next to Alice, out of breath. She leans over and grabs Alice's arm like a grammar-school girlfriend.

"I didn't want to interfere with anything."

Alice has had about enough of the entire Cherokee Nation organizing her love life. "What's that he's got on his belt?" she asks, nodding toward the chief. "Balls?"

"Naw, just tobacco and stuff. Plants. It's his medicine. They'll all smoke it directly. It isn't nothing bad."

"Well, I didn't think *that,*" Alice says. She wouldn't expect drugs; it has already struck her that there is no alcohol here. She can smell woodsmoke and coffee and the delicious animal scent of grease on a cooking fire, but none of that other familiar picnic odor. It's odd, in a way. A hundred pickup trucks on a Saturday night, and not one beer.

The chief raises his head suddenly and sends a high, clean blessing to the tree branches. His voice is so clear it seems to be coming from somewhere above his ears. When he paces to the east of the fire he seems to grow taller, just from taking long strides. He takes some tobacco from his pouch and offers it to the fire, speaking to the fire itself, the way you might coax a beloved old dog to take a rib bone out of your hand. The fire accepts his offering, and the chief paces some more, talking all the while. He fills a slender white pipe that's as long as Alice's arm. The old people move toward the fire, then nearly everyone else shuffles into single file behind them, making a line that circles the whole clearing.

Sugar leans to get up. "I got to go smoke the pipe now," she whispers. "Afterward, you come sit with me on the Bird Clan benches. You can't sit with Cash, he's not Bird, he's Wolf Clan." She winks at Alice. "Just as well. You can't marry inside your clan."

Sugar hurries to join the line, leaving Alice feeling bewildered and slightly annoyed. She surely had no idea she belonged to a clan. Also she's apparently the only person for miles around, besides Cash, who isn't making wedding plans.

The chief hands the pipe to the first old man, who closes his lips on the stem, closes his eyes, and breathes in. Then he rotates the pipe one complete turn, parallel with the ground. It's an odd-looking gesture that takes both hands. He hands the pipe to the woman behind him in line, the one who was debating Grasses with Letty. The old man walks five or six careful steps toward the east and takes a place at the edge of the clearing. When the woman has gone through the same motions, she joins him. One by one each person takes the pipe; even children do.

Alice spots Annawake in line behind a barrel-chested boy and a slew of kids, and there is Cash, looking like a tall, congenial weed among a cluster of chrysanthemum-shaped women. He seems round-shouldered and easy with himself each time he takes another little step forward. It's a slow process. Alice keeps her eye on two little twin girls dressed in identical frilled square-dancing skirts, moving patiently forward in the line. When their turn comes, the mother touches the pipe to her own mouth first, then holds it to her children's lips, helping each one to rotate it afterward. When the last person in line has smoked the pipe and everyone moves to sit down, Sugar motions Alice over to what she says are the Bird Clan benches. "Third ones from the east, counterclockwise," she points out with her finger. "So you can find them again."

"Well, it's a good enough seat, but I don't see what makes me belong here."

Sugar stares. "Alice Faye, you're just as much Bird as I am. Grandmother Stamper was full-blooded. You get your clan from your mother's line."

Alice never met her mother's mother, a woman of questionable reputation who died dramatically and young somehow in a boat. As the story is told, she didn't even own the clothes she drowned in; Alice hadn't especially thought this woman might leave her belonging to a clan. She doesn't argue, though, because the chief has begun to pray, or talk, again. With his arms crossed he paces back and forth on the bare dirt circle, sometimes looking up at the sky but mostly addressing the fire. His words seem very calm, more like conversation, Alice thinks, than preaching. Sugar says he is preaching, though. "He's saying how to be good, more or less. Everyday wrongs, and big wrongs. Don't be jealous, all that business," she confides. "Same stuff he always says."

Alice feels transported, though. His words blend together into an unbroken song, as smooth as water over stones. It is a little like those holy-roller churches she loved, where, when someone fell into a swoon, you *felt* their meaning; in the roof of your mouth and your fingertips you felt it, without needing to separate out the particular words.

A blue-tick hound walks across the clearing in front of the chief and lies down with a group of dogs near the fire. They all hold their heads up, watching him. Now and again a latecomer truck pulls up through the woods, joining the circle, and respectfully dims its lights. The focused attention in the clearing feels to Alice like something she could touch, a crystal vase, small at the ground and spreading as it goes up into the branches of the oaks.

All at once the chief raises his voice high, and something like a groan of assent rises up through the crowd and the glass is shattered. There is only quiet. Then babies start up with fretful cackles, and old men stand up to shake the hands of old women they didn't see earlier, and the dogs all rise and walk off toward the kitchens.

"Now we get to dance," Sugar says, excitedly. A dozen teenaged girls come out, checking each other seriously and adjusting side to side as they line up in a close circle around the fire. They're all wearing knee-length gingham skirts and the rattling leggings made of terrapin shells filled with stones. Alice is taken aback by how much bigger these are than the training shackles Sugar showed her; they bulge out like beehives from the girls' legs, below their dresses. They all begin to move with quick little double sliding steps, giving rise to a resounding hiss. Several old men fall into line behind them, nodding and singing a quick, perfect imitation of a whippoorwill. Alice feels chills dance on her backbone. The old men begin a song then, and the young women step, step, step, counterclockwise around the fire. As other people come into the circle, they take up hands behind the singers and shackle-bearers, making a long snake that coils languidly around the fire. All at once, when the chief holds up his hand, everyone's feet stop still in the dust and the dancers whoop. It's the sound of elation.

"Oh, that looks fun," Alice cries to Sugar. "Can't you do it?"

"Oh, I will, directly. You should too. You don't have to wait to be asked, just go on up any time you feel like it."

Another dance begins right away. The song sounds a little different, but the dance is still the same gentle stomping in a circle. Only the girls with the turtle-shell legs do the fancy step, concentrating hard, with no wasted motion in their upper bodies; everyone else just shuffles, old and young, pumping their arms a little, like slowed-down joggers. There are several rings of people around the fire now, and the crowd is growing. Alice is fascinated by the girls who remain in the inner circle by the fire, in the honored place, working so hard. This forest feels a hundred miles away from the magazine models with their twiggy long legs. These girls in their bulbous shackles have achieved a strange grace, Alice thinks—a kind of bow-legged femininity.

The dancing goes on and on. An old man produces a drum, and the music then is made up of a small skin drum and deep, mostly male voices and the hiss of the turtle shells above it all like a thrilling high wind. When Alice asked Cash, earlier, about the dance and the music, he said it would be music that sounds like the woods, and Alice decides this is right. No artificial flavorings. It's the first time she has witnessed an Indian spectacle, she realizes, that had nothing to do with tourism. This is simply people having a good time in each other's company, because they want to.

"What are the songs about?" she asks Sugar. To Alice they sound like "oh-oh-wey-yah," and sometimes the chief sings out in a sort of yodel. His voice breaks and rises very beautifully, and the crowd answers the same words back.

"I couldn't really tell you," Sugar answers, at last. "It's harder to understand than regular talking. Maybe it don't mean anything."

"Well, it would have to mean *something*, wouldn't it?"

Sugar seems untroubled by the idea that it might not. "Let's go," she says suddenly, grabbing Alice by the hand. "Just go in after the shackles," she instructs. "Don't get in front of the girls." Alice wouldn't dare.

She follows Sugar in, trembling with nerves, and then there she is, stomp dancing like anybody. At first she is aware of nothing beyond her own body, her self, and she watches other people, imitating the way they hold their arms. But she's also aware that she's doing a strange and unbelievable thing. It makes her feel entirely alive, in the roof of her mouth and her fingertips. She understands all at once, with a small shock, exactly what it is she always needed to tell Harland: being there in person is not the same as watching. You might *see* things better on television, but you'll never know if you were alive or dead while you watched.

Once in a while, Alice remembers Cash and feels a thrill in her stomach. She looks around for him, but can only see the people in front of her and those beside her in the snake's other coils. The song turns out to be a short one, and Alice is disappointed to see that when it ends everyone leaves the clearing and settles back down on the benches of their respective clans. Even after such a short time, her calves feel pinched. It's like an all-night workout on the Stairmaster she has seen advertised on Harland's shopping channel. A Stairmaster with a spiritual element.

While the dancers take a break, a young man stretches a hose from a spigot in one of the kitchen shelters, looping it through the trees, and attaches onto its end the kind of spray nozzle people use for gardening. He carefully hoses down the dirt floor of the dance area, beginning with the eastern part where the chief stood and paced, and working his way slowly around the clearing. He never sprays any water into the fire.

The fire seems to Alice like a quiet consciousness presiding. It's not like an old dog, after all, because it commands more prolonged attention. It's more like an old grandmother who never gets out of her chair.

Sugar is busy gnawing on a chicken wing and introducing Alice to everyone in sight. Alice is too tired to remember names, but she notices Sugar is very proud about pointing out Alice's connection to the Bird Clan.

"I know we had the same grandmother," Alice tells her finally, when all the Tailbobs and Earbobs have drifted away. "But you're forgetting I'm not Indian."

"You're as Indian as I am. Daddy was white, and Mama too except for what come down through the Stamper side."

"Bloodwise, I guess," Alice says, "but you married Roscoe and you've lived here near about your whole life. Don't you have to sign up some-where to be Cherokee?"

"To vote you do." Sugar holds the chicken wing at arm's length, turning it this way and that as if it were some piece of sculpture she were working on. "You have to enroll. Which is easy. You've just got to show you come from people that's on the Census Rolls, from back in the 1800s. Which you do."

"Well, even if that's true, it don't seem right. I don't feel like an Indian."

Sugar places the chicken bones in a bag inside her purse, and touches a napkin to her mouth. "Well, that's up to you. But it's not like some coun-try club or something. It's just family. It's kindly like joining the church. If you get around to deciding you're Cherokee, Alice, then that's what you are."

Alice can't believe it's 2:00 A.M. and people are still driving in. The crowd has grown to several hundred. The turtle-shell girls are assembling around the fire again, and when the dance starts, Sugar and Alice are among the first up. Alice feels endurance creeping up on her gradually. This time the singing lasts longer, and she forgets about her arms and legs. It's surprisingly easy to do. The music and movement are comforting and repetitious and hypnotic, and her body slips into its place in the endless motion. For the first time she can remember, Alice feels completely included.

The instant a dance stops, she becomes aware of her body again, her muscles and her sleepiness. She understands how, if she kept dancing, she could keep dancing. A keen, relaxed energy comes from forgetting your body. She sees how this will go on all night.

Midway through the next song, she realizes Cash has moved into the line behind her. She smiles as she moves her body through the siss-siss of the turtles. He is back there for a while, and then by the time another song begins, someone else is. She sees Annawake out to the side of her, once. She thinks she sees Boma Mellowbug too, without her feather. For a while she tries to keep tabs on where Cash is, but then she forgets to think about it, because she can't quite locate *herself* in this group either. She only knows she is inside of it.

At the end of each song the voices stop and then there is only the watershell hiss, vibrating inside a crystal jar of quiet. It's a sound that loses its individual parts, the way clapping becomes a roar in the hands of a crowd. It is as many pebbles as there are on a beach. Alice's life and aloneness and the things that have brought her here all drop away, as she feels herself overtaken by uncountable things. She feels a deep, tired love for the red embers curled in the center of this world. The beloved old fire that has lived through everything since the beginning, that someone carried over the Trail of Tears, and someone carried here tonight, and someone will carry home and bring back again to the church of ever was and ever shall be, if we only take care of it.

At home, with morning light seeping under the yellow-white shades in Sugar's spare room, Alice lies in bed hugging her own beating heart, afraid of falling asleep. She takes stock of where she is, without believing any of it. Her black suitcase yawns against the closet door, exposing a tangle of innards, and Sugar's ironing board stands near the bed under a pile of wrinkled laundry, burdened like a forward-leaning pack mule.

If she sleeps, the magic could be gone when she wakes up again in this room. She might be merely here, in a cousin's ironing room, with no memory of what has happened tonight. It seems like a fairy tale, and the stories say spells get broken and magic doesn't endure. That people don't really love one another and dance in the woods for no other reason than to promise goodness, and lose track of themselves, and keep an old fire burning.

27

FAMILY STORIES

A YOUNG WOMAN WEARING A lot of beads and a complicated hairdo leads Alice and Sugar through the basement hallway of the Cherokee Heritage Center. She unlocks the door to a small room with a huge oak table in the center.

"You need help finding anybody?" she asks. Alice has noticed that the girl is trying not to chew the gum in her mouth while they are looking. Is that what old women look like to the young? Their fifth-grade teacher?

"No thanks, hon, I've done all this before," Sugar replies.

Their guide leaves them, chewing her gum earnestly to make up for lost time as she heads back upstairs to the gift shop. The big table is covered with old brown ring binders, sprawled out hodgepodge across one another like farmhands taking a break. One wall of the room is covered with an old-looking map of the Cherokee Nation districts, and some sort of film-viewing machine crouches against the other wall. Lined up across the back of the room are antique wooden cabinets of the type that might sit in a country doctor's office. Alice feels exactly that kind of nervousness—as if she's about to get a shot, for her own good.

Sugar sits down in one of the plastic chairs. "This here is the index for the Dawes Rolls," she says, picking up a ring binder thick enough for a toddler to sit on at the dinner table. "1902 to 1905," she reads. She straightens her glasses, licks her thumb, and begins to page through it.

"Are you sure we ought to be doing this?"

Sugar looks up at Alice over her glasses. "I swear, Alice, I don't know what's become of you. You used to make me sneak out to the beer joints on a double dog dare, and now you're scared of your shadow doing just a ordinary everyday thing."

"I don't want to break any rules."

"For heaven's sake, sit down here and look. This isn't nothing in the world but a long list of names. People that was living here and got allotments between certain years."

Alice sits down and scoots her chair toward Sugar, who is holding her chin high so she can see the small print through the bottom window of her bifocals. She looks like a proud little bird with a forties hairdo.

"I'm just going to show you your grandma's name. She's not going to reach out of the grave and tickle your feet."

"She might, if she knew I was trying to cheat the Cherokees."

"Alice Faye, you're not cheating."

Alice gets up and moves restlessly around the room, leaving Sugar to her search through the roll book. "What's this?" she asks, holding up a yellowed, antique-looking newspaper covered with strange curlicues.

Sugar looks up over her glasses. "The *Cherokee Advocate*. That's old, they don't run it anymore. That's what the writing looks like for the Cherokee. It's pretty, isn't it? I never did learn to read it. Roscoe does."

Alice studies the headlines, trying to connect their cursive roundness with the soft guttural voices she heard at the stomp dance. "They had their own paper?"

"Land, yes," Sugar says, without looking up again from her book. "It was the first newspaper in Oklahoma. The Cherokees got things all organized out here while everybody else was cowboys eating with their jackknifes, Roscoe tells me. Them big old brick buildings we passed by in Tahlequah this morning? That was the Cherokee capitol. Oh, look, here she is, right here." She motions Alice over, holding down Grandmother

Stamper under her fingertip. "Write down this enrollment number: 25844."

Alice digs in her purse for a pencil, licks the end of it, and dutifully records this number in her address book under the "Z's," since it seems unlikely she'll ever get close to anyone whose last name starts with a Z. For that matter, the whole address book is pretty much blank, except for three pages of crossed-out numbers for Taylor.

"Now all you've got to do is prove you're descended from her. Having the birth certificate is the best, but she didn't have one. What we did, when Roscoe helped me do this, was we writ to the records office down in Mississippi and we got the record of where she was drownded at. And then we just took that on down to the tribal recorder's office and explained how she was my grandma, and that was that. I think I showed them some family pictures and stuff. They're pretty understanding."

Alice stares at the book of names. She can't put a finger on who, exactly, she feels she's cheating. All the people on the list, to begin with, and the fact they are dead doesn't help. She wishes Sugar hadn't mentioned the business of coming out of graves and tickling feet. "It doesn't feel right to me," she says. "I always knew we were some little part Indian, but I never really thought it was blood enough to sign up."

"It don't have to be more than a drop. We're all so watered down here, anyway. Did you see them blond kids at the stomp dance, the Threadgills? They're signed up. Roy Booth over here at the gas station, he's enrolled, and he's not more than about one two-hundredth. And his kids are. But his wife, she's a quarter, but she's real Methodist, so she don't want to sign up. It's no big thing. Being Cherokee is more or less a mind-set."

"Well, maybe I have the wrong mind-set. What if I'm just doing it to get something I want?"

"Honey, the most you're ever going to get out of the Nation is a new roof, money-wise, and you might have to wait so long you'll go ahead and fix it yourself. There's the hospitals and stuff, but nobody's going to grudge you that. They'll collect from your insurance if you have it, no matter who you are."

Alice feels her secret swelling against her diaphragm from underneath, the way pregnancy felt toward the end. She is even starting to get the same acid indigestion. "Sugar, you're a good friend to me," she says. "I appreciate that you never have asked why I came here."

"Oh, I figured a bad marriage, whatever. Then when you asked after Fourkillers I thought you must be looking for Ledger, for some kind of cure." Sugar holds Alice steady in her gaze, and puts a hand on her forearm. "Everybody's got their troubles, and their reasons for getting a clean start. People's always curious for the details, but seem like that's just because we're hoping somebody else's life is a worst mess than ours."

Alice feels a pure ache to break down right there on the roll books and tell all. But she's so afraid. Sugar might withdraw that hand on her forearm and all the childhood hugs that stand behind it. A month ago, Alice wouldn't have thought any person alive would argue that Turtle belonged to anyone but Taylor. Now she sees there are plenty who would.

"My reasons for coming are different from anybody's you ever heard of," she tells Sugar. "I want to tell you, but I can't right yet. But what I'm thinking is that it could help my cause to sign up here and be Cherokee."

Sugar cocks her head, looking at Alice. "Well, then, you ought to do it. I don't reckon you have to say you're sorry for coming along and picking a apple off a tree."

Alice knows she has to pick the apple. But in her heart, or deeper, in her pinched stomach, she knows it will hurt the tree.

The afternoon is humid and buggy. Alice waves her hand around as she walks, to chase off the gnats that seem to spring right out of the air itself. She wishes she'd worn her shorts. Though when she pictures an old lady in baggy shorts walking down a dirt road to the river, waving her hands wildly, she comes up with something close to Boma Mellowbug. It's just as well she wore her double knits. She wants to make a good impression.

Alice asked Annawake if they could meet someplace besides the café in town; she's not crazy about having every Tailbob in sight overhear what she wants to discuss. Annawake suggested her Uncle Ledger's houseboat. Now Alice is fairly confident she's lost. Just when she arrives at the brink of serious worry, she sees the flat glare of the lake through the trees, and then the corrugated tin roof of what looks like a floating trailer home with a wooden veranda running all the way around. Thick ropes bind it to the shore, and thinner lines run from boat to treetops like the beginnings of spider webs, from which all kinds of things are hung: men's jeans with their legs spread as though they mean to stand their ground up there; and buckets, too, and long-handled spoons. She spies Annawake sitting on the edge of the porch with her legs sunk into the water.

"Yoo hoo," Alice calls, not wanting to startle Annawake, who looks at that moment like a child lost in the land of pretend. Annawake looks up and waves broadly, and Alice is struck by how pretty she is, in shorts and a velvety red T-shirt. Last time, in the café, Annawake showed sharp edges, a cross between a scared rabbit and the hound that hunts him, and her hair seemed deliberately shaggy. Between then and now she has had it trimmed into a glossy earlobe-length bob, and her maple-colored skin is beautiful.

Alice walks across the wobbly-planked bridge from bank to boat, hanging on to the coarse rope handrail to keep herself from falling in the water. The side of the boat is lined all around with old tires, like bumpers.

"You call this a lake?" Alice asks. "I could just about throw a rock to the other bank."

"Well, I guess at this point you could call it a glorified river," Annawake admits. "Did you have trouble finding us?"

"No." She looks around to locate the "us," but sees only Annawake and a lot of dragonflies. Annawake had said Ledger had to go bless a new truck in Locust Grove.

"Do you mind sitting out here? The mosquitoes will be here pretty soon, but the water feels great."

"Don't mind if I do." Alice sits beside Annawake and catches her breath, then takes off her tennis shoes and rolls her pants legs to her knees. When she plunges her feet into the cold, it feels like a new lease on life.

"That haircut looks real good," she tells Annawake, feeling motherly in spite of herself.

Annawake runs a hand through it. "Thanks," she says. "I kind of went crazy and cut it all off when I went to law school. I think I was in mourning, or something. Seems like it's growing back now."

"That was a good idea to meet out here. It's nice."

"Well, it's private. We used to come out here when we were kids, for the summer, and we felt like we'd gone to California. We thought it was a hundred miles to Uncle Ledger's. If anyone would have told me you could walk out here from town in half an hour I wouldn't have believed it. Because nobody ever does."

"Didn't even take that long. Twenty minutes."

"You're a fast walker."

"I always was. If you're going someplace, I figure you'd just as well go on and get there."

She and Annawake look each other in the eye for a second, then retreat.

"So, you've got something to tell me."

"To ask, really," Alice says.

"All right."

Alice takes a breath. "Would it make any difference about who gets to keep Turtle if I was, if her mother and I were enrolled?"

Annawake looks at Alice with her mouth slightly open. After a while she closes it, then asks, "You have Cherokee blood?"

"We do. I found my grandma yesterday in that roll book."

"The Dawes Rolls," Annawake says. She blinks, looking at the water. "This is a surprise. I thought I knew what you were coming here to tell me today, and this is not it."

"Well, would it make any difference? Would that make us Indian?"

"Let me think a minute." She runs her hand through the hair at her temple, pulling it back from her face. Finally she looks at Alice with a more lawyerly look. "First of all, yes, if you enrolled then you would be Cherokee. We're not into racial purity, as you've probably noticed. It's a funny thing about us eastern tribes, we've been mixed blood from way back, even a lot of our holy people and our historical leaders. Like John Ross. He was half-blood. It's no stigma at all."

"That just seems funny to me, that you can join up late. Wouldn't it seem like showing up at the party after they've done raised the barn?"

"I guess it could be seen as opportunistic, in your case." Annawake gives Alice the strangest grin, with the corners of her mouth turned down. "But generally there's no reason why enrollment should be restricted to full-bloods, or half-, or wherever you'd want to make a cutoff. Anybody who lives our way of life should have the chance to belong to the tribe. I *sure* don't think outsiders should tell us who can be enrolled."

"Don't it kind of dilute things, to let everybody in?"

Annawake laughs. "Believe me, people are not lined up on the Musko-gee highway waiting to join the tribe."

"So I'd be as Cherokee as any soul here, if I signed up."

"Legally you would be. And I'll be honest with you, it couldn't hurt your case."

"Well, then, I'm going to enroll."

"But that's kind of missing the point, where your granddaughter is con-cerned. You'd be Cherokee legally, but not culturally."

"Is that the big deal?"

Annawake presses her fingertips together and stares at them. "When we place Cherokee kids with non-Indian foster parents, we have a list we give them, things they can do to help teach the child about her culture. Take her to the Cherokee Heritage Center, get Cherokee language tapes, take her to Cherokee National Holiday events, things like that. But that's just making the best of a bad situation. It's like saying, 'If you're going to adopt this baby elephant, you must promise to take it to the zoo once in a while.' Really, a baby elephant should be raised by elephants."

"She isn't an elephant. She's a little girl."

"But if she's raised in a totally white culture, there's going to come a time when she'll feel like one. And she'll get about as many dates as one. She'll come home from high school and throw herself on the bed and say, 'Why do I have this long, long nose?' "

Alice wants to argue that there are worse things, but she can't immedi-ately think of any. She still doesn't want to buy it, though. "If I'm Chero-kee, and Taylor is, a little bit, and we never knew it but lived to tell the tale, then why can't she?"

Annawake lays her dark wrist over Alice's. "Skin color. Isn't life simple? You have the option of whiteness, but Turtle doesn't. I only had to look at her for about ten seconds on TV to know she was Cherokee."

Alice crosses her arms over her chest.

"Alice, there's something else. I was going to call you in a couple of days. It turns out we have compelling reason to file a motion to vacate this adoption." She watches Alice carefully as she says this. "Someone has come to me asking that I help locate a missing relative who could be Turtle." She continues to look Alice in the eye.

"Oh," Alice says, feeling her heart pound.

"You didn't know about this?"

Alice's mouth feels dry. "No. Nobody would think to tell me about it. Sugar wouldn't, nor anybody, because there isn't a soul except you that knows what I'm here for."

"I see." Annawake looks back at her hands. "Well, we don't know for sure. All we have to go on really is the child's age, and the circumstances of her being removed from the family. The child they're looking for might be someone else entirely. But to tell you the truth, I think it's likely to be Turtle. I have grounds enough to subpoena Taylor and require her to bring the child here for identification."

Alice stares at the flat river where upside-down trees are dancing and cattails reach down toward the blue sky below them. There is a whole, earnest upside-down world around her feet.

"I thought you already told her she had to come here with Turtle."

"No. I suggested it, but I haven't filed the motion yet. What I'd like most is for Taylor to go ahead and do the right thing on her own. For the good of the child, I'd like to handle this with a minimum of antagonism."

"Well, Taylor's already done antagonized. She's living on the lam. That's the truth. I have to wait for her to call me. I don't even know what state she's in."

Annawake shakes her head slowly. "I keep thinking there has to be a way to explain this so it doesn't sound to you like we just want to tear a baby from a mother's arms."

"Well, what else is it?"

Annawake looks thoughtful. "Do you remember that surrogate baby case a few years back? Where the woman that gave birth to the baby wanted to keep it? But the judge awarded custody to the biological father and his wife."

"That made me mad! I never did understand it."

"I'll tell you what decided it. I read that case. The biological father stood up and told the jury his family history. He'd lost everybody, every single relative, in concentration camps during World War II. That baby was the last of his family's genes, and he was desperate to keep her so he could tell her about the people she came from." Annawake looks sideways at Alice. "That's us. Our tribe. We've been through a holocaust as devastating as what happened to the Jews, and we need to keep what's left of our family together."

Alice watches the water, where dozens of minnows have congregated around her calves. They wriggle their tiny bodies violently through the water, chasing each other away, fighting over the privilege of nibbling at the hairs on her legs. It feels oddly pleasant to be kissed by little jealous fish.

"You think I'm overstating the case?" Annawake asks.

"I don't know."

"Have you ever read about the Trail of Tears?"

"I heard of it. I don't know the story, though."

"It happened in 1838. We were forced out of our homelands in the southern Appalachians. North Carolina, Tennessee, around there. All our stories are set in those mountains, because we'd lived there since the beginning, until European immigrants decided our prior claim to the land was interfering with their farming. So the army knocked on our doors one morning, stole the crockery and the food supplies and then burned down the houses and took everybody into detention camps. Families were split up, nobody knew what was going on. The idea was to march everybody west to a worthless piece of land nobody else would ever want."

"They walked?" Alice asks. "I'd have thought at least they would take them on the train."

Annawake laughs through her nose. "No, they walked. Old people, babies, everybody. It was just a wall of people walking and dying. The camps had filthy blankets and slit trenches for bathrooms, covered with flies. The diet was nothing that forest people had ever eaten before, maggoty meal and salted pork, so everybody had diarrhea, and malaria from the mosquitoes along the river, because it was summer. The tribal elders begged the government to wait a few months until fall, so more people might survive the trip, but they wouldn't wait. There was smallpox, and just exhaustion. The old people and the nursing babies died first. Mothers would go on carrying dead children for days, out of delirium and loneliness, and because of the wolves following behind."

Alice uncrosses and crosses her arms over her chest, understanding more than she wants to. She knows she is hearing the story Annawake has carried around her whole life long. A speedboat whines past, far away on the other side of the river. Long after the boat and its noise are gone, they are rocked by the gash it cut in the water.

"They figure about two thousand died in the detention camps," Annawake says quietly. "And a lot more than that on the trail. Nobody knows."

A bright yellow wasp hovers over the water near their feet and then touches down, delicately as a helicopter. It floats with its clear wings akimbo, like stiff little sails.

Annawake gives an odd, bitter laugh. "When I was a kid, I read every account ever written about the Trail of Tears. It was my permanent project. In high school Civics I read the class what President Van Buren said to Congress about the removal, and asked our teacher why he didn't have us memorize that, instead of the Gettysburg Address. He said I was jaded and sarcastic."

"Were you?"

"You bet."

"Well. What did President Van Buren say?"

"He said: 'It affords me sincere pleasure to be able to apprise you of the removal of the Cherokee Nation of Indians to their new homes west of the Mississippi. The measures have had the happiest effect, and they have emigrated without any apparent resistance.'"

Alice feels she could just slide down into the water without stopping herself. It's monstrous, what one person will do to another.

Annawake and Alice sit without speaking, merely looking at the stretched-out body of Tenkiller Lake, drawing their own conclusions.

"Somebody must have made it," Alice says at last. "You're here. I saw the newspapers and all, that they had."

"Well, on the good side, we had the run of the place for a while with no interference. By the late 1800s we had our act together again. If you're really inclined to be Cherokee you should go down to the museum and have a look. We had the first free public school system in the world. For girls and boys both. In secondary school they taught physiology, music, history, algebra, Virgil."

"Shoot, that's more than they ever taught me."

"In 1886 we got the first telephone line west of the Mississippi into Tahlequah. They didn't want to have to look at ugly lines, so they ran it through the woods and strung it from trees."

Alice laughs. "Sounds like some high-class people."

"It's no joke. We had the highest literacy rate in the whole country."

"It's pretty, that writing." Alice can nearly taste the mysterious curled letters that kept their silence on the crumbling newspaper she saw. "Is it hard to read it?"

"They say it isn't, but I never learned. Don't tell anybody. It pisses me off that Uncle Ledger never taught me."

"You're bringing down the literacy rate."

"Yeah, I told him that. Although it's kind of down around our ankles now."

"What happened? If you don't mind my asking. I mean no offense, but Sugar showed me all the fancy old capitol buildings and stuff, and I was thinking it looked like a hurricane hit this place since then."

Annawake snorts. "Hurricane *Yonega*."

"You can't blame every bad thing on white people," Alice says softly.

"Nineteen-ought-two, the railroad came in," Annawake replies, just as quietly. "Gee Dick and his band played for a stomp dance on the courthouse lawn, to celebrate the arrival of the first train. The first white folks stepped off the train and started poking around and probably couldn't believe they'd given us such a beautiful piece of real estate. No ugly telephone lines. Within four years, our tribal government was dissolved by federal order. The U.S. government started the Indian boarding schools, dividing up families, selling off land. You tell me, who do we blame?"

"I don't know. The times. Ignorance. The notion people always seem to get, that they know what's best for somebody else. At least that part's over, they're not moving you out anymore."

"No, now they just try to take our kids."

Alice feels stabbed. "Turtle was practically left for dead," she says. "My daughter saved her from starving in a parking lot, or worse. I'd think you might be grateful."

"I'm grateful that she's alive. But I'm not happy about the circumstances."

"Maybe you and me are just going to have to be enemies," Alice says.

"I don't think so. But I want you to understand how deep these feelings run. For this whole century, right up until 1978 when we got the Indian Child Welfare Act, social workers would come in here with no understanding of how our families worked. They would see a child who'd been left with someone outside the nuclear family, and they would call that neglect. To us, that is an insane rationale. We don't distinguish between father, uncle, mother, grandmother. We don't think of ourselves as having extended families. We look at you guys and think you have *contracted* families."

"That's true," Alice says, thinking of her empty address book. She can't deny it. It struck her back in Kentucky, when she wanted to leave Harland but couldn't think where else home might be.

"We couldn't understand why they were taking us apart. My brother Gabe, going to a man and woman in Texas when we had a whole family here. I've seen babies carried off with no more thought than you'd give a bag of brown sugar you picked up at the market. Just a nice little prize for some family. The Mormon families *love* our kids, because they think we're the lost tribe of Israel. Little pagan babies to raise up and escort you into heaven!"

Annawake's eyes are streaming tears. She looks up at the darkening sky. "These were our kids," she tells Alice, and the sky. "Thousands of them. We've lost more than a quarter of our living children."

There is a whole fleet of yellow wasps floating on the water now. A breeze too slight for Alice to feel causes them all to slide across the surface along the same diagonal. One by one, they lift off into the air.

Annawake wipes her face with the back of her wrist, and looks at Alice. "I concede your point that Turtle was abandoned. She wasn't stolen, she was lost and found. It's not the first time an Indian parent has given a child away, I have to admit that to you. There's a real important case, Choctaw *vs.* Holyfield, where that happened. But the way our law looks at it is, the mother or father doesn't have that right. It's like if I tried to give you, I don't know, a piece of the Tahlequah courthouse."

Alice hands Annawake a handkerchief. Young people never carry them, she's noticed. They haven't yet learned that heartbreak can catch up to you on any given day.

Annawake folds and unfolds the cotton square on her lap. "We see so many negative images of ourselves, Alice. Especially off-reservation. Sometimes these girls make a break for the city, thinking they'll learn to be blonde, I guess, but they develop such contempt for themselves they abandon their babies at hospitals or welfare departments. Or a parking lot. Rather than trust to family."

"It's a sad story," Alice says. "But if you make Turtle leave the only mama she knows now, you're going to wreck a couple of lives."

"I know that." Annawake looks down, tucking behind her ear a lock of hair that immediately falls out again. "I could also tell you that some wrecked lives would be made whole again. There's no easy answer. I'm trying everything I can think of to avoid legal intervention. I'd kind of cooked up an alternate plan, but it doesn't seem like it's working out." She gives Alice the same careful study again, looking for something.

"What does the law say?"

"That's easy. The ICWA says a child should be placed with relatives if they're available, or with other members of the child's tribe, or, third choice, with a member of another Native American tribe. The law is clear."

"How's your conscience?" Alice asks.

Annawake lifts her feet out of the water and splashes a little, causing the minnows to flee. "The thing is, I'm really not jaded and cynical. My boss thinks I'm a starry-eyed idealist. That's the whole reason I pursued this case, instead of minding my own business. At the time I met your daughter, I had never experienced a crisis of faith."

Alice looks up at the sky, so much brighter and more silent than the one reflected below. "I wish I could say I always knew what was right," she tells this mysterious child.

Annawake brushes Alice's hand so lightly she could have imagined it.

28

SURRENDER

DOROTHY

THUNDER POUNDS IN THE DISTANCE and rain coats the Dodge's windshield, drifting across it in sheets like the hard spatter against a shower curtain. Taylor bangs on the steering wheel. "This isn't a city, it's a carwash!"

Turtle looks away, out the window on her side. They are parked in front of the Kwik Mart, held hostage by the rain, hoping it might lighten up enough to let Taylor make a call from the pay phone.

Taylor grips the steering wheel hard, until the weakness in her forearms runs in slow warm-water currents up into her shoulders and neck. She blows out air. "I'm sorry, sweetheart. I'm not mad at you, I'm mad at the rain."

Turtle mumbles something, rolling Mary idly in her lap.

"What?"

Still looking away, she pronounces: "You're always mad at something."

"Oh, Turtle." Taylor has to bite her tongue to keep from snapping, "I am not!" If she weren't so miserable, she would laugh at her terrible mothering skills. She stares out the window on her side, toward the washed-out vacant lot next door, empty tonight. Apparently the criminal element has the sense to stay home in this weather. They probably have nice homes, Taylor thinks, and VCRs. As drug dealers, they would have a decent income. Probably they're home watching *America's Most Wanted*, with their heat cranked up to seventy-five degrees.

"How was school today?"

"Okay, I guess."

"That's all?"

"Yeah."

Taylor turns in the seat to face Turtle, tucking her feet under her. She taps Turtle on the shoulder politely. "Listen, you, I want to talk about it."

Turtle slowly brings around her face, with its question-mark eyebrows.

"What was the best thing that happened?"

Turtle thinks about it. "There wasn't any best thing."

"Okay, what was the worst thing?"

"Lisa Crocker made fun of my pants."

"Your bicycle pants? What's wrong with those? All the kids wear those, I've seen them."

"She says I wear them every day."

"Well, that's not true. On the other days you wear your jeans."

Turtle pushes her palms against her thighs. "The other kids have more than two pairs."

"I know, Turtle. I used to get made fun of in school too. Mama cleaned people's houses, and they'd give her their kids' outgrown stuff for me to wear. They thought they were doing us a favor, but I ended up going to school looking like a clown."

Turtle slides her eyes sideways and suppresses a grin. "With a big red nose?"

"I should have worn a big red nose. I copped an attitude instead."

"What's that?"

Taylor notices that the rain is changing from a major to a minor key, maybe letting up a little.

"Copping an attitude? Oh, it just means I acted real tough. Like I *wanted* to look like that, and everybody else was ridiculous for wearing their little matching sweaters and skirts."

Turtle thinks this over. "I don't think I can cop an attitude," she says.

"You shouldn't have to! Kids your age should not even like the *idea* of clothing. You should still be trying to throw everything off and roll in the mud."

Turtle looks attentively skeptical.

"I'm telling you, this Lisa Crocker character is a social deviant."

"She's just like the other girls, Mom."

"Good grief, they're all going to grow up to be like Barbie! Can you imagine what that means for the future of our planet?"

"I want them to be my friends."

Taylor sighs and strokes Turtle's hair. "I think it's harder to be an underprivileged kid than it used to be."

"One time I wore the school's pants," Turtle says. "Those gray sweater pants with letters on them. When I had that accident."

"Well, that's true. That wasn't much fun, though, was it?"

"No."

"I'm glad your stomach's feeling better these days."

Turtle is quiet.

"Aren't you feeling better?"

"No," Turtle says faintly.

"No?" Taylor feels a wave of panic.

"It hurts mostly."

"Oh, Turtle. This doesn't make any sense. You've never been sick before."

"I'm sorry, Mom. I just get the stomach cramps. I can't help it."

"Oh, Turtle."

"Mom, it stopped raining. Look."

It's true, the noisy assault is over, but the windshield is still blurred with a serious drizzle. "You poor kid, you've forgotten what good weather is.

You think a sunny day is when you only need a raincoat instead of an umbrella."

"No, I don't. I remember sun."

"Remember Tucson?"

"Yeah."

"What do you remember best?"

Turtle closes her eyes for a long time. "There isn't any best," she says, finally. "I liked it all."

"But we didn't have much money then, either. I think you only had one or two pairs of pants even in Tucson."

"We had Jax, though. And Lou Ann and Dwayne Ray, and Mattie, down at your store."

"That's true. We had them."

"Will they let us come back?"

"We don't have enough money for gas. And we can't tell anybody where we are."

"But if we did have gas, I mean. Does Jax and everybody still want us to live there?"

"I think he does."

"He's not mad because we went away from home?"

Taylor rolls down the window and closes her eyes and lets the hissing night lick her face like a cat. "That's what home means, Turtle," she says. "Even if they get mad, they always have to take you back."

Alice answers the phone at last.

"Mama, I've been trying to call you all different times today. Where were you?"

"Law, Taylor, I couldn't even tell you. Someplace called Lip Flint Crick, or Flint Chip Lick, something. On a picnic."

"A *picnic?* I thought you were supposed to be arguing with the Fourkiller woman."

"I did. But then we went on a picnic."

"You argued, and then you went on a picnic?"

"No, not with her. I've got me a boyfriend."

"Mama, I swear, I can't turn my back on you for one minute!" Taylor hears a bitterness in her voice like green potato skins, but she can't stop up the place it's growing from.

Alice is quiet.

"I'm happy for you, Mama. Really. What's his name?"

A flat answer: "Cash."

"Oh, that sounds good. Is he rich?"

Alice laughs, finally. "Believe me, Taylor, this is not the place to come if you're looking to find you a millionaire typhoon."

"Tycoon, Mama. A typhoon is a hurricane, I think. Or maybe it's that kind of snake that strangles you."

"Well, they got more snakes here than you can shake your tail at, but no millionaire typhoons. The man-about-town is a fellow wears a horse-hide suit. He's a sight. It looks like he got up too early and put on the bath rug." She pauses. "How are you all doing? I been hoping you'd call."

"Not hoping bad enough to sit around by the phone, I notice."

Alice's voice changes. "Taylor, you got a bee in your bonnet. I don't know what you're mad at me for."

"I'm not mad at you. Turtle said that just a minute ago. She said I'm mad all the time. But I'm not. I've just fallen on some bad luck and landed jelly side down." Taylor digs in all of her jeans pockets for a handkerchief, but doesn't find one. She rips a yellow page from the damp directory underneath the pay phone. "I think I'm getting a cold."

"You still got that job?"

"Yeah, but they won't let Turtle hang around in Ladies' Wear anymore. She has to go out in the parking lot and sit in the Dodge for a couple hours, till I get off."

"In the car? Goodness, aren't you afraid she'll get lonesome and drive herself to Mexico or something? Remember when we read that in the paper when we was driving across Nevada? That six-year-old that drove the family car to Mexico?"

"That wasn't a newspaper, Mama, that was one of those supermarket things with Liz Taylor on the front. They make all those stories up."

"Well, stranger things have happened."

"I know. But I don't think Turtle's thinking in terms of Mexico."

"Well, good. But you might ought to leave her some stuff in there to play with, just in case."

"I do. I gave her some packing boxes and stuff from the store. She doesn't complain, you know how she is. But I feel like a murderer. Everything I've been doing, for this whole crazy summer, was just so I could keep Turtle. I thought that was the only thing that mattered, keeping the two of us together. But now I feel like that might not be true. I love her all right, but just her and me isn't enough. We're not a whole family."

"I don't know. Seems like half the families you see nowdays is just a mama and kids."

"Well, that's our tough luck. It doesn't give you anything to fall back on."

"What's that noise?"

"Oh, nothing. The Yellow Pages. I just blew my nose on half the landscape contractors in the city."

"Oh, well. I reckon you showed them."

"Mama, I'm thinking about going home."

"Don't hang up yet!"

"No, I mean back to Tucson. I'm at the end of the line here. Jax offered to send me money for gas. If my tires will just hold out. I'm worried about my tires."

"Oh, law, Taylor."

"What?"

"I've got some bad news."

Taylor feels numb. "What is it?"

"I talked to Annawake Fourkiller. She says there's somebody, relatives of a missing girl they think is Turtle, and they want to see her. Annawake said she was going to send you a, what was it? Something Italian sounding. A semolina? Papers, anyway. Saying you have to show up here in court."

"A subpoena?"

"That was it."

"Oh, God. Then I *can't* go home." Taylor feels blood rushing too fast out of her heart toward her limbs, a tidal wave. She stares at the symmetrical rows of holes in the metal back of the telephone hutch. Her life feels exactly that meaningless.

Alice's voice comes through the line, coaxing and maternal. "Taylor, don't get mad at me for something I'm fixing to say."

"Why does everybody think I'm mad? I'm not going to get mad. Tell me."

"I think you and Turtle ought to go on and come down here."

Taylor doesn't respond to this. She turns her back on the wall of holes and looks out through the rain at her car. She knows Turtle is in there but the blank, dark windows are glossed over like loveless eyes, revealing nothing.

"Go ahead and borry the gas money and come on. There isn't nothing to finding us here. Take the interstate to Tahlequah, Oklahoma, and ask around for Heaven. Everybody knows the way."

Taylor still doesn't speak.

"It would just be to talk things over."

"Mama, there's nothing to talk over with Annawake Fourkiller. I have no bargaining chips: there's just Turtle, and me. That's all." Taylor hangs up the phone.

Taylor has been waiting so long with Turtle in the free clinic waiting room she feels sure they've had time to pick up every disease known to science. One little boy keeps licking his hand and coming over to hold it up in front of Turtle, presumably to give her an unobstructed view of his germs. Each time, Turtle withdraws her face slightly on her neck like a farsighted woman trying to focus on small print. The little boy chuckles and pitches crazily back to his mother, his disposable diaper crackling as he goes.

Every now and then, the waiting-room door opens and they all look hopefully to the nurse as she reads off someone else's name. In the bright passage behind her, Taylor hears busy people scurrying and saying things like "The ear is in number nine. I put the ankle in two." The longer they wait, the more vividly Taylor can picture piles of body parts back there.

At last the nurse calls Turtle's name, in the slightly embarrassed way strangers always do, as if they expect the child answering to this name to have some defect or possibly a shell. As she follows Turtle down the hall, Taylor wonders if she did wrong, legalizing this odd name. She has no patience with people who saddle their children with names like "Rainbo" and "Sunflower" to suit some oddball agenda of their own. But "Turtle" was a name of Turtle's own doing, and it fits now, there is no getting around it.

They wind up in a room empty of body parts. The glass jars on the counter by the sink contain only cotton balls and wooden tongue depressors. Turtle climbs onto the examining table covered with white butcher paper while Taylor lists her symptoms and the nurse writes them on a clipboard. When she leaves them and closes the door, the room feels acutely small.

Turtle lies flat on her back, making crinkly paper noises. "Am I going to get a shot?"

"No. No shots today. Very unlikely."

"A operation?"

"Positively not. I can guarantee you that. This is a free clinic, and they don't give those out for free."

"Are babies free?"

Taylor follows Turtle's eyes to a poster on the wall, drawn in weak, cartoonish shades of pink, showing what amounts to one half a pregnant woman with an upside-down baby curled snugly into the oval capsule of her uterus. It reminds Taylor of the time she cut a peach in half and the rock-hard pit fell open too, revealing a little naked almond inside, secretly occupying the clean, small open space within the peach flesh.

"Are they what? Are babies free?"

"Yeah."

"Well, let me think how to answer that. You don't have to buy them. Just about anybody can get one to grow inside her. In fact, seems like the less money you have, the easier it is to get one. But after they come out, you have to buy all kinds of stuff for them."

"Food and diapers and stuff."

"Right."

"Do you think that's why the real mom that grew me inside her didn't want me?"

"No, she died. Remember? Her sister, the woman that put you into my car, told me your mother had died, and that's why they had to give you up. You told me one time you remembered seeing your first mama get buried."

"I do remember that," Turtle says. She continues to study the peach-pit baby poster. Taylor picks up a magazine and is startled to read news about a war, until she realizes the magazine is several years old.

"Hi, I'm Doctor Washington," says a tall woman in a white coat who breezes into the room as if she's run a long way and doesn't see any point in slowing down now. She has long flat feet in black loafers, and a short, neat Afro that curves around her head like a bicycle helmet. She looks around the room quickly, as if she might in fact be anticipating a blow to the head. Her eyes settle on Turtle for a moment, but the rest of her body remains tense. She holds the clipboard in one hand and a pencil in the other, poised between two fingers, jiggling in the air.

"Stomachache?" she says to Turtle. "Cramps, diarrhea? For two or three months?"

Turtle nods solemnly, owning up to all this.

"Let's take a look." Actually she looks at the ceiling, appearing to give it her full concentration as she pulls up Turtle's T-shirt and probes her belly with long, cold-looking hands.

"Here?"

Turtle nods, making a crackling sound as her head grinds against the white paper.

"How about here? This hurt?"

Turtle shakes her head.

Dr. Washington pulls down Turtle's shirt and turns to Taylor. "How is the child's diet." She states it, rather than asks.

Taylor feels her mind blank out, the way it used to in school during history tests. She tries to calm down. "I make sure she gets protein," she says. "We eat a lot of peanut butter. And tuna fish. And she always gets milk. Every single day, no matter what."

"Well, actually, that might be the problem."

"What, milk?"

The doctor turns to Turtle. "How do you feel about milk, kiddo?"

"I hate it," Turtle says to the ceiling.

"What kind do you give her?"

"I don't know," Taylor says defensively, feeling as if the two of them are ganging up. "The store brand. Two percent."

"Try leaving out the milk from now on. I think you'll see a difference right away. Bring her back in, in a week or two, and if that hasn't taken care of it we'll check on other possibilities. But I think cutting the milk's going to do it." She writes something on the clipboard.

Taylor senses that Dr. Washington is about to move on to an ear or an ankle. "Excuse me, but I don't get this," she says. "I thought milk was the perfect food. Vitamins and calcium and everything."

Dr. Washington slumps against the counter, losing a few of her imposing inches and visibly shifting into a slower gear. "Cow's milk is fine for white folks," she says, looking directly at Taylor when she says this, "but somewhere between sixty and ninety percent of the rest of us are lactose intolerant. That means we don't have the enzymes in our system to digest some of the sugar in cow's milk. So it ferments in the intestines and causes all kinds of problems."

"Uck. I never knew that."

"Yogurt may be okay, and aged cheeses. You can give them a try. And some kinds of orange juice are calcium-fortified, that can help you out some with her calcium. If you're determined to give her milk, you can get the kind that's lactose-reduced. There's a large Asian-American population in this city, so you can find that in most of the markets."

"My daughter isn't Asian-American. She's Cherokee."

The doctor lifts her shoulders in an offhand shrug. "Asian, Native American, African, we're all in the same boat. A lot of times it doesn't present until adulthood, but it can start showing up right around her age."

Taylor can't understand how such a major truth could have passed her by. "I always thought milk was the great health food. The people look so perky in those commercials."

The doctor taps her pencil eraser against her cheek and looks at Taylor with something that could be loosely defined as a smile. Her eyes are so dark the irises appear almost bluish around the edges, and her half-closed lids give her a lizardish look. "Who do you think makes those commercials?"

"The guardians of truth," Taylor says, sulkily. "Sorry, I didn't think about it."

For the first time, Dr. Washington's superior-reptile look melts into genuine sympathy. "Listen, nobody does. I break this news to parents of every color, a dozen times a week. You were doing what you thought was best, that's the main thing."

Her white coat is standing up straight again, then gone.

Turtle slides off the gift-wrapped examining table and bounds out the examining-room door like a puppy let out of its pen. Taylor finds she can't get up from her chair. She is paralyzed by the memory of Annawake Fourkiller's final warning, in Tucson, before she drove away: "I bet she hates milk."

Taylor catches up to Turtle outside the clinic. Turtle is shading her eyes and looking straight up at the sky, which for once is miraculously unclouded. A jet has left a white, rubbed-out gash of a trail, ugly as graffiti.

"An airplane makes that," Turtle informs her, and Taylor wonders how she knows this. It's one of several million things they have never yet spoken of, precisely. Did she learn it in school? Then again, do you have to be told every single thing about the world before you know it? The idea of rearing Turtle exhausts Taylor and makes her want to lie down, or live in a simpler world. She would like for the two of them to live in one of those old-time cartoons that have roundheaded animals bobbing all together to the music, and no background whatsoever.

"You're right," Taylor says. "A jet plane."

"Why is it doing that?"

Taylor wonders which level of answer Turtle wants. Why does a jet churn up white dust in the sky? (She doesn't know.) Or, what is this particular jet's motivation? (This, maybe nobody knows.)

"Remember in Dorothy, when the witch wrote in the sky?"

"Yeah, I do," Taylor says. "In the *Wizard of Oz*. She wrote, 'Surrender Dorothy.' "

"Did that mean they were supposed to give Dorothy to the witch?"

"That's what she was asking for. Yeah."

"Are you going to give me to the Indians?"

"No. I'll never do that. But I think we have to go back and talk to them. Are you scared?"

"Yeah."

"Me too."

29 ☾

THE SECRET OF

CREATION

CASH MOVES THROUGH HIS KITCHEN the way a lanky squirrel might, if a squirrel could cook: stepping quickly from sink to stove, pausing, sensing the air. By comparison, Alice feels like the lazy squirrel wife, sitting at the table separating hickory nuts from their crushed shells. "Slow down, Cash," she tells him, smiling. "You're making my eyes hurt."

"I always do that to women," he says. "I'm just ugly, is all."

"Pish posh, you are not." Alice picks a nearly whole nut from the curled chambers of its shell and drops it into the bowl. For reasons she couldn't explain, the naked, curled little nuts remind her of babies waiting to get born.

Cash told her this log cabin was the original dwelling on his family's homestead. It has stood empty for years, and seemed the right size for him when he came back from Wyoming. It's all one room, with a kitchen at one end and a pair of parlor chairs flanking the lace curtain on the other end. For the summer he's moved his bed out to the porch, for air. His rifle, his toothbrush, and a lucky horseshoe hang over the stone fireplace. The cabin seems sturdy enough to stand through a tornado, or small enough to be overlooked by one in favor of the larger house that was built later on, where Letty now lives. The cabin has been occupied by most of Letty's children at one time or another; they were the ones who installed plumbing and strung out the electrical wire, which now supplies Cash's few light bulbs and—Alice was distressed to note—the little TV set that squats on the kitchen counter amongst the bowls and flour canisters. He did shut it off right away when she came in. She'll hand him that much.

"You don't have to get all them shells out. Just the big pieces," he tells her. "Are you watching this, now? You got to know how to make *kunutche*, if you're going to sign up to be Cherokee here in a while."

"Is that right? Will they give me a test?"

"Oh, I think so, probably. But if you decide not to enroll, then don't bother learning. No *yonega* would fool around with a thing that's this much trouble."

"Maybe I oughtn't to, then, and just go on letting you do all the work." Alice is startled to hear what she's just said, words that contain a presumption about the future. If Cash is in any way riled, he doesn't show it. He dumps the nuts with a clatter into a dented metal bucket and pounds them deftly with a wooden club, making a steady gritch-gritch like a cow chewing. The pounding club resembles a sawed-off baseball bat. Alice saw one in Sugar's kitchen and had no earthly notion what kind of cooking implement it might be. It looked so forceful.

"You pound it till it's powder, that's the way you start out," Cash instructs. "Then you roll it into balls about yay big." He holds up his right fist, wrist forward, to show her, looking to see that she has understood. "There's enough oil in it so it holds together good." He turns back to pounding, and goes on talking with a slightly breathless rhythm over the nutty gritching sound, which has now gone to more of a hiss. "When you get ready to fix it, you just break off a piece of the ball and add it to boiling water, and then you strain it through a good clean sock to get out the little bits of shell, and you mix it with rice, or hominy. It's kindly a soupy consistency."

"Sounds good," Alice says, reverently. In her life she has experienced neither men who talk a lot nor men who cook, and here is one doing both at once. She would have paid money to witness this, and not been disappointed.

"I love it with hominy," he adds. "It kindly puts you in the mood of fall, when you smell *kunutche*."

"Did your wife teach you how to make it?"

"Well, now," he pauses and stares at the wall calendar. "I guess my mama did. My wife did the cooking, mostly, but I always pounded up the *kunutche*. She said all that grinding hurt her bones."

Alice stands up and wanders the length of the cabin, wishing for family pictures or some other hint of what Cash belongs to. Her eyes rest on his toothbrush, which seems small and stranded up there, and his gun. "You shoot anything with that rifle?"

"Oh, a squirrel now and then, if he'll set still long enough to get hit. My eyes isn't what they was. Usually I'll miss three or four time, and then one'll keel over and die of a heart attack."

Alice wants to give him a hug. If men only knew, modesty makes women fall in love faster than all the cock-a-doodling in the world. She touches her earrings, whose tiny beads shiver away from her fingers. They were delivered to her one morning in an envelope marked only, "From a secret admirer." Sugar, who had stood breathing on Alice's head while she ripped open the envelope, instantly identified the turquoise-and-silver beadwork as Cash's. She said he had been selling earrings just like that to the trading post at the Heritage Center.

Alice sent Cash back a note that said, "Many thanks and a special hug from your mystery date." She gave it to Sugar to mail at the P.O., and was mortified later to find that Sugar had run into Letty in town and asked her to hand-deliver it.

"Sugar says you do beadwork for the trading post. That a fact?"

"I do a little. It relaxes me at night."

"Somebody sent me these earrings. Can you imagine? Some fellow must think he can knock me over with a feather."

Cash grins. "I got your note."

"I'll bet Letty opened it up and read it first."

"Looked like it. She's not as professional as she used to be." Cash's face broadens under the eyes with a smile that seems to be settling in and getting comfortable.

"I guess I ought to try my hand at that," she says, coming over to stand next to him. "Either that, or sing for my supper. Of the two I think you'd ruther me mash nuts."

He positions her hands on the club, then stands back to watch. "I don't know about that. You got a real nice talking voice. I was thinking the other day, if I had a telephone I'd call up Alice just to listen at her voice. I bet you could sing like a bird."

"A turkey buzzard," Alice says.

"Now, you stop right there, I don't believe you. I'd pay a dollar to hear you sing 'Amazing Grace.' Or 'Don't Set Under the Apple Tree.' Here, it helps sometimes if you put more shoulder into it."

He stands behind her with his arms over hers, gripping her hands gently and pushing downward. The precise hissing sound returns to the kitchen, nut powder urged against metal. Alice feels a similar sound in her chest.

"You'd ask for your dollar back when I was done," she says.

Cash eases the pressure on her hands. "I wouldn't. Even if you did sound like a turkey buzzard, I wouldn't care."

Alice leans her head back against him at the same moment he lifts his arms across her chest, holding her there and dropping his face into the crown of her hair.

"Cash," she says.

"Hm?" He turns her around, keeping her within the circle of his arms. She looks up at his face, which at close range without her reading specs is blurry, except for the window-shaped lights in his eyes.

"You might be able to knock me over with a feather," she tells him. "It'd be worth a try."

Cash's cabin is in deep woods, a quarter-mile behind Letty's back garden. From his iron bed out on the screen porch, Alice wonders how it would be to wake up every morning to the sight of nothing but leaves.

"Did you hear what happened to that Mr. Green?"

"The ostrich rancher?" she asks. "I heard his ostriches like to sashay around and drop their feathers on the wrong side of the fence."

Cash runs a finger down Alice's nose. Without his glasses his eyes look soft and hopeful, like they're in need of something. Alice honestly can't remember the last time she was naked under the quilts with a man who was awake, but even so, neither she nor Cash seems to be in any big rush. It's such a pleasure just to realize they've gotten this far. And to listen to talk.

"He tried to break into Boma's house to get that feather back," Cash tells her.

"Lord! Was she home?"

"No. They was all at a wedding. Can you imagine? Reading about a wedding in the paper, he must have done, because he sure wasn't invited. And going over to burglarize the groom's own grandma?"

"Well, did he get it?"

"He got it all right." Cash rolls over onto his back and laughs, then clucks his tongue. "I oughtn't to laugh. He's in the hospital."

"With what?"

"Nine thousand bee stings."

Alice gasps. "And still no feather, I'll bet."

"Naw. It'd be like Boma to send it to him in a big vase of flowers, though. With a get-well card from the bees."

"Hope you're back in the pink soon, *honey,*" Alice says, getting the giggles.

"We're bad."

"We are," Alice says. "What would our kids think of us?"

The lines around Cash's eyes go soft, and he seems to drift for a moment. She traces the honed ridge of his breastbone with her finger, feeling deeply sad for whatever it is that takes him away, sometimes, at the mention of his family. She would do anything to ease that burden. She finds his hand, which was resting on her waist, and holds it against her lips. "I'm sorry," she says. "For whatever it is."

Cash moves forward to kiss her. He tastes like woodsmoke and the color of leaves. When he touches her breast, she feels the skin of her nipples gather itself in. She is pierced with a sharp, sweet memory of nursing

Taylor, and when he puts his mouth there she feels once again that longing to be drained, to give herself away entirely. Slowly Cash moves himself
against her, and then very gently into her, and she feels the same longing
coming through his body to hers. They rock against each other, holding
on, and the birds in the forest raise their voices to drown out the secret of
creation.

30

SIX PIGS AND

ONE MOTHER

ALICE WAKES TO THE SOUND of voices inside, in the kitchen. Half of Cash appears in the doorway to the porch, his shirttail out, a smile on his face. He holds a spatula in his left hand, poised like a flyswatter. "How do you like your eggs?" he asks.

Alice, feeling confused, looks around as if she might have laid some eggs she's not aware of. "Who's that in your kitchen?"

"Kitty Carlisle."

"Kitty Carlisle lives in Oklahoma?"

"Naw. She's on 'Good Morning America.'"

Alice runs a hand through her hair, trying to get her bearings. She was in some dream with water and furry animals. "What do you need the TV on for?"

Cash shrugs. "No reason. Just for the company, I reckon."

"Well, I'll get up and keep you company." She begins to

gather up her limbs, testing to make sure of their four separate locations.

"No, you just set there another minute. I'm going to bring you breakfast in bed. I'll bring your coffee on out, as soon as you tell me 'sunny side up' or 'over easy.' "

She thinks. "Over hard, with the yolk broke, if you really want to know. Lord, breakfast in bed? I reckon if I was Kitty Carlisle I'd have me a frilly housecoat to put on."

"I'll bring you my bathrobe," he says, disappearing. Alice licks the roof of her mouth, looking at the leaves all pressed like happy spying faces against the screen. She feels she has died and gone to the Planet of Men Who Cook. Cash returns with an old flannel bathrobe, blue plaid, and settles it on her shoulders. She hugs it around her like a lady in church with a fur stole, and with her free hand accepts a cup of coffee. The first black sip arouses her throat and lungs.

Cash is busy moving things around. He sets a coffee table carefully beside the bed and covers it with plates of eggs, ham, toast, butter, and huckleberry jam. He pulls up a stool on the other side. Alice puts her arms through the sleeves of the bathrobe and sits up on the edge of the bed, facing him, so she won't feel like an invalid.

"I'm not used to being catered to," she says, smiling at her plate. "I'll try to tolerate it, though."

For a while they are quiet, making small clinking sounds with their forks. Cash blows on his coffee. A bird somewhere in the leaves asks, "Chit? Chit? Chit?"

"I been wondering how long a visit you're here for," he says finally.

"Oh, at Sugar's? I don't know. I guess till I wear out my welcome. I didn't really come just to visit Sugar, to tell you the truth. I had some business."

"With family?"

"No, with the Cherokee Nation. I don't know if it's with the Nation, exactly." She cuts into her eggs, which are perfect. Most people don't believe you really want broken yolks, and they won't go through with it; they'll keep it whole and runny for your own good. "I had some dealings to do with Annawake Fourkiller. It's something we have to settle about my daughter and granddaughter." Her heart pounds. She didn't decide to tell

Cash, she only knows that she's going to. "I have a little granddaughter that she saw on TV. You know Annawake?"

"Oh, sure. Her Uncle Ledger is the medicine man. You seen him at the stomp dance, didn't you?"

"Sure."

"That little Annawake used to follow him around like a calf." Cash chews his toast. "At the dance, when Ledger would get up to speak, she'd stand right up in front of him and holler out sermons."

Alice finds she can picture this. With Cash, it's easy to get derailed from a confession. "I guess she's going to be the next one, then."

"No, it's somebody younger. I don't know who yet, but they's already picked him out. It starts when you're too young to remember. The medicine man puts the medicine on you, and then when you're older you don't remember it, but it kindly influences how you grow. Later on, you get the training."

"Well, that seems dangerous, don't it? What if the kid that was all picked out to be the next preacher turns out to be a motorcycle hood?"

Cash seems very serious. "That wouldn't happen. The medicine man can tell from the child how they'll be. You don't want one that's real loud, a fighter or anything. You want one that's more quiet."

They return to their breakfast. Alice hears Kitty Carlisle, or someone at any rate, muttering to herself in the kitchen.

"How long were you and your wife married?" she asks.

"Oh, since we was too young to know a hawk from a handsaw. I met her at the stomp dance after I left boarding school. She come from over around Kenwood way." His whole body tilts slightly backward with the pleasure of memory. "Law, I'll tell you, I only started going up there to meet girls, and for the food. They cooked good food at the dances back then: bean balls, squirrel dumpling. Eggs. People went over and stayed all day. They'd come in the wagon and on horses. They'd put up a tent, put up long benches and put a quilt on it and sleep on that. I used to always go early, to play ball."

"Play ball?" Alice asks.

"They play a kind of ball game, before the dance. Did you see that big tall pole with a fish on the top, carved out of wood? Down there in the clearing at the stomp grounds, where the dirt's all beat up underneath."

Alice nods, because her mouth is full. The good thing about Cash is, you can eat big bites while you're listening to him.

"It's girls and women against boys and men. That's how they play. You throw the ball or sling it up there with a stick, and try to hit the fish. It's too hard for little kids and old people. It's kindly serious. I don't know how to explain it, quite. Keeping your body in good shape is part of being a good person, you could say. But back then I paid too much attention to trying to be the best one. Ever time you throw the ball and hit the fish, your side gets a point."

"Don't the boys always win out?"

"No, ma'am, they don't. You should see some of them girls. Now Annawake, she's a killer. And my wife was. That's how we met, playing ball. I won a point, and then she did, we went on like that for a whole game, so we figured out we'd have to get married."

Alice laughs. "Seems like a better reason than most kids have."

"I quit going for a while, after she died. I didn't tell you, but the other night, when we went over together, that's the first I been for a while."

"Why's that, Cash?"

"I couldn't tell you. I was gone away, and then after I come back it seemed too hard. It reminded me of the funerals."

"They have funerals at the stomp grounds?"

"Well, sure. They carry the casket around the fire three times, the same direction as you go when you're dancing, and then they carry it walking backwards, three times. I guess you're going back out of life the same door as you come in. And then you go to the cemetery for the burying. There's buckets of tea outside the cemetery, so when you go out you can wash your face and hands in the tea to wash off the grieving, and leave it there."

Cash looks sunk in misery. Alice says gently, "It don't seem like you left it all behind."

"Well, maybe they was too much of it come all at once. Four year ago, we had three funerals in the same season: my mama, well of course she was old. Then my wife, of the cancer. And then my oldest girl, Alma. She drove her car off a bridge and landed it upside down in the Arkansas River. She had a little bitty girl, when she done that. She left the baby behind that night with her sister, the one that run off with a no-count boy to Tulsa and don't talk to me no more. I kept on calling her up for a while. She was mean as she could be, but I had to call, because I was worried about Alma's baby. Lacey, her name was. But durn if one day she didn't up and give that baby away. She goes to a bar one night and hands her over to some girl passing through in a car."

Alice feels the breath knocked out of her, exactly as if she had fallen off a roof. She can't pull in air.

"The younger people have got bad problems, I'll be the first one to tell you. Monday mornings the jails are full of 'em. A lot of these kids think liquor is made for one purpose, to get drunk as quick as you can."

"How do you know she gave the baby away?"

"She told me. How do you like that? She tells me, 'Pop, I'm moving to Ponca City, could I use your truck next weekend? I done give Alma's baby away.' I felt so discouraged I just packed up my truck that same weekend and drove out of here. I couldn't stand to look at my own kin."

Alice puts a hand on her chest and gets her breath back. She has to say it before she thinks twice. "Cash, my daughter has that girl."

Cash puts down his coffee cup and looks at Alice. He doesn't for an instant disbelieve her.

"That's what I come here for," she tells him. "Annawake saw Taylor and the little girl on TV telling the story of how she got adopted. Annawake figured some way she belonged to the Cherokees, and she tracked them down. Taylor run off. They're living on the lam now so she won't have to give her up. She loves her, Cash. My daughter's been as good a mother to that child as ever you're going to find."

"Lord God in Heaven," Cash replies.

"I can't figure out what to think," Alice says.

"No, me neither."

"My brain's gone off somewhere. Are you fixing to be mad? Because I have to tell you where I stand. My daughter hasn't done a thing in the world wrong. She's protecting her child, like any living mother would do, man or beast."

"No," Cash says. "She ain't done wrong. I'm just trying to picture that Lacey's somewhere all in one piece. Walking, I guess. Lord, what am I saying? Walking, talking, picking up sticks. She'd be six and a half."

"She's not a Lacey. Not for love nor money. Her name's Turtle."

"Well, what kind of a name is that?"

"What kind of a name is Able Swimmer?" Alice fires back. "Or Stand Hornbuckle, or, or Flester Dreadfulwater!"

Cash ignores her. "It just don't seem real," he says. "After I come back here from Wyoming a little while ago, I talked to them girls down at Child Welfare about trying to find her. They said they might have a bite on the line, but I didn't hold for much hope. Lord God in Heaven. Us coming together like this, not even knowing."

He stares at Alice while the trees grow outside.

"Letty set this all up," he says. "She must have knowed."

"No, she didn't, Cash. Not a soul knew my side of it but Annawake. I didn't even tell Sugar."

"Well, how in the world?"

"I don't know," Alice says. "I'm suspicious of miracles. There's near about always something behind them."

"Sugar didn't know?"

"No. I swear on the Bible."

"I figured this business with you and me was something Sugar and Letty cooked up. Otherwise, Letty wouldn't have knowed you was fair game."

"Then it was Annawake," Alice says suddenly. "It was. She had to have done this. She said she'd been working on Plan B, I'll swan, I could tan her hide! She's trying to find a way around doing her rightful duty by Turtle."

Cash looks wary. "What is her rightful duty?"

Alice stares back, comprehending his position. "Nothing's settled, is it?"

Cash lays his knife across the edge of his plate. "No. Nothing's settled."

Alice has spent all Sunday afternoon with her teeth clenched and unkind intentions in her heart, hunting down Annawake. She feels like one of those Boston Stranglers you can read about. The first thing she did when she came home to Sugar was spill the whole story, start to finish, leaving out only the details of last night with Cash, which were nobody's business. Sugar agreed she ought to give Annawake a good talking to, for meddling. They enlisted Roscoe to drive over to Annawake's place in Tahlequah. Sugar sat in the cab between Alice and Roscoe, squeezing Alice's hand as if she were having a baby instead of about to lose one.

In Tahlequah, Sugar and Roscoe waited in the cab while Alice knocked on the door and talked to a heavyset girl holding a baby, who said Annawake was down at the Nation offices. They drove down the highway to Nation Headquarters, only to find the place deserted. There was one secretary in the whole place, who pointed them to Annawake's office across the street. It was locked. Alice tried to peer in, but saw only houseplants. She festered in the truck for nearly an hour, waiting, before deciding to drive back to talk again to the heavyset girl, who seemed, in all fairness, just as sweet as she could be. She said Annawake had come and gone again, fishing this time, down at her uncle's houseboat. Alice climbed back in the cab and surprised Sugar and Roscoe by claiming to know the way to Ledger Fourkiller's. When they dropped her off at the path running down to the river, they offered to wait, but Alice waved them on.

"I know my way. If she's not here, I'll just walk on back."

"Well, honey, that's miles and miles," Sugar had protested before they drove off. "And dark. You're liable to run into a skunk."

But Alice feels determined as she sets off down the path, skunk or no skunk. If she ran into one right now, he'd have to take his chances. She doesn't really expect to strangle Annawake once she finds her, but she hasn't ruled out the possibility.

Annawake has given up the pretense of fishing. Nothing down there is hungry, and to be honest, neither is she; it seems reasonable to call a truce. She swirls her legs in the water, watching the reflected stars tremble in each other's company. The water is warmer than the air, and moves against her skin as if it cared for her. She tries not to think how long it has been since she was hugged by someone who wasn't a relative.

She hears steps on the footbridge, or rather, feels their vibrations approaching, the way a spider knows the commerce of her web. "Ledger?" she calls out.

A human silhouette appears in the darkness at the edge of the porch, and it isn't Ledger Fourkiller. Smaller, meaner, not at home. Her heart thumps.

"Well! If it's not Miss Lonelyhearts."

Annawake knows the voice. Thinks hard.

"It was you, wasn't it? You set up me and Cash."

"Alice Greer?"

She approaches as slowly as a dog outside its territory, until she is standing five feet away, hands on her hips, both angry and hesitant.

"You're mad? I saw you two giggling like kids at the Sanitary Market. I thought you'd be sending me a thank-you card."

"That was a sly, sneak-handed business you did. You figured I'd take a shine to Cash and wouldn't want to take his baby away from him."

Annawake feels this woman's anger sharpened like a hunting knife. "Did you ever think it might work out the other way? That he might like *you* that much?"

"I don't think that's what you were aiming for."

"Can we sit down and talk it over?"

Alice hovers for a moment the way a female dragonfly will, before committing her future, laying her eggs on the water. Finally she plunges. Sits and takes off her shoes.

Annawake paddles her legs slowly back and forth. "To tell you the truth, Alice, I couldn't tell you what I was thinking. I don't think I *was* thinking, for once. I just followed my gut. I thought my Indian-white relations project needed a human touch."

"And me and Cash went like lambs to the slaughter."

"I didn't think it would take you so long to find out what you two have in common. I figured you'd tell him right away."

"Well, maybe us old folks don't just jump into things the way you kids do."

"Sounds to me like just the opposite. You were so busy jumping into things you forgot to state your business."

Unbelievably, Annawake hears Alice swallow a giggle.

"I guess I overstepped," she tells Alice. "I'm sorry."

In the very long silence, an owl calls from upriver. Annawake can picture its wide-open eyes, hunting. Stealing scraps of sight from the darkness.

"You probably didn't mean no harm."

"Believe me, I had a lot of help from Letty."

"That Letty," Alice agrees, with grudging humor. "She'd stick her nose in a grave if she thought there was still hope of warm gossip."

The adrenaline that rushed Annawake's limbs when she first saw anger in the dark is receding now, leaving her body with a longing to stretch. She arches her back. "Every town probably needs a Letty," she says. "Somebody to lubricate things, and then count backwards from nine every time a couple of newlyweds have a baby."

"Margie Spragg. That's who it was in Pittman. She was the phone operator for the longest time. It about killed her when they put in the dial tone."

"It's a public service, what those women do. Sometimes people have communication problems with their own hearts."

"Well," Alice says. "Nothing's settled, still."

"I know."

"Taylor's on her way. She called me from a truck stop in Denver."

"Is she?" Annawake feels curiously apprehensive. For months she hasn't been able to recall Taylor's appearance, having met her so briefly, but now, suddenly, she does. The fine-featured, trusting face, the long dark hair, the way she held perfectly still while listening. She remembers Taylor standing at the window curled forward with animal fear, and she imagines her in a telephone booth in Denver, curled forward with the receiver under a sheet of dark hair.

"I figured you'd be jumping for joy," Alice says.

"Oh, I'm not much of a jumper. I oftentimes have communication problems with my heart."

"Letty ever try to help you out on that?"

Annawake holds her hand in the air. "Don't even ask. Letty Hornbuckle has tried to fix me up with everything in this county that stands on two legs to pee. Unfortunately, that's not my problem."

"Oh."

Alice is now swirling her own legs through the water, creating crosscurrents that jostle the stars together in the water until Annawake can fairly hear them ringing.

"Look. There's the Little Dipper out there in the middle of the river, upside-down. See her?"

"I can't see good at night."

"You can see it in the sky, though. Straight up from that one dead oak that looks white, over there on the bank."

"I think I do see it," Alice says, in a voice thinned out from looking up.

"Don't look it straight head-on. Look a little off to one side, and it will be brighter. Uncle Ledger showed me that."

"Sure enough," Alice says in a minute. And then, "I'll swan. I can see all seven of the Seven Sisters, when I do that."

"You people! That must be why whites took over the world. You can see all seven of the Seven Sisters."

"What, you can't?"

"We call them the Six Pigs in Heaven."

"The what? The *pigs?*"

"It's a story. About six bad boys that got turned into pigs."

"Well, that must have made them think twice. What did they do to get turned into pigs?"

"Oh, you know. They didn't listen to their mothers, didn't do chores. Just played ball all the time. So their mothers cooked up something really nasty for them to eat, to try to teach them a lesson. Have you seen those little leather balls we use for playing stickball?"

"Cash showed me a real old one. It was all beat up, with hair coming out of it."

"Exactly. Animal hair. The mothers cooked up a stew made out of that, and fed it to the boys when they came home for lunch. The boys were disgusted. They said, 'This is pig food!' And the mothers said, 'Well, if that's true then you must be pigs.' The boys got up from the table and went down to the stomp grounds and ran in circles around the ball court, just yelling. The mothers ran after them, ready to forgive their rowdy boys and forget the whole thing, but right in front of their eyes the boys started turning into pigs."

"Law," Alice says earnestly. "They must of felt awful."

"They did. They tried to grab their sons by the tails, and they begged the spirits to bring them back, but it was too late. The pigs ran so fast they were just a blur, and they started rising up into the sky. The spirits put them up there to stay. To remind parents always to love their kids no matter what, I guess, and cut them a little slack."

Alice looks up for a long time. "I swear there's seven," she says.

The owl hoots again, nearer this time.

"Maybe so," Annawake says. "The Six Pigs in Heaven, and the one mother who wouldn't let go."

31

HEN APPLES

In the road ahead, a dead armadillo lies with its four feet and tail all pointed at the heavens. The stiff, expectant curl of its body reminds Taylor of a teddy bear, abandoned there on its back. She reaches into the glove compartment and puts on her sunglasses so Turtle won't see her eyes.

Alice is backseat driving from the front seat, because she knows the roads. Turtle got used to the front seat on their long drive from the Northwest, and has now staked out a place between her mother and grandmother. She flatly refused the backseat when Taylor suggested it. Earlier today, Taylor confided to Alice that Turtle seems to be in a baffling new phase of wanting to have her own way; Alice replied, "About durn time."

"That was your turn right there. You missed it," Alice says.

"Well, great, Mama. Why didn't you let me get another mile down the road before you told me?"

Alice is quiet while Taylor turns the wheel, arm over arm, exaggerating the effort it takes to pull the Dodge around. Taylor can't stand it when she and Alice are at odds. The three female generations sit staring ahead at the Muskogee Highway, torn asunder, without a single idea of where the family is headed.

Alice speaks up again, this time well before the turn. "That stoplight up there. You'll turn into the parking lot right after that. Her office is in there next to a beauty shop, says Turnbo Legal something or other on the door."

Taylor pulls into a fast-food restaurant before the light. "I'm going to drop you two off right here, okay? I need to talk to her first. You can have a snack and play around a little bit, and come on over to the office in fifteen minutes or so. That sound okay, Turtle?"

"Yeah."

"No milk shake, okay, Mama? She's lactose intolerant."

"She's what?"

"She can't drink milk."

"It's because I'm Indian," Turtle says with satisfaction.

"Well, aren't you the one?" Alice asks, helping her out of the car, doting on Turtle as she has since their arrival in Oklahoma. The two of them are getting on like thieves, Taylor observes.

"Fifteen minutes, okay, Mama?"

"Right. We'll see you." She pauses before slamming the door, bending down to peer under the top of the doorframe at Taylor. "Hon, we're all upset. But you know I'm pulling for you. You never did yet let a thing slip away if you wanted it. I know you can do this."

Taylor pushes her sunglasses to the top of her head and wipes her eyes, suddenly flooded with tears. "Do you have a hanky?"

Alice shakes a wad of pale blue tissues out of her purse. "Here. One for the road."

"Mama, you're the best."

"You just think that cause I raised you." Alice reaches in to give Taylor's shoulder a squeeze, then closes the door. Turtle is already off, her pigtails whipping as she runs for the glassy box of a restaurant. Taylor takes a breath and drives the two final blocks to her destiny.

In the row of commercial fronts, between a realty office and a place called Killie's Hair Shack, she locates the law office. It seems deserted, but when she knocks on the glass door, Annawake appears suddenly behind the glare. The door slants open. Annawake's face is an open book of nerves, and her hair is different, a short, swinging black skirt of it around her face.

"I'm glad you made it," she says, throwing a glance at the parking lot, seeing the Dodge and no one else coming.

"She'll be here in a while," Taylor says. "I left Turtle with Mama across the street at a restaurant so I could tell you some stuff first."

"That's fine, come on in. Taylor, this is Cash Stillwater."

Taylor has to look twice before she sees the man in the corner sitting under the rubber tree. His worn, pointed-toe boots are planted on the carpet and his shoulders lean so that he seems drooped somehow, like a plant himself, needing more light.

"Taylor Greer," she says with urgently insincere friendliness, extending her hand. He leans forward and meets her halfway, then sags back into his chair. His dark face seems turned in on itself from shyness or pain, behind the gold-rimmed glasses.

Taylor sits in one of the chrome chairs, and Annawake clears her throat. "Cash has asked us to help find his granddaughter, Lacey Stillwater. I guess Alice might have told you that."

"Mama said there was maybe a relative. I don't know how you'd prove something like that."

"Well, there's blood testing, but I don't think we need to go into that at this point. Cash would just like for me to give you the information he has. His grandchild would be six now, seven next April. She was left in the custody of Cash's younger daughter, an alcoholic, after his older daughter died in a car accident. The child was given to a stranger in a bar north of Oklahoma City, three years ago last November. We have reason to believe that stranger might have been you."

"I can't say anything about that," Taylor says.

"We have no hard feelings toward you. But whether or not your adopted daughter is Cash's grandchild, there are some problems here. If the child is Cherokee, her adoption was conducted illegally. You didn't know the law, and I don't hold you responsible in any way. I'm angry at the professionals who gave you poor advice, because they've caused a lot of heartache."

Taylor is so far past heartache she could laugh out loud. At this moment she is afraid her heart will simply stop. "Can you just go ahead and say it? Do I have to give her up, or not?"

Annawake is sitting with her back to the window, and when she pushes her hair behind her ears they are pink-rimmed like a rabbit's. "It's not a simple yes or no. First, if she's Cherokee, the fate of the child is the tribe's jurisdiction. The tribe could decide either way, to allow you to keep her or ask you to return her to our custody. The important precedent here is a case called Mississippi Band of Choctaw *versus* Holyfield. I'll read you what the Supreme Court said."

She picks up her glasses and a thick stapled document from the desk behind her and flips through it, turning it sideways from time to time to read things written in the margins. Suddenly she reads: "The U.S. Supreme Court will not decide whether the trauma of removing these children from their adoptive family, with which they have lived for three years, should outweigh the interests of the tribe, and perhaps of the children themselves, in having them raised as part of the tribal community; instead, the Supreme Court must defer to the experience, wisdom, and compassion of the tribal court to fashion an appropriate remedy."

"So," Taylor says, trying not to look at the silent man under the rubber tree. "What does the voice of wisdom and compassion say?"

"I don't know. I'm not that voice. Child Welfare Services has the final say. They can give or withhold permission for a child to be adopted out. Assuming we're sure of jurisdiction here. Once we have all the facts, I'll make a recommendation to Andy Rainbelt in Child Welfare, and he'll make the decision."

"Do I get to talk to him?"

"Sure. He's planning on meeting you this afternoon. And I've agreed not to make any recommendations until I've heard what you have to say."

Taylor is aware of being the white person here. Since her arrival in Oklahoma, she has felt her color as a kind of noticeable heat rising off her skin, something like a light bulb mistakenly left on and burning in a roomful of people who might disapprove. She wonders if Turtle has always felt her skin this way, in a world of lighter people.

"Sir?" Taylor speaks to the man, Mr. Stillwater.

He leans forward a little.

"What was your granddaughter like?"

He crosses an ankle on his knee, looks at his hand. "I couldn't tell you.

She was small. Me and my wife, we looked after her a whole lot when she was a little bit of a thing. I'd say she was a right good baby. Smart as a honeybee. Right quiet."

"Did she ever talk?"

"Well, she started to. She'd say 'Mom-mom,' that's what she called her granny. Little baby words like that." His eyes light then, behind his glasses. "One time she said 'hen apple.' That's what I called eggs, to tease her, when we'd play in the kitchen. And one morning I had her with me down in the yard. One of the hens was stealing the nest, and I was looking for it, and she crawled off through the bean patch and into the weeds and here in a minute she hollers, 'Hen apple!' Just as clear as you please." He wipes the corner of his eye. "My wife never would believe me, but it's true."

Taylor and Annawake avoid looking at each other.

"Then after her mama died, seem like she quit talking. Of course, I didn't see a whole lot of her. She was with my other daughter and a young fella over to Tulsa."

Taylor bites her lip, then asks, "Did she go to her mother's funeral?"

He stares at her for a long time. "Everybody goes to the funerals. It's our way. The funeral is at the stomp grounds, and then the burying."

"Do you have any pictures?"

"What, of the funeral?"

"No. Of the child."

He folds himself forward like a jackknife and slides a curved brown wallet from his pocket. He flips through it for a moment like a small favorite book, pauses, then pulls out a tiny photograph, unevenly trimmed. Taylor takes it, afraid to look. But it has nothing of Turtle in it. It's merely a tiny, dark infant, her features screwed with fresh confusion. Her head is turned to the side and her wrinkled fist holds more defiance than Turtle ever mustered in her life. Until last week.

"Here's her mother, my daughter Alma. First day of school." He reaches across with another small photo, and she takes it.

Taylor makes a low noise in her throat, a little cry. It's a girl in saddle shoes and a plaid dress with a Peter Pan collar, standing tall on a front porch step, shoulders square. Her eyebrows hang an earnest question mark on her high forehead. The girl is Turtle.

Taylor holds the photograph by its corner and looks away. She feels she might not live through the next few minutes. The photo leaves her fingers, but she doesn't watch him put it away.

Taylor says, "The girl I've been raising came to me when she was about three. She had been hurt badly, before that. The night she came to me she had bruises all over her. That's the reason I kept her. Do you honestly think I should have given her back? Later on when I took her to a doctor, he said her arms had been broken. It was almost a year before she would talk, or look at people right, or play the way other kids do. She was sexually abused."

Mr. Stillwater speaks in the quietest possible voice to his boots. "I was afraid to death, when they took her to Tulsa. That boy beat up my daughter. She was in the hospital twice with a broke jaw." He clears his throat. "I should have gone and got her. But my wife was dead, and I didn't have the gumption. I should have. I done wrong."

There is a very long silence, and then a yellow leaf falls off the rubber tree. All three of them stare at it.

"I've let her down too," Taylor says. "In different ways. I made her drink milk even though I should have seen it was making her sick." She continues looking at the curled leaf on the floor, released from its branch. "Since all this came up, we've been living on the edge of what I could manage. I had to leave her alone in the car sometimes because I couldn't afford a sitter. We didn't have enough money, and we didn't have anybody to help us." Taylor tightens and releases her grip on the wadded blue tissue in her hand. "That's why I finally came here. Turtle needs the best in the world, after what she's been through, and I've been feeling like a bad mother." Her voice breaks, and she crosses her arms over her stomach, already feeling the blow. How life will be without Turtle. It will be impossible. Loveless, hopeless, blind. She will forget the colors.

She feels Annawake's eyes turned on her, wide, but no words.

When Taylor's own voice comes back to her, she hardly recognizes it or knows what it will say. "Turtle deserves better than what she's gotten, all the way around. I love her more than I can tell you, but just that I love her isn't enough, if I can't give her more. We don't have any backup. I don't want to go through with this thing anymore, hiding out and keeping her away from people. It's hurting her."

Taylor and Annawake gaze at each other like animals surprised by their own reflections.

Suddenly two shadows are at the door, tall and short. Annawake jumps up to lead them in. Turtle is hanging so close to Alice's knees they bump together like a three-legged race. Her eyes are round, and never look away from the man in the corner.

"Turtle, I want you to meet some people," Taylor says through the hoarseness in her throat.

Turtle takes a half step from behind Alice, and stares. Suddenly she holds up her arms to Cash like a baby who wants to be lifted into the clouds. She asks, "Pop-pop?"

Cash pulls off his glasses and drops his face into his hands.

32

THE SNAKE UK'TEN

"WHERE'D YOU GET A PRISSY name like Lacey from, anyway?"

"I don't know," Cash tells Alice, keeping his hands on the wheel and his eye trained ahead. "It was Alma thought of it. I think she liked that TV show with the lady cops. Lacey and somebody."

"Oh, if that don't beat all." Alice jerks herself around in the seat, facing away from him. She was more or less stuck for a ride home, since Taylor and Turtle had to go straight over to Cherokee Headquarters to see the man in Child Welfare. Annawake said her car was broken down and she was waiting for her brother to pick her up. That left Cash. She should have walked.

"She's so big," Cash says. "I can tell just how she is. The kind to keep her mind to herself, like her mother did."

They pass by fields of harvested hay that is rolled up for the winter in what looks like giant bedrolls. A barn in the middle of a pasture is leaning so far to the east it appears to be a freak of gravity.

"Are you going to go ahead and get enrolled, and get your voting card?" he asks.

"Might as well," Alice declares to the passing farms. "So I can get my roof fixed."

"Don't start talking to me about Indians on welfare."

"I wasn't."

"Well, don't. My people owned mansions in Georgia. They had to see it all burned down, and come over here to nothing but flint rocks and copperheads." Cash's voice rises to the pitch of a tenor in church.

"I can't believe I ever got mixed up with a family that names babies after TV shows!" Alice cries, just as loudly. "Kitty Carlisle in the kitchen. You can keep your Kitty Carlisle. I already had me one husband that was in love with his television set. Not again, no thanks!"

"Who was asking?"

"Well, I just didn't want you to waste your time."

As angry and heartbroken as she is, Alice feels something hard break loose down inside of her. She feels deeply gratified to yell at someone who is paying enough attention, at least, to yell back.

The Tribal Offices sit just off the highway in a simple modern arrangement of red brick and concrete slabs, with shrubs hugging the sidewalks. Taylor expected something more tribal, though she doesn't know what that might be.

Turtle holds tightly to her hand as they make their way around the long sidewalk, looking for the right entrance.

"You remember your grandpa, do you?" Taylor asks, talking to fend off approaching terror.

Turtle shrugs. "I dunno."

"It's okay if you do. You can say."

"Yeah."

"What else do you remember?"

"Nothing."

"Your first mother?"

Turtle shrugs again. "He's the good one. Pop-pop. He's not the bad one."

"You remember a man that hurt you?"

"I think I do."

"Turtle, that's good. I want you to remember. Remember him so you can throw him away."

Their shoes make soft, sticky sounds on the warm sidewalk. Turtle steps long to avoid the cracks. This building must be half a mile long, with entrances for every possible category of human problem. Health Care. Economic Development. Taylor can't believe the way life turns out. She has been waiting years for the revelation that just came to Turtle, and now it has happened, while they were walking along half distracted between a row of juniper hedges and the Muskogee Highway.

At last they find Child Welfare. Inside, the building is carpeted and seems more friendly. Receptionists sit at circular desks in the wide corridors, and pictures on the wall show the Tribal Council members, some in cowboy hats. When Taylor asks for directions to Andy Rainbelt's office, the receptionist gets up and leads the way. She wears low heels and has the disposition of a friendly housewife.

"This is his office here. If he was expecting you then I imagine he'll be on in here in a minute. He might be hung up with another appointment."

"Okay, thanks. We'll just wait."

But before they've sat down, they hear the receptionist greet Andy in the hall. He ducks in the doorway, smiling, huge, pony-tailed, dressed like a cleaned-up rodeo man in jeans and boots. Which is fine with Taylor. She prefers bull riding to social-worker interviews any day of the week.

"I'm Andy. Glad to meet you, Miz Greer. Turtle." His handshake is punctuated by a large turquoise ring on his index finger. When they sit, Turtle finds her way into Taylor's lap. Taylor hugs Turtle to her, trying not to look as off-center as she feels.

He leans forward on his elbows and just looks at Turtle for quite a while, smiling, until she has finished examining the floor, the doorknob, and the ceiling, and looks at Andy Rainbelt. He has kind, deep-set eyes under arched eyebrows. "So tell me about your family, Turtle."

"I don't have one."

Taylor earnestly wishes she were not alive.

"Well, who do you live with, then?"

"I live with my mom. And I have a grandma. I used to have Jax, too, back when we lived in a good house."

"Sounds like a family to me."

"And Barbie. She used to live with us. Barbie and all her clothes."

"Now, is she a real person or a doll?"

Turtle glances up at Taylor, who nearly laughs in spite of the dire circumstances. "She's both," Taylor answers for her. "She was a friend. Kind of clothes-oriented."

"What kind of things do you do for fun at your house?" he asks.

"Barbie played with me sometimes when Mom was at work," Turtle explains. "We made stuff. And clothes. She always ate Cheese Doritos and then went and throwed up in the bathroom."

"What? She did that?" Taylor feels ambushed. "I never knew that. Every time she ate?"

"I think every time."

"So that was her secret!" Taylor looks at Andy Rainbelt, feeling as if she might as well throw up too. "I guess we must sound like a pretty weird family."

"All families are weird," he says. "My job is to see which ones are good places for kids."

"Barbie is out of our lives, completely. I know it sounds bad that Turtle was exposed to that. I don't know what to tell you. She baby-sat for a while, while I was trying to get started in a new job. But she's gone."

"She took all our money," Turtle adds helpfully. "The guy that catches gooses had to take our electricity because we didn't pay."

Taylor knows her face must look like the cow in the corral who finally comprehends the slaughterhouse concept. "I was working full-time," she explains. "But somehow there just still wasn't enough money. It's probably hard for her to remember, but we had a pretty good life before all this happened."

Andy looks patient. "Listen. I hear everything in this office. I'm not grading you on what you say. I'm watching, more than listening, to tell you the truth. What I see is this little girl in your lap, looking pretty content there."

Taylor holds her so close she feels her own heart pounding against Turtle's slender, knobbed spine. "It's real hard on her to have to be separated from me. I just want to tell you that, for your records."

"I understand," he says.

"No, I mean it's terrible. Not like other kids. Sometimes Turtle lies in the bathtub with a blanket over her head for hours and hours, if she thinks I'm mad at her." She squeezes Turtle harder into her arms. "She went through some bad stuff when she was a baby, before I got her, and we're still kind of making up for lost time."

"Is that right, Turtle?"

Turtle is silent. Taylor waits for some awful new revelation, until it dawns on her that her daughter may be suffocating. She relaxes her hold, and Turtle breathes.

"Yeah," she says. "The bad one wasn't Pop-pop."

"She just met Mr. Stillwater. I mean, met him again. Her grandfather. I guess she's started remembering stuff from when she was little."

Andy has a way of looking Turtle in the eye that doesn't frighten her. Taylor is amazed. A giant who can make himself small. "Some tough times back then, huh?" he asks her.

"I don't know."

"It's okay to remember. Scares you though, sometimes, doesn't it?"

Turtle shrugs.

"Nobody's going to hurt you now."

Taylor closes her eyes and sees stars. She wishes on those stars that Andy Rainbelt could keep his promise.

Late that same afternoon, Taylor and Alice walk the dirt shoulder of the road out of Heaven. Turtle came back to Sugar's and fell into a hard sleep, but Taylor wanted to get out of the house for a while.

"I'm sorry you broke up with your new boyfriend," she tells Alice.

"Lord, what a soap opry," Alice declares. "All the fish out there, and I have to go for the one that's related to Turtle."

"Mama, that's not just bad luck. You were set up."

"Well, still, he didn't have to be so handy, did he? And related some way to Sugar?"

"To hear Sugar tell it, she's related some way to everybody from here to the Arkansas border. If they were determined to get you two together, it was bound to happen."

"Well, that's so. But I still have to say I got the worst darn luck in men."

"I'm not about to argue with that." Taylor has begun picking long-stemmed black-eyed Susans from the roadside as they walk along.

"The thing is, it's my own fault. I just can't put up with a person that won't go out of his way for me. And that's what a man is. Somebody that won't go out of his way for you. I bet it says that in the dictionary."

Taylor hands Alice a bouquet of orangey-yellow Susans and begins picking another one.

"It's the family misfortune," Alice says. "I handed it right on down to you."

"I called Jax," Taylor says, feeling faintly guilty.

"Well, honey, that's good. I mean it, I think he's tops. What's he up to?"

"His band is sort of breaking up. Their lead guitar quit, but they're getting an electric fiddle. Kind of going in a new direction, he says. He's trying to think of a new name with a country element. Renaissance Cowboys, something like that."

"Well, it beats the Irritated Babies all to pieces."

"Irascible Babies."

"What's that mean, irascible?"

"Irritated, I think."

"So I had the right idea, anyway."

"Yeah, I'm sure you did."

"And you forgave him for going to bed with that what's her name? That landlady gal?"

"Mama, I'd given him permission to do whatever he pleased. I told him when I left in June that we weren't, you know, anything long-term. So how could I hold it against him?"

A passing pickup truck, whose paint job looks very much like whitewash, slows down, then speeds on by when the driver doesn't recognize the two women carrying flowers.

"Mama, I've decided something about Jax. I've been missing him all summer long. Whether or not we get to keep Turtle, I've decided I want to start thinking of me and Jax as kind of more permanent."

"Well, that don't sound too definite."

"No, it is. I mean, I want us to be long-term. He's real happy. He wants to get married. I don't know if *married* is really the point, but you know what I mean."

"Well, Taylor, that's wonderful!" Alice cries, sounding ready enough to be wrong about men this once. She sings "Dum, dum da dum," to the tune of "Here Comes the Bride," and ties knots in the stems of her flowers, pulling each one through the next to make a crown. When it's finished she holds it out in her two hands like the cat's cradle, then places it on Taylor's dark hair. "There you go, all set."

"Mama, you're embarrassing me," Taylor says, but she leaves the flowers where they are.

"What changed your mind about Jax?"

Taylor uses her long bouquet like a horse's tail, to swish away gnats. "When the social worker asked Turtle about her family today, you know what she said? She said she didn't have one."

"That's not right! She was confused."

"Yeah. She's confused, because I'm confused. I *think* of Jax and Lou Ann and Dwayne Ray, and of course you, and Mattie, my boss at the tire store, all those people as my family. But when you never put a name on things, you're just accepting that it's okay for people to leave when they feel like it."

"They leave anyway," Alice says. "My husbands went like houses on fire."

"But you don't have to *accept* it," Taylor insists. "That's what your family is, the people you won't let go of for anything."

"Maybe."

"Like, look at Mr. Stillwater. Cash. He's still just aching for Turtle after all this time. I hate to admit it, and I'm not going to say I think he should have her. Turtle is mine now. But he doesn't accept that she's gone. You can see it."

Alice *has* seen it in Cash. She saw it long before she knew what it was. A man who would go out of his way.

Taylor has woven her flowers into a circle, and she crowns her mother with it. Alice reaches deep into herself and evinces a dramatic sigh. "Always the bridesmaid, never the bride."

A string of cars crackles by on the gravel, all following an old truck that is fairly crawling. The drivers stare, each one in turn, as they pass.

"Where's that sign?" Taylor asks.

"What sign?"

"The one that was in that magazine ad, remember? With Sugar, when she was young? You've showed me that fifty times."

"That sign that says WELCOME TO HEAVEN." Alice looks thoughtful. "You know, I haven't seen it."

"Maybe this isn't really Heaven!" Taylor says. "Maybe we're in the wrong place, and none of this is really happening."

"No, it's Heaven all right. It says so on the phone book."

"Shoot, then they ought to have that sign up. I wish we could go pose in front of it. Maybe somebody'd come along and take our picture."

"I wonder if they tore that down. I'll have to ask Sugar. I bet anything they did."

"Does that mean we're not welcome anymore?" Taylor asks.

Two more cars pass by, and this time Alice and Taylor smile and wave like Miss America contestants.

Alice says, "I reckon we'll stay till they run us out of town."

Some kind of fish jumps in the river. Annawake stares at the ring of disturbed water it left behind. "Uncle Ledger, just tell me what to do," she says.

Ledger is in his overstuffed chair on the porch of the houseboat, smoking his pipe. Annawake paces the planks silently in her moccasins.

"You never would let me tell you what to do before," he says through pursed lips, sucking his pipe stem. "Why would you start now?"

"I always knew what I was doing before."

"If you knew what you was doing before, you wouldn't be stumped now."

She sits down on the deck, then lies down, looking up at the sky.

"Did I ever tell you you looked like a plucked chicken, when you cut all your hair off?"

"I was mourning Gabriel. I thought somebody ought to."

"If you want to do something for Gabe, talk to Gabe."

"Gabe's in Leavenworth."

"What, they don't allow phone calls?"

Annawake looks up, startled. He means it. "I don't know. Yeah, I guess they do."

"Well, then, call him. Or go visit. Tell him you miss him. Organize a damn bust-out and bring him on back here."

Annawake feels something like round stones shifting inside her, settling into a new, more solid position. "I guess I could."

"Sure you could. If you got something to work out, then work it out. Don't take it out on the rest of the world by looking like a chicken."

"Thanks. Everybody always said I had your looks."

"Annawake, you're not as respectful as you used to be."

She sits up, but sees the light in his eye, so she can lie back down.

"Tell me a story," she says. "About a little lost girl whose mother is prepared to give her away, rather than go through any more hassle with Annawake Fourkiller."

"I'll tell you." He leans back in his chair, which once in its life was green brocade, before twenty summers of sun and rain. "Speak of lost children in low voices," he says. Annawake pulls herself up. He has slid over into Cherokee, and she has to sit up straight to follow him. "They say long ago there was a child claimed by two clan mothers. They carried the child to the Above Ones. They came with long cries and moans, both of them saying the child belonged to their own people. The mother from the plains brought corn, and the mother from the hills brought tobacco, both of them hoping to sweeten the thoughts of the Above Ones when they made their decision."

Ledger stops talking and merely stares at the sky for a time. His legs are splayed in front of him, forgotten, and his pipe dangles in his hand, still sending up a thread of smoke as a friendly reminder.

He goes on suddenly: "When the Above Ones spoke, they said, we will send down the snake Uk'ten."

Annawake leans forward with her arms around her knees, narrowing her eyes to listen. She wishes she had her glasses. She understands Cherokee better with her glasses on.

"We will send the snake Uk'ten to cut the child in half, and each clan can carry home one half of the child."

"Wait a minute," Annawake says.

"The mother from the grassland happily agreed. But the mother from the hill clan wept and said no, that she would give her half of the child to the plains clan, to keep the baby whole. And so the Above Ones knew which mother loved the child best."

Annawake pulls off a moccasin and throws it at Ledger, hitting him square in the chest. She pulls off the other and just misses his head, on purpose.

"What, you don't like my story?" He sits up startled, crossing his hands over his chest.

"Some old Cherokee story you've got there. That's King Solomon, from the Bible."

"Oh. Well, I knew I got it from someplace," he says, patting his pockets for matches to relight his pipe.

"It's a *yonega* story," she says.

"Is that true? Did a *yonega* write the Bible? I always wondered about that. It doesn't say on there, 'The Bible, by so-and-so.' "

"I don't know. Maybe it wasn't a *yonega*. I think it was a bunch of people that lived in the desert and fished for a living."

"If they lived in the desert and caught fish both, you better listen to them."

"Give me my shoes back."

He leans back to collect the one that flew over his shoulder, and tosses the pair. Annawake pulls them on over her bare feet and buttons them at the ankles.

"I've got to go down to the Council Chambers and give my recommendation in half an hour. And you haven't told me a thing."

"Not a thing, no."

"Except that maybe I don't want to jump for joy to see a baby cut in half. Which she's going to be, either way."

"Can I tell you something, little hothead?"

"What?"

"There's something else growing back with your hair."

"What's that?"

"Sense. Used to be, you wanted your side to win all the time."

"They taught me that in *yonega* law school."

"Must be. You never had a bit of it in you before. I never saw you knocking down your own brothers to hit the score in a stickball game."

"Okay, then, if you knew me so well, you never should have let me go to law school. If you knew it would just bring out my worst nature."

"If you have a frisky horse you put him in a race. You don't put him behind a plow."

Annawake gets up, dusts off her knees and her seat. "What do you know from horses, anyway? You're a Cherokee, not some war-whooping featherheaded Sioux."

"I know enough about horses. I know you want one that has a good heart."

"I hear Dellon's truck up on the road. He's driving me over to Headquarters. I'd better go."

"Annawake, you've got you a good heart. Run with it. Your whole life, you've been afraid of yourself." He is looking right at her. Not through her, like most people do, to the paper doll that is Annawake Fourkiller, but *into* her.

She stands with her mouth open, waiting for a word. Nothing comes. Then, "How did you know?"

Ledger seems entirely occupied with his pipe. He waves her off. "Birdy told me."

Dellon is idling with the radio on. He turns it down when she gets in. "So did Ledger blow smoke on you and bless you for the hunt?"

"He blew smoke all right. He aggravates me. Nobody ought to be that smart."

"Yeah, well, Annawake. That's what some people say about you." He rolls his eyes. "I wouldn't know who."

"If I'm so smart, how come I'm miserable?"

On the radio, Randy Travis's croony voice dips low over someone who's been gone for too long.

"You just need you a man, that's all," Dellon says.

Annawake exhales sharply. "I've had enough men in my life to last me about seven lifetimes. Think about it, Dell, growing up with all you guys, and Daddy, and Uncle Ledger. All those penises! You all had me surrounded like a picket fence."

Dellon shifts in his seat uncomfortably. "It wasn't *that* bad, was it?"

"No, Dellon, it's nothing personal against your body organs. But men are just not necessarily always the solution."

He stares at her until his truck runs into the ditch. He glances up and swerves back. "I'm going to have to put that in my pipe and smoke it awhile," he says.

She gives him the smile that has been knocking boys dead for twenty-seven years, with absence of malice. "You just do that."

33

THE GAMBLING

AGENDA

THE MEETING THAT TOOK PLACE previously in the Council Chamber room must have been concerned with the Bingo question. On the blackboard at the front of the room someone has written in narrow, forward-slanting letters:

TODAY'S AGENDA—GAMING ON TRIBAL LAND, YAY OR NAY? PRESENTATIONS

1. Cyrus Stonecipher. "The pritfalls of gambling, a story too often told"
2. Betty Louise Squirrel. "BINGO, everybody wins!"

Annawake Fourkiller and Andy Rainbelt sit at the long speakers' table down in front with their backs to the chalkboard, apparently unaware of the gambling agenda. Andy Rainbelt seems festive in a blue calico shirt with satin ribbon trim at the yoke, similar to the one Annawake wore the day she and Taylor met. Taylor can remember exactly how she looked. Today she's a different person, in black-rimmed glasses and a haircut that seems worrisome to her. She keeps pushing it out of her way.

Turtle, Taylor, and Alice are sitting together in the red movie-theater chairs that fill the small auditorium. Turtle swings her legs so the toes of her sneakers drum out a steady *tha-bump* against the empty seat in front of her. The rows are set in a V-shape facing the speakers' table, with an aisle down the center. Those in attendance have assumed a wedding interpretation, in which the center aisle divides the two families; the seats on the other side are filling up briskly. Cash is over there and so is Letty, in a red dress with an imposing row of gold buttons down the front; countless other friends and relations have trailed in with children and greetings and messages for their neighbors. Boma Mellowbug is wearing a man's pinstriped suit and a baseball cap, looking very sporting. She holds the hand of an old, extremely thin man whose hair hangs between his shoulder blades in a white plait as thin and prickly as binder's twine. The heavyset woman who waited on Alice and Annawake in the coffee shop hustles in, leaning into Letty's row in a businesslike way to inform Letty that the half-size dress patterns are in at Woolworth's in Tahlequah.

"What *is* half-size, Aunt Earlene?" asks a young woman who's nursing a baby. "I always wondered that."

Earlene turns her back and speaks over her shoulder, reaching her hands around to her waist and the back of her neck to demonstrate. "It's when you've got less inches from here to here than you have in the inseam and the bust measurements."

"It's for when you're shorter than you are wide," says Roscoe.

"You hush," Letty tells him. "I don't know why Sugar feeds you."

Earlene plumps herself down next to the nursing mother. The baby is making a good deal of noise at his task, sounding like the squeaky wheel determined to get all the grease.

Sugar comes in late, long after Roscoe has taken the one vacant seat next to his sister-in-law Letty, and she seems uncertain where to go. She takes Alice's side at last, but a seat on the aisle, as close as possible to the Stillwaters.

The talking falls to a hush when a small woman in heels and a white silk blouse clicks in and takes her place at the front table next to Andy

Rainbelt. She has a good deal of hair, which she shakes when she sits down, as if it might have gathered dust somewhere along the road to this point. Annawake puts on her glasses, squares the pile of papers in front of her, and stands up. She looks out at the small assembled crowd and smiles oddly. "Have you all decided this is Stillwater versus Greer?"

The auditorium owns up to this by its silence.

She leans forward on the palms of her hands, peering out over her glasses, looking just like a lawyer in blue jeans. "Well, it isn't. This is not a court battle, it's just a hearing. I'm Annawake Fourkiller, you all know me here. I was hired by the tribe to oversee its interests in this case. This is Andy Rainbelt, who has jurisdiction as the appointed representative of Child Welfare Services. And this is his boss, Leona Swimmer, here to make sure we all do our jobs."

Leona Swimmer nods very slightly, apparently wishing to acknowledge nothing more than that she is, in fact, here.

Annawake goes on. "Mr. Rainbelt and I have conferred, and we're prepared to make a recommendation about the child known as Turtle Greer, also known as Lacey Stillwater."

Turtle stops swinging her legs. Taylor squeezes her hand so hard that for once Turtle knows herself what it's like to be bitten by those turtles that don't let go.

Annawake looks down at Andy. "Did you want to say anything?"

"No, you go ahead," he says. Leona Swimmer is craning her neck to read the blackboard behind her. BINGO, everybody wins! Taylor can just imagine this Betty Louise Squirrel. Some charmed, perky type whose tires never go flat and whose kids never get chicken pox. Taylor pictures her as an actual squirrel, in an apron.

Annawake speaks in the level sort of voice that takes practice to achieve. "There are two principal legal considerations here. First of all, the adoption of the child by Taylor Greer was improperly conducted. There was no malice on her part, but even so it was illegal. I've filed a motion in state court to invalidate the adoption."

The nursing baby lets out a small strangled cry. His mother moves him to her shoulder, patting and bouncing him there to get the air bubbles to rise according to the laws that govern babies.

"Secondly," Annawake says, "we've determined that the child is Cash Stillwater's granddaughter, Lacey Stillwater. She recognizes him, and bears a strong family resemblance."

"Isn't that so," moans Letty in a low, breathless tone as if receiving the spirit. Cash is perfectly still. He can't feel his hands, and wonders if he's having a quiet, unnoticeable kind of coronary.

"Given those facts," Annawake says, "we have to consider Cash Stillwater to be the child's legal guardian. If this were contested, a court would undoubtedly find in favor of Mr. Stillwater. The Indian Child Welfare Act clearly states that our children should stay within our tribe, and whenever possible, with their own relatives. In this instance the natural mother is dead and the father is unknown, so the obvious choice would be to assign guardianship to the grandfather."

Cash still hasn't moved. Taylor has stopped breathing.

"There's a complication in this case." Annawake picks up a ballpoint pen and clicks the point in and out, in and out. "The child has formed a strong attachment to Taylor Greer, the only mother she's known for the past three years. Mr. Rainbelt evaluated the adoptive setting, and after consulting with a psychiatrist, he feels it would be devastating to break this extreme attachment. He recommends counseling for the child, who suffered a period of abuse and neglect before she was abandoned and subsequently adopted. Counseling will be undertaken at the expense of the Nation. That's one of our duties to this child. Mr. Rainbelt suggests it would be valuable to the healing process, too, for her to spend time with her grandfather and other relatives."

Annawake holds the pen at arm's length and suddenly stares at it as if she had no idea of its purpose or origin.

"So," she says finally. "You can see."

No one in the audience makes any indication that she or he can see.

"You can see we have conflicting considerations here. Keeping the child in her own culture, and not disrupting her attachment to a non-Cherokee mother. We want to reinstate this child—who should be called Turtle, since she's grown to be a fine little person under her adopted mother's care, and that's the name she connects with her conscious memory of herself—we have to reinstate her as the granddaughter and legal ward of

Cash Stillwater. We recommend her legal name be recorded as Turtle Still-water. So, we've figured out *who* she is. We've come that far."

Someone in the audience exhales. The baby emits a tiny belch.

Annawake takes off her glasses and looks at the ceiling as if in prayer. There is nothing up there but soundproof tile. No evidence of the Above Ones or the six bad boys who got turned into pigs, for whatever reason. The faces in front of her are wide open, waiting. She remembers wanting to be her Uncle Ledger, as a child, during the sermons. This is how it would be.

"I think we're looking at one of those rare chances life gives us to try and be the very best that we are," Annawake says. "The outside press, when they look at this case, will be asking only one thing: what is in the best interest of the child? But we're Cherokee and we look at things differ-ently. We consider that the child is part of something larger, a tribe. Like a hand that belongs to the body. Before we cut it off, we have to ask how the body will take care of itself without that hand.

"The Indian Child Welfare Act was designed principally to protect the tribe from losing its members. Our children are our future. But we want them to grow up under the influence of kindness and generosity. Some-times we have to put the needs of an individual in second place, behind the needs of the community. But we should never put them out of our mind entirely. What we have to do is satisfy the requirements of the tribe, without separating Turtle completely from the mother and grandmother she's come to love and trust."

Relatives and friends of Turtle Stillwater maintain a perfect silence.

Annawake puts down her glasses and pushes her hair behind her ears. "I'm going to go out on a limb here. Andy and I just cooked up an idea about fifteen minutes ago, right before this meeting. There's a precedent in these adoption cases for assigning joint custody. Sometimes it works, sometimes it's a mess. But we're going to go ahead and give Cash Stillwa-ter legal guardianship of Turtle Stillwater, with the recommendation that Taylor Greer has shared custody. We're willing to work with both families on an agreeable custody arrangement. Last year, in the case of a Navajo child adopted by a family in Utah, the tribe allowed the child to spend the school year with her adoptive family and summers with her grandparents on the reservation." Annawake looks from Cash to Taylor; their faces look peculiarly identical. She bends down to confer quietly with Andy.

Andy Rainbelt doesn't stand, but nods, and Annawake speaks again. "Andy plans to continue on as Turtle's personal Indian social worker, and do follow-up evals to see how this custody deal is affecting her. He wants to stress that Turtle won't be separated from her adoptive family until she's ready to do that. But we're going to require the guardians to come up with a plan fairly soon that places Turtle here on the Nation at least three months out of the year."

Alice Greer blows her nose. Letty pulls out a lace handkerchief and blows hers also, with substantially more showmanship.

"Obviously," Annawake says, "with joint custody, everything depends on how well the two custodial parties are willing to cooperate. And whether or not the cooperation extends indefinitely into the future. I would hate to see this case ever go to court." She looks down at the papers in front of her. "I think that's about all I have."

After a moment of shell-shocked quiet, Boma Mellowbug lifts her voice into a long, rising whoop, the signal for ending the sermon and starting the dance.

"Thanks, Boma." Annawake smiles and sits down.

No one moves. Taylor takes her first breath of the too-thin air of the rest of her life—a life of sharing Turtle with strangers.

"This is your chance, people," Andy says. "You're allowed to speak up if you have suggestions or questions or just want to promote the general welfare. That's why we open these things up to the whole family."

Cash slowly finds his feet, facing front. "I have a suggestion. I suggest that if me and Alice Greer was to get married, then the little girl could still be seeing her grandma when she comes for the summers."

Alice's face drops open on all its hinges. So does Letty Hornbuckle's.

"Now wait a minute, Cash," Letty says, standing up, gripping the seat in front of her like a church pew. "You hain't knowed her but three weeks."

Cash turns on his sister like a bull would, seeing that red dress. "Letty, now you look here. You're the one started this whole business with her and me in the first place. You ought to be ashamed of yourself."

"No, now goodness me, I helped," Sugar says, pulling herself up as high as her humped back will allow for. "Letty, you're not being fair to Alice. She's my cousin. If they love each other, we ought to go on and let these kids get married." She turns and speaks to Alice. "I helped set it up, too. I made up some of that stuff I said about Cash itching to get to know you."

Annawake is smirking. "I hate to bring this up, Letty, but *I* gave you the idea of getting them together. Remember that day I brought back your pie plate? I just hit on it when I was talking to Alice downtown in the coffee shop one day, and spilled the sugar."

"Honey, don't you worry about that sugar," Earlene says. "That wasn't nothing. Floyd Tailbob threw a whole fresh cup of coffee on Killie Deal one time in there, on a Easter Sunday. Don't even ask me how he done it."

Alice is standing with her mouth open, waiting. When Earlene has finished with Floyd Tailbob and Killie Deal, she asks, "Did anybody ask me if I *wanted* to marry Cash?"

All bosoms and shirt fronts turn to face Alice.

"Do I get a say-so here? Because I already made up my mind a long time ago, I don't want another husband that's glued to his everloving TV set. I have my own principles to think about." Alice sits down.

Annawake looks at Taylor. Andy Rainbelt is smiling broadly, exposing a wonderful gap between his front teeth. Taylor can hear him saying, *All families are weird.* She couldn't agree more. She's ready to grab Turtle and run for it, except she knows where that road ends.

"I just have one thing to say," Sugar announces. "If they do get married—I'm just saying *if*—then I think we ought to have the pig fry at my house. Because Letty's in the middle of getting her a new roof on, and that and a pig fry all at once would be too much to contend with if you ask me."

"Well, Sugar, it's Cash putting the roof on!" Letty cries. "Don't you think he's going to finish up a shingle job in time for his own wedding?"

The man with the white ponytail tells Earlene, "That was Flester that spilt his coffee on Killie Deal. I read about that in the paper."

"No, you did not. You're thinking of when he showed up with coffee all down his shirt sleeve when he was running for Tribal Council."

Leona Swimmer speaks up for the first time. "Now, why would either one of those things be in the paper? Could somebody tell me?"

Everyone turns to examine Leona. She looks very elegant and commanding, like a schoolteacher.

"Tribal politics, Leona," Roscoe tells her with polite impatience. "You know that as well as I do."

"Now, hear ye!" shouts Cash. "If this meeting is over with, which I'd say it pretty much is, I'm inviting Alice and everybody else here in this room to come over to my place right this minute and witness something I'm about to do."

He turns and walks out of the room. There is a moment of stupefied silence, then a neighborly stampede.

Taylor understands she has lost something she won't get back. Cash Stillwater is Turtle's legal guardian. No matter what.

Taylor can still remember the day when she first understood she'd received the absolute power of motherhood—that force that makes everyone else step back and agree that she knows what's best for Turtle. It scared her to death. But giving it up now makes her feel infinitely small and alone. She can't even count her losses yet; her heart is an empty canyon, so she puts her effort into driving.

Somehow she has ended up as caboose in the long line of cars following Cash's penny-colored pickup truck. She and Turtle seem to have been forgotten for the moment. It dawns on her that she could pull out of line now and head west, and not a soul would notice. But they're way past that point now. From now until the end of time she is connected to this family that's parading down Main Street, Heaven. One day soon she will lie in bed with Jax and tell him every detail of this day. The Renaissance Cowboys have got nothing on the Stillwaters, for entertainment value.

"Wait till we tell Jax we want him as your official daddy," she says to Turtle. "What do you think he'll do?"

"Maybe put his pants on his head and sing 'Happy Birthday' to himself."

"Yeah, maybe."

"Does that mean you're still my mom?"

"I am. But I have to share you with your grandpa now. He's going to have a big say in how you're raised."

"I know. So I can be a Cherokee when I grow up. Andy Rainbow told me."

"You like Andy?"

Turtle nods. "Those people in there? Were they Pop-pop's family?"

"Yep. *Your* family, to be exact."

"They're crazy."

"I know," Taylor says. "But they'll probably grow on you."

The one traffic light in town turns red on her, just after all the others have passed under. Taylor turns on her headlights so people will think it's a funeral, and floors it right on through the red. Nobody much was coming, anyway. If she gets separated from the others now, she'll never know how her life is going to come out.

Cash walks out the back door of his cabin carrying his television set, and with a vigorous wordlessness, sets it on a stump. It sits there not quite level, its short black cord hanging down in a defeated manner. While Cash stomps back inside, the witnesses arrange themselves in a semicircle facing the blank green eye. Nothing in this world, Alice notes, will get people organized and quiet faster than a TV set, even when there is nothing to plug it into but a tree stump.

Turtle takes a hop or two toward the TV, but the girl with the baby on her shoulder gently pulls her back. Taylor reaches forward and takes Turtle's hand.

Cash appears again, carrying his rifle. "You all move back," he says, and they waste no time.

"He's done lost his mind," Alice says calmly to Taylor.

"You better marry him, then," Taylor whispers back.

Cash stands a few feet in front of them with his feet wide apart. His shoulders curl forward, hunched and tense, as he lifts the rifle and takes aim. He remains frozen in this position for a very long time. Alice can see the gun barrel over his shoulder, wavering a little, and then she sees his shoulder thrown back at the same instant the gun's report roars over the clearing. Her ears feel the pain of a bell struck hard. The woods go unnaturally still. All the birds take note of the round black bullet wound in the TV screen, a little right of center but still fatal.

Alice's heart performs its duties strangely inside her chest, and she understands that her life sentence of household silence has been commuted. The family of women is about to open its doors to men. Men, children, cowboys, and Indians. It's all over now but the shouting.

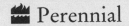 Perennial

Books by Barbara Kingsolver:

SMALL WONDER: *Essays*
ISBN 0-06-050407-2 (HarperCollins hardcover)
ISBN 0-06-051146-X (unabridged audio)

Twenty-three essays celebrate nature, family, literature, and everyday life while examining the genesis of war, violence, and poverty.

ANIMAL DREAMS
ISBN 0-06-092114-5 (paperback)

Codi Noline, a dreamless woman, discovers the unexpected when she returns home to Grace, Arizona to confront her past and face her ailing father.

THE BEAN TREES
ISBN 0-06-091554-4 (paperback) • ISBN 0-06-017579-6 (Anniversary hardcover)

This novel about the peculiarities of family introduces Taylor Greer, a spirited young woman who finds an abandoned child in her car.

HIGH TIDE IN TUCSON: *Essays from Now or Never*
ISBN 0-06-092756-9 (paperback) • ISBN 0-694-51577-9 (audio)

Twenty-five essays focus on Kingsolver's favored literary themes of family, community, and the natural world.

HOMELAND AND OTHER STORIES
ISBN 0-06-091701-6 (paperback) • ISBN 0-694-51656-2 (audio)

A rich and emotionally resonant collection of twelve stories that explore the themes of family ties and the life choices one must ultimately make alone.

PIGS IN HEAVEN
ISBN 0-06-092253-2 (paperback) • ISBN 1-5599-4722-5 (audio)

The contested adoption of a Native American child raises powerful questions about individual rights and the need for community.

THE POISONWOOD BIBLE
ISBN 0-06-093053-5 (paperback)

Kingsolver's bestselling epic novel which chronicles three decades in the life of an American family who travel to the Belgian Congo as missionaries in 1959.

PRODIGAL SUMMER
ISBN 0-06-095903-7 (paperback)
ISBN 0-06-019966-0 (large print) • ISBN 0-694-52437-9 (unabridged audio)

Three stories of human love woven together within a larger tapestry of lives inhabiting the mountains and struggling small farms of southern Appalachia.

Available wherever books are sold, or call 1-800-331-3761 to order.